THE RUNAWAY BOY

Manoranjan Byapari was born in the mid-fifties in Barishal, former East Pakistan. His family migrated to West Bengal in India when he was three. They were resettled in Bankura at the Shiromanipur Refugee Camp. Later, they were forced to shift to the Gholadoltala Refugee Camp, 24-Parganas, and lived there till 1969. However, Byapari had to leave home at the age of fourteen to do odd jobs. In his early twenties, he came into contact with the Naxals and with the famous labour activist Shankar Guha Niyogi. Byapari was sent to jail during this time, where he taught himself to read and write. Later, while working as a rickshaw-puller in Kolkata, Byapari had a chance meeting with the renowned Bengali writer Mahasweta Devi, who urged him to write for her journal *Bartika*. He has written twenty-seven books since. Some of his important works include *Chhera Chhera Jibon, Ittibrite Chandal Jibon* (memoir), the *Chandal Jibon Trilogy* (novels) and *Motua Ek Mukti Senar Naam*. Until 2018, he was working as a cook at the Hellen Keller Institute for the Deaf and Blind in West Bengal.

In 2018, the English translation of Byapari's memoir, *Ittibrite Chandal Jibon* (*Interrogating My Chandal Life*), received the Hindu Prize for non-fiction. In 2019, he was awarded the Gateway Lit Fest Writer of the Year Prize. Also, the English translation of his novel *Batashe Baruder Gandha* (*There's Gunpowder in the Air*) was shortlisted for the JCB Prize for Literature 2019, the DSC Prize for South Asian Literature 2019, the Crossword Book Award for Best Translation 2019 and the Mathrubhumi Book of the Year Prize 2020. He was appointed chairman of the newly instituted Dalit Sahitya Akademi in Bengal in 2020.

In 2021, Byapari was elected a member to the Bengal Legislative Assembly as a Trinamool Congress candidate.

V. Ramaswamy is a literary translator of voices from the margins. His previous translations include *The Golden Gandhi Statue from America: Early Stories, Wild Animals Prohibited: Stories, Anti-stories* and *This Could Have Become Ramayan Chamar's Tale: Two Anti-Novels* (shortlisted for the Crossword Book Award, 2019), all by the anti-establishment Bengali writer, Subimal Misra. He was awarded the inaugural Literature Across Frontiers-Charles Wallace India Trust Fellowship at Aberystwyth University to translate the Chandal Jibon novels. He was selected for the inaugural translation fellowship of the New India Foundation in 2021.

MANORANJAN BYAPARI

THE RUNAWAY BOY

Translated from the Bengali by V. Ramaswamy

First published in Bengali in 2008 in the magazine *Hatey Bajare*

First published in English as *The Runaway Boy* in 2020 by Eka, an imprint of Westland Publications Private Limited

Published in English as *The Runaway Boy* in 2022 by Eka, an imprint of Westland Books, a division of Nasadiya Technologies Private Limited

No. 269/2B, First Floor, 'Irai Arul', Vimalraj Street, Nethaji Nagar, Allappakkam Main Road, Maduravoyal, Chennai 600095

Westland and the Westland logo are the trademarks of Nasadiya Technologies Private Limited, or its affiliates.

ISBN: 9789395767095

10 9 8 7 6 5 4 3 2 1

Typeset by Jojy Philip, New Delhi 110 015

Printed at Radha Press, Sahibabad

Charaibeti, charaibeti

Keep moving, keep moving on!

CONTENTS

GARIB DAS

1

Rice

It was dawn. Crimsoning the eastern sky, the sun emerged like a golden orb over East Bengal's marshlands. The golden orb floating on the water swayed to the push of the gentle easterly breeze. A flock of cormorants flew across the sky, their wings unhindered and free. Who knew where and how far they would take them! Carried by the current, a country boat floated far away along on the vast river. The boat was loaded with a veritable mountain of coconut and areca. Its journey would end when it reached the town of Barisal.

The scenery all around was very pretty. Nature had adorned this time of day in such a way that—if men did not ruin it—it was a most excellent time for singing as well as praying. And for that matter, poetry too.

Like every morning, Mr Shibnath Bhattacharya rose from sleep at this time—which was called Brahma-muhurta, or 'the moment of the Lord of Creation'. After that, squatting on the canal-bank in the frisky breeze of dawn, he finished his morning task. Then, breaking a neem twig, he brushed his teeth and returned to the open space in front of his house, where the harvested paddy was threshed. He walked briskly there for a while. He had been badly afflicted with arthritic aches of late. The ayurvedic physician had advised him to take a morning walk.

There were only a few trees in this spot, so clear sunlight fell there. If the body absorbed the sunlight and breeze of dawn, one stayed fit and free of ailments. It was said that this sunlight also had the power to prevent leprosy. Shibnath Bhattacharya was mortally scared of that disease. His revered father had rotted and finally died of that.

At exactly the same time, another man trudged ahead along the bed of a river, much smaller than the one in the distance, although somewhat larger than the canal. He walked very slowly, silently. He was bare-bodied and barefoot, and wore a short dhuti that fell short of his knees. The dhuti had never seen the likes of soap. It was either washed in water or boiled with the ash made from burning palash flowers. Nothing more than that lay in its fate.

There was a clump of dry hair on his head—that had never seen a drop of oil—and a jungle of prickly beard and moustache on his face, from being unable to shave. Hunger, diffidence, weariness and humiliation, compounded over many centuries, seemed to weigh down over his body. He felt buried under a mountain of callous iniquity. It was as if all his limbs, and his entire existence, had been devoured by a limitless, indescribable deprivation. It seemed the great famine of 1770 had not yet lifted its talons from his life. Which was why his ribs jutted out. His eyesight was also failing. His eyes seemed lifeless; he looked like a dead fish.

It was futile to look for any hope or light, or any dream or desire in his eyes. A constant grief and distress welled in those eyes: how to endure the harsh snarl of time, how to survive.

One time, who knows when, perhaps there had been dreams and desires in his eyes too, and hope and joy. All that was gone. Now there was only despondency, and a mute cry that tore his chest—a cry that no one wanted to hear, or that no one heard or even understood if they did. That's why people like him were extremely unhappy. They were extremely unhappy folk.

The man now cast his gaping, lustreless gaze in all directions, as if searching for something. What was he looking for? What he was searching for, was food. Where was that to be found here? The thin skin of his unfed, starving belly was shrivelled and sunken. His bony chest heaved up and down, like a blacksmith's bellows, from the effort of walking. There was a rasping sound to his breathing. One could count the ribs on the man's chest, one by one, and say how many there were. But within this chest too, lay a heart. He wept for his near and dear ones, he wept at his own inadequacy too.

Not being able to spot what he wanted to see with his wide-open eyes, he emitted a deep sigh from his crumbled chest: 'Oh God! You have no pity!'

But there was pity earlier. God had great pity and mercy, and hungry folk went to woods and thickets and found fruits, tubers, yams and various kinds of things. Now, even that wasn't to be found. Even God seemed to have turned His face away from a vast community of people. They were the indigenes, the sons of the soil of this land, born to labour. But human society had declared them to be untouchable Chandals, people to be shunned.

The man's feet were full of cuts. His legs were grimed with dust, dirt, earth and slime, and a few blades of fresh grass. A small leech appeared to have attached itself near his ankle, perhaps while he was crossing some field or drain. When the spot began to itch, he plucked out the leech, threw it far away and wiped his hand on his dhuti. Seeing the man walk, one would surmise that he had walked like this all his life, across many paths. He was exhausted and worn out from all the walking.

Actually the man was not so old, he was only a few months short of thirty-one years. But dire poverty meant perpetual hunger and starvation, malnourishment and sickness. These had dug their fangs so hard into every crossroads, turn and path, every tiniest moment of his life, that despite his few years, he resembled an old man. Now no one would imagine that he had once been the strongest man across ten villages. He could once lift an entire sack of paddy on to his head at one go. He could cut all the paddy growing on a bigha of land in half a day.

The man was now walking westwards. The east is associated with sunrise and the west with sunset. That symbolic description was apt for the way the man walked. He dragged his body along, like a beast of burden. He seemed to be walking towards his final conclusion—a solitary journey, on which there could be no companion.

Mr Shibnath Bhattacharya had now finished brushing his teeth. He flung the neem twig in the direction of the marsh. It made a slight splashing sound before sinking. The sun had now risen to the top of the palm tree. There were many more cargo and passenger boats on the river. People had started setting out for work. The milch cows had been milked by now. He would breakfast on fresh milk, puffed rice and bananas. Suddenly his eyes went towards his own feet. No—it was not a snake or a leech or a scorpion. Prostrated before him was a man, or something resembling a man. Yet he moved back a couple of steps. He did not want to risk being touched. Earlier, people of all these communities were forbidden to even cast their shadow anywhere. But all that was in the past. The Brahmins of those times could lead a contented life simply with puja and worship. They did not have to look after land, property and farming like they had to now. And so these people, of the untouchable Pode and Chandal castes, were required now for various purposes. It wasn't possible to follow all the rules and customs now. But of course, people were after all people. Could their eternal make-up ever disappear? He became despondent. Seeing a Chandal's face at the very start of the day on such a beautiful morning ... who knew how the day would go! Inwardly, he recited the Gayatri, the all-powerful mantra, *Om bhurbhuvah svaha, tatsaviturvarenyam ...*

The prostrated man too knew that, had it been earlier times, if he so much as came up to a Brahmin, the babus would have lashed him for that offence with a whip made from the scales of the shankar-fish. The whip still hung on the walls of some babus' sitting-rooms. But now they couldn't use it on any and every pretext. In places like Faridpur, Khulna and Barisal, people of lower castes carried themselves with great pride as members of a religious organisation called Matua, centring around the Thakur family of Orakandi. They had become united. It was not at all a good sign. Suppressing his annoyance as far as possible, Shibnath Bhattacharya said softly, '*Ki byapar, re! Sokkal belay baoner paye dhula nite aichhosh ekkare khali haate!* What's the matter? The first thing in the morning, you come to collect the dust of a Brahmin's feet, and you come empty-handed!'

Exhausted by the journey and hunger, the man said most penitently, '*Shorilda koy din hoilo thik nai. Shei joinyo bile gange jaite pari nai. Jaile dui-chairda koi magur ...* I've been unwell for the last few days. That's why I couldn't go to the lakes or the river. Or else, I would surely have brought you a few koi-fish and catfish ...'

'Forget about the fish,' said Shibnath, silencing the man. 'Why couldn't you bring a bunch of brinjals and okra from the fields?'

The man wailed, 'No, master, if I could have found any, would I ...?' Shibnath Bhattacharya turned his face away. What more remained to be said. When the wretch hadn't come to give something, then what had he come for? Why had he walked over two miles, through fields, banks, water and slime? He had surely come to ask for something. Between one man and another—and especially between all these low-caste folk and upper-caste people—there could only be one kind of relationship, that of give-and-take. The Brahmin was at the top of the upper castes. The lower castes would receive blessings, counsel and advice from them, and give gourds, pumpkins and fresh fish in return. A boy from the Brahmin household, who knew how to read and write, would write letters on their behalf and read out documents, and in return the low-caste man, who was illiterate, would give him a befitting fee. That was the rule, the law, the religion, and in that lay religious merit.

This low-caste man had done nothing in accordance with the rule and law. Perhaps it was because of that transgression that he was crouched on the earth with a melancholy face. As Bhattacharya babu was about to go inside the house, the man screeched in distress: '*Kortamoshai aapner kachhe etta bishom bipode poida eto sokal aichhi.* Master, I came to you so early in the morning because I've fallen into a terrible calamity.'

What was new about that, Shibnath thought to himself. Unless there was a calamity, who would leave his work and rush here? '*Koiya phala ki bipod.* Tell me, what's the calamity?'

The man said, plaintively, 'No food's been cooked at home for two or three days. Haven't eaten the last two days. My wife is pregnant. She hasn't eaten anything either. She's going to deliver today or tomorrow. In her condition, if she doesn't eat, who knows if she'll live or die! Master, you must save our lives. Please lend me a couple of seers of rice. I'll work on your field at the time of cultivation and repay you.'

Shibnath Bhattacharya did not pay any heed to the man's entreaty. What was the use of hearing all that! In this country, the people of these castes had no other tale—the same thing all their lives, the same old story ... He gazed at the flock of multi-hued birds flying over the marshland. The morning's sunlight flashed off their red-blue plumage. How it shone! Wouldn't be bad if a fine bird like that could be made a pet. Chhidambala had once gifted him a mynah. It was a really nice-looking bird. It had also started saying a couple of words. But then the cat killed it.

'Master, do say something.'

Shibnath was brought back to the ground of reality from the realm of musing. He said, 'I can see you've come with a lot of hope. But what can I say now, tell me! Can't say no—but I can't say yes either. You know it's going to be a year since my Ma died. The anniversary is next month. We are Brahmins, so we have to follow religious duties and customs. It's against the rules to give or receive anything at this time. So what can I say to you now?'

The man was illiterate, but he wasn't entirely unintelligent. He could figure out that, like a wily eel, Bhattacharya babu was using the pretext of his Ma's death anniversary to slip out of giving him a loan. He was supposedly adhering to the stricture against giving anything; but where was the rule when it came to receiving something? Hadn't he asked him, just a while ago, why he hadn't brought anything? If he had brought something, would he have refused it?

Realising there was no hope, the man rose to his feet, wiping the dust off his backside. He wondered which door he would go and stand in front of next. He had to get some rice quickly, by any means whatsoever. His wife was pregnant, and she had not eaten for two whole days. Looking at her belly and various other signs, Janak's Ma—a mother of seven—had said it would be a son. 'I'll change my name if it turns out to be untrue,' she had said.

Janak's Ma had said a boy did not move much while in the womb, he stayed still, whereas a girl moved around a lot; sometimes she kicked so hard that it seemed she would break open the womb and emerge. The man had got frightened seeing his wife's belly, swollen but still. Had the baby in his wife's unfed body died and swelled up? He put his ear to her belly to try to find out whether it was still alive. It was. It was alive, it was healthy. Janak's Ma had confirmed that too. 'But give your wife rice at once. Or else both the fruit and the tree will die.'

Right then, just as the first light of dawn was about to break, as the warblers were about to emerge from the darkness and fly out, without telling his wife anything, the man had set out on the road. His sole motive was to get some rice. Rice—that could be cooked and eaten. Rice—that could fill the stomach. Because not eating meant dying.

This was the year 1953. As a result of the Direct Action Day of 1946, the country had been partitioned. And now crafty people in both the Hindu and Muslim camps were preparing for another action. The times were extremely unstable now, dangerous and full of uncertainty. Until just a few years ago, the situation was not at all like this. A storm had blown in from nowhere, and within moments everything had been turned upside down. The whole atmosphere had changed. People and their attitudes had changed. The times that had befallen the country, its society and people, were so bad that people's very thoughts and human values had been fundamentally transformed. If such a transformation had involved a qualitative improvement, it would have been called a revolution or renaissance. But this regression could only be judged by historians to be an anarchic, dark and barren epoch.

Just a few years ago, this landmass had witnessed as many as two terrible disasters: the great famine and the great partition. The result had now arrived, in the form of a third catastrophe: flight. In fear and terror, East Bengal's lost people left the land and homesteads of their forefathers, and began fleeing to an unknown country, to a land of strangers and a future of unending humiliation. They were going to India.

In such times, people were anxious only about themselves. This man's kinfolk were all as utterly impoverished as him. Who would hear his tale of hunger and suffering? Who could extend a helping hand? Those who were somewhat better off, those who had some means, if they wished, they would have been able to lend him two or five seers of rice paddy. But they were no longer there. All of them had left for the other Bengal. Left behind were those who—like this man—were impoverished, starving, stricken by fate. That was why the man had set off in the direction of the neighbouring village, towards Bhattacharya babu's house.

Thanks to their caste networks, the upper-caste folk of East Bengal had easily accessed the opportunity to be educated and successful. Sensing in advance the country's political trend and direction, they had been able to wind up everything as soon as possible and move to the other side. But not everyone did that. Some people remained in East Pakistan even now, despite the fear and dread. And they remained with all their power intact. Shibnath Bhattacharya was one such powerful man. He had decided that as long as he was alive, he would not leave the country, even though his elder son had gone to West Bengal and already ensconced himself there. His second son was also talking about going. But Shibnath Bhattacharya's final word was, 'I won't go. If I go it'll be for just a few days, for an outing'. However, many years later, at the time of the Liberation War, after witnessing the rape of his youngest son's elder daughter and the looting of their valuable furniture and possessions by the Pakistani army, he could not remain any longer in that country. In his ripe old age, breaking his own vow, he crossed over to the other Bengal, and died shortly after.

But for now, seeing the man going away, Shibnath called out to him: 'Listen! I can't give you anything for free, and I know you won't take anything for free either. However, there's a way according to the shastras so that all sides are taken care of.'

'What is that way?'

'You work, and I'll pay the price.'

'What's the work?'

'Ma's anniversary is approaching. Cut down that mango tree and make a pile of fuel-wood. In exchange, I'll give you two seers of rice. What do you say? Can you do that? If you can, go and do it.'

'I'll do it.' Inwardly, the man thought to himself, 'When there's no question of not being able to do it, then one just has to be able to do it.'

Spade, axe, cleaver and saw were all there in Shibnath Bhattacharya's house. After all, it was his family homestead and who knew what would be needed, when. Axe in hand, the man got down to an unequal battle. The medium-sized mango tree was still green. Cutting a green tree should not have been very difficult. The difficulty lay in the painful spasms of his starved stomach. So it took him a whole day. But the man's agonies could not fell him. He prevailed over the mango tree.

Shibnath Bhattacharya's youngest son was seventeen years old. He sprinkled Ganga-water over the pile of chopped wood to purify it. Mother Ganga's powers were infinite. The holy water would wash away the pollution of the wretched Chandal's touch, and everything would become clean and pure. After that, holding his hands out high, he poured out about two seers of rice into the gamchha held out by the man. He felt pity for him. Without taking his father's consent, he ventured to invite the man who had laboured so hard to cut the tree for his grandmother's anniversary ceremony, which was to take place on the coming twenty-second of Chaitra. 'Come the next morning and clear the soiled banana leaves. Take whatever food's left over.'

This son of Shibnath was studying for his matriculation. Shibnath wished to educate him further and then send him to take up some big job. Yes, there was some instability all over the country now, but it wouldn't remain that way forever. Nothing ever remained the same forever. The situation would definitely change. Those who were leaving the country and fleeing today would return. That would definitely happen, it had to happen. That was simply the law of time: if it was summer today, it would be the rainy season tomorrow, and winter the day after. Social life too was subject to time. This madness of today—it would become completely peaceful tomorrow. Shibnath Bhattacharya had read the Mahabharat. In the epic, Dharma, in the guise of a crane, had asked Yudhishtir: 'Who is truly happy?' Yudhishtir, who had been driven out again and again from his homeland, wandered through various lands and knew the agony of giving up one's home, had replied, 'He is truly happy who can live in his own land, even if he has only leaves to eat at the end of the day.' Shibnath Bhattacharya was of the same view. However, his children did not agree with him. Except for this youngest son of his.

Shibnath's son was a fine boy. Contrary to the atheistic and *mlechha* bent of mind to be seen everywhere nowadays, he was steeped in religious thoughts. He knew that it was laid down in the shastras that the Chandal was just another lowly creature, not unlike crows and dogs. It was only just to treat them in the same way. He had done nothing wrong by inviting him to eat the stale food left over from his grandmother's ceremony. He would have done wrong if he had given him fresh, hot, tasty food to eat instead.

2

Gagan's Ma

It was the moment when the light of day had been extinguished and the moon and stars were about to shine in the night sky. The moment seemed to have wrapped itself around the earth with an ashen gloom. Like something bearing a mysterious, unknown portent. It was unbearable. How amazingly silent everything was! As if a thick blanket of stillness had been laid over all turmoil and tumult. It was like the calm before a storm. Lightning would surely erupt in a flash just after this and strike down.

The man walked through that gloom, like a manifestation of a curse, of a famine. He was one of the millions of people of this country who were considered to be 'surplus' population, who confronted drought, floods and epidemic every year, and died like worms and insects. How they walked or talked, their very existence or non-existence—none of that mattered the least to the country.

The man—he had a name, given to him by his father. A name that, like the names of all the people of his community, was lowly, inferior and despicable: Garib, meaning 'poor'. Shri Garib Chandra Das was his name. Whether it was clothes on the body, slippers on feet or brains in his head—that is to say, whatever was necessary to survive and advance in society with dignity—not the smallest trace of any of that was in the ambit of such folk. The only thing he had was a crumbling shanty to lay his head under. The man, that is, Garib Das, walked fleet-footedly towards the shanty. He hoped to reach home before it got too dark.

His address! His village! His hut. A shelter that was barely of a man's height, made by daubing slimy mud on wattle. A thatch roof erected over four bamboo posts. Hadn't the thatch of the roof been changed last year, who knew whether or not it had been a year since ... A thatched hut ought to be changed every year. Or else, even if it staved off the sun, it couldn't cope with rain. The shelter was eight feet long and six feet wide. In one corner of the room stood a rolled-up, hand-made, date-palm mat. Hanging on a string were two torn, dirty kanthas that were full of dust. The mat and kantha provided them the only rest they got when they slept at night. Other than that, there was no other possession in the entire space. There was a cooking area on another side, where a fire could be lit using twigs. To speak of cooking utensils, all they had were an earthen pot to cook rice, a clay pan and an earthen water-pot. Garib Das had purchased all these at the time of the Baruni mela for—two and two, four, and three makes seven—seven small copper coins. Some things he had made himself. Like a long-armed bamboo ladle to stir the rice, another ladle to serve the dal, made by inserting a long stick through holes made on the two sides of a coconut shell, and a large shell to serve vegetable curry. All this comprised his household effects. They ate their rice using banana leaves for plates.

There was water and more water everywhere around them. On the water-edge was a dense forest of hogla grass, inhabited by jackals, wild cats, snakes and leeches. Wild boar and porcupine were also spotted there sometimes. During the rainy season, the water rose till the door of one's hut. With the water came several kinds of water-borne diseases, like malaria, dengue, gastroenteritis and cholera. There were no hand-pumps here. Drinking water meant water from the river, drains or ponds. As a result, the people here literally died like cats and dogs. No one here had any cultivable land. Everyone worked on other people's land. In return, they received four or six annas as wages. Some people went around catching fish in the rivers and drains. So that was Garib Das's village, his address.

Garib Das had no time now to think about the country or society or anything like that. His only thought was reaching home quickly. His pregnant wife Bimala was at home, she had not eaten for three days, counting today. He had to feed her rice at once. Inwardly, he called out to his revered Harichand and Guruchand: 'O Lord, may I find my wife well when I return home.' His thoughts were so intensely focused on how he could help his wife and soon-to-be-born child that he forgot all about treading carefully. All the poisonous creatures lay in wait on the ridged paths of the fields at this time: cobras, vipers, krates, and so much else. If he trod on one, there wouldn't be any time even to ask for water. They took one's life away with a single swipe. But such fears had vanished from Garib's head. Bimala could go into labour any moment now. His starving wife had completely wilted, like a severed gourd plant. And yet Garib Das had gone away, leaving her all alone, without telling her anything. Now he had to rush and cook the rice for her. There was salt and chillies at home. Hot, steaming, starchy rice tasted very nice with salt and chillies.

Night had set in by the time he reached home. Another dark night in rural Bengal's long, anarchic night that prevailed from the riots of 1946 to the violence of 1964 ... As he neared his house, Garib Das heard a heartrending sound. Someone was speaking loudly, and someone was moaning and weeping in agony. As he went closer, he suddenly heard the shrill cry of a baby. Standing near the door, waiting for Garib Das to return was Gagan's Ma, chattering away to herself. She was a distant aunt of Garib Das's, and she was known locally as 'Gagan's Ma'. The old woman was quite infamous in the locality for being a loudmouth. To spell it out, she wasn't afraid of anything or anyone. And when she spoke, it was as if brass bells were clanging in her throat. As soon as she saw Garib Das, Gagan's Ma began flaying him rudely: '*Koi chhili bebak dinmanda? Boudar ei rohom obostay ekla ghore phalaiya keu jaiy? Gele jodi to boila geli na kyan? Bodhbuddhi ki tor kon kale hoibo na! Padha, chiroda kaal padha hoiya thakbi! Kothay koy beda mainsher dosh dosha aar maiyya mainsher ek dosha. Aer chaiyya bodo bipod aar achhe naki! Dhare kachhe kono ghor bario nai je dakle manush jon aibo. Tor chouddo purusher bhaigyo bhalo je somoy moto mui aiyya podchhilam. Naile etukkhun duidaiy bhobo pade choilya jaito!* Where were you all day? Does anyone take off, leaving his wife all alone in this condition? If you had to go, why didn't you tell her and go? Will you never have any brains? An idiot—all your life you'll remain an idiot. Do you know, it's said a woman's labour pain equals ten torments suffered by men? Is there any greater danger than that? There aren't even any houses nearby to call out to. It's the good fortune of fourteen generations of your ancestors that I arrived on time. Or else both of them would have gone to the other shore by now!'

Garib Das laid down the bundle of rice wrapped in his gamchha. It wasn't just rice but life itself that was tied in the bundle. Then, as if to explain, he said, 'No work for the last two months—what will we eat? No fire's been lit at home for two or three days. I had to try and get some rice. Bimala seemed to be all right yesterday, so I thought I'd be back quickly. Who knew then that it would take a whole day? How is she now? I don't hear her—is she well?'

'She is. She's all right. You've had a son, you've become a father. You've got what you wished for from God all these days.' Pausing awhile, she laughed loudly and then said, 'But you have to give me a sari.'

'I'll give it,' Garib Das promised. 'Give your blessings, Khudi Ma, that my son lives. I'll give you a sari.'

'When will you give it?'

'Let me get some money in hand.'

'I hope you won't say, "Let my son grow up first ...", I hope you'll work and slave, and then buy it for me!'

'I won't say that, Khudi Ma. I swear I won't say that.'

'When you were born, your Baba had promised me a sari. He didn't even give me rags, let alone a sari! So many years have gone by, you didn't give me one either. Let's see what you do now.'

In this while, the dense knot of anxiety gathered in Garib's chest had dissolved. The light of joy spread all over his face. That light obscured the hunger pangs of his stomach, which felt like a gaping ocean of nothingness. His wife was well. His son was well. Then how could he not feel well!

Now he was eager to get the news from Gagan's Ma. 'When did you arrive, Khudi Ma? Is everyone at home well? The date-thorn that had pierced Suren-da's foot—how's his foot now? Won't Gagan go to Pirichpur any more? He was earning quite well there ... a wage of five quarters plus meals isn't bad at all.'

Gagan's Ma replied, 'Everyone's fine at home, Suren is able to walk a little now. Mukunda Kabiraj's medicine worked. Gagan's stopped working now; he's whiling away his time under the pretext of getting married. In the current situation in the country, when it's not certain whether we'll live or die—tell me, how can I get my son married?' After a pause, she continued, 'I came just after noon. I thought I'd take your advice and return home. But could I leave? I found your wife wailing in agony in the empty room, like a goat being slaughtered. How could I leave her and go away?'

Garib Das said, 'We'll talk later. Quickly cook some rice now, Khudi Ma. We can talk after we've eaten.'

'Where did you get the rice from?'

'From the Bhattacharya house.'

'Did they give it just like that?'

'Do they give anything to anyone just like that? Shibnath babu made me work the whole day in exchange for the rice. That's why it took so long.'

Gagan's Ma then asked, 'I heard that almost everyone in his family has left for India. Isn't he going?'

'Who knows what he'll do. From whatever I could gather seeing his household, I don't think he'll go.'

The conversation was moving in the direction of what Gagan's Ma had come to discuss. But she deferred it. The whole night lay ahead; she could talk all she wanted later. The fellow had just returned after working all day and, besides, a monstrous hunger must be assailing the starving girl's stomach after having delivered her baby. She ought to cook rice for them first. But before that, there was an essential custom to be performed, to welcome the new life that had come into the world.

She said, 'Garib, I'm cooking the rice. Do something, see if you can arrange for two drops of honey.'

'Honey! What do you need honey for?'

'Don't you know anything? How would you know! Even your parents didn't know,' Gagan's Ma said testily. 'You're a father now. Don't you want to see your son's face? It's the first time you are going to set eyes on your child. Won't you offer him something sweet? When a baby's born, it's customary to put some honey into its mouth. If it has honey, its speech will be sweet and its life will be beautiful.'

Garib Das said in a most helpless tone, 'Where will I find honey now?'

'How can I tell you that,' Gagan's Ma retorted angrily. 'You should have got it from somewhere two or four days ago, kept it ready at home. See what you can do now. It's your son—what more can I say ...'

'Must one put honey in his mouth?'

'You must.'

'What if one doesn't?'

Glaring at Garib Das with fire in her eyes, Gagan's Ma said, 'All these are the customs of our forefathers. They've said, "The life of one who doesn't have honey at birth turns bitter." There's no joy or peace in a life that's bitter.' As she spoke, Gagan's Ma's voice turned sombre. 'Being a father, don't ruin the boy's life for want of a drop of honey. Go, get it from wherever you can, by any means. Just one drop.'

Tears welled in Garib Das's eyes. His chest heaved and he wept when he thought about his own harsh life. No honey had entered his mouth either at the time of his birth. Whatever else it may have been, but it wasn't honey for sure. It was the same for his father too. So his son wouldn't get any either. Honey, a drop of genuine honey, honey that couldn't be found in any odd honeycomb. Where could he find that? People like Garib Das did not know where honey could be found. For want of honey, all their lives they would remain at the bottom of the bottomless sea of suffering. The lives of these folk were terribly accursed. The inauspicious moment of their birth would stalk them until the moment they died. There was no succor for any of them, no reprieve from this inevitability.

Garib Das sobbed, 'Khudi Ma, oh dear Khudi Ma, did you give honey to Suren and Gagan? If you did, then why aren't their lives sweet? Tell me!'

Suren was her elder son and Gagan the younger. Gagan ran the moneylender's boat and Suren climbed date palms, extracted the juice and made jaggery, which he went around selling in markets. They too could not claim a life that could be called sweet. Gagan's Ma knew that. Even so she muttered, 'Learned people have said so. One should heed what they've said.'

One should. But how could one? Where was honey to be obtained from? Where could one get the honey that made life healthy, beautiful and prosperous? At one time, Garib Das had a reputation for being the strongest man across ten villages. He could work like an ox. He worked like that too, but he didn't get a fair wage for his labour. That's why he couldn't eat two fistfuls of rice, twice a day, to fill his belly. Starved and underfed, his strength had whittled away. Whatever remained—with which he had been able to cut down the mango tree today—was of no use at this time. Most of those who could pay for his toil and sweat had left for the other country. As a result, there was no rice now in Garib Das's house. How could there be honey in the house when there wasn't even any rice?

That's why the lowly, low-caste, starving Garib Das could not feed the magical elixir made from flowers to the new life that had arrived in his house today. The new life would remain bitter and devoid of flavour.

'Khudi Ma, dear Khudi Ma, forget the custom! We are struggling with a great famine, it's a very bad time. We have nothing to wear, no thatch on our roofs, no food in our bellies. Those rules and customs are not for us. We'll have to live and die without any of that.'

⚬❧⚬

Long ago, there were no people here. There was only water everywhere. In the womb of this bottomless mass of water that extended to the very horizon, Mata Basumati, Mother Earth, slumbered, who knows how long she lay there. One day, she suddenly woke up. Mother Earth raised her head slowly and gazed at the sky, the sun, the moon and the stars. Sunlight fell on her body. Unknown to anyone, the land gradually turned dry. The marshland became suitable for human habitation.

At that time, after wandering through many roads and many lands, and suffering many hardships, a band of nomadic people—who had been compelled by the stipulations of the shastras to adopt nomadic lives—finally reached this inaccessible region that people were unaware of. They were entranced by the beauty and majesty of Mother Earth. There was plenty of land suitable for cultivation, and plenty of sweet grass for cattle fodder. When they scattered a handful of seeds on the land, it returned a thousand-fold at harvest. There was a limitless store of water all around, and if one merely stretched out one's hand, there was a surfeit of fish to be had. Seeing all this, the people gave up their nomadic existence and settled down in this uninhabited region that was inaccessible to the upholders of religious law. They hoped to live there permanently.

Those were days of great joy and contentment. If one went down to the water with nets, there were plenty of fish. On the land were enough fruits within hand's reach, and if one laboured on the land, unending supplies of paddy, sesame, jute and mustard were reaped. Nature had granted a hundred kinds of food to sustain life. In that era, people's lives were very peaceful and free of anxiety. Everything was simple and straightforward. After a whole day's toil, people returned home in the evening and got together for story, song, laughter and joy. And then they sank into a deep, happy slumber at night. Weren't there any troubles then? Of course there were—there was disease, grief, nature's fury. All the troubling things that are there today were also to be found then. But the dastardly skill of appropriating the fruit of another man's labour was not there. There wasn't the cunning endeavour of man's subjugation by man. The place was free of all these ills of the outside world.

Man was like a tree. Just like a tree had roots planted deep into the earth, man's roots were planted in the environment and the society he lived in. What he consumed via those roots was deemed cultivation, culture, sanskar, folk customs, religious practices, as well as many formal practices. All these people, whose lives centred around labour, were simple and straightforward, affectionate to guests and sensitive to others' suffering. Just as no one was wealthy in their society, there wasn't anyone totally destitute either. There was no thief or crook, or godman, or beggar in the society. There weren't any prostitutes, pimps, drunkards or gamblers. People were very good then; they were content. They had named this village *Pother Shesh*, or Journey's End, with much love and affection. This was where, after traversing many roads, their journey had finally ended.

But word of this place did not remain secret for very long from people outside. Coming to know about this well-watered, bejewelled womb of land, abundant with fruits, they slowly began arriving in ones and twos. And so, within a hundred or hundred and fifty years, this uninhabited frontier zone was transformed into a full-fledged human settlement. Not all of those who came were engaged in cultivation or cattle-herding. There were also weavers, blacksmiths, washer-folk and barbers. Finally came the band of traders, businessmen and middlemen, and Brahmins adhering to puranic life, as well as priests and godmen.

All of them were extremely clever, and as a result of direct and indirect connections with sages, kings and royalty, they were immensely powerful too. Thereafter, each day, in various ways, they skillfully pushed the original dwellers to a corner and grabbed their lands, places, crops and resources. After just a few generations, one day, the original residents saw to their amazement that they had nothing left. The outsiders had grabbed everything. They had all become landless, and found it difficult to survive without physical labour. They had possessed land, which was the source of their food, and which they had loved like a mother. Now they were motherless. After pouring labour and sweat on this land, come harvest, they had to carry the paddy and deposit it in other people's granaries, for which they received a pittance in wages. Contempt and humiliation were hurled at them. Their bellies and their hearts were bereft.

Shri Garib Chandra Das was a descendant, the current representative, of the original inhabitants. His father was Shri Har Kumar Das. Their address: Pother Shesh. Even now, Garib Das vividly remembered that long ago—he was five or six years old then—they still had had a little bit of land that was cultivated twice a year. The harvested paddy sufficed to feed them the whole year. The English government had given them for their land a deed—affixing a seal—granting them the right to occupation. Every year, the nayeb collected the tax on that. That land had now gone into Mr Roy's custody. A black-coated lawyer had stood in court and, with the aid of various bits of information, evidence, papers and documents, established that two years ago, Har Kumar Das had sold the land to him and that for the last two years, he had been illegally occupying and cultivating the land.

Now Garib Das's only sustenance was labour. As long as Mr Roy's family remained in this country, Garib Das found work on their land for a few months of the year. But now that they and others like them, who were affluent, had all left for India, he did not get work on all days. He was one of six brothers. The others worked independently, catching fish from canals and lakes because they could not feed their families with what they earned from labour. It was more profitable to catch fish. Consequently, they were slightly better off than Garib Das. At least their stoves were lit once a day. That was in the evening. They soaked the rice left over after the meal at night in water, and ate it the next morning.

A casting-net was required to catch fish. Garib's net had been stolen a few years ago, and he couldn't make another one. That would require at least five rupees worth of string and a month or a month and a half's knitting. Garib didn't have either the money or the time. And so his family suffered great deprivation. From which he was just not able to find release. It was as if an octopus called poverty had spread out its eight poisonous arms and grabbed him. And now another belly had joined this terribly poor family. Birth was not a matter of joyous festivity here. Rather, it was a burden, a trouble, a cause for anxiety. Garib Das was now in distress on account of that anxiety: What would happen? How could this light of the clan be kept alive?

This was Garib Das's first child, who was born thanks to the blessings of the soothsaying Matua sage, Hiraman Gosain. He had said, 'This son will bring glory to the name of your family and raise it to the very sky. Just see, you won't be poor anymore, you'll have a large house with a tin roof, a twenty-two yard long net and a large fishing boat. You'll have everything.'

Yes, he'd have all that. He'd have everything. This boy would bring all that when he grew up and learnt to work hard and earn. Until then, for just those few years, that small life had to be held close, like a lamp on a stormy night. Such a hope was every low-caste man's. The same tree of hope grew in everyone's heart: My son shall achieve what I could not. He will bring us happiness, prosperity and fullness. But the fullness that had been dreamt of by Garib's grandfather, his father and now by him—his son and grandson too would only dream of that. From the time they were born—as a result of that very crime of being born—any fullness would forever elude them. No one would be freed of the curse of birth.

Garib Das's father, Har Kumar Das, was once on his way to the weekly market in Nirojpur. He sold coconuts and areca from his trees, and bought salt, tobacco, oil and spices. There were large wholesalers in this market, who loaded goods on large boats that went all the way to Khulna, Jessore and Dhaka. As Har Kumar was going by boat along the river, he spotted a girl of about eight, bathing on a riverbank. Oh, it couldn't be just a girl—she looked like Ma Lakshmi herself! Her eyes, nose, face, complexion and the hair on her hand—how beautiful they were! Just her hair had Har Kumar Das entranced. He imagined the fair-skinned girl standing with a sky-ful of black clouds atop her head. When the boat reached the nearby jetty, he went ashore. He enquired about the girl. Her name was Bimala, her Ma had been widowed very young, and she was her only child. Caste and gotra too matched. Soon after, on an auspicious day, paying a dowry of twenty-one rupees, Har Kumar Das got his youngest son, Garib, married to Bimala, and brought his beautiful daughter-in-law home.

Garib had just entered his seventeenth year. He was a broad-shouldered, strapping youth. His wife was half of him, not only in age, but also in height. If he stood up, she reached his waist, or a bit above it. Seeing that, the old women of the neighbourhood couldn't help laughing. 'Oh dear, what a lovely match—just like Shiva and Parvati!'

In time, the girl came of age. She came to live in her husband's house. Now all six brothers, including Garib, were married; some brothers had children too. All the brothers lived under the same roof for thirty-three days, and during that period, no one else entered their lives. It was extremely difficult for six girls—hailing from six families, having grown up in six kinds of environments with six kinds of mentalities—to get along. And so came the day when each one separated their utensils and set up separate households. There were about forty families in Har Kumar's hamlet. He was slightly better-off—it wasn't clay utensils which were used in his kitchen, but aluminum ones. His wife's nose-ring and earrings, which she wore when she fetched water from the riverbank in a brass pot, were made of gold. Har Kumar divided all his possessions into six equal parts. A set of fishing nets, thirteen ducks and about ten seers of paddy fell to Garib's share. It was agreed that Har Kumar's wife would live with the younger son, Upen, and Har Kumar would not have any fixed place of his own; he would stay and eat in any house he wished.

After everyone went their separate ways, Garib Das took his wife and set up house in a slightly vacant area, near the wooded part in the eastern side of the village. He wanted to raise chickens, ducks, goats, cows and pigs there, which he couldn't do without vacant space. But that longing was never to be fulfilled. For want of what was needed to fulfill it: capital.

He had been married to Bimala for seven or eight years. An anguish had slowly begun to form within her. It was being said that her physical make-up was apparently like that of a barren woman. Whose face people did not want to see at the start of a journey, or at the auspicious moment of beginning an important task. There were whispered conversations to this effect in women's circles. Perhaps a similar concern had begun to emerge in Garib's mind too. That was when Bimala became pregnant. And there had been no danger or hindrance; Garib Das's first child had a perfectly normal delivery. By custom, today was the day to bask in that joy. But Garib Das could not do that. The innards in his belly were crushing him to death like a python. After starving for so long, he was wracked by spasms of pain. And when he tried to speak, it was as if half the words emerged from his ears rather than from his throat. Flames of fire seemed to dance before his eyes. So how could there be any joy or pleasure in the heart? Now there was only one worry, and it sat weightily on his mind: How would he keep the child alive? What would his future be like?

'*Koi, ki korbi?* What are you going to do?' Gagan's Ma called out.

'What will I do? There's nothing to be done. Whatever's in his fate will happen.'

Gagan's Ma stared at Garib's face. The night's darkness lay dense on that face. There was light, which fell on the leaves of the branch of the kadam tree above his head. That was the light of fireflies, coming alight and then extinguishing. Other than that, there was no light anywhere. Only deep, impenetrable darkness. It was as if this dark night was a veritable metaphor for life.

Garib stood silently for quite a while beneath the kadam tree. Then, becoming somewhat restless, he advanced towards his crumbling hut. Bimala was lying in a corner of the verandah, near where the cooking space was. He tried to look at her face, but he could not see anything. A terrible darkness had enveloped Bimala and her newborn baby. She was silent now. Not crying anymore. Who knows, perhaps by now she had fathomed that nothing was gained by crying. At this time, society and people would not attach any value to her cries. Tears were the most useless, cheap and insignificant thing in the world today. Maybe that's why she had fallen asleep.

Then it seemed like Bimala had woken up. From her anguished moans it was clear that she had survived. On her right, the earthen pot with smouldering paddy husk emitted a thin wisp of smoke. The smoke repelled mosquitoes.

He stood there for a while and called out to Bimala: 'Hey, can you hear me? I'm back. I had gone to fetch rice. I got the rice. I'll give you cooked rice in a little while.' He did not have any news bigger than that to convey. After that, Garib stepped down into the courtyard again. He saw clouds gathering in the sky. It looked like a rainstorm would arrive soon. It was as if the night that had enveloped Bimala and her newborn child, thick and black, was some fierce, deceptive, headless demon. A night that knew no mercy, justice, love or compassion.

By then Gagan's Ma had placed the pot on a stove in a corner of the courtyard and lit it. She wanted to finish cooking the rice before it began raining. Her experienced eyes, which had seen plenty of clouds and rain, sensed that with such clouds there wasn't going to be undisturbed peace tonight. It was just a little bit of rice, it didn't take long to cook. She ladled out a bit of rice and gruel on a banana leaf for Bimala, took some herself, and gave most of it to Garib Das. After that, there was no chance to look in any other direction! Blowing into the pile of rice, Garib stuffed handfuls into his mouth as he sat in the darkness.

After snuffing out the hunger in his belly, when Garib Das spread out his gamchha on one side of the verandah and lay down, Gagan's Ma finally got the opportunity to speak about the important matter that had brought her to his house that noon. 'O Garib, everyone says we won't be able to live in this country any longer. All my relatives and acquaintances are going away to India one by one. I believe the miyas are going to start rioting again. Both Subol and Radhakanta have decided to leave next month. Gagan told me, "Ma, go and talk to Garib-dada once. We'll do whatever he does."'

Four of Garib Das's brothers had crossed over to the other Bengal. Only he and his younger brother Shashikanta remained. Shashikanta was adamant: 'I won't go. Whether I survive or die, it's in this country that I'll stay. Can one just suddenly say that this country is not ours? If the country where my father, grandfather and forefathers grew up can't be ours, then no other country can.' Shashikanta's courage bolstered Garib's confidence. But then, seeing the terrified people all around, all his confidence was deflated like a pricked balloon.

He said, 'I've not been able to decide anything yet. I think I'll go and have a talk with Majid and Mamud tomorrow, or the day after. They may be Muslim, but after all, they are my brothers. We belong to the same family. I'll do whatever they say. If they say, leave, then I won't stay any longer.'

'Just let me know after you talk to them.'

'I will.'

It had begun raining now, accompanied by a gale. Garib could not sit on the verandah any longer. He went inside, carrying his gamchha. It seemed that he wanted to move away from all the dangers, disasters and dilemmas of the world and hide himself in a dark corner. Gagan's Ma thought of going to Bimala and consoling and cheering her. Garib stood alone in the darkness, as if facing himself and asking: Why is it like this? Why do things turn out the way they simply should not? He did not know the answer. He just could not figure it out. Why had all the millions of low-caste, impoverished, destitute folk like him, who had no land, property, wealth or resources to speak of, who had to eke out two handfuls of rice, twice a day, by toil and sweat—why had they become victims of the rage of another group of people who were just like themselves? How had they turned so belligerent and violent?

3

Nandu Gosain

There was no violence or malice in the beliefs, ideals and culture in whose bosom Garib Chandra Das's forefathers had been raised. Sons of the soil, their lives were centred entirely around labour, and they had ornamented this with their own human touch. Theirs was a society whose credo was to live and let live. In this society, people's lives were tranquil so long as the attitudes of outsiders—who despised a life of labour—could not infiltrate their culture.

In the habitation established by this group of low-caste people—who had been declared to be untouchable and polluted in the scriptures of the Hindu faith—in a region of rural Bengal that was completely surrounded by water and more water, there were no notions of high or low, or social divisions. There were no thieves, prostitutes or beggars, there was neither wealth nor poverty. All these gained currency after the arrival of the upper-caste folk, and especially the priestly class. It was they who compelled people to become their slaves, made them into thieves, beggars and whores. And with them came ailments like blood pressure, heart disease and deadly conditions like gonorrhoea. They were the ones who first imposed on people the notion of the crime of one's very birth, and of being touchable and untouchable. Over which no one had any powers or control. According to their laws, a class of people had to burn endlessly in the fire of humiliation and revulsion merely by being born: you are low-born, you are untouchable, unclean, polluted.

Love breeds love and hatred breeds hatred. Whose poison fruit was caste hatred? When they consider us non-human, why should we consider them human! When they felt no compassion, responsibility or duty or even pity towards us, why should we have any for them! When they did not accord any value to our lives, did not grant us any dignity, why should *we* grant them any?

Once Garib Das had travelled north with some people from his village on a wood-cutting mission. Baghai Karati, the sawyer, who had his own saw, had taken him along. They had worked for a whole month, cutting trees and making planks. As Garib did not have much experience in regard to wood-work, he had received somewhat lower wages than the others, and the work he did was also somewhat different: he cooked for everyone, and prepared the hookah for them. He wasn't married then, and he had a penchant for travelling, so he did not mind the low wages and the non-strenuous work.

One day, after Garib had finished his work, he and three others went for an outing to the riverside ashram of the spiritual guide, Nandu Gosain. After Gosain's parents had died when he was very small, he had gone away to Mathura as a sadhu's disciple. He had stayed there for a few years, and when he was a bit older, he had returned to his own country and set up an ashram. He did not renounce the world, he was married, a householder, and yet a sanyasi. His credo: life's salvation lay in doing one's work with the Lord's name on one's lips. The man had travelled through many lands, he had been in the company of many people, and so he was wise. Garib and his mates all had the same question—the question that assailed their inner being: 'Why do the Brahmins and Kayasthas keep calling us "Chandal", why do they despise us?

Why is there such misery for us in human society when we too are human?'

Gosain had a little bit of cultivable land. Together with his wife, son and daughter, he worked on the land and also practised a bit of homeopathy, and was able to sustain himself thereby. When Garib's group reached there, they saw that some other people had arrived before them. They had spread out a mat on the immaculately-wiped, mud-plastered courtyard and were seated. And Gosain was telling them about an amazing vehicle, whose name was railway. Apparently the huge vehicle emitted smoke from its mouth, and a thousand people could travel together on it. Even more incredible, it moved faster than a horse along two iron tracks, but never fell down.

Nandu Gosain was delighted to see Garib Das, Baghai Karati, Shyamacharan Kirtaniya and Bipad Bala. Welcoming them warmly, as if he had known them for ages, he said to them, '*Aishen bhaktobrindo*, come, disciples, may my knowledge be sanctified by the blessings of your holy feet. Please sit, all of you, drink some water.'

Har Kumar Das's father had told Har Kumar, and Har Kumar had in turn told his son Garib Das: 'The man who calls you his own can be recognised at once. There's no lack of a seat, breeze from a palm-leaf fan, water to quench one's thirst and sweet words in the house of one's own.' A date-leaf mat lay spread out on Nandu Gosain's courtyard. Wayfarers passing through the village, as well as some of those who were travelling by boat on the river, stopped there to rest and to say or hear a few words. Garib and his mates sat down on the mat. A person sitting there was smoking a hookah. He offered it to them saying, 'Here, master, have a smoke.'

Nandu Gosain enquired, 'Which parts are you from? I've never seen you before.'

After a brief explanation of where they lived and the work that had brought them there, Baghai Karati finally asked about the grave matter that tormented him. He said, 'Gosain, you have travelled through many lands, you've heard many wise people. I want to ask you something. I've heard from my father and grandfather that apparently we are of the Namasudra caste, that we are apparently the descendants of Kashyap Muni, so we belong to the Kashyap gotra. Then why do Brahmins and Kayasthas call us "Chandal"? And why do they treat us like animals?'

Nandu Gosain was silent for a while, and then he said, 'You all have come to me with a lot of hope. I don't know where or how you heard about me, but I am no scholar. I don't read any shastras or puranas. But I acquired some knowledge by hearing what some people said. I won't say I don't know the answer to what you want to know. That's my own question too. Why do they call us "Chandal"? I can only say what I have heard from various people. But I don't know how true or false that is.'

'Tell us that, we'll listen,' said Shyamacharan.

Nandu Gosain began, 'This world of ours, all the living creatures, trees, leaves, rivers, canals, people, cows, insects, birds— the one who made all of these is Brahma. One of Brahma's sons was Marich. Marich's son was Mahamuni Kashyap, and Kashyap's son was Namas. The Namasudras are the descendants of Namas Muni.'

'Gosain, we hear, why only hear, we see it too, that when a Brahmin has a son, he becomes a Brahmin too. When we are descendants of Namas Muni, then why are we Sudra and not Brahmin?' asked Bipad Bala. This was something that he had thought about a lot. 'Why do people of high castes consider us to be equal to dogs? Why do they despise us?'

Coughing a bit and looking, as much as was possible in the moonlit night, at the faces of all those present, Nandu Gosain said, 'That's a very long tale.'

'Please tell us. We've come only to hear you.'

'One of Brahma's sons was Ruchi. Ruchi's daughter was Sulochana. When Namas Muni came of age, he was married to Sulochana. She bore Namas Muni two children. Both were sons. One boy was named Uruvan, and the other Kirtivan. They grew up as the days and years went by. Once, Namas Muni left them behind and went away to the forest. He became so immersed in meditation that he lost track of time and stayed in the forest for days, months and years. By the time he completed his tapasya and returned home, almost fifteen years had passed. It was this that led to disaster ...'

Like possessed souls, Baghai Karati, Garib Das and company were sitting in the dark and looking single-pointedly at Nandu Gosain's face. They listened to every word of his with rapt attention. As if they didn't want to miss even a single word. A little while ago, someone had handed them a hookah. No one had puffed on the hookah and the fire in the bowl had died. But a fire burned in their minds. The tale of their caste's origins had inflamed them.

'The shastras say that every man is a Sudra at birth. After his *upanayan*—do you know about the *upanayan* ceremony? The thread on a Brahmin's chest, when he wears it, he's born for the second time. After that, when he acquires knowledge, he becomes a novice. And finally, after he attains self-realisation, he becomes a Brahmin. Those are the four stages to becoming a Brahmin, the four steps. In those days, one did not become a Brahmin simply by being born in a Brahmin household. He had to prove before Brahmin society that he possessed nine qualities. Only then was he accorded the status of a Brahmin.'

Those who were seated on the mat did not utter a word. None of them had the education or knowledge to say anything on the subject. Whether what Gosain said was true or false, they just had to hear him out.

'So the first stage of advancing towards becoming a Brahmin is the *upanayan*. Which, according to the shastras, must be performed by the age of fourteen. Once that age is crossed, the *upanayan* cannot take place. Because Namas Muni could not return from the forest in time, his sons' *upanayan* could not take place. They remained Sudras. But after all, they were Namas Muni's sons. Hence Brahma granted them a boon, whereby, despite being Sudra, all their descendants would be called Namasyas. Before any mantra was uttered, the name "Nama" would be uttered, in obeisance. Those who are known today as Namasudra are their descendants.'

Baghai Karati asked, 'If our past is so worthy of pride, then why is our plight so wretched today? Namasudras don't have clothes to hide their nakedness, no food in their bellies, no thatch on their roofs or medicines when they're sick. There's only nothing and nothing everywhere—no education, no guidance, no regard, no dignity.'

'That's because of a terrible conspiracy.'

'Conspiracy by whom?'

'None other than the Brahmins. The plight of the Namasudras today must be attributed to the craftiness of the Brahmins who lived during the period between the Pala and Sena dynasties. Those two kingly dynasties are renowned in history books. After the Pala dynasty came to an end, and some time before the Sena dynasty took over, for a brief while, Bengal came under the control of the Sur dynasty. I don't know for sure, perhaps they didn't rule over the whole of Bengal, perhaps their jurisdiction only covered a few districts. The Sur dynasty was Buddhist. Due to their enthusiasm, the Buddhist faith spread through the entire Bengali-speaking land. People of the Buddhist faith do not worship idols. They do not believe in God. They consider killing animals to be sinful. People's adherence to that faith did not diminish even after the defeat of the Pala dynasty. It kept growing. It was as if the tide of Buddhism was sweeping over the entire Bengali country.

'But the king Adi Sur was a zealous devotee of Sanatan Dharma. Soon after he became king, he decided to halt the spread of Buddhism and restore Sanatan Dharma to its former glory. To fulfill his wish, he decided to hold a mahayagna, or a grand fire-oblation. But that couldn't happen simply by deciding to hold it, because that required Brahmins who were well-versed in the Vedas. There were no Brahmins to speak of in Bengal then. There was no puja or recitation from sacred texts in Buddhism. Since performing pujas and reciting from sacred texts could no longer provide a livelihood, Brahmins had taken up other professions. Those who could not do so were left to others' mercy, but by then they too had lost their faith and conviction. The Vedas and puranas, the practice of recitation of texts—all of that had disappeared.

'So what could be done now? How was the mahayagna for the revival of Sanatan Dharma to be performed? Eventually, after making enquiries, Adi Sur found out that Brahmins of suitable proficiency were to be found in the kingdom of Kannauj. An emissary was sent to Kannauj, bearing Adi Sur's appeal.'

Pausing awhile, Nandu Gosain observed the expressions on the faces of his listeners and then said, 'I hope no one is finding it difficult to understand what I'm saying.'

'No, not at all. Please continue,' said Garib Das, the youngest of the lot, on behalf of everyone. He was enjoying the tale. He had never heard anything like this before.

'So the emissary went to Kannauj, but the king there, Virbhadra, did not pay any attention to Adi Sur's appeal. Bengal had already fallen to atheism—the believers of Sanatan Dharma outside of Bengal considered those of the Buddhist faith to be atheists. Nothing of dharma and karma remained in that country. Brahmins going there would go astray and lose their religion. Who would bear the responsibility for such a sin? Virbhadra told the emissary to go back and inform his king that Brahmins could not be sent to an irreligious kingdom. That would be sinful.

'King Adi Sur then steeled his mind. He realised that if one could not get what one wanted through fair means, then one had to adopt foul means. He would go to war and bring back the five Brahmins required for the ceremony. Have any of you heard the name of the twelve bhuiyas? Once upon a time, there were twelve kings in Bengal, and one of them was Pratap Roy. He had an army of twelve hundred men, all low-caste, who used to march to war with shields and spears. They were called dhalis, after the shields they bore. Adi Sur too had an army of low-caste soldiers like that.

'I made a mistake,' Nandu Gosain said and paused, and then correcting himself, he said, 'Low-caste and high-caste were all fabricated by the Brahmins. I don't believe in high and low. I said that only to simplify it so everyone can understand. Please don't mind.'

'Oh no, we won't. Please carry on.'

'So then, from that army of low-caste soldiers, seven hundred and fifty-six expert soldiers were ordered to don their battle gear. You know what they say in politics? Everything is fair in war. And so, sparkling white threads were planted on the chests of the army of seven hundred and fifty-six, and they all bestrode cows. One day, all of them went and gathered in front of Virbhadra's court, demanding battle. Virbhadra fell into a great dilemma. They were not armed. But if the Kannauj army attacked Adi Sur's soldiers, then either cows or Brahmins would be killed. And it was written in the shastras that killing Brahmins and cows were the gravest of sins. Those who killed them dwelt eternally in hell. Even if a Brahmin committed a heinous crime—robbery, murder or rape, the king could at most drive him away from his land; no more than that. How was Virbhadra to know that none of those who had come in the guise of Brahmins were really Brahmins? With no option but defeat, he accepted the condition of sending five Brahmins to Bengal. Later, the five Brahmins decided not to return to their land. They married five girls from Bengal and settled down in the country. It is the descendants of those five Brahmins who are accorded the name "Kulin", who are different from all the other Brahmin dynasties. They do not marry or have any social relations with the others.

'When the five Brahmins from Kannauj came to Bengal, they brought along five servants, to carry their belongings, to do all their work and execute their orders. They did not return to their land either. They too stayed back together with their masters, and got married in this country. Actually those five servants were of the Sudra caste. But on account of being in the company of and servicing people of high origins, their caste underwent change. They were placed below the Brahmin, but somewhat higher than the Sudra. From them arose a new caste in Bengal, which was called "Kayastha".

'Be that as it may, after bringing the Brahmins who were learned in the Vedas, Adi Sur's oblation took place without further hindrance. The king was extremely happy. Now it was the turn of the seven hundred and fifty-six soldiers—who had risked their lives, ventured abroad and brought back as many as five priceless gems in the form of the Brahmins—   to be suitably rewarded. "Speak, what do you want?" Sticking his neck out, the chief of the seven hundred and fifty-six soldiers stepped up before the king. He said, "Maharaja, we seek nothing else from you. We have just one humble submission: please don't take back what you granted. This sacred thread was a gift of your mercy. Maharaja, please don't ask us to remove it. Permit us to wear it on our chests forever."

'King Adi Sur was a righteous man, who never forgot his benefactors. He said, "Go ahead and wear the thread. Henceforth, you too will be regarded and valued as Brahmins in this country." On the king's decree, everyone acquiesced and accorded the army of seven hundred and fifty-six the status of brahminhood. But the Namasudras objected. And why was that? This is what they said: "Maybe we didn't get the thread because of an insignificant mistake. But after all, we are descendants of Namas Muni, we have pure Brahmin blood in our bodies. By what quality or virtue can they become superior to us? If it's on account of winning in war, then they can become Kshatriya. But how can they become Brahmin? We don't consider them Brahmins. If you wish to execute us, so be it. But we shall never bow down at their feet and show deference."

'And thus began the discord between the neo-Brahmins and the Namasudras. Which continued throughout the reign of the Sur dynasty. There was no sign of it ending.

'After that came the reign of the Sena kings. Ballal Sen became king. One day Ballal Sen arranged for a big feast for people of all communities, to accord full social status to the son of one of his mistresses. The invitation was sent to the leaders of the Namasudra community too. The important leaders of all the caste communities attended the royal feast, but no one from the Namasudra community went there. They turned down the king's invitation, saying they would not attend a feast associated with a mistress's son.

'Was he not the king! Ballal Sen took great offence. The band of neo-Brahmins, who were never accorded the status of Brahmins by the Namas, took the opportunity to incite the king's ire further. They said, "Maharaja, please announce that people belonging to communities that do not attend the royal feast shall be severely punished. Their caste shall be taken away." The king issued instructions accordingly; yet no Namas attended. The infuriated king punished the entire Namasudra community for the crime of disobeying the royal decree. Henceforth, they would be known in society as "Chandals". They would have the same status as the "Chandals", that is to say, those who cremated dead bodies or carried out the execution of criminals. That's the reason why the Brahmins and Kayasthas despise the people of the Namasudra caste, and refer to them as Chandal and untouchable.'

After speaking for so long, Nandu Gosain's lips were now covered in saliva. Turning towards the hut, he called out to his wife, asking her to bring a pot of water. 'Bring the tobacco box too,' he added.

The hookah was refilled with tobacco, and a piece of burning charcoal was placed in its bowl. Nandu Gosain took a few puffs, as the hookah hubbled and bubbled, and exhaled a lungful of smoke. Then he handed the hookah to another man. Seeing his expression, one could gather that Nandu Gosain had not finished what he had to say. There was much that remained to be said. After a while, he resumed speaking.

'This Hindu faith—it has four levels. Above everyone is the Brahmin, below him is the Kshatriya, and below him the Vaisya. Do you get it? Those who perform pujas and recite texts are above everyone else. Below them are those who go to war, and below them are those who engage in business. And below everyone is the Sudra, whose only role is to serve those three castes and carry out their orders. In other words, they are slaves. This is what is called the varna system.'

'So why is the Kayastha caste just below the Brahmins?' asked Baghai Karati.

Gosain said, 'At the time I'm talking about, there was no caste called Kayastha. They came much later. At that time, in order to keep the people of the Sudra caste down forever, those among the Brahmins who were the most crafty had created elaborate rules and customs. When does a man become knowledgeable? When he avails of education. They wrote the shastras and laid it down there: No Sudra could ever try to get an education. If he did, that would be a grave crime. I think most of you must have read the Ramayan, and heard the tale about Shambuk Rishi. He had recited the Vedas. That was why Ram had beheaded him. You would also know all about Eklavya in the Mahabharat. How craftily his thumb was severed because he was more illustrious than someone like Arjuna, who belonged to the Kshatriya caste. There are many such instances of Sudras being subjugated. 'So, just as on the one hand, it was laid down in the law that Sudras could not pursue education, there was also another law whereby no Sudra could acquire any wealth or property, and if he did so, a Brahmin could dispossess him with impunity. When people have no wealth or property, when they are completely bereft and destitute, how will they survive? They can survive only at the mercy of Brahmins, by working for them. The law for the high-castes has also been laid down in the shastras. If they provide any food to a Sudra, that must only be leftovers from their own food, and it must be served in a broken utensil. When people of a community are consigned to living in this way, nothing remains of their humanity.

'There are hundreds and hundreds of customs and laws like this. Can those who consider the Sudras as lowly as crows and dogs ever imagine, even in their worst nightmares, that they would marry off a daughter of their household to a low-born? They can't. To ensure that something as untoward as that never happens, so that no girl from their society chooses a Sudra for a husband, there are arrangements for stringent monitoring and severe punishment. That punishment is capital punishment. Yet, sometimes, forgetting their status, girls from Brahmin households would give birth to offspring from a Sudra's seed. In the shastras, the caste created for such offspring was "Chandal". There was no place for them in the *chaturvarna* or four-fold caste system. They were lowlier than Sudras.

'There was no place for them in human settlements; they were forced to live on some isolated riverbank. They raised pigs and dogs, and ate the flesh of these very animals. They would conceal their shame with clothes gathered from corpses. They could not have any name other than one that evoked contempt and made them appear lowly. They could not live in one place for very long; they had to keep wandering all the time. Even if their shadow fell upon a Brahmin, the punishment for that was death.'

Nandu Gosain's voice had grown hoarse now. 'Ballal Sen's one fiat consigned millions of people of the Namasudra community to the section of human society that was considered inferior to insects and worms. It was said that a kingdom is destroyed for a king's sins. For the sin that Ballal Sen had committed that day, the country of Bengal fell into the hands of Muslims. Fearing merely eighteen Muslims, Ballal Sen's son, Lakshman Sen, gave up his kingdom and fled by swimming across the river. If the Namas had stood by the king with spears and shields on that day, he would not have had to flee. Ever since the reign of Ballal Sen, high-caste folk, who include descendants of those seven hundred and fifty-six neo-Brahmins, have referred to the Namas as "Chandal", and scorned and despised them. And they had no remedy or way out either. But it turned out that there was a way, and that was by becoming a refugee from that kingdom. Muslim rule had begun in the country by then. A major section of the Namas—it is said that there were apparently nine hundred thousand of them—gave up their Hindu faith and converted to Islam. None of the Muslims that you now see everywhere came from Mecca or Medina. All were Hindus. Some went willingly, and some were pushed to convert.'

Garib Das's heart thumped now. There was an incident of someone being pushed to conversion in his clan too. Which was why Majid and Mamud were his brothers despite being Muslim. Garib did not want to think about that now. That was most painful.

Nandu Gosain said, 'The Muslims ruled for seven hundred years. Nimai Pandit, in Nadia, exercised his brain and established a new faith, and thus saved the low-caste folk from the religious oppression by Brahmins. He was able to hold them back from crossing over to Islam. Or else there would have been no Hindus left in Bengal. He did the Hindu religion a great service. If nothing else, the number of people in the ranks of the enemies of Hindus did not increase. As it is, if one aggregates across both Bengals, the population of Muslims is greater than that of Hindus.'

It was late, so Garib Das and company made to leave. Nandu Gosain repeatedly offered them food and bedding for the night, but they had to leave for their own village early the next morning. There were others in their group. If they did not return in time, the others would be enraged. But even after returning, Garib Das remained inwardly in Nandu Gosain's ashram. How much the man knew! Hearing his words, a sense of pride had awakened inside him. Whatever may be our present—we aren't worthless. Our past is something to be proud of. Whatever has befallen us today, whatever is going to happen tomorrow, is all the result of the conspiracy of the high-castes. And then Garib Das recalled the incident that had sundered his family into two. One of which was Muslim, and the other, not quite Hindu despite being Hindu—untouchable, Nama.

4

How Rup Kumar Became
Rupchand Miya

Garib Das's father, Har Kumar Das, was one of three brothers. Har Kumar was the eldest, after him came Ram Kumar, and Rup Kumar was the youngest. Compared to his brothers, Rup Kumar was somewhat more courageous, and also somewhat more restless. Once something got into his head, he couldn't forget about it easily. He couldn't rest until he had accomplished it. In rustic language, such people were called *gowar gobindo*, meaning headstrong. He had been married only about two years ago. He had brought home a beautiful wife, who wore a dangling nose-ring. He had got married, so now he would have children. What would happen then? Would his son grow up to cast a net and get into water, mud and slime? Or would he plant paddy saplings and plough others' lands and fields? Rup Kumar knew what such a life was like, how difficult it was. The lives of folks like him were not worth a whit. Blood-sucking leeches and snakes on land, the razor-sharp, saw-like teeth of sharks and crocodiles in water—if his child didn't succumb to all that, he would die of starvation. He would succumb to cholera or kala-azar or smallpox, without treatment or medicines. As long as he was alive, no father could push his son towards such a life. Perhaps some could, but Rup Kumar would not. He would raise his son to be a man among men. He would raise him to be like the sons of babus. They combed their hair immaculately, they went to school to study with a fountain pen clipped to their pockets. It was said, 'the one who learns to read and write, from horse carriages shall alight'. Rup Kumar's son would be a man who alighted from horse carriages. He would send him to the Mashiyahati Christian School to study. The boarding facilities there were extremely expensive. Not everyone could afford that. That's why their sons could not become babus. There were a couple of schools here, within a radius of about four miles, but untouchable and low-caste children were not admitted there; only the sons of Brahmin and Kayastha families studied there. If by any chance a boy from a low-caste family went there to study, everyone created such a ruckus that he was compelled to leave within a couple of days. It wasn't like that in the Mashiyahati School, where everyone was allowed entry and had equal rights too. The school was founded by an Australian missionary. He narrated the teachings of Jesus to the children for an hour every day, and hoped that when they grew up, each one of them would become a follower of Jesus. The teaching and standard of education in the school were extremely advanced. Rup Kumar's desire was to admit his son to this boarding school and raise him to be an educated man. That would cost him twelve to fifteen rupees every month. By working on fields or catching fish, it wasn't just difficult but impossible to earn even half a rupee a day. And so he decided to get into business.

One day he went to his elder brother, Har Kumar, and said to him, 'Dada, I'm going to Cuttack.'

Cuttack was a district outside Bengal, in another province, Orissa. How would a person like Har Kumar know that! Hearing his brother utter such a strange name, he forgot about the hookah he was puffing and incredulously asked, 'Where did you say you're going?'

'To Cuttack. That's the name of a place.'

'Where's that? How far away is it?'

'It'll take about a month to go there and return.'

'So why do you want to go there? What work do you have there?'

'Satindra, Mahadev, Bijoy and some eight or ten other people are going to Cuttack. I'll go with them.'

'But what is it that's taking you so far away?'

Rup Kumar was a well-built and strong youth of about twenty or twenty-two. His physique had not been lovingly built by consuming milk, butter and ghee. It had been formed by the labour and sweat of struggling against sun, rain, cyclone, cold and various kinds of natural dangers. His strong body, like a seasoned bamboo pole, housed both strength and courage. He said, 'Apparently buffaloes come very cheap in Cuttack. If I bring two buffalos and sell them here, the pair would fetch the price of a thirty-two foot net and a boat. That's how Gopal Midda made his fortune. I'm going to get into the buffalo trade.'

'Will Gopal Midda be going with you?'

'He's not needy anymore. Why should he go?'

'Then who knows the way? Who will take you along?'

'Someone or the other who knows the way will come along. Or else how would one have the confidence to go!'

His brother's words made Har Kumar's heart thump in fear. It was not the present era of aeroplane, train, bus and motorcar. It was a time when people reposed faith solely in the Almighty. In those days, thugs and thieves lay in wait on the highways, who killed men as if they were killing flies and mosquitoes. Besides, there were tigers, bears, snakes and scorpions, there were deadly diseases and ailments. Wasn't it just three or four years ago that Meghnath Biswas had gone to Gaya to perform the funerary rites on behalf of his father and ancestors, and never returned? No one knew where he'd gone, or what happened to him.

Har Kumar said, 'Listen, boy, there's no point in being greedy. It's said that greed is sinful, and sin brings death. If you work devotedly on the little land we have, you can feed and clothe yourself. Baba used to say that even gold from running a business is only a tiny part of what farming yields. If God wills, you can earn as much from an acre as you'll earn in a year from business. There's nothing like farming. If you plant a single grain, the land gives back a hundred-fold. There's no shortage of fish either in the canals and lakes here. Don't be impulsive. Stay at home and be content with the hard-earned fruit of toil. Forget these fanciful plans.'

Raising his voice a little, Rup Kumar replied, 'The way we live—can you call that living like humans? I want to test my fate once. I'm going. However much you forbid me, I'm not going to obey. I'm going.'

'It's time for your wife to have children now. Have you thought about what would happen to her if you came to any harm?'

'What can happen to me? So many people travel all over the country. If nothing happens to them, then what can happen to me! It's not as if I'm going alone, there'll be plenty of people with me. It's just a matter of a month. All of you are here to take care of Jamuna. Please don't forbid me.' Disregarding all his elder brother's counsels, Rup Kumar set off for Cuttack. Perhaps sitting somewhere unseen, the Master of his destiny smiled wryly.

They went some way by boat and then walked a great distance. Leaving East Bengal, they entered West Bengal. Of course, there wasn't any East or West back then—it was all just Bengal, the Bengali-speaking country. They planned to cross Mednipur district, in southern Bengal, and enter Orissa. The band of eight or ten men walked the whole day, without pause. At the end of each day, when darkness fell, they looked for a tree and stopped there to rest. They had taken along rice, dal, oil, salt and so on. They camped on the bank of a river or canal or pond, gathered twigs and cooked some rice. They poured water into any rice left over after the night's meal. The morning after, eating that stale or *panta* rice with salt and chillies, they would set off again. In this way, walking on and on, day after day, they reached the border of Orissa.

At that time in India, various kinds of death-traps were laid on roads and highways. Multitudes of life-threatening germs moved around in the water and in the air, as if simply to kill people. One such water-borne disease was called cholera. The germs of this disease spread the quickest, and were the most infectious and fatal of all. Once the disease struck a corner of some village, it would devastate the entire village like a conflagration. People used to drop like a swarm of locusts. The entire village would become desolate. No wonder the terrified folk had given it the name *modok*, 'epidemic'.

It was said that cholera had once struck a village called Bharatkati in Barisal district. The whole village of three hundred and twenty families had turned into a cemetery within a month. There wasn't anyone left even to light the lamp in any household shrine in the evening. Jackals and vultures used to tear the flesh off the dead bodies lying scattered everywhere. Many stories of ghosts and evil spirits from here had spread to neighbouring villages, which made people tremble with fear.

It was Rup Kumar's misfortune that even before the terror of Bharatkati had faded from public memory, he fell victim to that deadly killer disease. As he sat beneath a tree, far away from home, he began vomiting. The vomiting was accompanied by acute diarrhoea, watery as rice water. None of the people Rup Kumar had accompanied were his relatives or kin; they were merely acquaintances, people from the same village. Besides, out of simple-mindedness, insensitivity, selfishness and shortsightedness, a terrible fear licked the hearts of the people: the fear of death. I've come leaving behind my wife and children at home. Tending to a person struck by cholera, what if I too get the disease? What will become of my family if I die! Who will look after them? Who will feed and raise them?

So they kept a safe distance. Although they were inexperienced, callous and anxious, they did make some efforts for the first two or three days. But Rup Kumar's condition did not improve. There was no sign of the sickness leaving him. It kept getting worse. Little by little, like a severed gourd plant, the strong youth wilted away.

What shouldn't have happened did finally transpire. One member of the band took another aside and said in a tremulous voice, 'The signs are not at all good. I don't think he'll survive the night. Who knows what fate wills! When someone dies in an inappropriate place or time, people find fault with their planetary configuration. Death owing to such faulty fate-lines turns one into a ghost. I wonder whose ominous face I saw at the inauspicious moment when I set out from home! If Rup Kumar dies and becomes a ghost, not a single one of us will stay alive. He will break everyone's neck and bury us in slime.'

Another timid fellow-traveller said, 'Shall I tell you something…'

'Yes.'

'When he's not going to survive, when there's no sign at all of his surviving—what's the use of any more attachment? Let's flee. Let's save our own lives while we can.'

'What will we tell Har Kumar when we're back in the village?'

'We'll tell him that Rup Kumar contracted cholera on the way and died. After all, it's a long journey—how could we carry his dead body this far? We'll say we performed all the prescribed rites and then immersed him in a river.'

After some discussion, the rest of the group agreed with the plan. In times of calamity, one loses one's good sense. Those distraught, frightened, superstition-ridden men could not fathom then what a grave error they were about to commit, what a dangerous seed they were planting—for history, for all time, for their heirs, for their society, country and people. They left the dying Rup Kumar under a tree in the desolate darkness of night and fled. But Rup Kumar wasn't destined to die just then. The determiner of destinies wanted him to play a key role in a terribly painful drama. A cruel, pitiless foundation was thus laid towards the emergence of another Kalapahad-like destroyer of idols.

After Rup Kumar's companions left him behind, the night turned to dawn. A Muslim mendicant was walking to the mosque along the ridge separating the paddy fields for the early morning Fajr prayer. Startled by the distressed cries of the dying man, he came to a halt. Going near the tree under which Rup Kumar lay, the medicant realised that it was not just a man who was dying, but the conscience of human society too. The servant of God then bent down on his knees before the dying youth. He forgot where he was headed for. This was the first prayer that he had missed in his adult life of forty years. But he had faith in Allah. Allah would surely forgive him. Because he was most merciful.

He carried Rup Kumar bodily to his own house. He brought a hakim, and arranged for medicines. The treatment continued for a month. In the struggle between Yama and the man, finally the man emerged victorious. Humanity won. Rup Kumar was slowly rid of the disease. One day Rup Kumar said to the compassionate Muslim man, 'I've been away from home for long. Everyone at home must be anxious. Please permit me to go now.'

The Muslim man had begun to love Rup Kumar like his own son. But he was only 'like' a son. After all, he wasn't his own son. By what authority would he hold him back? Holding back the tears welling up in his eyes, he said, 'If you visit these parts some day, you must come to my house. Look upon it as your own house and come by.'

Rup Kumar too invited the mendicant to visit him. 'If you ever go to Barisal, you must come to our house. You brought me back to life. If my Ma and brothers see you—they'll simply worship you. You're not a man, for me you are God incarnate. If it weren't for you, I wouldn't be alive today.'

The mendicant said, 'I'm nobody, nothing at all. You live because of Allah. He is your protector. If you must sing praises, sing His praises. I only did what Allah made me do. I'm nobody, there's only Him—He's everyone's Master.'

Rup Kumar paid his respects to the pious Muslim, bowing down to touch his feet and then touching his own head to be blessed with the dust of his feet. Then he departed for home. The day he reached home—according to the Hindu shastras, by dint of the mantric powers of a Brahmin, his soul, holding a cow's tail, should have crossed the mythic river Baitarani and reached the celestial abode, Vaikunth. Seeing the selfsame Rup Kumar bodily present there, people were suspicious at first—this was surely a ghost! Apparently plenty of incidents like this had occurred in Bharatkati. Eventually, after all kinds of questioning, people realised it wasn't a ghost—it was the real Rup Kumar. And then, in the natural course of events, the village boiled over. Rup Kumar's brother Ram Kumar was notorious for his fierce temper. Flailing a cleaver used to slaughter goats, he rushed towards where Satindra, Mahadev and Bijoy lived. 'As soon as I find those bastards, I'll cut their heads off with a single blow. My brother died! Such a terrible lie! My Ma was in convulsions with grief for her youngest son. I've had to see his wife wearing a widow's garb. I'll avenge that today! Won't spare any of those bastards!'

The villagers stopped and pacified him with sane counsel: 'Stop, Ram, don't lose your head. Yes, this has to be accounted for. But don't we have a forum for resolving issues in the village?' On everyone's urging, he calmed down then. But his anger did not subside. Finally, Har Kumar, Ram Kumar and some of their relatives jointly made a complaint to the village council, whose head was Manibhushan Bhattacharya, the father of Shibnath Bhattacharya, who we encountered in the beginning of this tale. 'Master, we seek justice in this matter. Or else there will be violence and bloodshed.'

Manibhushan Bhattacharya was a man of stern disposition. He used to attend the village council with a brass-encrusted stick. Whoever does not heed me will heed this stick. And everyone heeded his ruling. Was there any option but to heed him? The chief rent collector, revenue collector and inspector of police were all under his thumb; who would have the guts to defy him? If he said water flowed upwards, everyone would nod their head and say, when the master says so, it surely flows upwards—how can he be wrong?

Manibhushan heard the arguments of both sides on the matter. Then he said to Satindra, Mahadav, Bijoy and the others, 'You returned leaving Rup Kumar behind. Cholera is an epidemic, and you say that you got scared seeing his condition. I accept that the disease is indeed one to be afraid of. Why, I would have been scared too. Getting scared and running away, leaving him behind—I don't see any fault in that. But you didn't tell the truth—that is your fault. If you had told Har Kumar that you didn't know whether Rup Kumar was alive or dead, then he wouldn't have had to arrange the funeral. He had to bear the unnecessary expense for Rup Kumar's last rites. So it is a grave fault. I can't see any option other than asking you to pay a fine.'

He announced that all the eight persons who had travelled with Rup Kumar were to be punished. 'Each of you shall pay a fine of a hundred rupees. Ma Kali's temple will be restored with that money. The sin you have committed will be atoned thereby.'

A hundred rupees was a lot of money in those days. For a monthly salary of ten rupees, an entire household was retained to work under the *baromeshe* or 'twelve-month' system. Hence, in order to pay the fine, the homesteads of several of the eight families in question had to be sold off. But the restored temple was indeed something to behold. And on the days of special pujas, Manibhushan worshipped Ma Kali in the temple, reciting Sanskrit mantras in his sonorous voice. Hearing the decision, Satindra, Mahadev and company had quaked in rage: 'Oh Ma, you can drink the blood of so many folk, but you could not devour Rup Kumar! And now, instead of one life, so many lives will be lost. Do as you please, but do give us one chance now, oh Ma. If you really exist, then do let us meet Ram Kumar once. Once we bring and sacrifice him before you, we won't suffer any more grief.'

Several years passed by. Gradually, the furore that had erupted around the marshlands subsided. The environment slowly returned to its former state. Then it was suddenly revealed that the house where Rup Kumar had found shelter when he was sick, the house where he had eaten and drunk and was restored to life before returning home, belonged to a man who was not of the Hindu faith, but a beef-eating Muslim, a *nede*. This came to light when, unable to get over his attachment to Rup Kumar, the pious Muslim set out one day with the address Rup Kumar had left him. He reached Pother Shesh, and thus was everything revealed.

Mahadev, Bijoy, Satindra and the other five persons who had been fined got together and appeared before Manibhushan Bhattacharya. 'Master, you are the head of our village. No one seeking your intervention gets anything but justice from you. We accepted the punishment given by you for whatever we did with bowed heads, willingly or unwillingly, whether we were at fault or not. We did not object then. But we shall object now, if Rup Kumar is not held accountable for the sin he committed.'

'What did Rup Kumar do?'

'He ate in a miya's house. No one can say whether he didn't eat beef too. Tell us how can such a man continue to be Hindu?'

Manibhushan Bhattacharya became very thoughtful. This was a complex dilemma. Which he could not resolve by himself. He was compelled to call Mr Roy, Mr Dutta and all the other notable people of the community. A quarrel between brothers, a wife's bad character, a cow eating someone's grain—the problem that had erupted now was vastly different from such hassles. All those could be resolved in a trice, but not this one. The matter in question was about pollution, and the Sanatan Dharma. So the leaders of society had to be of one view. Consequently, there were rounds after rounds of discussion, advice, reasoning, argument and counter-argument.

Mr Roy contended: 'Consider the case of poison. Some consume it willfully, knowingly. And some do so unknowingly. But the fact is that when it finally reaches the person's stomach, it will have its effect. Or consider the case of fire. Whether someone touches it willingly or unknowingly, they will be scorched. Whether Rup

Kumar ate it willingly or unknowingly, the fact remains that he ate polluted food. When that food reached his stomach, it must have had its effect. In that case, there's no way Rup Kumar can be considered Hindu now.'

Mr Dutta added: 'Once someone has consumed food and water served by a Muslim, they cannot remain within the Hindu faith. Rup Kumar has lost both his caste and religion.'

One person had been eager to speak for a long time. As soon as Mr Dutta concluded, he said, 'It's clear that Rup Kumar has lost his caste. But his wife—what's her name, Jamuna—she has a child too. What will happen to them? What are the rules in this regard in the shastras?'

The question was directed at the Brahmin, Manibhushan Bhattacharya, for who else had the right to speak before a Brahmin did on the subject of the shastras. But the questioner was looking at Mr Dutta. Hence he took on some of the responsibility of answering. 'I think the wife will not lose her caste. What do you say, Mr Bhattacharya?'

Mr Bhattacharya responded, 'A woman is a part of the supreme power, the mother of the universe. She has no caste. Women are like water. Water has no shape and only assumes the shape of the utensil it is poured into. There are several proofs of this in the shastras. If the wife disavows Rup Kumar, then it's possible to set right her fault in having unknowingly associated with him for so long. The blessings of five Brahmins can wipe away all her sins.'

As soon as Har Kumar found out about that, he realised that a grave danger was imminent. He raced to Manibhushan Bhattacharya's house, as if his very life were at stake. He broke down and wept at his feet: 'For God's sake, please save my brother. Have mercy. Perhaps he was unconscious as a result of his disease. He knew nothing about the man who took him away and gave him food and water. He did not commit the sin of eating a miya's food willingly. Please pardon him for not knowing anything.'

But his tears had no impact. Castigating him, Manibhushan said, 'Is this a matter in which one can be pardoned? In the Hindu shastras, the cow is a holy mother. Three hundred and thirty million gods and goddesses reside in her body. You will never fathom how sinful are those who butcher this holy mother like goats and eat her meat. The crime committed by Rup Kumar by eating and drinking from the hands of that mlechha *nede*—if I pardon that today, seeing that many others will walk the same path, they will start eating together with the miyas. Our religion, and Hindu society itself, will go to the dogs then. As the head of the community, I cannot allow that to happen.'

So Rup Kumar became an outcast. His brothers' and Ma's tears, appeals and entreaties could not stop his disownment. Earlier, there were no Muslims in the village of Pother Shesh. They lived on the other side of a fairly wide river, and in terms of numbers, were twice the population of Pother Shesh. Now one Muslim household had arrived in Pother Shesh as well. The community leaders, who were the upholders and protectors of Sanatan Dharma, had created, blessed and smoothened the road to their entry. They had all been born of the same parents, they had lived in the same house, shared the same courtyard and kitchen, drank water fetched from the same riverbank, and had been fed by the harvest of the same field. And yet Rup Kumar became untouchable, water touched by whom could not be consumed. That was what he became to his own kin. His own kin, who themselves were considered by the faith which they were so proud of and arrogant about, the Hindu religion, to be untouchable—those from whom water could not be consumed—Chandal, Nama. For whom temple doors were closed, school doors were very far away, and uttering a mantra was a crime.

After that, Rup Kumar changed his name to Rupchand Miya. And his wife Jamuna became Jamila Bibi. Of course, she was counselled not to become *nede*. Roy babu—in whose courtyard, as many as two huge piles of paddy were threshed after harvest, with threshers so tall that when womenfolk tried to look at their tops, the ghomtas on their heads slipped off—the same Roy babu had told Jamuna, 'I'll give you a hut on the fringe. Live there with your child. I'll send you food as well.' Jamuna did not agree to the attractive proposal. She became Muslim together with her husband.

People never learnt to live together with other people and love one another as easily as they learnt how to hate and abuse. They had somersaulted together on the same earth, breathed in the same air, standing beneath the same sky. They had laughed and cried over the same sorrows and joys, shared equally the same contentment and been devastated by the same diseases and natural disasters. But once a finger was pointed at Rup Kumar, the same neighbours and kinsfolk made him an alien. They began heaping on the helpless man the hate and humiliation they themselves had for so long received from the high-castes.

Neither Har Kumar nor Ram Kumar wished to do so, but on the orders of the village elders, a side of the courtyard fronting Rup Kumar's unit was partitioned, and saplings of acacia were planted along the divide. The acacia's thorns were poisonous, so no one from the other side could enter this side. Finding a salubrious environment, the plants grew. Gradually the roots spread deep into the soil. Thus the shrub grew, yielding no flower or fruit but only millions of thorns. Thorns that poisonously pricked people's bodies and minds, making them bloody, wounded and full of pain.

However, although Rup Kumar became a Muslim, for as long as he was alive, the flesh of a cow never entered his house. The conch shell was blown in his house at dusk, with the ritual ululation too. Jamuna continued to apply sindoor in the parting of her hair and wear the shankha-bangle on her wrist. As children, her sons used to stand afar and observe in banishment the Narayan puja being conducted in their uncles' courtyard. They accepted the puja prasad offered to them on banana leaves. But as soon as Rup Kumar passed away, all that came to an end. His five sons consciously disavowed every kind of Hindu custom, and each one became a staunch Muslim. The first expression of their resolve was to demolish the raised column with the holy tulsi where a lamp was lit at dusk. Then they smashed all the images of gods and goddesses, ritual pots and suchlike, and dumped everything into the river. After that, they slaughtered a female calf. The meat was cooked, and they ate it for all to see. On the occasion of Eid, five large boatloads of people, invited from across the river, came to participate in the ceremony organised by them. Ready for use in their boats were cleavers, cane shields and spears made from laths of areca. If any kaffir tried to hinder the religious ceremony, a fitting answer would be given. Rup Kumar's family had hitherto been completely alone and isolated. The Hindus had driven them away, but the Muslims had drawn them close. After the Eid ceremony, there was no longer any distance between them. The moulvi sahib announced, 'From today they are Muslims. Muslims are brothers unto one another. It is a Muslim's duty to protect another Muslim.'

Thereafter, religious functions, gatherings and discussions were regularly organised in Rup Kumar's courtyard. The Holy Koran was recited. During the religious discussions and speeches, speakers poured fierce hatred and scorn upon caste prejudice. They poured out all the agony, fire and flames of the humiliation and insults suffered for many ages. But what had once been caste prejudice—that very thing now raised its head in a new incarnation, donning the garb of communalism.

5

Acacia Thorns

A major tradition in East Bengal's folk culture was *kobi-gaan*, or poetry in song. Many great masters of poetry had been born here, with the outstanding ability to make up a song on any subject, extempore, and sing it out on stage to a rapt audience. Society, customs, politics, religion, as well as jokes and jest, were among the varied subjects touched upon in such songs. *Kobi-lorai*, or the battle of poets, was part of this too. One major *kobi-gaan* poet was Ganpati. He had made a name for himself in a short while. Har Kumar once invited him and organised a performance. Har Kumar had made many mistakes in life, and organising this *kobi-gaan* performance was another such mistake. Even in his wildest imagination, he did not think that by way of charming merriment, Ganpati would say things that would ignite the flames of rage among the Muslim community. Ganpati knew how to make songs, he knew how to sing, but he didn't know about things that were better left unsaid.

That midnight, just as the performance was coming to an end, replying to a question from his opponent, Ganpati suddenly said, '*Ghaora shoja gutaay, aar meya shoja jutaay!* The bull butts straight, and a miya is shod straight!'

Ganpati had sought to enrapture the audience by saying this in a tremulous voice, because his opponent just didn't want to accept something. Time and again, he pretended not to hear. Hence, the first part of the retort was directed at him—meaning, you won't get it unless you are cuffed a few on your face and shoulder. But by trying to rhyme the word in Bangla for 'butt' with that for 'shod', he invited calamity. A person asked, 'I got it that the bull butts straight, but I didn't understand the part about the miya being shod straight.'

Ganpati was a peddler of words. He knew how to string them together. He said, 'Once, in a *kobi-gaan* session, I had said this. There were Hindus as well as miyas there. After I said this, one miya charged at me, as if to beat me up. Finally I said to him, "Miya, why do you get angry? If you listen carefully to what I say, you'll get why all of you are shod straight. We eat rice on the upper part of the banana leaf, you eat it off the opposite side, the lower part. We wear the dhuti with a pleat, while you have no pleats on your lungi. We pray facing the east, while you offer namaz facing the west. We keep a moustache, while you chop it off. We read from left to right, you read from right to left. We are consigned to fire when we die, you go to a grave. So just see, in everything you are the opposite of Hindus—but the way we insert our feet in shoes, you too do that the same way. You don't wear it on your hands. That means that even though you are the opposite in every respect, when it comes to wearing shoes, you are completely straight." The man then agreed to my phrase. So do you get it now, why miyas are shod straight!'

Ganpati wanted to make people laugh by narrating the story. And some people did laugh. But those who had been compelled to live across the acacia thorns did not find it funny. Subsequently, the phrase became something like a slogan. Whenever a few Hindu fanatics gathered together, if the subject of Muslims' insolent attitude arose, someone or the other would say, '*Halar jait khali jutaay shoja.* The bastards' race is straight only when it comes to wearing shoes.'

When this story crossed the river and reached the Muslim hamlet, people from there arrived, together with a moulvi, to give a fitting reply to the people on the Hindu side. Accompanying them were fifty servants of Allah, bearing spears. They converged in Rupchand Miya's courtyard. After talking about this and that, the maulvi began his real speech.

'Once I had to go to Parichpur. In an assembly there, I said all Hindus are the offspring of bulls. One Hindu went red in the face with anger. I said to him, "Why do you get angry, don't you call the cow your mother? If the cow is your mother, then the bull has to be your father. So it's true, isn't it?"'

The maulvi's talk was broadcast so loudly via a tin loudspeaker that all the Hindus gathered across the boundary of acacia thorns, and further away, could hear it. As they heard it, they made a mental count of whether they had the strength of numbers to take on the fifty spearmen gathered in Rupchand Miya's courtyard.

The moulvi continued, 'I didn't tell him anything more. So folks, those who call the cow, mother, those who consume the cow's shit and piss in the name of *panchagavya* or "five holy cow-products"— just think about the kind of people they are. What kind of caste and religion they belong to! If one gets a mother merely by drinking milk, then what's the poor buffalo's fault? You drink its milk too. What's the goat's crime? Call it mother too! Make the cow the elder mom, the buffalo the second mom and the goat the younger mom. The bull the elder dad, and the ram the younger dad.'

Har Kumar was still alive then. But he did not wish to live any more. A few months ago, his brother Ram Kumar had died of a snakebite. Living in grief, humiliation and despair, Rupchand too didn't survive long. Finally, it was cholera—which had once spared him after almost taking his life—that returned to end his life. What could the helpless, aged Har Kumar do all alone? His hearing and eyesight were impaired now. But he could sense that secret preparations for fratricide, for another Kurukshetra-like battle, had begun. Arrangements were being made for one brother to bathe in the blood of another. The roots of the poisonous acacia shrubs that had one day been planted in the courtyard of his house had now spread to hearts. The bushes grew, as did their thorns.

Rupchand had five sons and three daughters. The eldest son was Mamud. He had a calm and thoughtful disposition. He had observed his father's unbearably sad life from close quarters. By then he was old enough to understand the situation. He had seen him die helplessly too. On a night of unceasing rain, Rupchand had died in a fit of vomiting and shitting. Not a single kin had disregarded the acacia thorns and come to his door, for fear of becoming an outcast. Their feet were shackled by the chains of religion and caste. The sight of his dead father left a permanent wound in Mamud's psyche. That wound would never heal. It would torment him and make him weep forever.

Momin was two years younger than Mamud. But in terms of physique, he was much bigger. He was obstinate and brave, and prone to anger like Rupchand. On that night of ceaseless rain, he swam across the river and carried the news of his father's death to the Muslim hamlet on the other side. But the people there did not go at once with him. They said, 'Tell us why we should go. It's true the Hindus drove your father away. But he didn't really become a Muslim after reciting the *kalma*. He remained in limbo between the two communities. Till the day he died, he harboured the hope in his heart that the Hindus would take him back. So why should we go for someone who wasn't truly one of us?'

Momin said to them, 'My father was thick-headed. He could not understand. Please come along. Let his last rites be over, and then we five brothers will rectify the mistake he made. There will be no sign or symbol of the Hindu religion in any corner of our house.' After that, people from the hamlet arrived by boat and buried Rupchand near the riverbank according to Islamic rites. It was Momin whom the village folk feared the most. If the fire of communal riots, which was now raging all over the country, was ever lit in this village, Momin would be the prime arsonist. Touching the soil of Rupchand's grave, he had vowed—'The bastards didn't let you die in peace. I won't let even a single one of them live in peace. I'll make them suffer ten times as much as you suffered in death.'

Majid was the next brother after Momin. He was of the same age as Har Kumar's son Garib Das. When Rup Kumar was disowned, neither Garib nor Majid had been born. If that unfortunate incident hadn't occurred, the two of them would have played together. They would have gone fishing together. But now, despite being cousins, they were far apart. They saw one another from afar. In between stood the fear of becoming an outcast.

Although Har Kumar was saddened by Momin's rage, he could not blame him. His was the only Muslim household in the entire neighbourhood. No one mingled with them, laughed with them, played with them or stood by them in times of hardship. When they were children, Momin and his brothers used to break the acacia barrier and come running to play with the children in the village. The Hindus used to scold their children and move them away. They considered Momin and his brothers as despicable as those afflicted with leprosy. As children, they did not know why such severe punishment was being meted out to them. Companionless in childhood, solitary during adolescence, and an object of contempt in his youth, Momin grew up to be a vengeful person. His desire for revenge made him akin to a hungry tiger. As soon as he found an opportunity, he would pounce.

In this remote region—surrounded by water and forest, lacking communication with the outside world, and somewhat distant from the ambit of the law—quarrels, discord, violence and riots between neighbours, brothers and kin wasn't something new. For that reason, people used to say, '*Dhan, khoon, khal, teen niye Barisal*. Paddy, blood and canal, the three comprise Barisal'. All that had happened before would happen again. However, earlier, when quarrels took place, they used to end soon. But now they wouldn't. The poison of political motives had entered this region. Plans were afoot to kill large numbers of people—criminals, as well as the innocent, children and the elderly. No one would be spared. They wanted numbers now—a thousand, two thousand, ten or twenty thousand. Some people wanted to touch new heights by standing atop a mountain of dead bodies. And so, a deep conspiracy was afoot all over the country to make the two communities fight one another. In Calcutta, Bihar and East Bengal. On one side was the Hindu Mahasabha and on the other, the Muslim League—both parties were inciting people in the name of religion, to kill. As a result of which, as many as three terrible riots took place. People died like flies. Some of the interests of the political leaders were fulfilled, while some remained. That's why more riots were going to take place.

No riot had happened in the village of Pother Shesh yet. But everyone lived under a pall of terror—who knew when it would begin? Would the flames of the riots cross rivers and canals and strike their village? Rupchand's sons were all adults now. They were incited by outsiders: 'This country now belongs to Muslims. The police, army and political leaders are all Muslim. Everyone wants Hindus to leave the country. If they don't go of their own accord, they'll have to be thrashed and driven away.' The desire for revenge, accumulated over many years, burned fiercely in their minds. Who knew when it would explode ...

Har Kumar died the year the country was partitioned and Bengal too was divided, with one part becoming East Pakistan. But, of course, before that, his sons gave up the joint family, and each one set up a separate home in convenient places. The situation in the country was more volatile than ever. Hindus were not getting justice or recourse from police stations and courts. As a result, some of those who had still not left East Pakistan began to sell their land and homesteads and leave for India. People had been leaving right from 1947, and that continued without letup, with at least some leaving each and every day. But people in Pother Shesh didn't know much about that. They looked upon their village, and the region, as being in East Pakistan, where even the three terrible riots could not make any mark. But now they were afraid. Now they began to feel they couldn't stay much longer. It would be terribly wrong to stay.

⁂

It was in the grip of such a fear that Gagan's Ma had come to Garib Das's house the day his son was born. Except for Shashikanta, all of Garib's brothers had gone away to India. They would certainly have written to their brother about the opportunities and facilities there. If Garib left, she would go too. But Garib Das was unable to make up his mind.

One evening, a few days later, Garib Das walked—with some trepidation—towards his cousin Mamud's house. Mamud had now moved to another part of the village, having built a two-roomed hut with a corrugated tin roof. After his first wife died, he had remarried. His second wife's father had sixteen bighas of farmland. He had helped out his son-in-law with tin roofing, wood and bamboo.

'Dada, how are you?'

Mamud had just returned from the marketplace. He was sitting on the verandah and fanning himself to dry his sweat. Turning his head to look at Garib Das, he said, 'Yes, I'm fine. How are you? Is everyone at home well?'

'Yes, everyone is ... sort of ... whatever you people permit.'

Mamud smiled wistfully. 'As if we are the masters looking after you ... The Lord Almighty is the one who looks after everyone. The way He wants to keep each one. Isn't that correct?'

'Yes, when you say so, it must be.'

Garib Das did not know what to say next and was at a loss for words. As if to relieve him, Mamud said, 'So tell me, what brings you here suddenly? You never came to my house before! Come and sit on the verandah.'

Garib did not step on to the verandah. Was it because of the eternal custom which had grown, little by little, over a very long time, in his ignorant mind and now loomed large? Standing below the verandah, he said, 'Dada, I'm hearing all kinds of things from everywhere. People are saying that the kind of riots that took place in Noakhali will now happen in our area too. I was terrified to hear that. They say people will slaughter people like goats.'

Wiping the sweat on his face with the gamchha in his hand, Mamud replied, 'I too hear that in the marketplace. It's not just you, anyone who hears it will be terrified. If there are riots and killings—when people slit one another's throats in a mad frenzy—is there anything certain about who'll die and who'll live? Is it only Hindus who'll die? Won't some miyas die too?'

As he spoke, Mamud filled tobacco in his hookah. Blowing on the burning piece of charcoal in the bowl of the hookah, he extended it towards Garib. 'Here, have a smoke. But whether miyas kill Hindus or Hindus kill miyas—this business of killing is not good.'

Garib began to ruminate out loud. 'I just can't understand why miyas all over the country have risen as one in fury like this. I hear miyas from Bihar or some such place are going to come here to riot. In what way have people from here harmed them? Isn't this simply madness?'

'Of course, it's madness!' Mamud retorted. 'Sometimes I think this madness is inevitable, and that there's no other option besides such madness. Can you explain why, for no fault and no reason, miyas get such scorn, all their lives, from Hindus? Some day or other, they are bound to lose their heads. If you have to live together, it's necessary to feel a little bit of kinship in one's heart. Do the Hindus have that? Tell me, do they consider Muslims to be human? The way one man should treat another—do they grant that to any Muslim, or will they ever? Then how can they live together in the same place?'

Garib could not understand why Mamud was agitated today. It was completely contrary to his nature. Even if he did not see him frequently, he did run into him once or twice every month or two in the marketplace, and whatever the subject, he always spoke calmly. But today—'If we stand in their courtyard, after we leave, the Hindus sprinkle cow-dung-water there for purification. If we happen to touch them, they bathe at once. But that's not needed when dogs and cats go near them; no sprinkling of cow-dung-water for them. It's needed only when it comes to us miyas. When there's such contempt for us in the minds of Hindus, do you think miyas will kiss your cheeks in response? The country was partitioned because of the Hindus' hatefulness. Such a terrible riot took place in 1946. But have the Hindus changed even one bit since then? This country now belongs to miyas. Why will they let you stay if they are not accorded the dignity due to them as human beings? They are avenging ages of humiliation and oppression. Can you blame them? Why should those whom you never considered your own, call you their own today? The one who is not your own is an outsider. The one who is an outsider does what an outsider will.'

Garib Das had never heard or thought about all this in this fashion. Actually, for the delicate cells of the mind—from where thoughts emerge—to be cultivated and developed, a healthy environment is needed. Thoughtful and intelligent people are required in the vicinity, with whom one can exchange thoughts. Such people were lacking in Garib Das's community. Till date, this community had not produced a single person who could raise their voice against the uncivilised practices carried on in the name of the Vedas, Puranas and the Hindu religion: 'Enough, no more, stop now! Or else we shall force you to! Your scriptures, texts and books full of laws that denigrate people so much—they are not mine, I shall kick them into the river! I shall not bow down anymore before a god who has made me as lowly in society as a worm. I shall bow only to myself. And I shall acknowledge only the one who acknowledges me.'

The Hindu religion was nothing but violent Brahminism in another garb. In this geographical terrain, it was the Buddhists who had first stood up against that. But they were non-violent, unarmed and weak. That's why they were blown away like straws by the fierce assault of Brahminism. But the Muslims were a race of armed and courageous warriors. Only they had been able to deliver a powerful blow to the Brahminical powers in the region. Today, no one had the courage to denigrate or disregard them. If anyone did so, he could not live in East Pakistan anymore. Now, Muslims had raised their clenched fists and said, 'Either accept us as equals, or pay the price.'

Garib Das lacked education or enlightened guidance. He was very far away from cultivated sanskars and culture—living as he did in a region surrounded by water—a very ordinary man belonging to a community of labouring folk. Lacking any cultivated consciousness, he couldn't sense or understand, let alone reach, the inner anguish of a person like Mamud. From the time he was born, he had seen that if he went and stood in the courtyard of a Brahmin or Kayastha, they sprinkled cow-dung-water after he left. If he touched them, they bathed. Seeing all this, he had formed the notion that this was the rule, this was normal, and in accordance with the shastras. It had never occurred to him that this could be a matter of such mental anguish and humiliation. Long ago, someone had told him, 'They are high-caste, wealthy and educated because of their merits in past lives. And our being low-caste, too, is the fruit of our actions in past lives. Whatever God has destined for anyone at the time of birth has to be accepted. Destiny cannot be altered in any way. It is a test of God. If, despite all the suffering, hardship, deprivation and poverty, I desist from doing anything sinful, if I have faith in God, then in the next life He will make me high-caste, he will make me wealthy and handsome.'

If Mamud had been Rup Kumar Das's son, he too, like Garib Das, would have believed in and relied upon such notions. But he was the son of Rupchand Miya. He did not consider the writ of the Vedas, Puranas, Brahmins and priests to be true. He did not believe in the existence of past lives. He knew and believed that man had just one life. All give-and-take belonged to that one life. And everything else that tormented someone—was created by man.

After hearing Mamud, Garib said, 'Dada, I don't know how to read or write. I'm just a thick-headed, ignorant man. I work during the day and then sleep at night. I thought this is how life would always be. I don't harm anyone, and so no one would harm me. But who knows what led to what. Things have changed in the village and everywhere. Now even though I've done nothing wrong, I feel as if I have done much wrong. On roads and highways, people look at me so strangely. I'm afraid to be out in the open. I don't find any contentment or relief in work anymore. I'm terrified that someone may come and slit my throat.'

Heaving a deep sigh, Mamud said in a tone full of despondency, 'What else can you do but be cautious when you go out. People say, "the kingdom is destroyed for the king's sins". The Brahmins, Kayasthas and other high-castes committed a sin by oppressing and exploiting people, and for that sin, not only are they dying, but they're also killing you. If those bastards didn't exist, there would have been no notion of high and low, no discord and disaffection between people. Everyone would have been able to live in harmony. But whether Nama or Pode—no one broke away from the laws made by them and mingled freely with miyas, like fellow men. Whatever happens will be the fruit of what was sown. There will be riots, there will be bloodshed. What else can you do but take care of yourself ...'

Like an idiot, like the one in the joke who asks whose father Sita was, at the end of the narration of all the seven chapters of the Ramayan, Garib said, 'Please try to dissuade those who are talking about riots and arson. Tell them, let's continue to live in harmony like before. It's living together in harmony that brings happiness.'

'In the name of Allah!' Full of annoyance, Mamud said, 'Who am I talking to! What did I tell you? I wonder whether you heard me or understood anything I said! How can there be harmony? We obey our pirs and maulvis, while you toe the line of Brahmins and Kayasthas. They have established countless barriers to keep people from living together in harmony. Will any Hindu family give their daughter in marriage to a miya's family? Will a miya's daughter be accepted as a bride in any Hindu family? Will the religious leaders ever accept that?'

Before Garib could respond, Mamud's brother Momin arrived. He had a small axe in hand. He had come there to cut a bamboo pole from the clump in his brother's courtyard. Seeing Garib there, he said loudly, 'How come you're here, bhaichhab? I hear you're going away to your house in India. Are you looking for a buyer for your house here?'

Trying to dilute Momin's jibe, Garib Das said, 'My house in India! Why should I go there? Where is that place?'

'You'll find out where India is. No one knew about it before. But now everyone's running there. Haven't you heard, this country has now become Pakistan, the land of the pure? There'll be no place here any more for impure people. Everyone other than Muslims is impure. They are all kaffirs. Allah doesn't like kaffirs. So why should followers of Allah like them? If anyone has to live here, they must recite the kalma, become a miya and eat beef.'

'What if I don't?'

'Haven't you heard about what happened in Muladi? All the Hindus there were taken to a room in the school and confined there. After that they were brought out, five at a time, hacked to pieces and thrown into the river. Two hundred finished off in a single night. If Allah wishes, the same will happen here too. Haji-saheb is waiting to act. He says, all the Muslims who've come from Calcutta and Bihar don't want to hold back any longer. They want a final settlement soon. We say, bhai, if you give us the signal, there can be a riot tonight itself.'

Garib was truly afraid now. Not a word of what Momin said was untrue. In a trembling voice, he said, 'Whatever they might say, however much they may try to misguide people, we are brothers after all. The same blood flows in our bodies. Isn't it said that brothers stay together? Who's small and who's big, who's high and who's low ... all these laws of society ... Hindu and Muslim, riots and violence—I'm not talking about any of that, nor do I pay any heed to it. I've come to my brother at a time of danger in the hope of receiving some sound advice.'

'It's sound advice that I'm giving you,' Momin said testily. 'If you're attached to notions of caste and to what the Puranas say, go the same way as everyone else. Escape. It's not only you, now that they are facing the heat, many people are calling us 'brother'. Brother indeed! If we're brothers, will you be able invite the miyas, Mamud and Momin, to your pujas, harvest ceremony and fairs? Will you be able to take them into your kitchen? You won't. Then what kind of brothers are we? The Brahmins and Kayasthas are dearer to you than us. When they give you their leftovers to eat, you accept it as a blessing. You touch the dust of their feet to your head. But if you go and stand at their door, they won't come anywhere near you for fear of being touched or of your shadow falling on them. You beg them to perform the funeral ceremonies for your parents and to recite mantras at your sons' and daughters' marriages. Mantras! Won't the mantras protect you now? They say they can bring a clay idol to life with mantras; so why are they running for their lives now?'

Mamud scolded Momin: 'Keep quiet, Momin!' But Momin didn't stop. It was as if the fire of his rage was bursting out of his mouth like blood and bile. He said, 'Har Kumar and Rup Kumar, our fathers, were brothers. They had the same father, they were brothers of the same womb. But Har Kumar forsook that brother for fear of losing his caste. He couldn't stand by his brother. His brother lay dying, but he did not come even once to check on him. Have we forgotten that day! We haven't!'

Garib realised that there had been terrible injustice. He said, 'Things were different in those days. My father didn't have the courage to stand up to that handful of old fogeys, the Brahmins. But a lot of social customs have changed in the last twenty years or so. Like I've come today. Earlier, I wouldn't have been able to come, for fear of who might see me and what people would say. But now I know that even if anyone sees me, they won't say anything.'

'I agree that things have changed. But whatever's changed is because of us, miyas. If we hadn't stood up, nothing would have changed. Things would have continued as they were.'

'That's not correct. Not everyone changed under pressure. Many Hindus have also changed inwardly.'

'How much have they changed by themselves, without any pressure? Have the bonds of caste become any looser? We were Hindus earlier. If we want to become Hindus again, will they take us back? Will they let us enter the temples of their gods and goddesses? Will Brahmins and Kayasthas take our daughters into their homes? Will they make boys from our homes their sons-in-law? Will they eat with us?'

'All that hasn't happened yet.'

'So, then?' After pausing to catch his breath, Momin continued, 'I used to think and talk about living together in harmony. But harmony cannot be only on the surface. The most important thing is the union of minds, and after that comes union of blood. Harmony cannot endure unless there's union of blood. Will the Hindus agree to that?'

Brimming with outrage, Momin said, 'Tell me, bhai, was there any sin or injustice on our part? How did we lose our caste? A man was dying of cholera under a tree. Those who travelled with him left him to die and fled—were they human? Those men didn't lose caste. But another man took the dying man to his own house and saved his life. A man as humane as that belongs to the highest caste. His brow should have been adorned with flowers and sandalwood-paste in reverence. Not only did he not get that respect; on the contrary, the person he cured was labelled an outcas, so low that whoever he touched and gave food and water to lost his caste. That's Hinduism. I think that unless the whole race of bastards is wiped out, there can't be any wellbeing in the world.'

Unable to say anything more, Garib sat down mutely on Mamud's verandah. He had come a long way, and had been standing for a long time. His legs ached. As soon as Momin stopped, Mamud said,

'Don't cause him any more anguish with your words, Momin. Our anguish is a hundred times greater than the anguish you feel, Garib. It comes out in the form of anger when we speak. Go, Garib, go and enquire in the miyas' quarter. You'll see that half the Muslims in the country were driven out by the Hindus themselves under various pretexts, and so they became Muslims. The other half were oppressed so much by the Brahmins that they were compelled to embrace another faith. That's why they hate the Hindus so much. They are the ones who want to cleanse our country of Hindus. No one ever bothered to find out how they suffered, never tried to put an end to it. There's no use crying now.'

Momin added, 'Now the tide has turned. Those whom you were subjugating are now subjugating you. Now, however much anyone cries, it's of no avail. We too were crying one day, but who came then to wipe our tears? So why should we wipe their tears now? Rather, we'll make them cry instead. All the Hindus have to leave this region and go away. Or else ...' Twirling his axe in the air, he seemed to convey how dire the consequence of not going would be.

Garib stepped down to the courtyard. Above him was the sky. But he realised that this sky was no longer his. The soil beneath his feet wasn't his either. He was an unwanted creature in this country now. Looking through the gaps between the leaves of the mango and jamun trees there, his eyes moved to the northeast corner of the sky. He saw a black cloud emerging there, which would soon turn into a storm. The very air seemed to be pregnant with an inauspicious portent.

6

Flight

A Bedford lorry sped along the road. It had begun its journey at the crack of dawn when the sky was still grey, and it had not stopped since then. Now the blistering sun of the month of Baisakh was directly overhead. It wasn't simply heat but some merciless rage that was streaming down from the sun, which would be quenched only after it had burned the whole universe to not into ashes. Beneath the inflated rubber tyres of the lorry was a bumpy, cratered road of rubble and stones. The run-down vehicle bounced up and down violently as it sped along the road.

The owner of the lorry was a Punjabi, a former military contractor. During the Second World War, he had been contracted to supply food and meat to the army. He had roamed various parts of rural Bengal to buy mutton on the cheap, and delivered it to army barracks in this same lorry. Now, just like those military goats, a band of people and their household effects, mattresses and mats were stuffed in the lorry. Sitting atop the pile of belongings, like inexperienced travellers on camel-back, the people swayed, trembled and wept. Terrified that they might be thrown off the moving vehicle, each one was supplicating his or her respective deity. None of them knew when this journey would end or where, or how far they would be taken before they got down. They had heard that they were going to a 'camp'. But what that meant and where it was—they did not know.

The dry road of the Rahr region of Bengal was red like scorched earth. The lorry raced along the road like a crazed horse. The road was carpeted in fine dust because many lorries had plied along the road before this, just as the driver of this lorry had many times. A cyclone-like cloud of red dust enveloped the lorry, as if keeping pace with the roaring, speeding vehicle. The hot dust flying in the furious sun's heat covered the eyes and faces of the travellers. Their bodies too became red. They did not like that at all. It was as if despite their unwillingness, someone had forcibly pushed them into an untimely Holi play, in which people throw colour on unwilling folk simply to provoke them and watch the fun. There was dense forest on both sides of the road, and in the scorching heat of the noon sun, the tall trees stood silently on their single legs. The fire of the torrid Baisakh sun snapped at the leaves on their branches, seeming to endanger the very life of the trees.

After a long time, after journeying a great distance, and after the yearning for human contact in the people's distraught eyes had turned to naught, the lorry and its travellers came upon an Adivasi village. The village had about twenty or twenty-five houses made of thick, earthen walls, which had been built with much toil by labouring folk and covered by thatch laid on bamboo rafters. The people who lived there belonged to the Santhal tribe. Hearing the sound of the lorry, the Santhal men, women and children emerged from their houses, and looked incredulously at the people atop the vehicle. Who were these muddy, exhausted, dejected people? Why were all these people being taken along this road every now and then? Where were they from?

They were the dispossessed: refugees. This was their identity now. An identity that was soaked in disaffection, neglect and humiliation. Just a few days ago, they too had homesteads—

shelters, however modest, to survive through winter, summer and the rains. Now they had nothing. They were paying the price of India's Independence, something incomprehensible to the common people. A part of Bengal had been cut away and discarded—and in that cut-off part, all their rights as citizens had been buried alive. Their identities, their homes and their human dignity too. They were now parasite. They were refugees begging India for shelter. That was where they were being taken now. To a shelter that was called a 'camp'.

Seeing the fields, forests and wild-looking, semi-naked folk all around them, the people sitting atop the lorry were extremely unnerved. They were already frightened to start with; now they became terrified. Who were these people? Their bodily appearance, colour and garb were not at all like that of Bengalis. *Where have they brought us?* Their confounded eyes searched for familiar people, familiar soil, and the beloved waters to which they were eternally habituated. The river on which boatmen unfurled their sails and burst out singing Bhatiyali songs to their heart's content. The water from which countless silver-coloured fish were to be had. Where, where was that empire of water? Water—another name for which was life itself. Where was that life? No, for as far as the eye could see, there was no sign of any water. The fields, trees, plants, people and houses all seemed to be burning under the cruel assault of heat-missiles that exploded over the whole landscape. It was as if a fatal curse was raining down from the ball of fire burning overhead—devoid of mercy or compassion, pitiless, unrelenting. There was no cover over the lorry. No one had even thought of putting up a cover. After all, goats and cows did not require a cover; why should refugees? So the people sitting atop the lorry, those whom time and society had consigned to refugeehood, were burning in the heat of the sun. The hot wind blowing was like the poisonous breath of mythic serpents, scorching the exposed parts of their bodies.

Before this, no one from any of these families had ever undertaken such a difficult journey by road. They had only ventured out on boats. They had the experience of spending days and months living on boats, and if they so much as stepped down into their courtyards from their houses, their feet got wet. These people were gasping like fish out of water in this dry, parched and pitiless land. The truck sped along, passing by one place after another and snaking along bends as it steadily approached the end of its journey. But in the people's eyes and faces, and in their hearts and minds, there was a formless, unknown fear. Their dust-covered, muddy, emaciated bodies trembled in the stupor of that fear. *Where are we going? To which country? How far away is it? Is ugly fate going to cast us into some desert? What awaits us there? Will it herald a new life? An auspicious beginning? A reconstruction? Or will we only be very far away from our own country, our own land, consigned to a helpless life with an ocean of thirst within?*

Ever since morning, the people's dry eyes had been looking in all directions, searching frantically for some water to drink. Water—that was to be found in ponds and rivers, small and wide. But where were the ponds and lakes? Everyone was dying of thirst, but there was no water anywhere. Instead, what they saw on the horizon, which they mistook for water, was only a deceitful mirage.

The soil here was very illusive, deceitful, and insidious. Its sorcery laid a cruel death-trap all over. Under harsh sunlight, when the atom-sized light particles hit the horizon, then, as if in a frenzy, the soil began casting a deadly mysterious spell. Hatched under the hot sun, the dancing light on the sand particles—which were hidden in the earth's body—created an illusionary wave of water. When a thirst-crazed soul spotted such waves, which appeared to be flooding an illusory shore, he kept running in that direction like a lunatic in the hope of reaching water. But he never reached. As he kept advancing, thirstier than ever, the dancing water of the mirage too kept retreating. Finally, as the poor soul ran and ran in acute thirst, he lost his very life.

These travellers were the simple rural folk of East Bengal, who had lived until today with rivers and canals surrounding them. They did not know about the tricks played by the earth. And so, with an ocean of thirst in their parched throats, they gazed at the dancing waves of the mirage. *There's a river as wide as the Padma and Meghna! Wait just a little bit longer.* After that, their thirst would be quenched. After immersing and bathing in and drinking the water, their minds and bodies would cool down.

⌘

Tulsi, the wife of Subol Sutar from Kalakandi village, had been placed in one corner over the piled-up luggage, mattresses and bundles. She was seven months pregnant. She had been experiencing some pain since morning. After setting off from the village, crossing the border and arriving at Bongaon, and then going from there to Ranaghat, and then some other places—somewhere along the way, relatives, kin and neighbours had all got lost. But none of them could be blamed. People were only concerned about themselves now. In times of danger, everyone thought only about their own lives and those of their immediate families and children. They only wanted to rush to a safe place before anything else. Who cared for anyone else in such a time! Now, the few persons remaining known to Subol and Tulsi, people from their village and some relatives, were travelling on this lorry. If they were separated from them, who knew who they would end up with. What would happen if they could not get along with them, by way of language, thinking, behaviour and customs! At the halt in Ranaghat, five or seven families had also been waiting beside Subol and his pile of belongings. They were all people from Chittagong. The whole day, Subol could not understand a word of their language. How could he stay with them? How would he call out to them in times of danger or distress? How would he express his feelings of joy or anguish? That's why he had boarded this lorry.

Subol did not blame anyone for anything. The entire blame lay on his fate. Or else why would he have to leave behind a mansion-like, tin-roofed house, two-and-a-half bighas of paddy land, a twelve-foot boat, a twenty-foot fishing net and a dozen coconut and areca palms, and flee his country under cover of night, like a thief? Although their hamlet was peaceful, the foundations of his courage had been shaken on seeing the fierce flames that burned and turned the sky red on the northern side of Kalakandi village, accompanied by the cries of 'Allahu Akbar!' that rent the air. He realised that his peaceful village would not be peaceful any longer. The fire's wrath would claim it before the night ended. And so, holding Tulsi by the hand, he had slipped out along the muddy path through the paddy field. Once he reached the road, he realised that he was not alone. There were many others fleeing like him, leaving behind their age-old homes.

The thought of fleeing had arisen in Subol's village three or four months back. The inner conviction—that this was their homeland—which had remained unbroken for the last six or seven years, was suddenly rocked. Those who had foresight had secretly sold off their land and homesteads and, before anyone could get the slightest inkling of it, moved across the border—to India. Those like Subol, who were not as farsighted, who were more emotionally attached to their homeland, had stayed back.

For some strange reason, Subol had harboured a strong conviction that after some time, the chaos would come to an end, discord and disagreement would leave their land, and everything would be peaceful once again. The Muslims had wanted a country of their own, which they had achieved. So why would they engage in violence and bloodshed? Moinuddin Sheikh had voiced such a belief: 'Why are you afraid? There has been discord between Hindus and Muslims so many times and in so many places. Did anyone ever have to leave the country? Why would you leave behind your own home and go away to another country? Be without fear. Aren't we here? Let me see who dares say anything to you!'

Moinuddin Sheikh was an influential person in the region. Everyone knew him and respected him. He was fond of Subol Sutar. How could Subol disregard him? And so there had been no prior preparation for escape. But one evening, his head downcast, Moinuddin Sheikh had said embarrassedly to Subol, 'I had given you hope, but now I see that my words have no worth at all. No one heeds me. Yesterday, some leaders had come from the district headquarters. They were inciting the hot-headed sons of the miyas. They said, "Miyas have a right to everything in this country. Drive away the bastards and take over their land and homesteads. The law and the police are on your side." That's why everyone is dancing like crazed souls. One can't say what will happen now, or when. If there were two or five people, I could have held them back; but now there are hundreds upon hundreds of them. And it's not just people from this region. There are outsiders too. I hear there are miyas from twenty or twenty-five nearby villages, together with miyas who fled violence in India and came here. How many can I deter?'

There was no time to lose. The terrifying flames enveloping the Roy family's house, and the ear-splitting screams of the women of that household, burnt all his courage to ashes. Mr Roy had already sold off some of his land and property and sent away half his family to India. Even though the loss and destruction wasn't so much, whatever was destroyed was not so meagre either. Mr Roy's daughter-in-law could not be found. The arsonists had carried her away. No one knew whether she was alive or dead.

Although Tulsi hadn't been nurtured with milk and butter like Mr Roy's daughter-in-law, she was quite beautiful. She had just turned nineteen. She wasn't fair-complexioned, but she wasn't that dark-complexioned either. Her eyes, face and features were most attractive. Subol wasn't wealthy, but for Tulsi's sake, it did not take him long to exit from the southern side of the village once he saw flames rising from the northern side. One did not hear so much about riots and bloodshed nowadays, but there had been no letup in reports of robberies and rape.

In anguish, Subol had handed over the keys of his house to Moinuddin Sheikh. 'I'm leaving everything in your custody.' In a choked voice, Moinuddin Sheikh had said, 'It won't be like this always. This madness will surely stop one day. I'll look after your house. You'll get it back when you return. Don't worry.'

Could a man be free of worry simply because of those words— 'Don't worry'? Leaving behind home and homeland, setting off for an unfamiliar and unknown place ... But right now Subol was more worried about Tulsi. Her pain could worsen any moment. In which land devoid of shelter or friend would she deliver their baby?

Tulsi's thirsty pleas in the scorching heat made Subol look helplessly in all directions. Where was water to be found? He had never realised before, and in this way, how precious and valuable water was. He had never imagined that such dry, parched soil—for miles on end—could exist in this world. There was water in some corner of the Santhal hamlet, in some well, but the travellers did not even know what a well was. So even though they saw it, they could not recognise it. After all, one could not remain alive without water. The awareness that since there was life around them there had to be water somewhere, was buried under their anxiety. Subol consoled Tulsi, 'We've almost reached. Just be patient for some more time, you'll get water very soon.'

In the corner opposite from where Tulsi was perched was Radhakanta's seventy-six year old father, half-sitting, half-lying. Just the other day, the old man had gone around the entire neighbourhood, tapping the earth with his walking stick, the unvanquishable strength of his mind and body egging him on. He was enquiring after everyone, who was content and who was in distress, who was unwell, how the harvest had been in each one's field, and so on. The old man had never been ill to speak of. But he was stricken by mental illness now, arising from forsaking his homeland. Broken, crushed, supine and incapable of even standing on his two legs. The newfound taste of 'Independence' had sucked away all his mental fortitude, just like a leech sucked up blood from a body. As he lay on the lorry, tears streamed continuously from his eyes. The withered, ancient skeleton of the man crushed by his mental wound was collapsing under the wild bouncing of the speeding lorry. He felt as if his old body was being ground to powder by the crazy jolting. As he lay, he moaned, 'Oh Radhakanta, how much longer? I can't bear it anymore! I think I am dying!'

The driver of the lorry was frantic. He had no time at all. He had to drop the passengers and return with the empty lorry as quickly as possible for a second trip. Some time had been lost on the way because of a problem with the vehicle's gearbox, which had to be repaired. He was driving the lorry at breakneck speed in order to make up for lost time. Time was of the essence. That's why the people stuffed in the vehicle were being thrown around like shelled peas on hot sand.

Along with Tulsi, the baby in her womb was also bouncing up and down in the severe jolting of the lorry. She had borne the pain so long by clenching her teeth, but now it had crossed all limits. The signs of impending delivery were writ large on her face and in her eyes. Garib Das's Khudi Ma, Gagan's Ma, as she was known, was highly experienced in such matters. With her assistance, hundreds of women had delivered babies without impediment. Like his son, Garib Das too had been born at the hands of this woman, a veritable earth-mother. Forgetting about the anxieties plaguing her own mind, Gagan's Ma now became agitated seeing Tulsi's condition. She started screaming out, 'Subol, what are you waiting for? Hurry up and tell the driver to stop! Tulsi's going to deliver now!'

Hearing Gagan's Ma's shrill screams, the fear-crazed Subol cried out to the driver as loudly as he could, 'Sir, sahib, please stop! Stop the lorry!'

A government employee sat beside the driver. He was in charge of taking the refugees to a predetermined place. As soon as he heard Subol's cries, fearing some mishap, he said to the driver, 'Stop the lorry!' The driver slammed the brake. The lorry came to a standstill in the middle of the road with a tremendous jolt. Opening the door and thrusting his head out, he asked, 'What's happening? Why the shouting?' Just then came Tulsi's ear-splitting scream: *'O Ma, moira gelam, Ma go!* I'm dying!' The government employee stepped out to see what the matter was. Looking in Tulsi's direction and realising what the situation was, he shouted in annoyance, 'Why did you come in this condition? Does anyone do that? Come on, bring her down! *Joto shob jhamela!* Hurry up and bring her down!' Subol, Gagan's Ma, Garib Das's wife Bimala and a couple more women brought Tulsi down from the truck. They took her to the concealment of bushes at a slight distance. There, in a short while, Tulsi delivered her baby. It was a girl.

Quite some time was spent in all this. Everyone then climbed back into the lorry with Tulsi and her newborn daughter. The driver of the vehicle, incensed now because of the time lost, drove even faster. Only then did the people notice that while everyone had been preoccupied with Tulsi, Radhakanta's old father had died quietly at some point. So as to avoid the driver's ire, no one dared to ask him to stop the lorry.

Carrying the dead body of Radhakanta's father on one side and the new-born child on the other, the lorry sped ahead, raising a cloud of red dust.

7

Ghar-jamais of the Indian Government

Poets live in a world of imagination. They create an imaginary universe of their own with the help of beautiful words. Thus, with great ease they can write, 'all birds return to their nests, all journeys come to an end'. No, they don't end, not all journeys come to an end. Some journeys are interminable. Neither can the bird whose breast is pierced by an arrow, whose wings are torn in a storm, fly. It cannot return to its nest.

All these uprooted folk had set out on a road that had no end. Their journey would only lead them to a dead-end of unbearable humiliation and unspeakable agony. Who was responsible for that? Arrogant social leaders who lacked any farsightedness, political leaders with evil designs who were greedy for power—whoever it may be, it wasn't the people who were on the road now.

The Bedford lorry came to a halt. The driver got down and, addressing Garib, Subol and Radhakanta, thundered out an order in Hindi: 'Everyone get off! We've arrived at the camp!'

Temporary shelters had been created for the uprooted folk on a huge expanse of land. Red-coloured tents were crammed into the whole area, with an arrangement to house about seven thousand families. The camp was called Shiromanipur. This was in Bankura, a district of West Bengal. On one side was a dense forest of sal, which had been planted painstakingly by the forest department. Scattered here and there on the other side lay mango orchards, all in a state of neglect. On the third side lay two nearly dilapidated buildings of a former aerodrome, with a large runway for planes to take off and land. And opposite that was an immense field. Across the field, far away, was an Adivasi village, where a few thousand utterly poor people, belonging to a primitive tribe, lived. The Shiromanipur camp was situated within these four boundaries. Scattered all over the camp were large structures, made of bricks, stones and concrete. All these collapsed structures bore testimony to the fact that people had lived here earlier, who were not the indigenous people; they had not been destitute. They had been affluent enough to live in pukka houses. Who were they? One guessed that they belonged to the Indian army.

Bishnupur, the principal town of Bankura district, was not more than eight or ten miles away. It had once been the capital of the powerful Malla kings. The old palace was still there. The famous cannon at the entrance of the palace had been witness to the valour and glory of the Malla kings. There had once been a fierce battle between the Malla king and the English army. Who knows, perhaps this secret outpost had been built by them in the middle of the forest, not far from Bishnupur, because it was necessary for the battle. Alternatively, it was also possible that the call to the 1855 revolt by the heroic Santhal warriors Sido Murmu and Kanhu Murmu had agitated the indigenous folk here. They had attacked the representatives of the Raj with bows and arrows, axes and spears, with the objective of ousting the English rulers. Perhaps the English army had gathered here to defeat the rebels.

Whatever may have been the reason for locating a military outpost here, those who were here last were probably soldiers of the Sikh regiment. It was they who had given the region the name Shiromanipur, in order to keep the memory of their faith alive. Those soldiers were no longer there. Only collapsed structures lay in the place, given a name by them.

It was about four in the afternoon now. The sun was as hot as it had been earlier. All the refugees unloaded their belongings from the truck and huddled under the shade of a mango tree. The office and residential quarters of the government officials were right in front of where the truck had stopped. There were sheds with tin-sheet walls and roofs, which housed clinics, warehouses and dining halls. Looking at the sheds, one could surmise that they were temporary structures, erected in a hurry for immediate use.

In one shed, a bespectacled man with a thick register was sitting at a dirty wooden table. He was dark-skinned and dressed in a white shirt. He had a round face and big eyes, and had tufts of hair on his earlobes, in his nostrils and on his arms. Another man stood nearby, fanning him uninterruptedly with a large palm-leaf fan. He was also a refugee who had arrived a few days ago. He had volunteered to be a servant-at-large so that he could earn two or five rupees a month.

After a while, the dark-skinned babu, who was being fanned, shouted out, 'Line up! Everyone stand in a line and come forward!' He addressed them not as *apni* or even *tumi*, but *tui*—the way educated, high-caste people addressed the average illiterate, low-caste, impoverished person. Not with respect, or fellow-feeling, but contempt.

What's your name?

Father's name?

What's your address? From which district, police station and village have you come?

What's your occupation?

How many family members? Tell me each one's name and age.

Which caste?

Thirty families had just arrived by truck. More were likely to arrive. If they did not arrive today, they'd come tomorrow. Or else the day after. Those who dwelt in the political universe knew that many trucks would arrive now. A few hundred camps had been set up all over the Indian state of West Bengal. This camp had been set up after those were full. There were three more camps like this one in nearby Basudebpur. The one in Shiromanipur was the fourth camp in the region.

Garib Das was eighth in the queue for registration of names. Behind him were the others in his group. After completing the registration, he went and sat below a tree. How could he leave until everyone's details had been recorded. But the dark-skinned babu took so long to enter the names and personal details of the few people that it seemed he wanted to spend the rest of the day doing that. The fiery sun burning overhead all day long had finally penetrated Garib Das's head. And the fire beneath his feet was now setting his stomach on fire too. Early that morning, just before they had boarded the lorry, volunteers of the Sevashram Sangha had distributed some chira and jaggery, which he hadn't been able to eat more than a couple of handfuls of for want of water. Since then he had gone without food all day. Now, hungry and thirsty, he felt extremely weak.

Evening had descended. But the final light of the day still remained. After recording everyone's names, the dark-skinned babu rose and gave Garib Das a piece of paper that was supposedly a ration card. 'Go, show this at the warehouse and collect rice and dal.' Rice and dal was obtained, some salt was obtained too. This was called 'dole'. And each family was provided a tent. The dark-skinned babu showed them where their tents were to be erected. He explained in his own fashion, 'From now on, you lot have become *ghar-jamais* of the Indian government. Eat and have fun!'

Garib, Subol, Radhakanta and Gagan erected their tents next to one another. They managed to create a shelter to lay their heads under.

It had been four or five days since Garib had left his village and country. In all these days, he had not laid eyes on rice. He had survived on chira and jaggery. Now, after receiving the rice and dal, it was as if his heart was dancing in joy. The rice was reddish and thick-grained, mixed with grit and dust. But it was rice after all. Another name for which was *Lokkhir Dana*, 'Ma Lakshmi's grain'. Lakshmi was the Goddess who led one to one's goal, and so her grain ought not to be frowned upon. Garib had heard from his father that the one who frowned upon Lakshmi's grain invited her ire; he would starve to death. When Garib was a little boy, their situation had been better, and food was cooked twice a day in his house. They had some paddy land then, from which they fulfilled their year-long requirement of rice. Garib's Ma used to cook the rice. When the rice would begin to boil noisily, it was as if life itself blossomed with its aroma. Har Kumar used to lay the floor-seat on the verandah of the large room, and sit down on it to eat. He wasn't just eating—it was like puja, an act of worship. He never uttered a word then. First, taking some drops from a glass of water, he'd sprinkle it in a circle around the plate, as an offering to God, in gratitude for being blessed with food. After that, taking some of the hot rice in the tips of his fingers, he'd knock his forehead with his knuckles in obeisance, muttering the names of Ma Lakshmi and Ma Annapurna—the provider of food— before putting that into his mouth. 'Ma, you have granted us food today; grant us the same tomorrow as well, Ma.' Even if a single grain of rice fell off the plate, he would carefully pick it up. Garib Das was like his father. He too had the same devotion to food. And yet, why were Lakshmi and Annapurna unkind to him? He did not know what sin he had committed, to make them turn their faces away from him.

He said to his wife Bimala, '*Aei, shonchhos?* Do you hear me? I'll take care of the unpacking in a little while. But organise the cooking first. I'm dying of hunger. I'm going to look for some firewood and dry leaves in the jungle out there. You can make a hearth with some stones.'

Bimala was fair-skinned and petite. Despite the myriad deprivations and starvations, she was still pretty. Her eyes were like twin pools, full of natural simplicity. When she spoke, her voice brimmed with the diffidence of ages. Her Ma had taught her—'Girls shouldn't speak loudly, shouldn't walk fast, and shouldn't raise their eyes to look at anyone. For that matter, even while speaking to your husband, speak in an impersonal voice. Not directly. Because that's imprudent. That's modesty, meaning *lojja*, or shame. It's a woman's ornament.'

While responding to Garib, Bimala therefore addressed her son instead: 'Tell your father not to go too far into the unfamiliar forest. And he should return quickly. Once he's back, I'll leave you with him and go to fetch water. I can't cook without water.'

A few hand-pumps had been installed in the camp to meet the water requirements of the people there. Other than that, there was no trace of water anywhere. Bathing, washing, cooking and drinking, were all from the same source. Consequently, all day, for that matter, until late at night, there would be a long queue at the hand-pump. Garib returned to his tent with the firewood he had foraged. But by the time Bimala had fetched water after standing in the queue, washed all the utensils and began to cook, it was night. Garib squatted at the entrance of the tent, biding time in eager hope, a void as vast as the sky in his belly. When would the food be ready? When would his belly get hot rice? In time, the fire was lit and the rice began to boil. But after that, it kept cooking. The rice did not get cooked at all. It was as if it wasn't rice but bits of stone. After an hour and a half, it was still the same—uncooked. Suddenly, the smell of rice boiling in water hit Garib's nose. It had not come in his direction so far because the wind had been blowing in the other direction. As soon as he smelt it, Garib stood up, startled. What's this? Where's that unforgettable, entrancing aroma of rice? The aroma that makes the very air delightful and brings the dying back to life! ... The aroma for which the hungry man forsakes a fragrant garden of flowers! But what's this? It smells sour and rotten, gives you a headache! It stinks! It makes one sick to smell it, makes one want to vomit! As the smell emanated from every tent, a veritable storm assailed people's noses, making all those who had arrived today wonder: How can I eat this? Will I stay alive if I eat this?

Such thoughts did not remain for very long in Garib's mind. He consoled himself: It's nothing. Whatever it may smell like, after all, it's rice. Rice means life, rice means God's blessing. One must not find fault with it. The stomach has to be filled first with this. Good and bad can come later.

After the cooking was done, Bimala served the rice on an enamel plate and placed it in front of Garib Das, and then poured some dal over it. Just like the rice that hadn't softened, the grains of dal too stared out. Because the cooking had taken a long time, the firewood had run out, and so the dal could not be inspected in the dark to see if it was done. Was it the dal's fault that it hadn't dissolved, or was it because of the water?

Like his father, Garib poured a few drops of water from the enamel glass into the cup of his palm, and sprinkled it in a circle around his plate. After they had crossed the India border, a Marwari social service organisation had distributed a plate and glass to each person in the group. They were greedy to earn merit. They arrived wherever there were people in distress—in the hope of earning merit through charity. Whether it was drought, or floods, or epidemics— they landed up in the affected region with relief materials. Their constant prayer to God: O Lord, don't do anything whereby there's no more need to provide relief to people. Just carry on doing your work, and give us so much money that all these people feel blessed with just a tiny bit from that!

After the invocation and symbolic offering to the deity, as Garib brought the first morsel of rice mixed with dal to his mouth, the smell that shot out and assailed his nose made Garib realise that, let alone eating to one's heart's content, even stuffing it into the mouth somehow, merely to assuage the stomach's craving, was a loathsome task. After swallowing three or four handfuls—driven by hunger—

when he was about to take the next handful to his mouth, he felt as if his stomach was revolting. Yet he put the handful to his mouth— and at once a violent resistance sprang from his gut. He puked uncontrollably, right on the plate of rice.

It wasn't just Garib Das. Subol, Radhakanta and Gagan were all in the same condition. Everyone was shocked. 'What's this they've given us, which only looks like rice? Do humans eat this? Can they?' Carrying their plates of rice, they rushed to the dark-skinned babu. 'What kind of rice have you given us? Won't complain about the dust and grit ... but the foul smell ... How can we eat this rice?'

Although the dark-skinned babu was annoyed, he did not express it. He laughed and, speaking softly, explained to them: 'Tell me, what can I do? We can only give you the rice and dal that the government sends us, isn't it? I didn't grow this in my field, did I! I've given you the rice that we received. If the next consignment consists of basmati rice, I'll give you that. Just put up with the difficulty for a few days. It's said, isn't it, that health is above everything else, whatever it takes! Eat it, and after a few days, you'll get used to it. At first, you'll vomit a bit, your bowels will empty a couple of times. But don't worry, nothing more than that. Then you'll see you're fine.' Pausing to laugh, he continued, 'After all you aren't scions of any zamindars, you're peasant-folk. If you ate your fill one day, the next day you couldn't. If you die eating the rice— I'm not saying you'll die, that's just an expression—if you die, then at least you wouldn't have died of starvation, you'd have died eating rice. Tell me, aren't you truly fortunate!' He laughed again.

The dark-skinned babu had seen people eat that rice earlier too. After eating it, several people suffered loose motions. In a few days, some people recovered. Those whose powers of resistance were weak, would die. More refugees would arrive, and eventually the number of those who were not dead would only increase.

That night, seeing Garib sit before his plate and suffer as he tried to eat what was inedible, Bimala felt terrible. She said, 'Son, tell your father to take the Lord's name, hold his nose and swallow it down.' And Garib had said to himself inwardly, as he stared at his plate: 'Oh dear life, how you wept all these years for rice. And now that you've got it, you won't eat! Eat, oh life, eat and fill your belly. If you die eating this rice, so be it. So many die for not being able to eat. Why don't you eat and die!'

So Garib held his nose and swallowed that black meal down with water. However, as the night advanced, his stomach began to rumble and ache unbearably. Even before it was morning, he had to rush out to defecate. Later in the morning, someone or the other from the thirty newly-arrived families was rushing, with a pot in hand, towards the field. They realised, after wasting five or seven pots, that water too was precious here. Then they began tearing and using sal leaves instead of water.

While people were engaged in a deadly battle against the rice provided to them, and it hadn't yet been determined who would emerge victor and who would lose, they were inattentive to the attack of yet another enemy. The angry sun of the month of Baisakh shone with great fury upon the wax-impregnated tents, which became terribly hot. In the afternoon, the inside of the tent became as hot as a blacksmith's furnace. People wanted to rush out of the tent and run for cover in some shade. But where could they go? The sal forest was quite far away, and the little bit of shade under the mango trees had already been appropriated by those whose tents were pitched in the mango orchard. Lacking any other option, most people were compelled to stay inside the hot tents. These people, who had been nurtured by the relatively pleasant climate of the marshlands, were unable to withstand this fierce two-pronged attack. The death rate of those who were a bit weak, like infants and the aged, but especially the infants, rose like anything. Almost every night, from some tent or the other, one heard the ear-splitting wails of mothers who had lost their children. 'O my precious gem, golden one, O God, where have you gone leaving your Ma behind!'

In the midst of such a terrifying time, Garib's son—who had been named Jibon, meaning 'life'—fell very sick. When Garib got sick, it took him eight or ten days to recover. Bimala recovered in less time, in just five days. But there was no sign of Jibon recovering. His condition worsened by the day. It had begun with watery motions; after a few days, it turned into amoebic dysentery. After that, he began passing blood. He had a high fever. As soon as he squatted to defecate, his bowel emerged and jutted out. His bowel, red like the flowers on the cashew-nut tree, used to hang out until it was pushed back inside by hand.

This continued for about three weeks. The virulence of the disease kept increasing by the day. Finally, the little infant, who should have been running and jumping around all day on his tiny feet in his family courtyard, lay wilted on the bed, like a lifeless, severed stem of pui-spinach. He didn't move, didn't cry or speak. He simply lay with his mouth agape. Saliva oozed from his mouth. Flies sat on his face, licking the saliva.

There's no hope, thought Garib.

There was no count of the number of unsung children in the camp whom Yama, the Lord of Death, had laid on the funeral pyre. It was like an endless procession of death. A thousand or twelve hundred families had arrived at the camp by now. It was doubtful whether there was a single household which Yama had taken pity on. Whether it was someone's mother or father, or son or daughter—someone or the other had surely perished. There was a pond about a mile and a half to the north of the camp. The water was only knee-deep there. The dead bodies were taken to its bank for cremation. But because there were so many deaths, wood became scarce. There was no dry wood to be found in the forest. So there were no more pyres. All the dead bodies were buried. With so much weeping all around, the tears in people's eyes seemed to have run dry. Hearing all the wailing, people's hearts had turned to stone. Gradually, the ear-splitting screams of distress ceased to disturb the night's tranquility. People sobbed in secret, and waited for their own turn to arrive. They hadn't known that the lives that they had sought to protect so crazily could depart amidst such neglect and apathy.

So many people were dying in the camps—but what were the doctors doing? There was nothing they could do. Only medicines could do something. But where were the medicines? There were only three kinds of medicines in the camp doctor's clinic. There was a white syrup in a large bottle, looking a bit like lime dissolved in water. In another bottle was a red liquid, the colour of *alta*. And in a third jar were white tablets. If someone had a cut or a swelling or a burn, the doctor applied the red medicine, using cotton wool, and gave a few tablets. He would say, 'Take two tablets a day for three days. If you haven't recovered by then, come again.' If someone had fever, stomach-ache, dysentery or any other kind of ailment, the doctor poured out some of the lime-water into the bottle they brought with them, gave them two tablets, and told them the same thing: 'If you haven't recovered in three days, come again.'

No one was cured with those medicines. Garib Das's son, Jibon, did not recover either. He got more and more sick. One day, Garib fell into great anxiety seeing his son's condition. The way a stream of fresh blood gushed out of his body—it didn't seem he would survive the night. The light of Jibon's life was fading away little by little. With her son on her bosom, the sleepless mother, Bimala, sat like a stone image. An unceasing stream of tears flowed from the corner of her eyes as she gazed at her son. Tears—colourless, flavourless and unreasonable too. She didn't realise they had no value at this time. They achieved nothing at all.

Feeling utterly helpless, Garib Das squatted at the entrance of their tent. Before his eyes, his son was slowly sliding towards death, and yet he was unable to do anything. In order to suppress his inner anguish, every now and then he got up and paced up and down. Neither he nor his wife were in good health. But that did not matter to them. They only had one prayer now: '*Hey bhogoban mor polar peran bhikka deo.* Oh God, I beg you to spare my son's life.'

Garib Das had no close relatives in the camp. Some of his brothers had crossed the border a long time ago and gone to another camp. When Garib left his country, the few distant relatives who were with him had all scattered in different directions. Some of them had found shelter in camps one, two or three in Basudevpur, some in Garbeta and some in Piyardoba. And some had in their destiny the camps in Ghutiari Sharif, Khola or Doltala, in the southern part of the district of 24 Parganas.

Uprooted refugees found shelter in dozens of camps like these, spread across West Bengal. But even if there were no kinfolk of one's own, the grief, suffering, mental anguish and above all, anxiety about the uncertain future, had bound one person to another in bonds of kinship. Now they all belonged to one another.

In Garib Das's tent, Yama and man were locked in a bitter struggle. The night arrived with her face veiled by a black scarf, her eyes smeared with the nightmare of death. Because death, and those who worshipped death, had come to take the life of such a tiny infant, they needed concealment. They had concealment all right—that of the dense sal forest. No one had the slightest inkling about what transpired, day after day, in this faraway region, cut off by a forest from the rest of the world. Day was darker than night here. Thousands of people here were sick. Only one doctor had been assigned to them. By way of medicines, he had a red one and a white one—two kinds of liquid. In such conditions, people were bound to die. That's why Subol, Radhakanta and Gagan, from the adjacent tents, stayed up at night, their hearts full of anxiety. Garib Das's son was dying. He would not see the sunrise the next morning. How could a neighbour fall asleep at such a fearful time?

Coming out silently from his tent, Subol Sutar slowly went and stood before Garib Das. As if talking about a secret matter, he whispered, 'How's the boy now?'

Suppressing his tears, Garib said, 'He's still there. But it's time. He won't be around very long.'

'Don't say that! You're his father. Call out to God. He is the only Master. If God wills, your son will recover; he'll live for a hundred years!' Subol Sutar consoled Garib Das, and then he headed towards Radhakanta's tent. He called him softly, 'Hey, Radha-da, have you fallen asleep?'

'I'm awake. Is it time to go?'

'No, he's still alive. It looks like he'll be gone by daybreak. Come, let's go to the office and get a spade and a pick. We should keep them ready. Or else we may not get them when needed. What if someone takes them before us? We'll have to wait then.'

When all these people had given up their country and come away, they had been unable to carry with them a lot of valuable household items. Nothing besides their own lives and the lives of their family members and relatives' had seemed important then. So no one thought to take along a pick or spade, which were needed every day now. However, the thoughtful government had arranged for that. If they hadn't done that, what would have happened to the dead bodies when there was no more wood to be found in the forest? People would have thrown them here and there. That would be improper.

But now, with a few hours left for daybreak, Radhakanta felt hesitant to wake up the sleeping watchman and get the pick and spade. He said, 'We won't have to wait. Do you think they have only one or two picks and spades in the godown? Let it happen first; we'll go there after that.'

There were plenty of spades in the godown, but there were also plenty of people needing them. Everyone rushed to get them when needed, but not to return them. Subol said, 'I tell you, let's go and have them ready before day breaks.'

'We'll go later, sit down for a while. We'll go as soon as we hear Bimala weeping.'

Subol squatted in front of Radhakanta's tent and lit a beedi. He puffed on the beedi, but his ears were alert. The night advanced slowly towards dawn. But Bimala did not start weeping.

Radhakanta said, 'Such a tiny boy, yet he's battling so bravely with death.'

Subol said, 'We can't keep sitting. Let me go and lie down for a bit. I'll get up when the weeping and wailing begins.'

No one thought Jibon would live. His parents' anticipation of the final moment, the neighbours' mental preparation for his final journey—despite all that, and without a drop of any medicine, who knows how, tiny Jibon survived the night. Which was a matter of great astonishment for everyone. How was it possible! Perhaps it was such boys that people swore at, calling them *Jomer awruchi*, 'Yama's disgust'. Whom nothing could kill! Who lay dying—and then survived!

After surviving that night, Jibon lived. But the way he lived throughout his life—could that really be called living?

8

To School

Man is said to have drunk the divine elixir. Because even after being wiped out successively by drought, flood, epidemic, famine, gale, cyclone, earthquake, communal riots, revolutions and world wars—humanity survived. Although so many died, everyone else survived.

Garib Das was alive. His son was alive. His wife too was alive. And, like serving time in prison, albeit without hard labour, their minds and bodies rolled through several years. One day Bimala was going to fetch water in an earthen pot from the hand-pump. Unless she went for water early in the morning, there would be a long queue at the pump. After all, bathing, cooking, drinking and washing utensils—for so many people—required a lot of water. Having completed one round of fetching water, and pouring it into pots and pans in her tent, she had walked a few steps to make another round, when Garib called her. '*Aw Jiboner Ma*, how old is our Jibon now?'

Hearing Garib Das's question, Bimala's eyes rolled upwards to the heavens, as if looking askance at the one who dwelt there. *Ha bhogoman, aapen kemun mainshere polar baap banaichhen je nijer polar boyosh jaane na.* O God, what kind of a man have you made the boy's father, who doesn't even know the age of his own son! She said, with a trace of exasperation, 'When we came from the country, I was carrying a one-year-old in my arms; we've been here five years.'

Garib replied in a guilty tone, 'There are so many kinds of worries always buzzing around inside my head, I can't remember anything. But what I say is, since the boy is six years old, let's admit him to school.'

At the mention of 'school', Bimala was struck by terror. The pot in the crook of her arm fell to the ground. She said, 'No, no, not now. Let another two or four years go by. Let him grow older. My son has suffered a grave sickness. There's no flesh on his body, he's all bones. He's so weak—if he's thrashed by the schoolmaster, he won't survive. Keshto's father stopped Keshto's schooling precisely for this reason. The master slapped him so hard on his temple because he could not read the alphabet that he's become deaf in one ear.'

Garib explained to his wife, 'He didn't make him deaf deliberately! He only hit him, but somehow he got hurt in the wrong place. Boys are very naughty. Unless they are thrashed a bit, how will they learn to read and write? The master is not an enemy who thrashes for no reason. He only beats the students for their own good. The more he's beaten, the more he'll learn. The potter first cuts the earth with his spade, makes it squelchy by adding water, and then he kneads it with his feet. After that, he puts the clay on the wheel and turns it. He turns the wheel and makes pots, utensils and pitchers. When that's done, he puts them out in the sun. He dries them all day. At night, he puts them in a furnace. When they're burnt and red, they're hard and strong. People want those pots, they're useful. In the same way, if a boy has to be raised right, parents have to turn their hearts to stone and push him to school. If he gets beaten, so be it. If you keep him at home fearing the beating, he won't become a man.'

Bimala couldn't exactly understand the connection between becoming a man and learning to read and write. Back in the other country, Mr Bhattacharya's elder son had several qualifications—but was he a man? There was no kindness or compassion in him, one heard he had several other faults too. So then what was the use of all those qualifications?

In an attempt to convince his wife, Garib thought some more, and then said, 'If a man does not know to read and write, then even though he has eyes, he is blind. Should we make our son blind too, just because we are blind! That babu, the one who writes in the register in the office—it's because he learnt to read and write that he has a cushy job today. He doesn't have to stand in the rain or sun like us. People are always crowding around him, saying babu this and babu that, imploring him with folded hands. No, don't say no! I shall educate Jibon and make him a babu!'

In front of the hand-pump that Bimala went to for water was a fine metalled road, as level as a bowstring. It began at the aerodrome runway and, cutting across the middle of the camp, it led to the Santhal hamlet. The primary school was on that road. A fair-skinned master, with a limp, taught there. What he taught and how he taught was visible to all. He would pull some boy's ear and make him stand in the sun. He made some other boy do sit-ups, and he caned another boy till his backside turned red.

Her husband's intentions made Bimala want to weep as she thought about her son's impending bad days. Suppressing her feelings, she said, 'Educate him. It's your son, so beat him, or else have him thrashed to death by someone else! What more can I say! I'm going to fetch water.'

Garib Das stood firm upon his Bhishma-like vow. He would educate Jibon, come what may. After all this wasn't Barisal, that land of marshes and woods, where children had to cross canals, rivers and lakes, and walk two or three miles to go to school. And back in the country, it wasn't like the children of the untouchable Nama folk were allowed inside the school even if they went there. The school authorities would immediately flare up with grimaces and snarls. 'What on earth have you come here for? What will you gain by going to school? After all you're only going to catch fish and push the plough. Where's the need for schooling for that?' If the student did not flee at that rebuke, if he stubbornly hung on like a leech, the master would frighten him: 'If you're unable to learn, I'll have the skin off your back. I'll break as many as four canes on your back.' If even that didn't frighten the student, the master would then say, 'Go and sit quietly in that corner. Don't touch anyone, don't talk to anybody, don't touch the water-pot.' Here, at least it wasn't like that. The schoolmaster and students were all low-caste. But the thrashing was there. That had to be there. A stone could never become an idol without the wounds inflicted by hammer and chisel.

But Bimala! Many children in the camp suffered the terror of the skin off their backs, and made their parents suffer that too. There was nothing one could do about that. Garib reflected that the schools in the old country were like a dangerous forest, where children of Brahmins and Kayasthas roamed like a pack of hunting dogs. If one or two children of the Nama folk went there, their plight was like that of a meek hare. Everyone pounced upon them, abused them and beat them. If someone complained, the master found fault with him and beat him instead. Most children fled for their lives from that hostile educational system. They never advanced beyond Class 2 or Class 3. If a Nama parent was hell-bent on educating his child, he would send the child to Bagerhat College, which had been established by Gurchand Thakur, the great idol of the Namasudra community. There was no caste oppression there, no discrimination.

There was no caste oppression in this camp either. Those who indulged in that—the Brahmins, Kayasthas and Baidyas—did not want to live together with low-caste folk, on account of caste arrogance and economic well-being. They stayed far away from them. Only all the low-caste, destitute people were compelled to come here—those 'whose stale *panta* rice ran out even before salt could be fetched', those who were utterly bereft. Even though all the officers and government employees who had come here were high-caste, they were all from West Bengal. They were less casteist in their mentality, relatively speaking, than the upper-castes in East Bengal. They did not give much importance to caste divisions and prejudice, as much as they did to whether someone was educated and wealthy or not, that is to say, whether they were *bhadralok* or *chhotolok*. For them, 'poor' and 'illiterate' were synonymous with *chhotolok*; those who lacked means and education were *chhotolok*. That was why the dark-skinned babu, Bhuban Barui, addressed them with the disrespectful *tui*. It did not behove the dignity of a *bhadralok* to address a *chhotolok* deferentially, as *apni*.

For precisely the same reason, the dark-skinned babu accorded respect to Khagen Mandal, a Namasudra. He always asked him to sit on a chair when he came. Khagen Mandal was a relative of the undisputed leader of East Pakistan, Jogen Mandal. He was educated and well-off. If he wanted, he could have, instead of coming to the camp, purchased a house and stayed there. But if he did that, a few hundred families—who had fled their country, accompanying him—would become hapless orphans. He had chosen this harsh life on their account. Everyone in the camp heeded and respected Khagen babu. It was from him that Garib Das had heard that there was no wealth greater than education. Garib Das had high hopes. He would make his son a scholar like Khagen babu. He too would read the newspaper like Khagen Mandal. People would crowd at his door to hear all the news about the country and the world.

Khagen babu had one day narrated the story of how their community—that had come to be regarded as 'Chandal'—had in time been accepted as Namasudras in society and in government records. Whether their plight was on account of Ballal Sen's fiat, or for whatever other reason—the lives of East Bengal's suffering Namasudra folk had been witnessed first-hand by the humanist poet Rabindranath Thakur. In 1911, in his essay titled 'The Right to Religion', he had written: 'I went to the villages and saw that other castes do not work on the fields of the Namasudra folk, they do not harvest their paddy. They do not build their houses. In other words, in order to survive in the world, people expect others' assistance. Yet our society regards them as unworthy of even that. For no fault of theirs, we make their lives difficult and unbearable, and punish them every day, from the day they are born till the moment they die.'

Every morning, there was a crowd of people in front of Khagen babu's tent. They were there that day too. Garib had reached a bit later. He did not know what they were discussing. He sat down on the mat, beside Jagadish Biswas. Khagen babu was reading out from a book. Hearing him mention the name of Rabindranath Thakur suddenly, Garib's ears pricked up. Garib knew about many *thakurs*, or gods, but all those *thakurs* lived in heaven. He knew only of two *thakurs* who were men of this earth. They were Harichand Thakur and his son, Guruchand Thakur. Hearing the name of another *thakur* now, he whispered to Jagadish Biswas, 'Who's Rabin Thakur? Where's his ashram?' Jagadish Biswas gestured with his hands to Garib to keep quiet, and said, 'Just hear him now. We'll ask Khagen babu about it later. He must surely be some big sage or gosain.'

❧

The notable point here was that Rabindranath Thakur referred to the Namasudra folk as 'Namasudras', and not by any other name. Meaning that, when he wrote that essay, the Namasudra community had already gained formal recognition—as Namasudras—in government records. But it goes without saying that this did not happen so easily.

The first ever census in this country was conducted during British rule. Sex, age, caste and so on were all meticulously recorded. All the public servants upon whom the responsibility of the census devolved, were—for the usual reasons—high-caste. Disregarding the actual responses of the people of the Namasudra caste, they persisted in writing 'Chandal' instead of Namasudra in the place assigned for caste identity. They were simply adhering to the fiat prevalent from Ballal Sen's time. The Namasudra community exploded in protest.

At that time, in Orakandi, in the Faridpur district of East Bengal, Guruchand Thakur, the gifted son of Harichand Thakur, the founder of the Matua faith, had become widely recognised as the leader of the Namasudra community. Under his leadership, a strike was observed throughout East Bengal, which had a tremendous impact in Barisal, Faridpur, Khulna and Jessore districts. It was in these regions that the population of Namasudras was the highest.

A ray of light had entered the life of the Namasudra community then. With the help of the Australian missionary Meade sahib and the initiative of Guruchand Thakur, a high school was established in Orakandi. And a band of zealous youths strived and moved ahead rapidly, in their quest for social transformation. They were led by the *Louhopurush*, Guruchand Thakur. It was a time signalling a great awakening. Through the organisation of the Matua faith, the Namasudras began to express themselves in the form of a united force. Later, there was a fierce movement to change the community's name. They had thought that with the victory achieved through that movement, the indignity of bearing the yoke of the name 'Chandal' would also come to an end. Little did they know that even if the name were to be changed, there would be no change in the mentality of people from higher castes. Like a secret, subterranean stream, it would remain in the inner recesses of their minds.

Finally, as a result of the movement, the community was formally recognised under the name Namasudra in 1911. Whether out of hatred or habit, some public servants still recorded them as 'Chandal'. Which was why the colonial government declared that whoever recorded the caste identity of Namasudras as 'Chandal' or anything else—instead of Namasudra—would lose his job. The fear of losing one's job was indeed a great one, and so they did not have the courage to write anything else.

Garib Das had high hopes that his son too would read fat books like the one Khagen babu had read from. He imagined that when people saw him walking on the road, they would point towards him and say, 'That person there is Jibon babu's father ...' The school was in the camp itself. A long shed with a tin roof, open on all sides. The room had four sections, for the four classes from 1 to 4. No one had reached Class 5 yet, and so that was absent. The students spread out gunny sacks or mats on the floor and sat down in the shed. Exactly like the *tols,* or Sanskrit schools of yore. The drowsy, droopy children learnt the multiplication tables, and about Vidyasagar's childhood education. Garib Das was very keen that, come what may, he would definitely educate Jibon till Class 5. So that he could read the Ramayan, the Mahabharat and the Srimad Bhagawat with ease. If required, he would have a master teach him at home too. If Benu Haldar—who had passed Class 3 in colonial times—could read out the seventy-eight names of Krishna as well as the tale of Lakshmi, then how fat would the books that Jibon—educated till Class 5— would read be! Seeing Jibon, people would say, 'Do you know whose son he is? He's Garib Chandra Das's son ...' Thinking about his son's bright future made Garib Das almost tremble with excitement.

Finally, both husband and wife agreed that the *haate khori,* or 'chalk in hand' ceremony, for their son would take place the coming Tuesday, at the auspicious moment of sunrise. All of Monday, Garib Das was busy with the arrangements relating to Jibon's schooling. He had searched for and found a palm tree. Tucking up his dhuti like a loincloth, he had climbed up the palm tree. After all, it was from the top of the palm tree that the first lesson in formal education began. He cut and brought down a bundle of palm leaves. He then cut them into strips, dried them in the sun, and strung the strips together with a string. After that he left for the Santhal hamlet. There was a bamboo thicket there. The role of bamboo in children's education was not insignificant. He cut two thin stems from the thicket. One was about nine inches long. By sharpening one end, he would fashion a pen. The other stem was about a foot and a half long. With that, the lame master could take the skin off Jibon's back if he did not learn his lessons. Garib had observed that in the camp's school, not finding anything at hand, the master sent the child at fault, to fetch a branch from the nearby jungle. There could be snakes, scorpions and so many other things in the forest—what would happen if Jibon was bitten! Garib could not be so thoughtless! He would provide the master a stick beforehand to beat him with. He would tell the master, 'Beat him as much as you want. Just see that he doesn't die!'

While Garib Das was busy with all this, Bimala wasn't sitting idle either. First, she went to find out where she could get some goat's milk. No one in the camp had any cows or buffaloes. How could they keep a cow inside the tent! But there were goats. If Bimala tried, she might be able to get a little bit of goat's milk. She bought two-paise worth of milk from someone to make curd with. Before anyone stepped out for an auspicious task, a dot of curd had to be applied on their forehead. She would feed Jibon the rest. After all, curds kept the stomach cool. The one who had a cool stomach would also have a cool head. Only a calm and cool head could be educated. Not those who were hot-headed—they would only wield the plough, catch fish, toil on fields, beat their wives and work as toughs. Jibon's father wished for something different. And so, curd was important.

Returning to the tent with milk, Bimala had bent down at the stove. Once the previous night's cooking was over, she had sprinkled water on the stove and extinguished the fire. Now she poked inside the stove to retrieve some charcoal. She powdered that finely on the grindstone and added water. Then she sieved it through a piece of mosquito-net, and poured it into a glass bottle. That was the ink Jibon would write with. When she thought it was enough, she stopped. Of course, by then, because of the work as well as her excitement, she was drenched in perspiration.

When the little children in the vicinity saw all these preparations, they trembled in fear. Not a sound escaped their lips. To them it all looked like the sharpening of the cleaver before sacrificing the vowed goat on the night of Kali Puja. As if the cooking ingredients for that were being prepared. Most frightened of all was Tulsi's daughter, Kusum. Wondering whether Jibon would die tomorrow, or live, she was utterly perplexed.

Eventually, all the suspense came to an end. On the appointed day, at the specific hour, and without any kind of hindrance at all, the prescribed ceremony was completed. Early in the morning, Jibon was bathed and dressed in new clothes. Before that, Benu Haldar arrived. He had passed Class 3 in colonial times. It was with his help, to the accompaniment of much fanfare and the sound of conch shells and ululation, that Jibon's *haate khori* rite—symbolising the first act of writing—was performed. By dragging the bamboo-stem pen dipped in charcoal ink over palm leaf, Jibon performed the task that no one in Garib Das's family had ever achieved before. He wrote the first letter of the alphabet: ক, Kaw.

Garib Das's chest heaved as he stifled a sob, overcome by emotion. There were tears in his eyes. The entrancement of a proud father was writ large on his face. His six-year-old son had bravely and boldly made the impossible possible, which none of his forefathers had dared to do. He had written Kaw.

Benu Haldar, the Class 3 graduate of the English era, was the principal priest at the momentous event. He received a seer and a quarter of rice for that, which, strictly speaking, could not be the dole rice—because there was no merit in donating something that had been received as a donation. It had to be purchased. Before Benu left with the rice and the dakshina of five and a half annas, he said, 'Listen to me, Garib, just look at the letter Jibon wrote now. See how it shines, like a star. When women cook, they can press a single grain of rice and know whether the whole pot of rice is cooked. Just like that, by looking at that one letter, I can tell you about your son's future. I tell you, and remember my words later—when Jibon grows up, he will become a learned person. I can see it as clearly as if I'm looking into water.'

The next morning, Garib Das bathed his son, dressed him in a new shirt and shorts, combed his hair, and then, holding his hand, set off for the school. Jibon looked like a heroic warrior son, dressed for battle by his brave Ma. Bimala had tied the small bottle with charcoal ink to a length of string and slung it across his chest like a Brahmin's thread. A bundle of eight or ten palm leaves had been tied together and slung on the other shoulder. A torn gunny sack, folded four times, was given to him to hold in his hand; he would spread that out, to sit on. A wet rag was also provided, for wiping the palm leaves. And a nadu of roasted rice to eat at tiffin time.

The place where the school was situated was commonly known as the sal grove. And the part where Garib and company lived was referred to as the mango orchard. At the northern end of the mango orchard—at the farthest end of the camp—was a row of about ten tents. Garib Das lived in one of these. On the route from his tent to the school lay a large well on the right side, which was encircled by a high wall. It must have provided water for the military camp when it was here. But the water was unusable now. It was green in colour, full of moss and frogs.

Garib went past the well, past the hand-pump, and reached the broken, uneven road, which had at one time been smooth and metalled. But when he looked in the direction of the school, he was startled. The playfield in front of the school was completely desolate. There wasn't a single student there. It was well past the time school began—so why wasn't anyone there? And where was the lame master in his dhuti-panjabi? No one was tunefully reciting, 'one ones are one, two ones are two ...' No children screaming and fighting. It wasn't supposed to be like this. The school should have been teeming with students now. What happened today?

After waiting a long time, Garib found out from a passerby. No child would sing out the times tables in this school any more. They would not recite any more poems from memory. The ding-dong of the brass bell would no longer announce the school's goings-on.

The master would not come any more. He had been transferred to an Adivasi village far away.

Hearing the news, Garib Das collapsed on his haunches right there. His legs seemed unable to support him. It was as if the partition had heralded another terrible chapter in their lives. He wasn't aware how long he sat before the school, suppressing his sobs.

As he was returning, he heard a terrifying news from Subol, Gagan and Radhakanta. The refugees would no longer get any kind of assistance from the Government of India. The school had been closed down, the doctor's clinic was no longer there, and the provision of rice, dal and a few rupees—the last known as 'cash dole'—had been discontinued. All the governmental offices had been closed down. Since morning, the government employees had been loading their belongings on trucks and departing to the head office in Bishnupur. They were no longer responsible for the well-being of the refugees.

Garib Das—and everyone else—felt like trees struck by lightning. Or as if the earth beneath their feet had given way in a massive earthquake. They could only fall on their faces in helplessness. A mute cry rose in everyone's throats: 'Oh, what a calamity!'

After a long time, someone said, 'Let's all go and meet Khagen babu.'

9

Permanent Banishment

No one could fault the Honourable Government of India. The refugees could not complain that their abandonment had been sudden, or that it came about without giving anyone any option. It was merely the final outcome of a well-planned programme that had been executed in stages. The rationale of the political leaders, bureaucrats, advisers and government authorities was extremely clear, simple and unambiguous. It was meaningless, as well as impossible, to feed so many hundreds of thousands of people for so long. It may be kind, but it was impractical. Because this policy would only make people—who were at one time hard-working folk—lazy, unwilling to work and fond of being idle. Which was not in the best interests of the country and society, or the people themselves.

The government was extremely worried about the huge numbers of uprooted, lowly, illiterate, low-caste and low-class people, who had arrived after being displaced from the other Bengal, as a result of the partition of the country. If they had simply borne the oppressions, and somehow remained in East Pakistan, it wouldn't have come to this. But they were all piling into West Bengal. Why were they coming? By what right?

All these people belonged to the community that did not participate in the freedom movement. While the masses went to jail, suffered torture and went to the gallows—they were only concerned with their own bellies. All their lives, they thought only about what to eat. Those who only thought about themselves, who didn't bother about the country or the rest of the world—how would the common people of the country benefit from such selfish folk? Who would feed fodder to a cow that did not yield milk or a bullock that did not plough?

Once a representative of the Congress leader Suren Banerjee met Guruchand Thakur, the leader of the Namasudra community. The Swadeshi movement to boycott British cloth had begun with much gusto all over the country then. He said to Guruchand Thakur, 'You command the obedience of hundreds of thousands of people. Our movement would be strengthened if you joined the boycott.' Guruchand Thakur replied to him with a smile: 'What you say sounds nice and would also be good to do. But you know, only those people who have something can boycott. Let alone British goods, our people don't have the means even to buy local cloth! Go to people's houses and you'll see that men have only a coarse dhuti and women a single sari, and nothing else. They can't even take it off and wash it when it's dirty. What have these people got to do with the boycotting of British cloth? It's not for us; it's your movement.'

Guruchand Thakur's reply wasn't couched in diplomatic refinement. The Congress leader felt very offended. And after returning, he reported to the big leader that the Namasudras would not participate in the movement.

It is said that later, at the time of the Quit India movement, apparently some people had asked Guruchand Thakur to join it. He had supposedly responded by saying: 'The British have been in this country for about two hundred years. But what about the fact that from long before that, we have been enslaved by the folks with the threads-and-tonsures? Let them liberate us from that slavery first.

The British can be driven out after that. At least there's rule of law in the country now. The one who is at fault is judged. When the British go away, who will save the low-caste folk from the lot with threads-and-tonsures? It's because the British came to this country, that our sons and daughters were able to reach the school gates. They are learning to read and write. They get at least that bit of benefit. If your people are better than the British, let them prove it with actions.'

All this was true. And because it was true, it was unpalatable. And so, for the high-caste leaders presently in government, the Namasudras were unacceptable. They were creatures who deserved to be completely excluded. This wasn't Germany, or else, in the same way as the Nazis rounded up Jews and sent them to gas chambers as if burning waste materials, this refugee question too could have been solved. There was only one problem in doing that here—one had to stand for elections. If that had not been the case …

So when it wasn't possible to kill and bury them like it was done with the Jews, it was necessary to devise a means whereby they could remain on earth and yet be killed. The question was, what was the place, the soil, where they could be sent, so that the United Nations as well as all the other human rights organisations could be told: Look, we have rehabilitated them … Actually that would be permanent banishment! A programme that was guided not by empathy but only by official duty, expediency and hatred could never be wholesome, humane or praiseworthy. But that didn't happen either. The two regions of India which were severed to form the state of Pakistan were Bengal and Punjab. People were displaced from both the regions and became refugees. But compared to the refugees from Punjab, not an iota of governmental compassion came the way of the refugees in Bengal. The reason can easily be guessed.

Bengal's soil was very well-watered and fertile; it was valuable. Thousands and thousands of acres of this land were held formally or informally by the lords of the land. That land could not be acquired by the government to resettle the refugees in Bengal. Because each one of those very lords of the land was a pillar of politics. They had deep ties with the party in government now, the Congress. So if rehabilitation could not be provided in Bengal, where else could it be provided? After much thought, a suitable place was found. That was an appropriate place for the kind of people the refugees were.

Orissa and Madhya Pradesh were two of the most backward states in India. Within these states, the regions which were the most underdeveloped, lacking in communication, forested and hilly, where the land was rocky, stony and devoid of water, a drought-prone region, where the light of civilisation had not yet reached—Malkangiri, Koraput, Umarkot, and Paralkot—were the most appropriate places for the rehabilitation of refugees from East Pakistan. The primitive tribes there—Gond, Damdami, Halba, Muriya, Bonda and Koya—dwelt all naked or half-naked. In the eyes of civilised, cultured people, their religious practices were just as terrible as their language was incomprehensible. In the name of culture, unmarried youths there, both male and female, spent the night together in the same room. These were called *ghotul*.

This vast region was very sparsely inhabited. Because of attacks by wild animals and frequent deaths on account of malaria, gastroenteritis and other diseases, the growth of population was relatively low. But people were badly needed here. There were countless trees of precious sal and teak in all the forests, which were used for laying rail tracks as well as for making household furniture. There were mahua trees, whose flowers yielded liquor and fruits yielded oil. There were amla, haritaki and baheda trees, whose fruits were used for medicines. There were thickets of bamboo, from which paper was made. There were kendu trees, whose leaves were used to make beedis. Underneath the soil was dolomite, bauxite, iron ore, copper and so much else. In order to mine all this, hard-working folk were required, who could be paid a nominal wage and made to toil. There was a great paucity of such healthy, strong people here. If the refugees could be sent there, two birds would be killed with the same stone. That was why the Dandakaranya project was constituted, comprising all those areas in Orissa and Madhya Pradesh. Let the refugees be taken and left there, irrespective of the consequences. If they survived, well and good; if they perished, even better. One day, everybody was informed by the government office: 'Get ready. Now you will be provided rehabilitation. Everyone has to go to Dandakaranya.' The word 'rehabilitation' was the most joyful one. Rehabilitation meant house and hearth, ploughs, bullocks and arable land. But the very name 'Dandakaranya' was enough to make the heart tremble. Dandakaranya was the forest where Ramchandra had gone into exile. Who didn't know the perils that befell him when he went there! The seeds of doubt began to take root in the minds of only a couple of the camp's officers: 'Perhaps they won't agree to go there.' Another group was explaining to them: 'If they don't go, there's nothing more we can do. This burden cannot be borne permanently. We'll then have to put an end to all assistance and close down the refugee rehabilitation department. The country has just become independent, it's now time for us to stretch our arms and legs, and put up our feet and rest and relax. At this time, it's imperative that all such hassles be done away with in whichever way possible.'

According to the instructions from the higher authorities—no longer oral—a notice was put up on the board on a wall in the office of the Shiromanipur camp:

> *Through this notice, all the refugees in Shiromanipur camp are informed that by the kindness of the Government of India, a project has been initiated for your proper resettlement. All those who wish to be rehabilitated under the aforementioned project, named Dandakaranya, should register their names.*

Some people were sick and tired of life in the camp. They were distraught for land, a plough, bullocks, seeds and paddy. The terrifying name of Dandakaranya could not deter them. Trusting their destiny, they put down their names to go to 'DAK'. And the first group set off for that unknown destination. But the rest of the people rushed to Khagen Mandal—'What do you say?'

Khagen Mandal was an educated man. He kept himself informed about political and policy matters. Newspapers from Bishnupur reached him every day. He read the news reports out to everyone. He explained what different words meant. He drew out all that was unstated or hidden within whatever was stated. So now, many anxious people stood at the entrance of his tent. Everyone wanted to know his opinion.

He said, '*Eida kono punorbashoni na. Aida punnoh nirbashon.* This is no rehabilitation at all. This is simply permanent banishment. After crossing the border and coming to this country, they brought us to this sal forest in Bankura district. Now they'll take us from here and throw us among the demons in the forests of Dandakaranya. By sending Ram to that forest, the lame Manthara and Kaikeyi had rendered Ayodhya free of impediment and made Bharat the king. By sending us now to that forest, the lame Mantharas of today want to make India trouble-free. Those who want to go, should go. I won't stop anyone. But I'm not going. If I have to die, I'll die here. We didn't divide the country! The people who committed the sins for which the country had to be partitioned shall remain in Bengal, while we, who are not to blame in any way, are the ones who have to leave it! I'll never go. We shall fight and get rehabilitation in West Bengal itself.'

The people said, 'Then none of us will go to Dandakaranya either.' In the first call about five hundred families had left. The second time, about a hundred went. When the trucks came for the third batch, they returned empty. Some twenty families, who had registered their names at the last moment, changed their minds. 'We won't go.'

After this, another notice was posted on the notice board in the office. A time period was specified. The refugees were informed that once the specified timeline for the transference was over, the government would no longer bear any responsibility in regard to the families who were unwilling to go to DAK. Therefore, in their own best interest, the refugees should register their names in the office. They should not fall into the trap of any kind of instigation. But no one heeded the government's inducement. The time period for registering names was extended time and again. A documentary film made by a director with government funds, putting out the government's views, was brought from the town. With a screen put up in the field, the gushing waters of the Narmada river were shown with the exhortation—See the big river in Dandakaranya. Who said there's a water problem? They are lying. See how many fish there are in the water! Just cast the net and you'll catch large rui and katla! Images of the golden paddy fields of Chhattisgarh, famously referred to as a paddy bowl, were shown with the commentary saying these lands were in Malkangiri. Such fertile land there! Cows from Haryana were shown with the commentary—these are the cows in Paralkot, yielding twenty seers of milk twice a day. (Of course, that very year the seer measure was discontinued all over the country, with kilograms and decimal measures coming into effect.)

Despite all the allurement, no one was willing to go to that verdant, well-watered, fertile, golden land. Rather, three or four of the five hundred families from the first batch returned from DAK to the camp. The account they gave of that land terrified everyone. 'There's nothing but forests there, dada. What forests they are! As dark as night even during the day. Tigers, bears, snakes and scorpions—what isn't there in those forests! And what terrible snakes they are, they can swallow a whole live calf. There's all that, and besides there are the forest-dwellers. Oh dear, what they wear—it's like not wearing clothes at all. Whether it's men or women, they're all naked. Black-skinned. Just to see them makes you scared to death. Always going around with bows and arrows on their shoulders, or else small axes or some weapon or the other. And their language. Can't understand a thing of what they mumble.'

From them it was learnt that what was given to them as land was not land at all but rocky terrain. The earth there could not be dug with a spade. The land was so sloping that no water accumulated there. Besides rain, there was no other arrangement for water during the planting season. If the rain wasn't adequate, all the hard work was futile. 'There's nothing but death there for people like us. Even if you want to escape from there, you can't. How will you go, when there are no vehicles or carriages? All that is twenty-five or thirty miles away. How can you go so far carrying your belongings! You can only walk if you throw everything away. But that won't be so easy either. There are guards along the way. If they catch you, they'll thrash you and send you back to the same place. If you go through the forest, once you lose your way, you'll spend the rest of your life going round and round in the forest and die. And if you come in the way of a tiger or bear, you'll finally be free very quickly, with just a little bit of pain. If you fall into the clutches of any Adivasi during the planting season, they'll sacrifice you to their god, Angadev, to be granted a good harvest. Angadev is very fond of human blood.'

Fifty families had fled together, and eventually just three or four of them had managed to return somehow, after overcoming many hurdles and dangers. Who knew where the rest of them ended up. After hearing all that, who would want to go to Dandakaranya. And so, as a result—the school was closed. The office was closed. The officers and band of employees had disappeared. There was no more work for them at the Shiromanipur camp.

'What shall we do now?' Gagan asked Garib Das.

'Come, let's all go to Khagen babu. Everyone's gone there, it's been a long while since then.'

They arrived at Khagen Mandal's tent, Garib Das in front, and behind him Subol, Radhakanta, Gagan and several others. Khagen Mandal was probably fifty or fifty-five years old, but he looked much younger. He spoke slowly, but there was a conviction in his words that was capable of influencing people. The disastrous news was not unknown to him. But he did not want to spread the news and terrify the people. He also nursed a feeble hope that it was only a rumour. No one would do something so inhumane.

He said, 'This country became independent but we became subservient. Like convicts in prison. We have to eat what they pitifully give us and go wherever they take us. If you disagree, they get angry. We lost our homes to freedom's womb. There's a saying that the river destroys one bank and creates a new one. But both our banks have been washed away. The leaders of East Pakistan say, you aren't one of us; the leaders here convey to us through their actions that we aren't one of them. So what's the option now? If someone's going to tie your hands and legs and throw you in the river, will you keep quiet and accept that? Since we all have to die one day, come, let us all unite and try to do something.'

Someone asked, 'What shall we do?'

'Protest!' Khagen Mandal retorted. 'We have to agitate and put pressure on the state government. We have to assert that we are Bengali, we belong to the soil and water of Bengal. We won't accept being sent outside Bengal. We must be rehabilitated in Bengal itself.'

'Will they heed what we say?'

'I don't believe that all the people, all over this country, feel the same way about us. The heart of someone or the other surely beats for us with compassion. I'll go to Calcutta tomorrow itself. The senior leaders of the Communist Party, Jana Sangh and Hindu Mahasabha live there. I'll go and tell them our tale of woe. Won't anyone stand beside us? Won't anyone say that injustice is being done to us? If they put pressure on the government, then it can't go ahead with its plans. Let me go and give it a try.'

A man took out eight annas from the folds of his dhuti, and putting it down in front of Khagen Mandal, said, 'This work is not for you alone. It's for the good of all of us. Everyone ought to give whatever they can and provide for your expenses for going to Calcutta. I give eight annas.' Following his example, each person put eight annas in front of Khagen Mandal. The contributions came to twenty-two and a half rupees.

Khagen Mandal shouted out in jubilation, 'Victory to Baba Harichand Guruchand! May you be victorious!'

⚬⚬

It had been two months since the refugees' dole had been discontinued as punishment for refusing to go to Dandakaranya. The condition of the people at this time was very alarming. Once the final dole had run out, they had been surviving on boiled tubers, wild fruits and roots. Figs and fruits had become hard to come by in the forest nearby; mahua fruits too appeared to be scarce. What would people eat now? Hunger was an incurable disease, for which there was no medicine. Driven by hunger, people were insanely running around here and there, in search of any kind of food, and getting lost. But in such a desolate zone surrounded by forests, where would they get enough food to fill the bellies of thousands of people? The tender leaves of palm trees were finished, the water-lilies in the pond were finished; even the wild yam which made the insides of one's throat itch had all been eaten by the hungry folk. And so now, in every household, there was wailing and crying, no cooking, only fasting. Up in the sky, carnivorous vultures circled the camp. They smelt death. Their experienced eyes had seen the inevitable outcome advancing rapidly towards the band of starving, helpless folk in the camp. Driven insane by hunger, Sukharanjan Biswas, a young man of twenty-two, had hanged himself on a tree branch with a gamchha a few days ago. No, he didn't die of starvation. Death by starvation is, of course, a very controversial subject. There were two points of view among the specialists in starvation regarding the question of whether at all anyone, anywhere, could die of starvation in free India. Sukharanjan died because he couldn't bear the suffering of his wife and son. Some people would die here, but perhaps that would not be purely because of starvation. They would die because they ate inedible or poisonous wild fruits and roots. For instance, there was a yam called kharkol. Gagan's Ma cooked it and her throat became inflamed. For seven or eight days, no sound or word came out from the throat of someone whose voice was like the sound of a thunderclap; she couldn't even swallow water.

Until very recently, the camp had hummed with life. From every household one heard bhajans, kirtans and songs of recitation of the name Hari. Now all was quiet. Everyone was choked by unbearable hunger. Now, when a person came face-to-face with another, they stared at each other in distress. These perpetually suffering people had been deprived and starved in East Bengal too. But there was at least some hope there, that if not today, if not tomorrow, then at least the day after tomorrow, somewhere or the other, someone or the other would call them for work. Some wage would be obtained, with which rice and dal could be purchased. There was hope that a handful of rice could be borrowed from some neighbour or relative. Who would lend anything here? Who would give anyone work here? Everyone was in the same plight. There was, of course, a Santhal village, some three of four miles north, but the people there were even more destitute than the refugees. They themselves had been bonded to work and had gone off to various places. There was a Muslim village, five or six miles away on the eastern side of the camp; their condition too was not so good.

When Garib Das's dole hadn't yet been stopped, every fortnight, the quota for adults, of five seers of rice and atta per head, was available from the government warehouse. Although it had first made him sick, soon he had become used to digesting that rice. At that time, there was a man in the nearby Muslim hamlet, who knew refugees from East Pakistan had been driven out to West Bengal by some Muslims there. He knew that these refugees would have no love lost for Muslims and would nurse a terrible grudge. Yet the Muslim man walked all the way to the camp, with an empty bag in his hand. He too had an unbearable hunger in his belly. Who knows how many days it had been since he'd eaten. He crossed the field and entered the camp, and stood in front of the first tent he came upon. That was Garib Das's tent. Seeing an unknown, thin and dark-skinned, lungi-clad man, with a beard, Garib Das looked at him with some astonishment. With tearful eyes, the man had pointed and said, 'I live in that village. My name is Mamud. You can ask about me in the village. My children are starving, bhai. If you can give me a seer or two of wheat-flour ... You don't have to give it for free. Come the month of Ashadh, I'll return four seers in place of two.'

The direction Mamud had pointed to, saying 'that village', was too far away to be visible. By mentioning his name and address, he wanted to convince Garib Das that he really lived there. And he had offered to return double because whoever lends something does so out of the desire to gain.

Seeing the man and hearing what he said, Garib Das surmised that in the village he lived in, either there was no one who had the means to lend him anything, or that he had already borrowed so much from them that he couldn't go to ask for more. But it was true, and it was a harsh truth, that his children were without food. Or else he wouldn't have come running like that, to people he did not know, to people who followed a different faith.

Ashadh was three months away. There was no certainty whether the camp itself would remain three months hence. And what was the guarantee that Mamud would come to repay the debt three months later? Were there such honest folk to be found any more? Just as it was natural for such thoughts to enter the minds of the refugees, it should also have entered the mind of the man named Mamud. But evidently it hadn't. Since his children were starving, he did not have the sense of a normal, healthy person. He had set out with a bag in his hands, trusting in Allah. Allah was compassionate; he would surely intervene. It was trusting in Allah that he had entered the camp. Encountering Garib Das, without thinking about anything else, he had narrated his tale of woe.

But observing his emaciated body and pleading, Garib Das had seen him not as just another person but his own mirror image. This man called Mamud, which was his outcast cousin's name, was in dire need. That a man could request, claim or demand something from another man, regardless of caste, or country or language—he was merely doing that. He wanted to live. Like a burning man would raise his hands and plead to relatives as well as strangers: 'Help me!'

He asked the man with the same name as his cousin to sit down. He gave him water to drink, as well as some jaggery syrup. And before he left, knowing he would have to tighten his own belt, he gave him two seers of wheat-flour. Mamud left with the flour, and Garib Das soon forgot all about it.

Garib Das had forgotten, but not Gagan. He had witnessed the whole affair. When the month of Ashadh was over and it was midway through Shrabon and yet Mamud had not returned to repay the debt, he said, 'Garib-da, I have never seen a man as stupid as you. Someone whom you don't know, or know anything about, just came and asked, and you gave him a loan! You've lost all that flour, and you're in need yourself. If he meant to come, he would have come a long time ago. Just see, he's not going to come!'

'Let him not come,' Garib Das had replied. 'After all he didn't take my destiny, he just took a couple of seers of flour. Do you think he can ever forget about the loan I gave him when he was in distress? For two seers of flour, someone will remember me for the rest of his life. What could be greater than that!'

But proving Gagan's suspicions to be unfounded, one day in Shrabon, when it was raining heavily, the man named Mamud returned, wading through knee-deep water. In keeping with his promise, he had brought with him double the flour he had borrowed, as well as a bag with some vegetables from his own garden. Garib Das had taken back only the amount of flour he had lent, and no more. But he kept the vegetables.

When the people of Shiromanipur and the inhabitants of the Advasi village themselves were starving, how could beggars from outside find any food there? But to Garib Das, Mamud had felt like a friend, kin, family. India was a vast country, with hundreds of millions of people. From among them, Garib Das had found one, only one man, who belonged to his own community, to his own clan, one who was truly his own. Who, despite being a free citizen of a free country, was deprived of everything but the freedom to go hungry.

⁂

There had been no cooking in Garib Das's tent tonight. His son Jibon had cried himself to sleep. Bimala sat at the entrance of the tent, gazing blankly at the horizon. Her father had died when she was very small. He had gone to catch fish in the vast river, and his boat had sunk in a storm. Bimala's Ma had kept her alive somehow, by stitching people's torn kanthas, threshing their paddy, washing their clothes, cooking at ceremonies, and by feeding her merely rice foam at times. It was a life bereft of any joy or contentment. Never had Bimala ever laughed to her heart's content. Having never laughed, Bimala had forgotten about laughter. In a life where there was no laughter, there were only tears. Having swum in tears all her life, it seemed even her tears had run dry. Tears didn't flow any more. Now she only gazed around mutely. No rainbows appeared in her sight. There was only the grinding, headless, black monster of night. Endless night, without light, within which death's sharp fangs and claws lay in wait. The way out of which was unknown.

10

Inquilab Zindabad!

One day, Subol came running to give Garib Das the news: 'We'll be rehabilitated in West Bengal itself. A leader from Calcutta has come, wearing a sparkling dhuti, white as milk. Spectacles on his eyes. Just like a prince in appearance. He looks so wonderful! When he speaks, it sounds like the voice of God from the heavens!'

'Where's he? Hey Subol, where's our leader?'

Garib Das's starving body trembled in excitement. Not a political leader, but seemingly Lord Narayan incarnate, who, donning a new form, had descended on earth, to wipe away the tears of grief of these perpetually suffering folk. Now the accursed refugees would have homes, hearths and courtyards. They would get a little bit of cultivable land. Land that would yield harvest. People would eat to their fill and live. The great men who were called leaders had an amazing magic wand. Once they waved the wand, people's lives brimmed over with fulfillment. However, he had only one condition: whatever he said, and however he said it, had to be followed gratefully, without question. One could not have any doubts or misgivings in mind. It wouldn't do to be afraid and turn back. One had to be prepared to lay down one's life, if necessary.

Garib Das couldn't sit still until he saw from near and to his heart's content the incarnation, who had the power to make the impossible possible. He asked again and again, 'Where's he? Hey Subol, where's our leader?'

'He's sitting under the mango tree in front of Khagen Mandal's tent.'

Garib Das rushed towards the mango tree. Oh, this wasn't a mere mango tree; it seemed to be the famed Bodhi tree itself, under which had gathered a veritable dharma assembly, which the leader had illuminated with his presence. Having forsaken all comforts, his only objective was to bring happiness to the people in distress and take them on the path to liberation. For this, the very first task that the people had to do was to take refuge in the Buddha, and move ahead, obeying instructions.

Of course, just as there was opposition even to the Buddha, so did the leader too have detractors. They were not pleased with his role. They only abused and denigrated him. 'As if the *banchod* is a Prahlad from the clan of demons! Being an educated scion of a *bhadralok* family, why is he dancing around with coolies and labourers and destroying his own future? If you have such a penchant for politics, you could have got into any other political party—but why the Communists? Will that party ever be able to come to power?'

Prahlad Chakraborty was sitting, not on a chair but on a torn mat spread out on the ground. His white dhuti was getting muddy, but he seemed to be oblivious of that. He was also oblivious of the caste identity of those who touched him. When he was setting out from home, his old Ma—in whose veins the blood of the Choudhury family of Jessore district flowed—had spelt out to him in detail: 'Don't eat food from the hands of strangers; don't touch casteless and low-caste folk; always observe the religious injunctions on caste in everything you do.' If he observed all that, then he could not be in politics. Especially Communist politics. Let all those rules and customs be confined to home. Here he had to conduct himself according to the situation at hand. No one should think, even for a moment, that he was afflicted by caste pride. What was there in the past was still in existence today, and would continue in the future. With the passing of time, its form and colour had to be altered. The one who could do that would be successful.

Prahlad babu had come from Calcutta with an entire team. He found some accompanists from Bishnupur too. Everyone knew they were supposed to come today, but they did not believe it. Then someone arrived on a cycle with the news that they had got off the train and would arrive in the camp shortly. At once there was a great buzz in the camp. After that, the people counted the minutes and gazed eagerly in the direction of the road. Finally, the wait was over. He arrived.

Just behind where the office, godown and doctor's clinic used to be, was a large playground. When the office was in existence and the office babus were around, they used to play football in the playground. A kind of dais was erected on one side of the field, with wood cut hurriedly from the forest. Two or three persons who had come from Bishnupur, who addressed one another as 'comrade', tied a loudspeaker to one of the posts of the dais. After that they tested their voice: 'Hello, mic testing, one, two, three, four ...' Garib Das and those like him did not know what a mic was. In the public meetings and processions that they had seen earlier, the speakers spoke through a tin megaphone. Now, hearing the loud sound emanating from the mic, they were astonished. They thought that perhaps with that sound, the very throne of Indra, the king of gods, would be rocked.

Prahlad babu was tired from the journey. He was resting a bit now. Once the mic was in place and ready, he would start speaking. By now he had gained fame as an orator. A dramatic beginning, voice modulation, choice of words, use of analogies and examples, ornamental use of emotion—all the aspects of the art of speaking were at his command. In Indian classical music, there were six premier ragas, of which it was customary to sing one in the morning, one at forenoon, one in the afternoon, one in the evening and one late at night. The morning raga could only be sung in the morning; if it was sung in the afternoon or at night, it would not be pleasing to people's ears. Prahlad babu knew that. And because he knew that, he could win over people's minds.

Which song were all these uprooted people keen to hear; which stream of melody they could be immersed in—he could fathom that at once. He would sing that very song. It wasn't an important issue now whether or not, after a few years, he would sing another song altogether. The great poet Kazi Nazrul Islam, who had once declared, 'I am Bhrigu the rebel, and I stamp my footprint on the bosom of God!' had in later years sung, 'I shall lie at Ma's feet like a hibiscus', and surrendered himself. That was the gift of time. Men could not be blamed for changing. And especially not political entrepreneurs.

Khagen babu's young daughter, Lalita, brought some warm water in a bowl and placed it in front of Prahlad babu. He rummaged inside his bag, took out a small container and put something from that into the hot water. The water turned dark. After some time, he poured the water into a glass and took small sips. This thing was called tea. It was by drinking this that the British had conquered the world. Of course, Prahlad babu did not believe in theoretical analyses of world conquest. A country that did that was imperialist. Imperialism and communism were sworn enemies of one another.

However, he believed that his throat really opened up with the hot tea. Nor was he unaware that having too many cold things wasn't good for the throat. Because of that he had given up having curd with his meal. Especially cold curd.

After he finished his tea and the mic turned silent, he went up to the dais in regal style and, with full-throated and practiced ease, brought to bloom verses of poetry. In the manner of a valorous general on the battlefield, he expressed his great desire to become a martyr for the country and the well-being of people. In the course of all this, his milk-white panjabi got drenched in sweat.

'Bondhugon, do any of you know why I have come running from faraway Calcutta to be among you all today, after a long journey, overcoming many hurdles and obstacles, braving much hardship, and averting so many risks?

'I've come because I could not stay away. It's said that if one truly calls from the core of one's heart, then even God descends to this earth's dust, forsaking all the comforts and pleasures of heaven. I said, and I hope you could understand—if one truly calls, even God's seat is rocked. And he appears before the devotee and says, "Tell me what you want!"

'But I am merely a man. You people called me in your anguish, and so I could not stay away. You are in distress, you are helpless-deprived-exploited-persecuted-neglected-humiliated-insulted-raped-oppressed-famished humanity. My heart wept. You cried out and called me. You say, save us. You say, protect us. You ask for the restoration of human dignity in human society. Shall I disregard this cry of distress and remain content in a corner of my peaceful-beautiful-comfortable home!'

After reaching this point, Prahlad babu had to pause a bit. But that did not affect his speech at all. He wiped the sweat off his face and neck with a handkerchief. In that time, he thought about which word would be most appropriate now, whether it should be 'contemplate' or 'immersed', 'overwhelmed' or 'content'. And then he decided to say it in this way: 'Can I be entirely immersed and content in my own comforts?'

The sun had set by now. The rays of sunlight peeping in through the leaves of the sal grove on the western side of the ground vanished, and darkness began to descend. Someone lit a petromax lamp and hung it on a post of the dais.

Beside Garib Das sat Madhab Bala from Khulna. He whispered into the ear of Jagadish Biswas, who was seated next to him, 'He's only talking about himself ... when will he start talking about us?'

'He will,' said Jagadish. 'As soon as he's finished talking about himself, he'll come to that.'

'Can't bear the mosquito bites!'

'As if you have a mosquito net at home! Sit quietly!'

The leader, Prahlad Chakraborty, had asked a question. He knew he himself would have to provide the answer. The question was: 'Can I?' And his answer, 'I cannot.' He explained, with infinite patience and in the most beautiful words, why he could not disregard the call of oppressed folk and carry on living an undisturbed life in his beautiful mansion in south Calcutta. In his speech, that became longer and longer, there was poetry as well as philosophy and history. And then came the final and most forceful point. Which was added to the speech in the form of one of the nine *rasas*, the *raudra rasa*, that is, anger.

'You must not go! None of you should go to the terrifying forests of Dandakaranya! Whatever be the deprivation, sickness and starvation, whatever be the oppression—you must not give in to the injustice and the inhuman policy of the cruel exploiter class! Don't accept defeat, don't be despondent. You must not break down in fear. Know that eventually victory shall be yours! Stand up bravely, rise up! Build the inevitable people's movement! Make the hearts of those who sit on the throne in Delhi tremble! Force the Congress government to rehabilitate the refugee folk in West Bengal itself! Join your voices together and roar out, "We'll face sticks, bullets and tear gas, but we will not leave Bengal!"' And he concluded his speech with the slogan—*Inquilab Zindabad!*

Garib Das had learnt quite a few new words since coming to this country. Camp, cash dole, refugee, without, strike, procession, slogan, and now to his lexicon was added—*inquilab*. But what was the meaning of the word? After a while, when he got a chance, he asked Khagen Mandal, 'What's the meaning of that word he used?'

Khagen Mandal had gone to Calcutta and heard what the comrades said. He knew the meaning. 'The meaning of *inquilab zindabad* is revolution.'

'What's that? What does it mean?'

Khagen Mandal now thought about how he could explain in his own rustic way to dull-headed folk like Garib Das the meaning of words unknown to them, and said, *'Bujhla Garib, shob kothar maane hoy na. Maane hoyle taar gun thake na. Jemon dhoro Om, Heem, Kreem. Ache iyar kono maane? Jaar maane nai taite thake shokti. Shei rokom inquilab hoilo ekta beej montor. Baar baar jop korba dekhba mone darun jor paba. Ami Koilkata giya shuina aichhi ei montor koiya buke guli khaileo naki byatha lage na. Hari naamer moto mone mone jopba dekhba aar khida lagbo na.*

You see, Garib, not all words have a meaning. If they're given a meaning, they lose their value. For instance, *om, hrim, khrim,* do they have any meaning? They don't. That which does not have meaning has power. In the same way, *inquilab* is a seed mantra. Keep reciting it and you'll see you get tremendous inner strength. I went to Calcutta and heard that by uttering this mantra apparently you don't feel any pain even when you are struck by a bullet. Keep repeating it in your mind, like reciting the name Hari, and you'll see you won't feel hungry any more.'

After the meeting was over, Garib Das returned to his tent reciting the seed mantra. Seeing him, Bimala, who was sitting at the entrance of the tent holding her son close to her bosom, asked anxiously, 'Did you get anything?'

'What would I get?'

'Rice, dal.'

'Where will I get that?'

'You went, didn't you? Some people apparently came from Calcutta. Didn't they give anything?'

'They gave the seed mantra.'

'What happens with that?'

'How can I tell you what happens?' Garib paused for a while and then continued spiritedly, 'All my life I've recited the name of Hari. If one utters the name of Hari, apparently all the agonies of the world go away. But have they really gone away? Our agonies have only gone on increasing. Now I've heard something new, that apparently if you recite *inquilab*, the pangs of hunger go away. People think I'm a bullock, and tell me whatever they like. They think I can't tell this from that. Even though we have eyes, we are blind. We don't know how to read and write. Nor do we associate with clever folk. We are like bullocks.'

'So what will we do now?'

'There's nothing more to be done. As long as one's alive, just trust in destiny and wait.'

'I don't know how long we can survive like this.'

Even though Garib Das may not have known or understood anything, all the people in the camp had realised that by the power of that name, some sound arrangement would definitely be arrived at. Hari himself had declared: My name is greater than me. The one who recites my name is even greater. The shastras had said that even God was subject to mantra. And the mantra was the business of the Brahmin. The Brahmin, Prahlad Chakraborty, had declared that reciting *inquilab* was the solution to every problem, just carry on reciting it devoutly. Hence from the mouths of young and old, children and adolescents, one constantly heard the grotesque battle-cry—*inquilab zindabad!* Long live revolution! Everyone was reciting the seed mantra in full earnest. In the hearts of the half-dead folk, a new hope was kindled: We are going to live!

After a few days came Prahlad babu's instructions from Calcutta. 'It's time now, there can be no more delay, throw yourselves into the movement now!' The movement began. The camp came alive with meetings, processions and slogans. Some people sat on fast-unto-death in the room where the office had been. But word of that could not make its way even across the sal forest and reach the ears of government bureaucrats and the concerned individuals; or who knows whether they heard everything and remained deaf and mute. Day after day passed; soon it was the twenty-second day of the fast.

Actually if one thought about it, such a large number of refugees could be brought within the fold of the hunger strike at the time only because no one had anything to eat. Within their own tents too, they just sat without food. Although the fasting dais was a much better place than that. But this strike by a few thousand people did not have an impact on anybody. To them, the refugees' fast-unto-death was like eunuchs professing celibacy.

It was then agreed upon—when the government cannot hear our cry from so far away, we have to go to their door. *Kothay thaake shorkar moshay?* Where does Mister Government live? He lives in the tall and beautiful buildings in the city. The government folk shine in their well-fed and well-groomed splendour. They nap in the afternoon. Their sleeping conscience needs to be awakened. For that, everyone must go to Bishnupur, to Shorkar moshay, Mister Government.

There were three more camps a few miles away from Shiromanipur. They were called Basudebpur camps No. 1, No. 2 and No. 3. In those camps, too, were thousands of refugees whose dole had been stopped as punishment for being unwilling to go to Dandakaranya. After meetings and discussions, several thousand people from the four camps set off in procession towards Bishnupur, chanting slogans and with placards in their hands. All the government offices would be blockaded.

Blockade! Khagen Mandal said, 'Prahlad babu says, as long as the government does not agree to rehabilitate us in Bengal, we shall blockade all the government offices, police stations and courts. Come day or night, weeks or months, no one will move from there. We are dying, anyway. If required, we shall lie dead in front of everyone's eyes. But Prahlad babu says it won't come to that. After being confined behind closed doors at home and offices for three days, the officers will relent.'

Someone asked, 'What if the police arrive and take us away?'

Khagen babu replied, 'If they arrest us, then it'll be great fun. I've heard that people are fed twice a day in jail. So many of us haven't even laid eyes on rice for so many days. For as long as they keep us locked up, we'll at least get two meals to eat. And, they can't keep us there forever. If they had to put us in jail and feed us, why did they stop the dole? The day they release us, we'll resume our protest.'

Hearing mention of police and jail, Garib Das became worried. From his childhood, he was very scared of those words. All the people in the Namasudra hamlet were well aware of what the police were like. If a tiger attacked it left eighteen wounds, but if the police attacked there were thirty-six! That's why, as soon as they spotted the daroga's boat on the river, people ran away in whichever direction they could. Court, litigation and so on were the devil's own weapons, with which high-caste folk had ruined the lives of low-caste people. The police were the controllers of those weapons.

When, after hearing Khagen babu's call to protest, Garib Das had returned to his tent looking frightened, seeing his crest-fallen appearance, Bimala had asked him, 'What's happened? Why are you trembling?'

'Khagen babu said we have to go to Bishnupur to picket. Who knows what trouble we are going to get into, and whether we'll die or live …'

'You haven't eaten in so many days. How will you go? I tell you, you shouldn't go when you are so famished.'

'All the people from the four camps are going. Khagen babu has said that those who don't go to Bishnupur will be socially boycotted. No one will speak to them, or mingle with them. What will we do then?'

'What do Subol and Radhakanta say? Are they going?'

'Radhakanta has been exempted; he has a fever. Subol said he will go. Gagan is going too.'

'Then stay close to them, and be careful. You are very weak.'

11

How Will We Survive?

Bimala had accomplished a major task today. Accompanied by Subol Sutar's wife, Tulsi, she had walked all the way to the Santhal hamlet. They had come upon it by chance, while walking along the path that went past the woods; she had no idea a hamlet lay on the other side. Although the Santhals usually went around with bows and arrows on their shoulders, unlike the Naga, Kuki, Jarawa and Muriya tribes, they were not averse to or intolerant towards civilised folk. But who knows why Bimala feared them. A boy of about ten from the Santhal hamlet used to come to the refugee camp. He went around performing stunts and asked for rice or money. Using a bamboo stick that was four-fingers wide and two-and-a-half arm-lengths long, and emitting a weird sound, he used to beat himself hard. There were black welts all over his body, from all the beating. There was a class of people in society who enjoyed seeing others in pain. And there was a class who could not bear to see others in pain. The boy liked both kinds of people: those who made him stand in the sun and said—'I'll be counting, I'll give you a paisa every time you hit yourself!'; and those who trembled in fear and cried out as soon as they heard the sound he made—'Stop, stop, my dear, you don't have to do all that, here's some rice!' The boy could not remember who had initiated him into this performance of hurting himself in order to eat, before he met the class of people with perverted tastes and another with soft hearts. Thanks to that—when the refugees received dole, when the babus disbursing the dole were around, especially those who drove the trucks bringing rice and dal—he got along rather well. But not any longer.

It was the Santhal boy who had informed Bimala about where, in which forest, some food could still be found. Going in search of that food, she came upon a pond, which she had never imagined she would find. There were lots of water-lilies in the pond, at the base of which were plenty of edible roots. She didn't know how the Santhals cooked the roots. Those who knew hadn't yet started coming so far away from the camp. Bimala and Tulsi together brought back a basket full of the roots. It would last them several days. Giving Garib Das some boiled lily-roots to eat on the dented enamel plate, Bimala said to him, 'Don't fall into any danger, keep a watch over yourself. We are in an unknown land, none of our own people are around. Stay away from fights and trouble. Don't get involved.' As Garib Das set off towards Bishnupur after eating the lily-roots, she muttered inwardly, '*Joy Baba Inquilab, Joy Baba Zindabad.* May there be no dangers in his way. May he return home safe. I vow that if my man returns home safely, I shall perform five toils in your name.'

Long ago, when she was a child, Bimala's Ma had told her, 'The gods test people from time to time. All the dangers, diseases and ailments are a result of their wrath. If one can placate their anger, then misfortunes disappear. Only true devotion satisfies them. That's what they test, how devoted you can be. One of the ways of showing devotion is fasting and the other is toil. Toil means reciting the Lord's name while going around the courtyard, spinning round and round, continuously, until you collapse. People are already fasting, but if God is not satisfied with that, if He thinks it's mere cunning, then he demands the vow of toil. And not just one or two, but five.'

There was a metalled road from the Basudebpur camp on which buses and lorries plied. Reaching there, Garib Das saw that there were two equally long lines of people. The two lines moved ahead at the same pace. Between the two lines a man shouted with a megaphone in front of his mouth, 'Our demand must be met!' The people in the procession shouted back in the same tone, 'Must be met, must be met!'

'Sending refugees outside Bengal is unacceptable!'

'Proper rehabilitation must be provided in Bengal itself!'

'We'll face lathis, bullets and gas, but we won't leave West Bengal!'

'Inquilab Zindabad!'

Garib Das had arrived a bit late. So he had not been able to memorise the slogans. As he tried to shout the slogans while walking in step with the procession, he said it incorrectly time and again. Instead of saying 'is unacceptable', he said 'must be provided', and was scolded by the megaphone-man. But he made no mistake in shouting *'Zindabad'* after *'Inquilab'*. After shouting it out a few times, he now sensed that this was an even more powerful word than the great mantra of the name Hari. He felt a flush of heat inside him. He felt strong inwardly. He was sure that with the mantra's push, it wouldn't be difficult to make the crooked government bend to their will.

Prahlad babu had told Khagen babu, who in turn had told everyone about where, and in which country, by the power of this mantra, the government had not merely been made to bend but been completely overthrown. Now the common people there lived in great comfort. This was such an all-powerful mantra that unless one bent before it, one was destroyed.

The procession moved from Basudebpur to Bishnupur without any hindrance. But it could not enter the town. Hundreds upon hundreds of armed policemen stood in the way, in battalion strength. Word had reached them in advance, through informers, that a band of people of unruly disposition, who were hungry for sure, were all pouring into the town, like a flood. There was a possibility of breakdown of law and order. An outbreak of looting could not be ruled out either. Once they entered the town, it would be difficult to control them. So the procession ought to be blocked outside the town limits, on the open field. As a precautionary measure, the district magistrate had imposed Section 144, prohibiting assembly.

From the blocked procession erupted the slogan, 'We must not be blocked!' But the police did not pay attention. They stood wall-like in front of the procession. One group wanted to advance, another group would not let them advance. Consequently whatever had to happen happened. There was pushing and shoving from both sides. Someone from the procession threw a stone at the police. A pretext was all that was needed. The police found the pretext. They ran forward and began lashing out with their lathis. A few shells of tear gas were also fired. About forty refugees were hurt from the blows of lathis, of whom six suffered serious injuries. They had to be admitted to hospital in Bishnupur. And almost two hundred people were arrested. Garib Das was one of them.

When the police were hauling up the people and cramming them in groups into the police vans, many of them were quite happy inwardly. They were consoling one another: let it be, at least we'll get something to eat today. Khagen babu had said they provide food. But none of them knew that the government authorities in question were very clever. They knew that a cat should never know about a broken fence, or else there wouldn't be any milk left for the household. The cat would keep entering through the broken fence. So they did not take the agitating refugees anywhere near the food-plates in jail. They took them in vans and trucks—some twenty-five or thirty miles away from the town—to a desolate zone, and that too, not everyone together, but in groups of twenty or twenty-five persons, all in various directions. After that, they swung their lathis and made them get down from the vehicles. 'Go! See how it feels to walk back now!'

It was dusk when Garib Das's group reached a place called Saltora, and were made to get off. There was no habitation anywhere in sight, only forest and more forest. But the only saving grace was that there were no man-eating creatures in these forests. They spent the whole night there, under the open sky, with fear in their hearts, hunger in their bellies, and a mountain of anxiety in their heads. In time, night turned to day. None of them had any strength left in their bodies to speak of. They thought they would all die in that alien terrain. Vultures and jackals would tear and eat their flesh. But eventually they did not die. Like a snail dragging its shell, the hungry bodies inched ahead along the woods, forests and unknown roads. After walking all day, they reached the site of the erstwhile camp in the evening, and returned to their wives, sons and daughters. On the part of the administration, this initial assault was so fierce that the backs of the refugees were broken. Yet, braving their injuries, with broken backs and broken minds, they were trying to stand up. In gatherings, associations, meetings and processions, they had shouted out slogans as loudly as they could. One procession after another had stormed into the town, but it was futile. Their pleas and appeals failed to bring life to the body of dead humanity. In response, the administration had ratcheted up their resistance. They were thrashing them cruelly with lathis, massively using tear gas, and employing all other means of suppression at their disposal. Khagen Mandal as well as some others were arrested and thrown into jail. The fate that Garib Das had suffered was reserved for all the other agitators as well.

In order to raise the morale of the refugees, Prahlad babu once sent a singer from Calcutta. He went around the four camps singing, full-throated, without any instrumental accompaniment. '*Jaago, jaago*, awaken o awaken, destitute folk imprisoned and enslaved in starvation have risen, the conviction of freedom has arisen ....' Trying to convince the people that it would not be much longer, that the end of their sorrows and suffering was nigh. Don't halt, fight on. But people did not awaken any more. The movement did not grow stronger, gradually it began to wilt.

The famous French general Napoleon had said, 'An army marches on its stomach'. A movement is also a kind of war. A picket of unarmed, emaciated, starving people against an armed, strong, well-fed, fierce enemy ... How long could they carry on the battle? Starving folk can never win any battle anywhere. There was no greater enemy than hunger. Who has ever been able to defeat that enemy and stand fast in the battlefield! The refugees too could not. They lost to their own selves. What does hunger eat? Hunger feeds on everything. Love, affection, friendship, intimacy, principle, morality, ideals, vows, conviction, stale and rotten leftovers in the dustbin, everything—hunger can eat everything. In the end, it eats up the man's life itself. It eats him up and tears him to pieces. A torn-up man is of no use to himself, his country, society or anybody else.

After about six months of excitement, the movement died down. The silence of a graveyard descended upon the camp. There wasn't the slightest trace of any hue and cry, enthusiasm or animation. Hope and faith had ceased. People just lay wilted, gazing with mute eyes in all directions.

Following a month in custody, Khagen Mandal was released from jail. He returned to the camp all by himself, walking all the way from Bishnupur. Everyone knew that he was to be released unconditionally today, but no one was present outside the sub-jail to receive him. Those whom he had trusted deeply, those comrades had all vanished. After returning to the camp, he was telling his neighbours, in a most sad and pained tone: 'There's no hope for us. When the British were in the country, if someone fasted for two or four days for some demand, they used to find a way to resolve it through dialogue. The little bit of kindness and compassion that was there in the foreigners is lacking in the people of this country. This government has only one message, those who want to go to Dandakaranya should enlist their names, and nothing besides that.'

His voice choked as he spoke, as if there was a spasm of inner grief. 'Those who are running the country now, they are all high-caste folk who think we are no different from worms and insects, like flies and mosquitoes. They only want to see us perish.'

'What does Prahlad babu say?'

'Don't talk about Prahlad babu!' There was no more respect for that name in Khagen Mandal's words today. 'Don't they say, *roshuner goda shob ek jagay; tole tole shob eki.* All the garlic pods emerge from the same spot; everyone's the same at the bottom. There's no sign of him. He incited everyone and then moved away. I heard that he's gone somewhere and taken up some other work.'

∽

The tarpaulin tents, made of thick cloth coated with wax, had a short life. A tent lasted a year at most. When the camp office was in existence, every year, before the rains began, they could be exchanged for new ones. But they had not been changed this time. Who would do that? Now the scorching sun during the day burst in through the gaps laid bare in the torn tents. The rain would soon pour in. Some families, who were in a situation to go somewhere, had left the camp by now. Those left behind now were the ones who lacked any support or means, the utterly wretched. No harm would come to the country if they ceased to exist.

The hand-pumps in the camp had been out-of-order for long, and lay gathering rust. Forget about bathing, there was no water even to drink. No one had ever imagined that a civilised government in a civilised country could be so barbaric. When man was wild and uncivilised, living in the forest in pre-historic times, primitive culture had taught him: don't let even your greatest enemy go thirsty; give water even to a dying man.

Khagen Mandal had written an application, making a fervent appeal, taken everyone's thumb impressions on it, and submitted it in the sub-collector's office in Bishnupur. He had written, 'We are in great difficulty without water. Kindly arrange for the hand-pump in the camp to be repaired.' The sub-collector sahib crumpled and threw the application into the waste-paper bin. 'There are no people there, what's the need for hand-pumps?'

'No people there! What do you say, sahib? So many thousands there—aren't they people?'

'Why are they languishing there?'

'Then where will they go?'

'The file is still open, let them enlist their names. Let them go to Dandakaranya. There's plenty of water there.'

There was no option. One could go without food, but it was impossible to live without water. The people tried to quench their thirst somehow, fetching water from the well or two in the Santhal and Muslim hamlets. But even there, all kinds of problems arose, simply because of the pressure of numbers.

Finally, Khagen Mandal decided, he would leave the camp and go away. Some relatives of his had bought one or two katthas of land in a place called Thakurnagar in the northern part of 24 Parganas district, and somehow managed to build a structure to shelter in. He would go there. Before he left, he called everyone for the final time and told them, 'We were together for so long. I had hoped to spend the rest of my life with you, sharing our difficulties and joys. But that was not to be. What can one do about fate ... I'm going, and you all should also try to go wherever you can. I've heard some of our people have built shanties near the stations and along the rail-lines and canal-banks close to Calcutta. They are working and raising their children. See if you can do the same. There's nothing but death here ...'

Subol went to Garib Das and collapsed, weeping. 'Everyone's leaving us behind and going away; where shall we go? How will we survive, Garib-da?' The fleeting breeze carried his wails away, like it made the leaves in the sal grove flutter.

JIBON

12

The Stranger

A great man had once said—one must know how to survive. Survival is an art, a skill, it requires wisdom. And that has to be acquired. The one who can do that lives, and the one who cannot is doomed to vanish. That's the natural law that has existed from time immemorial. Time is ever subject to change. Whatever existed yesterday is not there today, just as what exists today will no longer be around tomorrow. With the passage of time, tastes, eating habits and lifestyles too have to be made appropriate to the changing times. They have to change. You can survive only if you do that. Look at the huge creature, the dinosaur—why did it disappear? It did because it could not adjust to the changed environment and climate. But the tiny ants survive despite all the storms, cyclones, earthquakes, collapses, calamities and cataclysms. Because although they are tiny, they know how to survive. The one who does not know that is certain to become extinct.

Garib Das's little son, Jibon, now knew the skills of survival. He had learnt how to defeat the great enemy called hunger. Who could match the one who knew how to kill hunger! Some of these skills had been taught to Jibon by a Santhal boy, Mongla, and some more by another boy from the refugee camp, Fatik. Whenever his hunger became unbearable, Jibon ran to them. They knew hundreds of ways to overcome hunger. Like a trusted friend or devoted disciple, they initiated him into that knowledge. Once, when he was terribly hungry, Mongla had roasted two large lyata fish on a fire of husk. With some salt and red-chilli powder, the fish wasn't at all bad to eat. Mongla's folk ate frogs, large rats caught from the ridges of paddy fields, squirrels, snails and cockles—all that and so much more formed part of their food. Jibon had tried and tasted most of these things and realised that he could eat them too. But he had been frightened when it came to the snake.

In order to make him lose his fear, Mongla had told him, 'Eat it. Nothing's going to happen. We eat it all the time.'

'Don't you know snakes are poisonous!'

'Didn't you see I cut the head off?'

He had cut off the head of the snake, peeled its skin, and cooked it with salt, chillies and turmeric. He had used a bit of oil too. It looked just like cooked eel. On Mongla's insistence, Jibon had tried some and found it tasted like that too. Still, he could not get more than one piece down his throat.

Mongla hunted for birds sometimes. Shooting stones from a small bow with perfect aim, he killed doves, sparrows, green pigeons and various other kinds of birds. He also laid traps to catch cranes. Whenever he went out to lay the traps, he took Jibon along. At the end of the hunt, the two friends had a grand picnic. Of course, they did not need to venture far for that. After all, the forest was Mongla's backyard.

Compared to Mongla's regal fare, Fatik's foods were very different, but also much tastier. On the two sides of the aerodrome runway that lay to the south of the camp were plenty of jujube-berry shrubs. Countless berries were to be found on the three- or four-feet tall shrubs. Once they were ripe, the green leaves of the plants were barely visible. Everything was red. If one shook the shrub with a long stick, the berries fell to the earth. They were great to eat with salt and chilli powder.

On both sides of the road that went from Basudebpur to Bishnupur, there were trees which had caterpillar-like hairs. They were laden with bunches of bright yellow flowers. If a branch was pulled gently, the flowers fell off. When one sucked at the base of the flowers, nectar emerged. How sweet it was! Utterly captivating! Jibon would walk along the road with Mongla, sucking the nectar. Jibon's life had begun without honey at the moment of his birth. But now, away from people's eyes, the seven-year-old Jibon endeavoured to make his life sweet by sucking nectar from unnamed flowers.

Fatik knew all about what was available at a particular time in any place. When the paddy on people's fields was half-ripe, they took the paddy between their teeth and sucked the milk-like liquid inside. That did not fill the stomachs, but it did take away hunger. Sometimes they pulled out fresh grass by the roots and chewed their base. It was very soft and tasted like coconut. The same kind of taste was also to be found in the stones of the tender dates. The green skin had to be peeled off and the stone chewed. It made a crunching sound when chewed. Just a little bit erased one's hunger. If one had too much, one got a stomach-ache. And of course, if there were ripe dates, there was nothing like that. But it was difficult to find ripe dates. People roamed around everywhere like rabid dogs, with the fire of hunger burning in their bellies, and cut the dates even before they could ripen. The dates never got the chance to ripen on the tree.

On both sides of the asphalted road were many trees with black berries. These berries, which were small and a bit astringent, were known as iron-berries. And inside the forest one found mahua flowers. One couldn't eat too many of the flowers. Although they were very sweet and tasty, if one ate more than one or two, one felt giddy, intoxicated.

Once Fatik had cut the top of a date palm and extracted the spathe. Its taste was something a hungry man would never forget.

Breaking with a crunching sound when bitten gently with the teeth, it was as if the spathe released a cascade of juice on the tongue. Large, ripe figs were to be found in the forest. Ripe mangosteens, kendu flowers and wild custard-apples too. There were mangoes in the mango orchard. However, not all the edible items were found at all times. But it was jujube season now. If one went to the forest now, one could find ripe jujube-berries.

⚮

Jibon and Fatik were on a mission to eat jujube berries today. This mission wasn't just a matter of eating, but also of play. It involved pride, and also had to do with popular religion and culture. The plans had already been made in the morning. Now, as the day advanced, the process of actualisation was commenced.

It was afternoon. Tulsi was lying inside the tent with her daughter, Kusum. Her husband, Subol, wasn't there. He had gone to Bishnupur, for wood-work with a carpenter whom he had found after great difficulty. If he earned two or three rupees, he would return to the camp after purchasing rice and dal. With nothing else to do all alone, Tulsi had lain down and fallen asleep. Her naughty daughter was wide awake, waiting with her ears pricked for when she would be called.

And the call did come: 'Kusum, come to play!'

Slipping out quietly from beside her Ma, Kusum came out of the tent, took Jibon by the hand and said gleefully, 'Here I am!'

Fatik was waiting nearby, under the shade of a mango tree. Coming towards them, he said, 'We'll pay Ram-Sita today. I'll be Ram. Kusum, you'll be Sita, and Jibon will be Lakshman. The three of us will play the part about setting off for the forest. We'll eat lots of fruits, we'll hunt tigers, and then we'll return home.'

Shashibala, one of the camp dwellers, used to sing songs from the Ramayan. In the days before the rations were stopped, when food was still being cooked, a jatra troupe had been formed, which performed during the Rathayatra or chariot festival. They had enacted the scenes of Sita's wedding, the defeat of Ravan and the Ashvamedha Yagna. The players in these parts used to put the red colour called *alta* on their faces and wear crowns made of tin-foil on their heads while enacting the roles of Ram and Ravan. Once, during a performance of the Ashvamedha, Fatik had played the part of the base of the oblatory fire. That had no lines. With a crown on his head, a flower-garland on his neck and colours on his face, he had crawled along on all fours on the makeshift stage that had been made on the playground. That scene had been performed quite a few times. So Kusum's knowledge of the Ramayan was no less than Fatik's. She knew who Sita was, and how Ram was related to her. So she now jutted out her lip in a pout, swung her plaits, puckered up her face and said with great antipathy, 'I won't play. Go away, you can play.'

'Why Kusum, why won't you play? We'll go to the forest. There's lots of flowers and fruits there. The berries are ripe and red ...' Jibon said, trying to persuade her.

'I told you I won't play. You go and play Ram-Sita.'

'Oh you stupid girl, boys can't play Ram-Sita. A girl's needed. Or else, who'll play Sita? How can we play without you?'

Kusum said she would play, but on one condition: 'If you play Ram, then I'll be Sita. If it's anyone else, I won't.'

Jibon tried to explain to her, 'Ram is the elder brother, and Lakshman the younger one. Isn't Fatik two years older than me? If I play Ram, then who will he be?'

The main reason for Jibon supporting Fatik was the bow and arrows, and in fact Hanuman's mace too, all of which Fatik had. What if Fatik got angry and refused to give the weapons? What was Ram without his bow and arrows?

But Kusum refused to relent. 'I won't be his wife.'

'Then whose wife will you be?'

'Yours.'

Jibon chided her once again, 'Oh you stupid girl, you won't be his real wife. It's only a play.'

'I won't, I won't, I won't. There, I swore thrice.'

There could be no further argument now. If someone broke a vow after swearing thrice, they would be consigned to hell forever. After all, the Ramayan was all about abiding by a vow. Jibon couldn't knowingly send Kusum to hell by making her break her vow.

Then Fatik said, 'That's fine, Jibon, you play Ram. Here's Ram's bow.'

'And what will you be?'

'I'll be Hanuman the brave.'

'If you play Hanuman, won't you need a tail?'

'I tore the border off Ma's sari and made a tail. Here it is.'

Finally, when it was the pleasant time of evening, they journeyed into the forest, the great archer Ramchandra, his pants torn at the backside, in the lead, Janak's daughter Sita, with her head full of lice, in the middle, and in the rear, the son of the Wind God, the undefeatable Hanuman, wearing a torn gamchha tucked up like a loincloth. Walking along the path beside the military well, they climbed up to the road on which the school used to be. After that they walked straight, northwards, until they reached the runway.

There they encountered a one-headed Ravan, whose name was Dhiren. He was the most roguish boy in the camp. For no reason at all, he was always beating up someone or the other. His family had a few goats. He took the goats to the forest to graze, and went around with a knife in his pocket. His father, Ramesh Dakua, used to go to Bishnupur to make beedis. Sharp knives were needed for beedi-making, so there were quite a few such knives in his place. It was one of those that Dhiren always carried and, from time to time, he used it to frighten the children in the camp. 'I'll shove this into your belly ...' If he cut the belly—how could one eat after that! That terrified the children.

Now Dhiren stood blocking the way of the venturing Ram and Sita. '*Aeyi*, where are you all off to? And what's this? Oh my my, isn't he playing Ram with a bow and arrows! Someone who hasn't yet learnt to pee is Ram!' Dhiren laughed and tore up the tin-foil crown on Ram's head. He broke all their weapons made from woody stalks, of which one was called the *ognibaan*, fire-arrow, and another the *barunbaan*, flood-arrow. Not being able to snap the bamboo bow, he cut the bowstring with his knife. He also tore the brave Hanuman's tail to shreds.

It was a terrible humiliation. Even the abduction of Sita by Ravan would have been more tolerable than this. She could have been rescued through battle. If Kusum's Ma, Tulsi, was informed, she herself could have fought and rescued Sita. What could the unarmed Ram do now, other than cry! He began to wail loudly—'Just you wait, you rascal, let your father return home. See if I don't go and tell him!'

'What will you tell him, my dear?' Dhiren stepped forward and boxed Ram's ear. 'Go and say what you like. I'm not scared.'

Beaten, defeated, the two great warriors returned home and sat brooding. They could not imagine how this could be avenged. An assault like that, for no fault of theirs, and especially in front of Kusum! Unless this was set right, their playing Ram and Hanuman was all in vain. But Dhiren Dhakua was much older than them. He was strong, too. Besides, he carried a knife. How could they overcome such an enemy empty-handed?

That day, the following day, and almost every day after that, the only thought in the minds of the two friends was how, by whichever means possible, they could exact revenge. Jibon said, 'Listen, here's something we can do. If we go to the Santhal hamlet and call Mongla, we can strike Dhiren. He has a bow and stone pellets. In the same way as Ram shot an arrow from afar at Bali, Mongla will be able to shoot a pellet at Dhiren and fell him.'

'Will Mongla come along for our sake?'

'If he hears that Dhiren beat me, he'll lose his head! Isn't it there in the Ramayan—kill him by any means. So what's wrong with getting Mongla on our side and attacking Dhiren? It's the same as us hitting him.'

It was decided that Mongla would be summoned. Mongla would wait with his bow beside the runway. As soon as he spotted Dhiren, he would shoot at him and slip away into the forest. Like Meghnath fighting from under the cover of clouds. That would be the correct strategy to adopt in the battle against the sharp knife.

⁂

That very evening, Jibon set out for Mongla's hamlet. Walking along the road from the camp, going past the cremation ground on the left and the fields stretching away endlessly on the right, he reached the Santhal hamlet. Mongla lived in the first house. He had no siblings. He had an elder sister, but she had got married and left. Jibon had never seen Mongla's father, he had heard that he had gone away somewhere to work, breaking stones. But he had met Mongla's Ma. She was fond of Jibon. Once, seeing Jibon's hungry face, she had brought two husks of corn from the field, roasted them and given it to him to eat.

Seeing Jibon, Mongla's Ma said, 'Mongla isn't here. I don't know where he is. Why don't you sit?'

Jibon did not want to leave without meeting Mongla. He waited. He waited all evening, but Mongla did not return. Finally Jibon said, 'I'm leaving now, I'll be back tomorrow.'

Until Jibon set off on the journey back, he hadn't realised how late it was. The refugee camp was about three miles away from the Santhal hamlet. In between lay the cremation-ground. More people were dying now than before, but no pyres were lit anymore in the cremation-ground. There was no wood. Now they dug up the area on the bank of the pond, buried the body and hurried away. So many people had died in the camp, but now, a person's death did not perturb people. Death was no longer something painful, it had become an everyday affair. Everyone would die one day. One had to assume when someone died that God had granted them life only until then. If one went to a large cremation-ground, like the Keoratala burning ghat in Calcutta, one saw dead bodies burning and the relatives of the deceased weeping as they performed the ceremonies. But the dwellers in the cremation-ground laughed, gossiped, played cards and smoked ganja. Women could be seen cooking. Little children played hopscotch there. Dead bodies did not create any disruption in their daily lives. The situation in the camp too was like that now. No longer did anyone wail over the dead body lying in front of them. They buried the body quickly, and that concluded the ritual mourning, before they rushed off in search of some means of survival.

Shortly after Jibon left for the Santhal hamlet that morning, a dead body had arrived at the cremation-ground. That was Garib Das's aunt, Gagan's Ma. She had been ill for a long time. But even in that condition, she had continued to rail against fate in her hoarse voice and roundly abused and cursed the heartless government. But everything was quiet now. Garib Das, Gagan and Subol had carried her body wrapped up in a torn mat, buried it and returned to the camp.

By the time Jibon reached the cremation-ground on his way back from the Santhal village, it was very dark. It was well past dusk. Besides, it was cloudy, so it was darker than usual. On one side of the road lay the unending stretch of fields. Those fields were undulating and full of small mounds. On the other side, was first a field, which yielded crops if water was available, and behind that was the protected forest of sal trees. There was no one on the road. Only the chorus of crickets could be heard. A wildcat with a rabbit in its jaws crossed the road and went off. Jibon was scared. And right then, he inwardly called out, 'O dada, Madhusudan!' He didn't know why he did that. But it seemed like he didn't want to let go of the little bit of faith he possessed, with the help of which he could make the journey back along this road shrouded in darkness.

⚮

Jibon's Ma, Bimala, did not usually say much, but in the days when the refugee dole was in operation, sometimes, after she had fed him, she used to take him on her lap and tell him stories. Jibon didn't know where she had heard all those stories. One day she told him the story of a sad mother and her sad son.

A mother and her son lived in a village. They had nobody in the world to call their own. They were extremely poor and their days were spent in sorrow and begging. When the boy was old enough, his mother sent him to school. At the time of the story, schoolmasters used to beat the boys as if they were cattle, and so they were very scared of going to school. There was also a dense forest on the way, in which wild animals lived. Although they didn't harm people, because he was a child after all, he was scared. Making up a story in order to give him courage, his mother then told him, 'Khoka, don't ever be afraid. An older brother of yours lives in that forest. Call him whenever you are in any danger. You'll see, he'll protect you. Remember, your brother's name is Sri Madhusudan.'

After that, whenever the boy went past the forest, he called out in distress, 'Where are you, Madhusudan dada, I'm very scared, protect me, dada!'

Just as the robber Ratnakar did not know that reciting 'mara', which meant death, was actually like calling out to Lord Ram, similarly, the boy too did not know that Madhusudan was actually another name for Hari, who dwelt in his celestial abode, Vaikuntha. One day, hearing his anguished cry, God could not help being moved. He descended to the dust of the earth and appeared before the child in the guise of a boy. He said, 'What's up, bhai, why are you calling me? Here I am! Come, let me help you cross the forest.'

Thereafter, helping the boy cross the forest became God's daily task. The story was actually a long one. Bimala had told her son this story out of deep conviction, so that Jibon had faith in God. Knowing what a great friend and protector of poor, sorrowful and endangered folk God was, she revered and had faith in Him.

Jibon loved his mother. He believed her. She hadn't yet begun to teach him to distinguish between action and reaction, truth and falsehood, real and unreal, imagination and reality, and freedom and faith. Jibon was still at an age when he got scared when he heard ghost stories, trembled at tales of ogres and became thrilled to hear stories about sleeping princesses awakening at the touch of a magic wand. 'My Ma cannot lie'—he still had eternal faith in his Ma. So now, on this journey through darkness, wary of danger at every moment, he called out to God: 'Dada Madhusudan!'

It wasn't only Bimala, Garib Das too knew lots of stories like that. Both of them had blind faith, an unwavering belief in God. From time to time, Garib too told his son several stories concerning God. He had told him, 'Whenever God visits the earth, he comes assuming human form. That's why people can't recognise him.'

Who was this that walked fearlessly, emerged from the forest, went past the pond in the cremation-ground and came and stood on the road in front of Jibon? It could be Bimala's Madhusudan, or it could be Garib Das's Narayan in a new form. Or he could be neither of them and simply another person. Whoever he was, Jibon felt a bit emboldened seeing him. His face wasn't visible in the darkness, but he guessed he was about his own age. How come such a small boy was so courageous that he could walk indifferently through forest and cremation-ground in the darkness!

Before Jibon could say anything, the boy asked him, '*Tui ke re*? Who are you?' In a single breath, Jibon told him his name, his father's name and where he had gone. But he didn't tell him why he had gone there.

On the stretch of road here was a small concrete culvert. The government had built it in order to ensure that the flood of rainwater along the drain, during the months of Ashadh and Shrabon, did not damage the road. The stranger sat down on the culvert. From his demeanour, it was clear that he intended to sit there for a while. Seeing him, Jibon had become hopeful of having a companion on the walk back. He still had to walk another mile along the road adjoining the forest, and it was very dark. It was probably only about seven, but the darkness enveloping them made it seem like late night. So the light of hope that had been ignited in Jibon's heart was extinguished. He could not decide whether to remain there or move ahead.

Full of disappointment, he asked the stranger, 'Won't you come along?'

'Where?' the boy replied, with a question of his own.

'To the camp.'

'Why? Why should I go to the camp?'

'Where do you live? Don't you live in the camp?'

Leaning back, the stranger put on an air, as if he was lounging there, and said, 'If I lived in the camp, wouldn't you have seen me sometime? Have you ever seen me there?'

Jibon could not see his face in the darkness. 'How do I know?'

Rocking back and forth, and thumping his back against the wall of the culvert, the stranger said, 'I don't live in the camp. I used to live there earlier, long ago. I don't live there now.'

'Where do your parents live?'

'They live in the camp.'

'Don't you stay with them?'

'No.'

'Why's that? Does your father beat you?'

'No. He used to earlier, he used to beat me a lot. He can't beat me now.'

'So why don't you go there now?'

'I don't because I don't want to.'

'Then where do you live?'

'In the forest during the day, and on this culvert at night. And when it rains, I'm under the culvert.'

'Aren't you afraid?'

'Of what?'

'Of those who live in the cremation-ground—what if they come and catch you?'

'Oh, so you're talking about ghosts! My dear, ghosts catch people—why would they catch me! They won't catch you either—aren't I with you!'

Jibon's body seemed to suddenly weigh heavily on him. He wasn't completely timid, yet he found himself trembling. Ghosts caught hold of people. Yet they didn't catch this boy—so what was he then!

The stranger was silent for a while. Then he said, 'Once I had terrible dysentery.'

'I had dysentery too. Ma told me I had almost died then.'

'You survived, but I—don't be afraid—I died. I died and became a ghost. Ghosts don't catch other ghosts.'

It didn't take Jibon long to realise that the boy actually wanted to frighten him by telling such lies. No, he mustn't get scared! At the very least, he shouldn't express his inner fear. Or else the boy would frighten him even more.

Jibon said, 'I don't believe it.'

'What?'

'That you're a ghost.'

'Tell me who you want me to swear by, I'll do that!'

'Swear on Ram.'

Laughing boisterously in the darkness, the boy said, 'You're very clever. You know ghosts flee as soon as they hear the name of Ram, that's why you asked me to swear on him. Ask me to swear on anyone else, Kali, or Mahadev—whatever you like!'

Jibon couldn't decide who else he could ask him to swear by.

The boy said, 'Do you know, ghosts eat whatever they find, including snakes and frogs? I eat everything too.'

Jibon replied, 'I've eaten snakes and frogs too with Mongla.'

'Have you eaten crow's eggs? I've eaten that. That's how they found out about me. Those who saw me eating the eggs began to talk about it. They were the ones who said, it must be a ghost! Ever since then, I have stayed away from people. When I'm a ghost, it's better to remain in the territory of ghosts.'

Jibon said, 'When people see me too, they say I look like a ghost.'

Now the boy seemed to be a bit annoyed with Jibon. He snapped, 'Won't you ever believe that I'm a ghost?'

Remembering something his father had told him, Jibon replied with great confidence, 'If you were really a ghost, I would have believed it. You're saying these things only to frighten me. But I won't get scared. My father told me that hunger, sleep and fear feed on themselves and grow.'

The boy sat silently for a while, and then he said, 'I don't want to frighten you. After I was sick, everyone said I had recovered. But I thought I had died on that very day. Died and become a ghost. I used to be very scared earlier. But then I thought—ghosts didn't have to fear dying all alone in the darkness. Man's greatest fear is death, but when that fear's gone, there's nothing to fear! When someone is not afraid of death, why men, even tigers are afraid of him! I thought to myself, people die and then become ghosts, so why not become one even before dying! There's some pain at the moment of death, after all it's an unnatural death. So let me defer that. I'll take it back after some time. Isn't it a great advantage to be a ghost! You don't feel hungry. And if you get hungry, you can eat whatever you like. You can fall asleep wherever you like. Become a ghost like me. If you become one, we can be friends.'

'How old are you?'

'Why, my dear, why do you want to know my age?'

'The way you talk, so knowingly, reminds me of the lame master in the camp school. Where did you learn all that?'

'Do you want to learn?'

'Tell me, who taught you?'

'No one taught me, I learnt it all by myself.'

The boy paused for a while and then said, 'People don't learn about everything simply by growing older. If that were so, all the people of the same age would think and talk in the same way. People speak based on the way they see things, the way they understand things. If you go and ask anyone in the camp, they'll tell you that there are ghosts in the cremation-ground. Ask me, and I'll tell you that's all rubbish. I've been on this culvert and under it for so long, if there were ghosts, wouldn't I have seen them! It's because I wanted to see the ghosts that I began to stay here. Now I've become a ghost myself!'

Jibon said, 'If you're going to stay here, then I should be going. It's late now. My Ma will be worried.'

The boy said, 'Come, I'll walk with you.' As they walked, the stranger continued, 'What did I ask you then? Do you want to become a ghost? Actually, there's nothing called ghosts, so do you want to be like a ghost? If you do, tell me now, then you and I will be friends. I'll be beside you and you'll be beside me. It seems you're all alone now; I am too. But if there's one and one, we'll become eleven. The children in school recite that one and one makes eleven. If the two of us become as good as eleven, that's a great advantage!'

Jibon said, 'I will.'

'You will?'

'I will. I'll become like a ghost and before anything else, I'll thrash Dhiren. He thrashes everyone, now I'll thrash him. Can I do that?'

The boy laughed loudly and said, 'I know a mantra, I'll teach it to you. If you utter that mantra, you'll be successful in whatever you do. Come tomorrow, I'll teach it to you. Will you come tomorrow?'

'I'll come.'

'When you come, remember to get some salt, some chillies and a cup or bowl. I've found mushrooms in the forest. We'll cook that and have a feast.'

'I heard that some people in Basudebpur apparently ate mushrooms and died ...'

'We won't die. After all we're ghosts.'

They had arrived near the camp. The rows of tents looked like tombstones from afar. There was no light in any tent. Lighting a lamp required kerosene. Where would they get that? It seemed there was no life there either. Everything was dead. Only some skeletal people seemed to be moving, wraith-like, outside the tents. One of whom was Garib Das. His son had not returned. So he was anxious. Pointing in his direction, Jibon said, 'My father's waiting for me. I'll come tomorrow, be there. Tell me your name, I'll call you by that name.'

The boy said, 'Your name—I'm the opposite of that. My name's Maran, meaning death.'

13

To Khola

Jibon had seen lots of boys in the camp, he had played with them and heard them talk. But the boy he had met today, Maran, seemed to be different from everyone else. He seemed to belong to an entirely different clan or community. He seemed to be someone like Sudhir Haldar, who lived in the Basudebpur camp. Jibon had heard about Sudhir Haldar several times from his father.

This Sudhir Haldar was a strange kind of man. People said he was apparently an atheist. How would Jibon know what the meaning of atheist was, after all he was only a child! Sudhir Haldar had his own unique version of the events taking place around them, folklore, hearsay, history and for that matter, the religious scriptures too. Whether people believed him or not, and whether or not they understood what he said, he carried on with whatever he had to say. He did not believe the tale about the Namasudra folk which was in currency, which was beloved to them and which they were thrilled to narrate. He used to say, 'The Namasudras have always suffered a feeling of inferiority because of their caste identity. It was to cover up that sense of inferiority that this story was created. And what's that story? That we are Namas Muni's descendants. That we too have pure Brahmin blood in our veins.' He did not believe that Brahmins emerged from the mouth, Kshatriyas from the breast, Vaisyas from the stomach and Sudras from the feet of Brahma, the creator. He said this was a story made up by the Brahmins so as to keep Sudras forever beneath their feet.

So what was true then?

Who knew where Sudhir Haldar had heard this tale, but he went around telling it to people:

'In this country of ours, there were no Brahmins or Kayasthas earlier, no high-caste or low-caste. All were equal, non-Aryan. Non-Aryan means those who are not Aryan. Who were they? All the Adivasis and Santhals that you see—it's them. Four or five thousand years ago, a group of people who were fair-skinned, came to this country from outside, who knows where they came from. The people of this country were dark-skinned, they were simple and peaceful by nature, their way of living was very guileless. They used to hunt in the forests, they gathered and ate fruits from the woods, danced, sang and laughed. But the fair-skinned people who came from outside were cruel, violent and aggressive. They were ahead of the people of this country in two respects: one, they knew horsemanship, and two, they were skilled in the use of weapons used to attack from afar, namely bows and arrows. Consequently, they could easily defeat the non-Aryans in any battle. Riding on horse-drawn chariots, attacking stormily, retreating and escaping swiftly in times of danger—such skills of warfare assisted them greatly. Later, of course, the non-Aryans too learnt these skills and some of them became even more adept than the Aryans. However, that came much later. Before that, the non-Aryans had heavy weapons made of stone, with which they couldn't do anything against enemies who were far away. So almost all the good parts of the country were taken over by them. After being defeated, the non-Aryans fled to the mountains, forests and impassable regions. It's not as if warfare continued uninterrupted; sometimes there was war and sometimes a treaty. Since the Aryans were cunning, they would engage in battle for a few days and then rest for a few days before attacking once again. But they could not defeat the non-Aryans and take over their territories all the time. Those whom they were unable to defeat were such brave battle strategists that the most important outpost of the Aryans, which was called Swarga, was also captured from time to time. The Aryans gave the name "Danav" to these brave non-Aryan warriors. And they gave the name "Devata" to the cleverest of their own great warriors. To the defeated non-Aryan warriors, who lived in forests and emerged from time to time to attack the Aryans before retreating back to the forests, they gave the name "Dasyu". And those who submitted to the Aryans and became servile were named "Das". Another name for which is Sudra.

'To be enslaved is something that makes man weak, inferior and dependent on others. One can do what one likes with such people. And that's what the Aryans did with the Sudras, making some low-caste, some even lower, some untouchable, while those whom they were pleased with were placed a bit higher, like the Kayasthas, the barbers and so on. Thus they created a thousand divisions among the Sudras. And abiding by those divisions, each Sudra considers himself superior to all others. Dhopa, Dom, Bhuimali, Tanti, Pode, Tiar, Jaliya, Malla, Bagdi, Duliya, Methor, Shikari, Barui—divided into a thousand categories, these people never mingled freely and spoke their minds with one another. Their children did not marry one another. They never met at social gatherings. Because of the lack of unity between them, only fifteen percent of the population, comprising high-caste folk, wielded the whip over the remaining eighty-five percent. And they'll keep wielding it. If you people think that simply uttering the name of Hari, Harichand and Guruchand will make your life beautiful and honorable, then do that by all means. You've been doing that for a hundred years, beating the drum and blowing the trumpet. Blow it some more! I'm not in your band. You can call me an atheist or anything else!'

Namasudras comprised the largest part of the Sudra population in East Bengal. They believed that by changing their name from the erstwhile 'Chandal', Harichand's son Guruchand Thakur had achieved a great task. But Sudhir Haldar was not of the same view. He said that had the Hindus not softened their former mentality a little bit, all the Namasudras would have become Christians.

The Australian missionary Meade sahib lived with them for many years and tried to convince them about the dignity and all the benefits they would gain by becoming Christian. The Hindu leaders had realised that they would not be able to hold on to the Namas. So they held out that sop and placated them. Through this means, irrespective of whether or not anything was gained by the Namas, the Hindu community did gain considerably. In the two Bengals together, in terms of population, Muslims were already in majority. The Hindus knew well what would happen if, in addition, another large section left the Hindu fold. So they consented to the change of name. But Sudhir Haldar used to say, 'What's the purpose of the name change, you'll still remain untouchable!'

Eighty percent of the people in the four refugee camps were Namasudras. How could they like the man who trivialised the greatest accomplishment of their most beloved religious leader, Harichand's son, Guruchand? That's why, despite living among his people, Sudhir Haldar was alone, lonely.

For some reason, Jibon liked Sudhir Haldar. In his child's eye, in his child's mind, the image of the man was of an altogether different kind from that of his own father's or anyone else around them. Now, seeing this boy, Maran, he thought he was a smaller version of Sudhir Haldar. Who had only just begun to stand on his own feet, but would in future, it appeared, disavow all that was old and walk in an entirely new direction.

⋙⋘

Jibon would go to the runway again today to eat jujube-berries. He wouldn't go alone, he would take Fatik along. And he would take

Kusum along too. He had to prove his manhood to Sita, who had been humiliated the other day. There was no need for the part about Ram breaking the great bow to win Sita, and so on. They would dash directly to the vanquishing of Ravan.

And so Jibon went and called Fatik: 'Tell me, Fatik, are we going to thrash Dhiren today? Do you want to vanquish Ravan? Will you take revenge for that day?'

Fatik replied fearfully, 'How will we do that? Dhiren is so much bigger than us. He's so strong. He eats rice every day. He carries a knife.'

'What can he do with his strength? The knife will be of no avail either. Don't they say—there's no one a spell can't fell! I've learnt a spell. If I go and say it before someone, they'll lose all their strength. They'll just stand like stone and get thrashed.'

'Won't he be able to fight?'

'He'll fight. But what of that? As long as you can thrash him to your heart's content.'

Fatik thought about it for a while and then said, 'But I won't be in front, I'll stand far away. You go before Dhiren and utter the spell. After that I'll come and beat him, beat him for as long as you say. I'll thrash Dhiren with his own stick.'

'Then go and call Kusum.'

Kusum was summoned. And now began the journey to battle. As agreed, Jibon led the way. Fatik's heart thumped and his legs trembled as they walked. He was scared. What would happen if Jibon's spell failed to work at the appropriate time? If that happened, Dhiren would grind them to dust. Like how his Ma used to grind muri on the grindstone long ago to make rice flour.

They encountered Dhiren, arrogant as usual, in the same place as the other day. Spotting the three tiny creatures, he looked at them contemptuously and roared out menacingly in the manner of a dacoit, 'Hey, where are you lot going?'

Fatik whispered to Jibon, 'Hurry up with the spell.'

But what did Fatik see? There was no spell and no transfixion! Instead, with a sheepish face and shrinking into himself like a frightened, cowering Chandal entering the Brahmin hamlet, Jibon advanced towards Dhiren. All the bravado he had professed seemed to evaporate. In a voice melting with humility, he said, 'Dhiren-da, we've come to eat jujube-berries. Would you like to eat some? Shall I pluck some and get them for you? Just see what a fine masala I've brought to eat the berries with!'

Observing such ingratiating behaviour with the prime enemy, Fatik felt like dying in shame. What a disgrace! The chillies he had got with such difficulty, pinching them out of his Ma's sight and sweating it out grinding them together with salt—here was Jibon opening the paper packet and holding up the tasty masala for him to smell! What could be worse than this!

Dhiren was extremely pleased now. It was like a defeated king paying tribute to the victorious one. He brought his nose down to smell the masala in the packet. Showing him the masala was just a ploy. Jibon threw it into Dhiren's eyes. And after that, whatever had to happen did happen! Dhiren started screaming out in agony, sat down right there and began rubbing his eyes like a madman. And then Jibon pounced on him. He rained blows, slaps and punches on him and called out to Fatik, 'Come, let's finish the bastard Ravan now!'

⤙⊱⊰⤚

The government had also set up a few large refugee camps—like those in Shiromanipur and Basudebpur—in the southern region of 24 Parganas district, in Ghutiari Sharif, Khola, Doltala and Ramdhari Bridge. In those camps too, all government assistance had been stopped because the refugees were unwilling to go to Dandakaranya. But the people in these camps had not fallen into the dire condition that Garib Das was in. Because these places were near Calcutta, the refugees could go to the city and find ways and means of eking out a living.

Three of Garib Das's brothers lived in the camp in Khola. Another brother had come there, but after his wife died, he took up sanyas and lived in the ashram of Mahananda Haldar in Palashi. The youngest brother refused to leave East Bengal. His only refrain—'Whatever you all may say, even if India's good, it's another country. Who's to say what will or won't happen in a foreign country! I'd rather live in my own country. If there are riots, if miyas cut us into pieces, at least I'll die on the soil of my country. That means more to me than becoming a king on foreign soil.' And so, he stayed back in East Bengal, clutching the soil of his homeland.

Garib Das had now decided to leave the Shiromanipur camp and go to his brothers in the camp at Khola. There was no work to be found in the Shiromanipur camp. One or two persons had learnt beedi-making, and they went to a shop in Bishnupur and made beedis. One person pulled a rickshaw. Some people cut wood and went to the town carrying piles of wood on their heads to sell to some roadside eatery. Earlier there was plenty of dry wood in the forest. But now there wasn't enough wood even to cremate those who died. So what would they sell? They would have to cut green trees. It wasn't as if some people hadn't done that too. One or two of them had been caught by forest guards and spent time in jail because they were unable to pay the fine. Garib Das too had sold wood on a couple of occasions. But he wasn't up to cutting green trees. However, that did not help his family situation. That's why he wanted to bid farewell to Shiromanipur.

While coming here from his country, Garib Das had brought along his only child, Jibon, carrying him in his arms. After that he had two more children. There were five members in his family now. How could he manage unless he earned at least two rupees every day! But earning even two rupees was difficult.

Six days before the day Garib Das decided to leave the place, Jibon had run away. It was about the boy that Garib Das was most anxious now. He was simply going to the dogs. He ate all kinds of stuff, who knows where all he went. Some people said that someone had once seen Jibon beneath the culvert near the cremation-ground. What did he do in the cremation-ground? Wasn't he afraid of going there? He had run away after throwing chilli powder into Dhiren Dakua's eyes and beating him up, and hadn't returned home since. He was scared Garib Das would beat him up.

Finally, with no other option, Garib appealed to the Santhal boy, Mongla. 'Dear boy, please find Jibon and bring him back. Tell him I won't beat him.' Jibon returned home on the seventh day. He had heard from Mongla that his father was looking for him. And so he had hugged the boy named Maran and told him sadly, 'I don't know where Calcutta is, I think it's very far away. Come along with me. Or else I'll never see you again.' Maran had patted Jibon on the back and told him, 'You should know that I'm always beside you. Just you see, whenever you need me, or even otherwise, I'll be there.'

The following day, with all his belongings packed into a bundle, Garib Das left with his family for Khola.

⌘

This was at the time when hostilities at the border between India and China had concluded. There was a major difference of opinion within Prahlad Chakraborty's party regarding whether it was India or China that was responsible. This would later result in a split in the party. Prahlad babu remained in one faction, contested elections and became a member of the legislative assembly.

It was the time when throughout Bengal the terrifying flames of a food crisis raged. The common people were venting their rage, protesting against inflation and food scarcity. The police of the newly independent nation had fired indiscriminately on processions of agitating folk. Calcutta's streets were awash with fresh red blood from eighty warm hearts. The situation in rural Bengal was worse. For months on end, people had not even seen rice. All the rice in the market had been cleverly hoarded away by greedy, profiteering traders. People died of starvation, or from eating wild berries, roots, tubers and yams.

In order to deal with the situation, some voluntary organisations had set up free kitchens. They dished out a plate of watery khichuri once a day. For which there was a queue a mile long. Those who had some money were also compelled to go without food because there was no rice available in the market. Something called milo—bits of broken corn—was sold in the market, as well as some white stuff that looked like sago which they called rice. Which even animals wouldn't eat.

It was the time when the Honourable Chief Minister of West Bengal, together with a friend of his, exhorted the people to eat green plantains and brinjals. They elaborated on how much protein, vitamins, calcium and calories there were in those two vegetables and how people would benefit from eating them. They were being ridiculed for that.

In the camps at Khola and Doltala, there was a cottage industry at the time, which was weaving mats with hogla grass. At that time, there was a dense jungle of hogla grass spreading over thousands of acres of marshland stretching from the Garia rail station almost until Bantala. The refugees bought hogla, cut it and carried it away. There were plenty of poisonous creatures in the hogla jungle, which also took the lives of some. Using the long hogla stalks, two people together could knit two mats a day. Which, at the time, sold in the market for three to four rupees.

Hogla and thread had to be purchased with the sale proceeds so that the next pair of mats could be made. The expenses of the family had to be met with whatever remained after keeping aside a rupee and a half for that purpose. There were five members in Garib's family—how could five bellies be fed with two and a half rupees? The price of rice itself was touching the sky. Thick-grained, red-coloured, inferior rice was a rupee and a half for a seer. And then one needed salt, chillies and fuel!

Garib Das sold the mats they made, and bought two seers of the broken grains of corn for the price of half a rupee a seer. Half a seer was lost after removing all the grit and dust in it. Whatever remained was boiled to make a thin gruel, which they sipped and consumed twice a day. There were no vegetables to go with that, nor any dal. Just salt, and sometimes one or two chillies. For the boy named Jibon, this was an unbearably difficult life. He woke up in the morning and sat down with his Ma to make mats. His father left to sell the pair of mats made the previous day in the market so he could purchase food. Of course, he could only sell them if he found customers! When he returned home with the corn after selling the mats, Bimala got up to prepare the meal. Jibon's father then sat down beside him to resume making mats. It took Bimala almost an hour to clean and wash the corn. After that, she put it to cook. By the time she finished cooking, Jibon and Garib would have knit another mat. Jibon would then go for a bath. That meant simply immersing himself once or twice in the pond. There was neither any oil nor any soap. A round, black cake of soap made of caustic soda was available for an anna. They could not afford to buy even that. If their hair became matted with dirt, they rubbed it with some fine clay. After the bath and after sipping some of the gruel, Jibon would sit down once again to make mats with either his Baba or his Ma. The knitting had to be completed before it was evening. The mats could not be knit after that. Where was the light? Kerosene was needed to light a lamp. Money was needed to buy kerosene. Where was the money? They could not even afford to buy matches to light the stove. They took fire from a neighbour's stove, who in turn would have taken it from someone else.

In the Bengali lexicon, there are some words to convey the degree of people's wretchedness, like *gorib, nirdhan, durgoto, kangal, haghor, sorbohara* ... poor, indigent, destitute, beggar, vagrant, deprived and so on. But all those words were too weak to convey the poverty of these people. They had known poverty in the past too. But the form of that poverty was not as terrifying, noose-like and life-threatening as this. That poverty hadn't weighed down like an immovable mountain on anyone's chest, and from which there wasn't the slightest chance of escaping.

This life was unbearable for Jibon. Is this what life was? What was the purpose of such a life? What was the fruit of this life? If life was another name for endlessly going around carrying a mountain of agony, like the hump on a camel's back, then what was the point of hauling it day after day, month after month, and year after year? Why wasn't putting an end to it thought about? Such adult concerns ravaged the mind of the child, Jibon. The answers to which he had no way of knowing. As he sat with his head bent low in the stuffy atmosphere of the closed room, stitching the grass mats, inwardly, he wanted to rebel against everything. He wanted to run away. But where would he go? There wasn't a single child his age who got the opportunity to play, or went to school. The hair on their heads matted for lack of oil, their bodies emaciated, wearing pants torn at the backside, they sat with their heads bent and knit the mats. Hunger raged in their bellies. If anyone was called to play, their parents barked out like dogs, 'Don't call him! Go away from here!'

Jibon observed the people living all around him. They seemed lifeless, like images made of stone, devoid of emotion. They had all become stooped and bent, as if under some terrible assault. They no longer knew how to laugh; not having laughed for ages, they had forgotten how to laugh. They had forgotten about chatter, stories and songs. No one dreamt anymore. Their eyes seemed to be dim, like the eyes of the dead. The people did walk around, but it seemed as if they had lost everything and were simply streaming into an immense, gaping maw of darkness ...

Garib Das had left the refugee camp in Shiromanipur and come to the erstwhile camp in Khola along with his family. That was around the beginning of the sixties. After that, with his brothers' help, he built a shanty on the bank of the salt-water canal that lay between Khola and Doltala. It was such a tiny shanty that one could not stand up inside, one's head would hit the roof. One had to crawl in through the makeshift door. Even the first hut built with leaves and vines by the inexperienced hands of cave-dwelling folk in prehistoric times, once they ventured out of caves, would surely have been stronger and better-looking than this. By living in such a dwelling, by bending and stooping continuously, one became permanently hunched and disfigured. The people in this dwelling would never be able to straighten their bent spines and stand tall in human society. No light of health, education, well-being or culture would ever enter such a dwelling. After just a few years, man would set foot on the moon. But another set of people on the same planet were regressing and gradually becoming rat-like creatures, living in burrows.

A few years passed by. By then, two more children were born to Garib Das, both daughters. The seven-member family could not survive on the money earned by making mats. Around that time, the high-caste refugees who had come from East Bengal had set up many colonies in the Jadavpur locality, on land that they had forcibly occupied. These people were of the babu class. They were averse to manual labour. And so, there was a great demand for manual labour for the construction of houses and roads in their colonies. Someone said, 'Garib-da, go to Jadavpur for work. You'll get good wages.' That man's name was Dhonai Sardar. He too went to Jadavpur for work. It was with him that Garib Das set off, carrying a basket and a spade, to start working as a manual labourer. He rose each day at 3 a.m., walked eight or nine miles to the Ghutiari Sharif station so he could catch a train at 5 a.m., and after a journey of an hour or an hour and a half, get off at the Jadavpur station and then walk again for about two miles to reach the Bagha Jatin crossing. After that, he would sit at the crossroad, like a cow at a pilgrim shrine, hoping for someone to call him for work. A few hundred people crowded around the crossroad in search of work. Not everyone found work every day. If Garib Das did not find work, he returned the same way, hungry and empty-handed. Travel on the train was without tickets, and so, because there were ticket checkers on the train during office hours, he did not get into a train until it was dusk.

If he found work, in the afternoon he spent half a rupee on a loaf of bread, a plate of alur-dam and beedis, and was able to return home with three rupees or two rupees and twelve annas. Those days were most joyful for his family. Real rice was cooked at home. With potato curry, if not dal. But those days were few, no more than ten or twelve in a month. Living on one meal or half a meal a day, or sometimes even fasting altogether, Garib Das began getting stomach-aches, which was known as gastritis, and which eventually led to an ulcer. He could not go out to work then, he lay in bed.

During this time, Jibon cast his eyes on their dwelling. On his parents and siblings. His Ma, Bimala, used to have long hair, and it was on account of seeing her hair that her father-in-law had brought her home as Garib's bride. For want of oil, her hair had become matted, and so she had had it shaved off. The final bit of cloth on her body was worn out and tattered. She had saved one or two saris from the time two saris a year were distributed from the government godown at the Shiromanipur camp. She had been using those all these years. Bimala had been quite fair at one time, but her skin now looked weather-beaten and coarse. She did not possess a blouse or even a petticoat. She somehow wrapped a piece of a torn mosquito net around her waist to preserve her modesty. She hid her semi-naked body inside the shanty all day. Even if there were a hundred necessities to attend to, she could not step outside in daylight. Shameless eyes, liked honed knives, lay in wait in the light of day. Jibon was at his wit's end thinking about how he could buy a sari for his Ma when the earnings from making mats was insufficient even to fill their bellies. How much longer would those tatters last? What would happen after that?

Jibon observed his father. The ribs on his chest could be counted now. He used to be famous as a strongman once, but now he was broken. Even when he breathed, he gasped and wheezed like a pair of bellows. His stomach-ache would probably have been cured if he saw a doctor, but he had no money to see a doctor. Jibon also observed his brothers and sisters. The way children of that age laughed, ran and played—they couldn't do any of that. They just sat dozing and drooping the whole day. Or they wailed and cried miserably. Some unbearable pain somewhere in their tiny bodies tormented them. They cried because they did not have at their command the language to express their pain. They went on crying. None of them said buy me some food, no one begged for toys; they didn't say, I'm hungry. Whipped by acute deprivation, the wounded, tortured sensibilities of the children had forgotten all child-like caprices, forgotten the eternal yearning to be loved.

None of them wore any clothes to speak of. Only the older boy, who was two years younger than Jibon, wore pants, which were torn at the backside. The one after him wore only a tiny pair of underpants, like Santhal kids. The next girl too wore the same.

He observed the refugee colony around them. It seemed that all the people living there were suspended in a procession of death. There was no way that anyone could cheat death. It would chase and catch them. Drag them to its jaws and chew them alive.

As Jibon sat in the semi-darkness of his shanty, with his stomach burning with hunger and mind burdened with a thousand grouses, he wondered whether he should run away like a crazy wind and go looking for some place in the world where there was life, light and hope.

After that, Garib Das's ailment grew worse. He would writhe in agony on the ground like a slaughtered goat. A homeopathic doctor was called. He gave some pills that looked like grains of sugar, took a rupee and left. That did not alleviate the ailment. It only led to the end of mat-making. The money needed to buy the hogla grass and thread had been taken away by the doctor. Once the mat-making stopped, so did the lighting of the stove. For want of food, a sister of Jibon's shrivelled up and died. Jibon's Ma did not have milk in her breasts; the famished infant in her arms had seemed on the brink for months. Jibon's two brothers too seemed to be standing in the death queue. Jibon realised that unless he slipped away from this abode of death, he too would perish. He had to survive, so that he could save the others. Jibon wasn't afraid of death. If it came, if he was chosen, let that be for survival—to save his parents, brothers and remaining sister. Let it be a death that would not be a mere death, but another name for fighting, for change.

14

The Cowshed

Morning signalled what the day would be like. Likewise, Jibon's life had begun in the womb of an anxious, fearful and starving mother. Deprived of the customary auspicious drop of honey at birth, his life would never see beauty and fulfillment. Man could not see his future, and so all he could hope for was that perhaps there would be some change, that something would happen, whereby his life would be completely transformed. If only Jibon could look into the future, he would have known what was in store for him.

This was towards the end of 1964, or the beginning of 1965. A man sat at a roadside tea-shop in Khola, and was talking about what a strange place this world was. 'The most difficult thing here is survival. Some things can be seen, while some things remain unseen. Although no one realises it, one's locality is surrounded on all sides by thousands of enemies. As soon as they get a chance, they will kill. There is nothing more difficult than surviving them. The next most difficult thing is to live well. Only a few people are fortunate enough to live well. Those who have enterprise, who have the courage to take risks, are the ones who are fortunate. It is said that God bears the burden of the fortunate, while the unfortunate ones have to carry their own burden.'

One's own burden! Life was nothing but a cruel mockery! A mountain of agony, a curse. Let's see whether this life could be steered away from the fathomless sea of suffering towards some other shore.

The sun had just descended to the horizon. In the pleasant, pale glow of the setting sun, the western sky was alight like the dying embers of a burning flame. At that moment, everything seemed to have halted, as if mourning something. As if a temporary silence was being observed in some condolence meeting. Not a leaf in any tree stirred; the birds that had returned at the end of the day to their arboreal abodes were silent. The chorus of crickets was also absent. Even in the ponds and lakes nearby, the water was still, without the faintest ripple. It was as if all habitations and all of nature had died. As if all of creation lay enclosed in a black, airless coffin of stillness. A dog moaned plaintively in that terrifying stillness.

It was at such a moment that Jibon set out on his journey. He didn't know where he would go. He wasn't certain why he was going either. He only knew he had to escape. He had to flee from the endless grief of this abode of death, he had to go somewhere far away. Where there was hope for survival. He had to search and find out whether there was even a tiny place like that in this vast earth. Instead of dying bit by bit each day, he had to make a final do-or-die bid and see where he could survive and find the means to save his parents, brothers and sister.

Nilkantha Gosai used to go to Calcutta to beg. One day he said, 'Do you know, dear Jibon—money flies in the air in Calcutta! Go and see how blissful people in Calcutta are! I just gaze in amazement! Buildings that touch the sky. Those who live there are like princes and princesses, all glowing in comfort. And why won't they be like that, apparently they bathe in milk and eat ghee and butter! Have you ever tasted ghee? Tastes like ambrosia!'

Jibon was going to Calcutta. Apparently a lot of people had grabbed the money flying around there and become rich. Being rich meant having lots of money. Jibon thought—when lots of people were grabbing money, why wouldn't he be able to grab some too! When they lived in Shiromanipur, and a storm arose while they were playing in the sal grove, no one but Fatik could beat him in the game of catching the leaves flying in the gust. If he could grab some money, the first thing he would do was buy rice, dal, potatoes and oil. And then he would buy a couple of saris for his Ma. Unless there were two, what would his Ma wear after bathing? He would buy medicines for his father's stomach-ache. He had heard that there were big medicine shops in Baruipur, near Calcutta. For his two brothers, kites and reels of string and lots of marbles made of glass, and a doll for his sister. For himself, he would get a harmonium and a flute.

Nurturing such hopes, Jibon was leaving today, leaving behind his parents, brothers and sister. Khola and Doltala were two separate villages. Between them flowed a canal, built off men's labour. Refugee settlements lay along both banks of the canal. If one walked westwards along the canal, there was first the Ramdhari bridge, with a metalled road running over it. The road ran between the town of Canning, on the banks of the Matla river—so named for its mad, wild ways—and Calcutta, via Baruipur and Garia. The No. 80 bus plied along this road. Just past the Ramdhari bridge, there was a narrow path curving to the right and going through fields. One could see the rail tracks far away, stretching straight as a taut bowstring. Trains, hauled by engines running on coal that emitted smoke and blackened the sky, plied along these tracks between Sealdah and Canning.

The paddy had been harvested. The fields were now covered with the sharp stubble of paddy stalks. His heart full of hope, Jibon, barely fourteen years old, walked along a narrow muddy path through the fields, oblivious of the bleeding soles of his feet.

When Jibon finally reached Ghutiari Sharif, the nearest station, it had already become quite dark. Brushing aside the unbearable stillness of dusk, the band of crickets had begun to sing their evening chorus. The flashing lights of fireflies hovered over the bamboo grove. Electricity hadn't yet reached these parts then. The lamp-posts at the railway station had kerosene lamps. The trains too ran only once an hour, or every hour and a half. Rural folk did not depend on towns so much then. So the station was quite desolate.

Jibon hadn't eaten anything the whole day. Besides, he was exhausted after walking eight or nine miles. He sat down on a wooden bench on platform No. 2. He didn't realise when he lay down and was carried away by the bottomless sea of sleep. He was oblivious of the trains that came and left. Late at night, he woke up to the flashing light of a torch and a loud voice: '*Aeyi khoka*! Where are you going, boy?'

Jibon's sleepy eyes stared back at the man, blankly.

There were some refugee settlements along the rail tracks near the Ghutiari Sharif station. About a thousand people lived there. But if one went past those, along the road, going southwards, after walking for about half an hour, one reached Notunpally, where a few thousand people resided. Although it was only people who had come from the other Bengal who lived in this locality, they were not 'refugees'. That was considered a derogatory term. They were ashamed of identifying themselves in that fashion. They may have been in some camp at some point of time, but they had come here after that, bought land at the proper price and made houses, ponds and cattle-sheds. Some had bought a bigha or two of cultivable land and were farming too. Why then would they identify themselves in such a humiliating way? After all, 'refugee' meant poor, shelterless, destitute folk, candidates for government succour. They professed sympathy for the refugees living without state dole along the rail track, but were utterly indifferent to their plight.

Ghutiari Sharif was a predominantly Muslim locality. There was a shrine here of a pir saheb known by the name of Ghazi Baba. A fair was held there every year on the day of his Urs, or memorial day. People came to the fair from faraway places. The shrine played a major role in the local economy. Who knows what evil design lay behind setting up a camp for the people driven out of East Bengal here. A few leaders of the Hindu Mahasabha frequented the place, hoping to incite the folk against the local Muslims and extract political gain thereby. Consequently, there was always an ominous, suppressed tension between the two communities. There was a lack of trust, and there was fear, which could explode at any time.

Notunpally was a bit far away from the station. This was where Dr Hemanta Chakraborty lived. The doctor was a very shrewd man. He made a calculated effort to maintain good relations with the local Muslims. Dr Hem attended not only to people but also to cows, buffaloes and poultry—in short, he was a master in treating all living beings. He knew that people were afflicted by only two kinds of diseases. One of which was secret and the other was visible. He treated secret diseases secretly and visible diseases visibly. However, in comparison to visible ailments, like fever, stomach-ache, cough and so on, he was more adept at treating secret ailments. The secret ailments of men were gonorrhea, syphilis, nocturnal emission, impotence, premature ejaculation, and so on. The secret ailments of women were leucorrhoea, urinary tract infection, frigidity and menstrual complaints. For this last category of ailments, he was— at least in this locality—seen as a reliable and good practitioner. If he was paid well, he worked silently and freed people from their ailments. In those days, this could not be done free of cost, like it is in government hospitals today. There was no public consciousness either about it. Birth control pills or condoms like Nirodh were not so easily available back then. And so, by curing a female patient, a doctor could easily buy five or ten kathas of land. Of course, that was if the patient was of that stature.

As he was returning home after attending to someone like that, who had been suffering from a secret disease, the beam of his torch fell on a boy lying like an unclaimed corpse on a bench on the station platform. He felt a strange stirring in his mind. Oh dear! Who knows whether it wasn't seeing such people that the poet Madhab had composed the song, '*Ekhon manob jomin roilo potito, aabaad korle pholto sona.* Now man lies fallen on the ground, if cultivated a harvest of gold would abound.'

Realising that the possibility of harvesting gold lay before him, he stepped towards the uncultivated human ground.

'*Aeyi khoka*, where do you live? Why are you lying here?'

Rubbing his eyes, Jibon said, 'I'm going to Calcutta. When will the train for Calcutta come?'

'You want to go to Calcutta? Why, my boy? Why are you lying here? Where do you live? Your father beats you, does he? Have you run away from home?' Dr Hem shot off a volley of questions. But Jibon could not answer even a single one. He didn't get a chance. He just stared blankly at the questioner's face.

Now Dr Hem asked, 'Are you a refugee?'

Jibon nodded his head.

Nothing more needed to be said. Dr Hem gathered everything from the nod of the head. He understood what the boy's ailment was and why he was lying there. What kind of doctor was he if he couldn't look at a man's face and recognise his ailment! He asked, 'Have you eaten?'

Jibon shook us head. 'I haven't eaten anything.'

'Do you want to eat rice? Come with me to my house, I'll give you rice.'

Rice! Rice was an incredible word. Jibon's chest heaved, and his eyes brimmed with tears. He could no longer remember when, how many ages ago, he had eaten rice. How long ago was it that his mother had cooked rice on a fire using twigs and leaves! His brothers and sisters would blow on the hot rice and wolf it down. Jibon had once scalded his tongue putting the hot rice in his mouth. After his father's stomach-ache worsened, rice was never cooked at home again. They had survived on a gruel of corn milo and the grain of some grass, full of grit and dust, probably poultry feed, for months on end. For the last seven or eight days, that too had come to an end.

After coming to Khola, Garib Das's brothers had initially helped him a bit. They had given him some ten or twelve rupees to get going and to buy hogla and thread. Now they had stopped helping them. It was said—who lays wood on a corpse every day, and who gives food to a beggar every day! Their economic condition too was not at all sound. How could they help? That's why Jibon had run away from home; he could not bear to starve any longer.

'Will you come to my house?'

Jibon was a refugee boy. Dr Hem was an educated man. From the single word 'refugee', he had seen both the boy's past and present, and he knew the word with which refugee boys and grown men could be felled. He let loose that deadly arrow. 'You can come to my house and stay as long as you like. You can eat rice twice a day. I have my own pond, I have cows. You'll get fish as well as milk ...'

Jibon stood up at once. Putting an end to any more talk, the doctor entrusted his heavy bag to Jibon. 'Be careful, see that you don't drop it. He walked ahead, flashing his torch, Jibon followed him silently. As one went past the shops and houses near the station, one could see a refugee camp on the right side of the rail track. People were asleep in all the huts now. Going past the settlement, there was a path cutting through the fields that lay on the left side. Herds of cows tramped along that, bullock-carts too. During the rainy season, there were knee-deep puddles and slime there. The puddles had dried up now and become fine as powder under the wheels of vehicles and hooves of cows. As soon as one set foot on the earth, dust rose to one's knees.

One had to walk along this path for twenty minutes to reach Dr Hem's house. The doors of the house were made of strong wood, the walls were of earth and the roof was tiled. Considering the locality, this signified affluence.

As they stepped down from the road to the muddy path, it occurred to Dr Hem that before entering the house, some practical information regarding the boy needed to be ascertained. Of which the most important was caste and clan. Although he was an honest man, Dr Hem was a Brahmin. He belonged to the highest caste. Whatever he did outside, he had to do for professional reasons. But that did not mean that the same could be practised within the house. That would not be correct, either. It was said that one should be a teacher in one's behaviour and a scholar in one's judgment. When he was born into the Brahmin caste, Dr Hem had to conduct himself accordingly, in his behaviour as well as judgement. After the country had been partitioned, almost nothing of caste norms remained. Cobblers, sweepers, Muslims and Chandals all mingled freely, they sat in the same shop and drank tea from the same cup.

This business of tea, Dr Hem reflected, was a cunning ruse by the British to destroy caste. One had heard that apparently cowhide was ground and mixed in it. That's why he never drank tea. As far as possible, he was careful, and especially within the house, he maintained the norms of untouchability and pollution. After all, a Brahmin could not fall into the ways of the *mleccha*.

Nilkantha Gosai, who used to beg in Calcutta, had said, 'We are descendants of the world famous sage, Namas. We are Nama by caste and belong to the Kashyap clan.' Jibon remembered that. So when Hem Chakraborty asked him, '*Aeyi khoka*, what's your caste?', he promptly replied, 'Nama by caste, and of the Kashyap clan.'

Dr Hem knew in advance what Jibon would say. It had to be either Nama or Pode—the people in the refugee camps belonged only to these castes—yet he had asked because he needed to begin somewhere so that he could come to the main point. As Jibon could not see Dr Hem's face, he thought that perhaps he hadn't heard him. So he said, more loudly this time, 'My father told me we are high-caste.'

'That's all right,' Dr Hem said. He shone his torch on the path ahead. He then continued, 'I am a doctor. I treat whoever is sick. I don't believe in caste and all that. There are only two castes really: women and men. But there are other people at home. They believe in caste. Besides, there's also God's shrine at home. That's why I say, as long as you're there, be a bit careful. Don't touch or put your hand on anything. You're just a boy, you don't know how to conduct yourself if you're staying in a Brahmin household. So let me explain. Stay as long as you like. Eat happily. That's perfectly fine. But just remain quietly in one corner. What do you say?'

'You have lots of rice at home, don't you?'

'Why do you ask me that, boy?'

'Didn't you say you'd give me rice every day?'

Smiling wryly, Dr Hem replied, 'Does anyone feed another just like that? Do you know what the price of rice is? And would anyone eat at another person's house for month after month just like that? Tell me? If you were to eat and just sit around, you'd get arthritis in your joints! So let me tell you what you will be doing. You stay like a boy in my house. There are a few cows, you'll give them hay and water. Take them out to graze. Won't you be able to do that? If you can't do that, there's nothing to be done, you can go away. And if you can do it, stay as long as you wish and eat. Unlike before, people don't like to work nowadays. That's why they starve to death. The one who can work hard never goes hungry. Tell me, how old am I? I'm fifty-two, but I still work eighteen hours a day. That's why I'm in good health. Didn't you ask whether there's lots of rice at home? All that's the fruit of my hard work.'

Jibon was silent. Dr Hem interpreted that to mean he would stay. His feet had now been shackled. These were indeed times when people were assailed by hunger. The entrancing magic of the 'vashikaran mantra'—with which anyone could be brought under control—had come to be attached to the word 'rice'. Whoever it was uttered to had no option but to bow down.

⌘

They reached Dr Hem's house and entered the courtyard. The door was locked from inside. But there was light at a window. Dr Hem stood in front of the door and called out loudly, 'Gayatri's Ma, where are you? Have you fallen asleep? Wake up! Open the door!'

Opening the door, a middle-aged woman stepped out into the courtyard with a lamp in hand. She did not have a blouse on, but there was a gold necklace around her neck. The woman yawned and was astonished to see Jibon through her sleepy eyes. She asked, 'Who's this?'

'I brought him along.'

'Where did you find him? Where's his home?'

'How would he have a home, he stays in the camp.'

'I hope he lasts. He's too small. It would have been good if he was a bit bigger, like the earlier one.'

'Where will I get a bigger one? Make do with this one, we'll see about that later …'

The woman kept the lamp in the courtyard and went back inside. She brought a gamchha and a pitcher and gave knew to Hem Chakraborty. She said, 'Wash up and come in quickly.' Taking them, Dr Hem said to his wife, 'Give the lamp to him—oh, don't touch—let it be there, he'll pick it up. Show him his place in the cowshed. Where the sacks of cow-dung are kept. Let him move the sacks and make some place to sleep. What with all the cow thefts happening everywhere these days, at least there'll be someone to keep watch.'

Mrs Hem was trying to ask something, but even before she could finish, surmising her intent by looking at her face, Hem Chakraborty said in a muted tone, 'Nama.'

Dr Hem's house consisted of a very large room with a tiled roof. It had a verandah all along the entrance. In front of the room, on the left side of the courtyard, was the kitchen. And along the right side of the courtyard was a long cowshed. To the right of the entrance to the compound from the public path outside was a large fishpond. Dr Hem went to the pond to wash his hands and feet. Mrs Hem took Jibon along to show him the cowshed. 'Take the lamp and go and sit there.' The cowshed was a large one. Dr Hem had twelve cows in all, including the calves. At the rear of the cowshed was the dung pile. Some of the dung was used in the form of dung cakes, for fuel, and the rest was used as manure on the land. Dr Hem had seven bighas of paddy land and a four-kattha fishpond. He employed workers to farm the land. After all the disbursements, the rice from the field saw them through the whole year.

As Jibon picked up the lamp from the ground and made his way to the cowshed, he began to feel dejected. Just a little while ago he had begun to feel happy, thinking he would like it here, but that had vanished in a trice. He felt as if someone had suddenly pushed him out of the world he had been familiar with all his life, into an extraordinary, unknown situation, regarding which he had no choice. And if he did accept that, it would severely wound his inner being. Even if the people among whom his childhood was spent were not all of the same caste or religion or community, they were not so orthodox in matters of pollution, or so full of hate for the low-castes. They had never considered him to be so inferior as to make him sleep in a cowshed that stank of dung. But these people did. Who were they? Why were they so stone-hearted? Were they not people like him? If not, what kind of people were they?

In the two camps where Jibon's short life had been spent, there wasn't a single Brahmin, Kayastha or Baidya. During marriage and funeral ceremonies, one or two Brahmins used to come, who knew where they came from. They could not flaunt their caste pride so brazenly before the people in the camp. Whether deliberately or otherwise, they kept themselves under check, to some extent. But these people, finding a helpless boy all alone—their inhuman conduct was something that could never be forgotten.

Hem babu's wife put down an enamel plate in front of Jibon with some rice and some *chorchori* made of potatoes, pumpkin and drumstick, and said, 'After you finish eating, wash the plate in the pond and put it in that corner. Take care of it. Tomorrow I'll give you rice again on the same plate. And take a sack from there, spread it out and lie down. Remember to put the lamp out.' She then left.

The cowshed was full of mosquitoes. And the smell of cowdung was suffocating. Jibon lay on the sack but could not sleep. Yet, however unbearable the night was, it had to end. In time, night turned to dawn. The mellifluous refrain of the azaan came wafting from the Muslim quarter. Jibon could not understand anything of the Arabic language it was in. Yet, who knows why, he felt cheerful. After that, he dozed off.

15

Gobor-Ganga

The eastern sky had just begun to light up. The sun had not yet risen. Mrs Hem woke up. She entered the cowshed, and bringing down the cowherd's staff kept between the bamboo rafters, she prodded Jibon with it and woke him up. 'Hey, wake up, get up now! Take all the cow-dung in the shed and put it into the dung-pile. Clean the cowshed thoroughly with the broom.' By the time Jibon finished these tasks, the sun had risen. Mrs Hem milked the lactating cows and issued the third instruction. 'Take the cows to graze. But be careful! See that the cows don't enter anyone's field. The fields nearby belong to miyas. They're a terrible lot. If a cow touches their crop, they'll kill the poor thing. Come for a while in the afternoon to quickly eat your lunch.' After that, she asked Jibon to hold out his gamchha, into which she poured some muri from high up. 'Eat this when you're in the field.'

Just across the public path in front of Dr Hem's house was a vast open field. To the left of the field was the village of Chakla. Javed, Khaled, Hamid and Habibur lived in the village, and they too brought cows to graze in the field. The cows did not belong to them. They took cows from other households to graze, for which they got some rice and a bit of money. When he went out with the cows, Jibon mingled with them. All of them together tended to everyone's cows, and they played haddu-du and dariya-bandha. They quarrelled and fought too. Who was it that had said once— 'Muslims are terrible people! They catch Hindus and slit their throats. Burn down their houses!' He did not believe all that talk now. His heart did not tremble any more at the mention of the names Muslim, miya or *nede*. He could not reconcile all that talk and hearsay with his present practical experience. He could not spot any difference between his own father, Garib Das and Javed's father, Anwar Mollah.

There was Javed's father. A devout Muslim who said his namaz five times a day. His back was bent and his body hunched forward when he walked. The shrunken skin over his unfed belly formed a sunken cavity. He was always bare-bodied. No oil in his hair, no smile on his face. He was a very ordinary man, ravaged by poverty. This Muslim man did not conform to any monstrous, imaginary notion of gore and terror. And it did not seem at all fitting if such conformity was forcibly imposed. Like Jibon's father, Javed's father too looked too old for his age. How could a sad and suffering man like him be an enemy of another suffering man? Why would he destroy his people and property? Or slit his throat? Why would he do that? What would he achieve by doing that? False, false, it was all lies, made-up stories! Hamid's sister, Zuleikha, why, she smiled just like Kusum! Chattered all the time, jutted out her lip with hurt pride, melted like wax in affection. Just the other day, on the occasion of Eid, Zuleikha had brought a bowl of siwain, covered with a banana leaf, for Jibon. So sweetly she had said, 'Eat it—but don't tell the Brahmin doctor! Or else, he'll thrash you.'

The addiction to food was the greatest addiction. All other addictions were like midgets before the addiction to food. Before Jibon knew it, two or three months had passed by. In this while, Jibon had been thrashed by Mrs Hem a few times. Once it was for the crime of wetting his bed in his sleep. Bed meant the jute sack, through which the piss had percolated and wet the dung cakes underneath. And once when, making the mistake of forgetting his caste identity, he had pinched Gayatri's cheek. Gayatri, the daughter of the Brahmin, who, although only eight- or nine-years-old, was full of caste pride. Gayatri was fair-complexioned. Her face was beautiful, her eyes too. Her hair would be tied in two plaits on two sides. She still bathed naked in the pond. She had finished bathing and had climbed up to the bank of the pond. Drops of water ran down her back from her wet hair. The water ran down her back, then lower, all the way to her feet. Seeing her chubby cheeks and doll-like face, who knows why, Jibon had felt a great desire to fondle her cheek, and he forgot Dr Hem's cautionary advice.

The girl had screamed as soon as her cheek was touched. 'Ma, come and see! Come quickly! The Chandal touched me!' Her scream was not one of affection, but one that could deceive anyone—as if Jibon had raped her. But Jibon committed the same folly again—he touched her cheek once again. But this time with a loud thwack. The mark of Jibon's five fingers was imprinted on Gayatri's soft, plump, fair-complexioned cheek. 'You bitch of a girl, why do you call me "Chandal" all the time? Don't I have a name? Can't you call me by my name?'

Mrs Hem was frying fish. Fish from their own pond. Hearing her daughter wailing, she rushed out of the kitchen. Aiming the metal spatula in her hand at Jibon—who had just returned to eat, leaving the cows to graze—she flung it in his direction. Perfect aim, like a knife thrown in a circus. It hit Jibon on his forehead. It cut his forehead and blood streamed down and covered his right eye. 'You have the gall, you dared to touch my daughter ... I'll beat you to death!'

'Why does she abuse me?'

'I'll thrash you again if you make up stories. Didn't you hear what I just said? If a Chandal is not to be called Chandal, then should he be called Brahmin? Just because you're being allowed to stay and eat here, don't think you can climb on our heads and dance! I'm warning you!'

Jibon had heard the Ramayan and Mahabharat being narrated. He knew the name of Guhak Chandal. He had heard the tale of Harishchandra, too, who had lost his kingdom and become a Chandal. Everyone regarded Chandals as untouchable. They lived in cremation grounds and burnt dead bodies. Neither Jibon's father, nor any of the others he knew, performed that task. They lived in the refugee camp and made mats or worked as labourers for a living. So how were they Chandal? He erupted in fierce protest—'We are not Chandal, we are Nama, descendants of Kashyap Muni!'

Dr Hem was not at home then. He returned after about an hour. Seeing the cut on Jibon's forehead, he did not think it was necessary to punish him. He'd had enough already. He said to his wife, 'Why do you throw spatulas and things like that in this fashion? Please don't do that! It just missed his eye …'

'So what? Can one control oneself when one's furious?'

'Control yourself! Be calm! Tell me, what would have happened if he lost an eye? Someone or the other would have taken him to the police station. The police would have come and taken you away.'

After a pause, he continued, 'I know, one can't help getting angry at the behaviour of these creatures. So if you're angry with him, hit him a few times on his back with the cowherd's staff. As they say, *shaap o morlo lathi bhanglo na* … the snake will be killed and the stick won't break either! Just don't throw whatever's in your hand!'

Having pacified his wife, he consoled Jibon. 'Suppose your Ma had hit you, what would you have done then? Gayatri's Ma is like your Ma. Even if she did hit you a bit—after all she didn't throw the spatula to hit you, she threw it just to frighten you. It hit you by accident. Don't brood about that. I'll give you a medicine that will heal the cut in two days.'

Jibon cried, not from the pain of the injury but from the anguish of the abuse. 'Why does Gayatri abuse me all the time?'

'Gayatri abuses you! What are you saying, boy? As if she's like that!'

'She calls me Chandal.'

Dr Hem laughed. 'Oh! Say that! So if she called you Chandal, what of that? Did that make a scar on your body? Let her say it as much as she wants, you mustn't get angry. And that puts an end to it. Look at me—if anyone calls me doctor or Brahmin, do I get angry?'

'But I am Nama ...'

'Yes, my dear, you are Nama. No one's told you and so you don't know that Namas are Chandals.' He then explained the matter to Jibon: 'When ice melts it becomes water, and again when water freezes it becomes ice. It's like that. You shouldn't get angry about that. Come, let me apply the medicine on your forehead.'

Jibon could not stay angry for long. Of what use was anger? All he could do was to give up the job and go away. But where would he go? He would be stalked by hunger wherever he went. When he was hungry, his body trembled like a banana leaf. His ears and head began to ring. He became dizzy. He did not feel like talking, working or playing. Out of fear of hunger, Jibon could not run away. It was as if hunger had tethered him, like a cow, to an inevitable compromise.

Man cannot survive without food. Jibon wanted to live. He had to survive and grow bigger. If he did not live and grow up, he would not be able to save his parents, brothers and sister. It was vitally important for him to survive in order to save everyone else.

Jibon had eaten the siwain Zuleikha gave him the other day because he was hungry. An ancestor of his had once become an outcaste for consuming the food and water offered by a Muslim. Jibon had closely observed himself before and after he ate the siwain. No, there was no change. Neither did he think of himself as impure or unholy. Rather, it was just the opposite. After eating something so tasty, made of milk, ghee, cashew nuts and raisins, his mind and body felt completely at peace. He felt content and strong. Long ago his father had told him, 'If someone gives you even stale rice to eat with love and affection, you should know that it's a million times better than the choicest food given heartlessly.'

And what if someone gave him the choicest food with love? The one who brought this choicest food was not a Princess Sujata of Buddhist lore, but a famished little girl of rural Bengal. She had given a share of her own assigned food to one whom the mullahs and maulvis labelled 'kaffir', someone who even the great Allah had no love for.

Jibon felt an unforgiving rage now towards all those liars who said that one lost one's caste if one ate or drank from Muslims. His caste had not vanished anywhere! He was still exactly the same as he used to be. If eating food destroyed caste, then by eating food in Hem Chakraborty's household for so long, his own caste should have been wiped out and he should have become a Brahmin! Like them, he too should have become hateful, abusive and oppressive towards others, for no reason.

No, Jibon could not become like these people, or those people, or like anyone else. Jibon remained the same ordinary Jibon. But an adult-like conviction now took root in little Jibon's mind. If everyone was simply human and nothing else, then he could never harbour the desire to harm anyone.

Khaled's grandmother also went around with the herd of cows, scooping cowpats into a basket. She also worked in the paddy fields, together with the womenfolk of Chakla, uprooting the stubble. That enabled her to cook the day's meal at home. She made fuel-cakes with the dung she gathered. She went to Ghutiari Sharif to sell that. One paisa for a cake and a rupee for a hundred. Ten dung-cakes free if a rupee's worth was purchased.

Khaled's grandmother always laughed at and made jokes about Jibon. 'Hey, boy, just grow up and become a young man. Once you learn to earn a living, I'll make you a son-in-law of our village! I'll marry you off to Zuleikha!' Hearing that, Zuleikha would curse her, 'You don't have to marry me off, you lustful hag! Why don't you marry him yourself?'

The old woman retorted, 'Who-o-re! You're running around him all the time and when I talk of marriage, you curse me! Ask your beau whether he wants to marry me! If he says, tomorrow, I'll say, why not today! At least I'll get someone to carry my sacks of dung!'

All this was in jest. These people loved such jest, and despite deprivation and penury, they were full of life. They were simple and straightforward folk. They were poor but they were upright. They gathered their food through hard toil. Why would they slit the throat of another person like them? What would be gained by doing that? Jibon could not fathom the complex calculation that lay beneath this vilification. And as much as he failed to comprehend this, so did his child's mind become filled with melancholy. He kept thinking—caste, religion, community—through all these, a balloon of poisonous vapours of mutual hatred had been inflated. If this balloon burst and ceased to exist, no one would come to harm. But instead, that very thing had been raised to an exalted status through various kinds of propaganda. Those who did such things were all scoundrels, racketeers, monstrous enemies of human society. They were the ones who were responsible for all the bickering, fighting, violence, destruction and bloodshed. If one was so keen to slit people's throats—slitting the throats of these scoundrels wouldn't be a crime at all!

Jibon reflected that Khaled and he were not each other's enemies. But when one stayed together and played together, sometimes, on some issue, there was bad blood, and they quarrelled and sometimes even fought. Why, just the other day, while playing haddu-du, there had been such a quarrel, and even fisticuffs—it could also happen again someday. But suppose Khaled, Javed and the others went back to the Muslim hamlet and reported, 'A Hindu beat me up!', and if someone in the village incited everyone, 'Come on, we'll thrash ten Hindus to avenge this!'—that would be terribly wrong! And if I incite Hindus by saying the same thing, that too would be terribly wrong.

A group of people was engaged in such wrongdoing. They were not ordinary people but scoundrels of the highest order. They did this in order to fulfill their personal interests and designs. Which spread like a secret virus among ignorant, unaware, foolish, unthinking folk. Jibon hadn't encountered many Muslims in his short life. There was his father's friend Mamud chacha, and now a few people from this village of Chakla where Dr Hem lived. But he hadn't been able to discern any special fault in them, which was not to be found in others. But they did have one quality, a special quality—they did not despise him like Dr Hem did.

One evening, it was very late when Jibon returned with the cows. He was normally never so late, he always returned when it was still daylight. Returning well before dusk, he would tie the cows to their posts, prepare the fodder and feed them. Cutting hay for so many cows took a long time. After that, he had to fetch water from the pond and pour it into the water-trough. Only then would he be done for the day. That day, a colourful *bokatta* kite had floated down to the grazing field. Jibon's heart danced in joy seeing the kite. He had never been able to buy a kite, and so he had never flown one. Luck had finally provided him the opportunity today. Flying the kite to his heart's delight, before he knew it the sun had set and it had turned dark. By the time he returned to the house, night had fallen. Night meant darkness.

Arriving at the house in darkness, Jibon saw that Amjad Ali, Nurul Huq and Rahmat Mollah were sitting in the verandah on the western side of Dr Hem's south-facing house. They were all about thirty-five or thirty-six years of age. They were all respectable and affluent people of Chakla village. Each of them owned forty or fifty bighas of paddy land. Nurul Huq had a small talking-box. It was called a 'radio'. No one else owned one in the ten or twelve villages nearby. Nurul Huq always carried that box with him. The box spoke, sang, narrated stories and jatras, poetic songs and so many more things! Whether or not it would rain, whether a cyclone was imminent, what fertilizer should be used for which crop to give a good yield—this talking-box provided all such information.

The verandah they were sitting in faced the metalled road that began at Kudali, where the path from the rail track led, and meandered to the locality of Naranpur in the middle of Chakla village. But no one walking on that road could see anything. The men were also speaking in muted tones, with diffidence, which was quite unusual. As if they were assailed by some sense of guilt for concealing their presence. There was an expression, *'Jaar golay dhan taar kothay taan*. The one who has paddy in his granary speaks with a rustic accent'. They had paddy in their granaries and also spoke in a rustic accent. People everywhere, on the streets, in the marketplaces and in the village council knew about that accent. But that voice was absent today.

Dr Hem Chakraborty came to meet them. Those who at one time used to consider it a sin if a Muslim's shadow fell upon them, who hatefully prohibited a Namasudra boy from entering the verandah of the house—it was one of them who had invited the beaf-eating Muslims! How low wouldn't he stoop for a manoeuvre! His voice was the embodiment of utmost humility. As if it was his compassion that had melted to form the very rivers Ganga and Jamuna. 'How fortunate I am today! I never even dreamt that you would actually grace my hovel with the dust of your feet! When Rahmat dada told me in the bazaar the other day that he would come to my house, I thought he was joking. And so I asked you again this morning whether you were coming. It was only then that I realised that you would really come to the house of a poor man like me. I don't have words to express my ... Let that be! It's almost ready, just a few more minutes.'

The whole house was filled with the aroma of boiling milk. Payesh was being made in the kitchen now. To that had been added cardamom, cloves, raisins, bay-leaf, cane jaggery and various other things. Which was why there was a wonderful aroma. The cow that

Dr Hem had purchased for a thousand rupees had calved a few days ago. The payesh was being prepared with the cow's milk. Rahmat Mollah had accompanied Dr Hem to Naranpur and bargained to get him the cow cheap. How could one repay the debt of that favour! Following what was customary in such matters, Dr Hem had said to Rahmat Mollah after concluding the purchase, 'What can I say after all the trouble you went to for me. I can never forget this favour. Come to my house when the cow calves. I'll treat you to payesh made with its milk.'

But that was some months ago. Dr Hem had long forgotten about it. How long could one remember who had helped him buy a cow, and what he had told him amidst all the daily hassles and commotions? But Rahmat Mollah hadn't forgotten about it. One day, he said, 'So doctor, the cow calved long back. Where's the payesh you promised?'

'Which payesh?'

'Which you said you'd treat me to?'

'Really! Will you eat from our hands?'

'If it's nothing impure, then where's it forbidden to eat that? Payesh is made with cow's milk. If you can have it, why can't I?'

'Then, let it be tomorrow—no, not tomorrow, I have to go to Kudali tomorrow. Come to my house the day after tomorrow. You'll come, won't you?'

'I told you I'll come. I'll come, but only after evening. I'll bring two friends with me.'

'Do bring them along. Why only two, bring ten! I live in the village next to yours. In times of danger, it's you folk who are our strength and hope. Who do we have as our own in this land other than you! You visit us, we visit you. Without such mingling—what kind of neighbours would we be!'

That's why they had come. They were invited guests. In the Hindu scriptures, it is said that a guest is like God himself. However, unlike normal, ordinary guests, Rahmat Mollah and his friends were unable to conduct themselves freely. As if there was some underlying discomfort. Perhaps the age-old customs were knocking at their mind's door. And hence they were a bit ill at ease, somewhat embarrassed. If anyone from Chakla village saw them eating at a non-Muslim's house, and a Hindu at that, who knows what they would report back in their neighbourhood. Who was to know whether they were partaking of payesh made of milk or turtle stew? Crabs, turtles and suchlike were impure foods under Islamic norms.

After a while, Dr Hem Chakraborty's wife ladled the payesh into three large bell-metal plates. With suppressed annoyance in her voice, she called out to her husband, 'Go and give them the plates.' The doctor brought the plates from the kitchen, crossed the courtyard and placed them before the guests on the side verandah. 'Here, please start eating.' Mrs Hem was arthritic. If she had gone herself to give the payesh and somehow touched the *mleccha* bodies, it would be horrible to have to go and take a bath at this time of night. And so, Hem Chakraborty decided that his taking the plates to the guests would be the wise thing to do.

Rahmat Mollah and his friends had come with an open mind. They were eating payesh with an open mind. Whatever may have been their hesitation or customs, all those were entirely their own social and religious matters—they had kept all that afar. In order to break the unshakeable rules of orthodoxy, one side or the other had to make the first move. So they had come. They had come under the cover of darkness today, hiding their faces like thieves. Tomorrow, they would come in the light of day with their chests puffed up in pride, like brave souls.

After they had eaten the payesh with great relish, licking the plates clean, they left. Dr Hem was pleased too. Among the refugees from East Bengal who lived along the rail tracks in Ghutiari Sharif, a few had by now become big guns in the Hindu Mahasabha. They were always engaged in inciteful talk. As a result, there was a kind of suppressed acrimony between the two communities, which could explode at any time. If riots ever broke out between the two sides, this payesh would protect Dr Hem from Muslim rage. That was his belief. But the doctor's wife was not so shrewd. She could not stomach the fact that those who had made her flee from her country, that race of beef-eating *nedes*, would come and sit in the verandah of their house and eat. They sat in the verandah today, tomorrow they would enter the kitchen! What would remain of their caste then? If one had to do this, why did one leave one's country at all?

After the guests had left, Dr Hem called Jibon. 'Hey boy, wear your gamchha and come here. First, take those plates to the pond. Wash them properly, scrubbing them with ash.' When Jibon had done that, Dr Hem said, 'You're back? Now wash the floor-mat and hang it to dry on the roof of the cowshed.' When Jibon had done that, Dr Hem said, 'Now get a bucket of water mixed with dung, and sprinkle it all over the verandah floor.'

After all the tasks had been completed according to Dr Hem's instructions, Mrs Hem ordered Jibon to fetch another bucket of dung-water and sprinkle it all over the courtyard. Or else, she said, she wouldn't be able to cross it to enter the house. She said that with such a tone of revulsion that one would imagine a mountain of excreta had been spread out on the courtyard, which was impossible to cross but for the life-saving dung-water. But Jibon's little eyes could not spot any dirt on the smoothly plastered floor of the courtyard that had been swept earlier in the day. The kitchen was across the courtyard. Dr Hem's wife stood at the kitchen door with a lamp in her hand. She could easily cross the courtyard space in the middle if she wished to, and enter the main room of the house. So what was preventing her from doing that?

Dr Hem knew what prevented her. A group of beef-eating *mlechhas* had walked through the courtyard, which had therefore lost its purity through their touch. After all, she was the daughter of an orthodox Brahmin; she could not tolerate any deviation from customs. Dr Hem could not abide by all that as strictly; he mingled with people of all castes. He said God wasn't blind, he saw everything. God knew why Dr Hem was compelled to commit this sin. God in all his compassion would surely forgive him for that.

He said, 'Bring it, boy. Get another bucket of dung-water. Sprinkle it the way Ma asks you to.'

While he was sprinkling dung-water over the courtyard as instructed, he could hear them. Mrs Hem's angry and grumbling voice: 'I'm telling you, this was the first time and let it be the last time! Make sure those outcastes never enter this house ever again! If you want to mix with them, do that outside. If you want to feed them, feed them outside. We left our country because of miyas. And now they enter this house! This Brajabala will never tolerate such an abomination! Don't forget that there's a shrine of Lakshmi now in the house. Oh, what a bother! Sprinkle the gobor-Ganga all over and purify the house now! I'll be cringing the next few days—who knows whether I'll be able to eat anything—who knows what all they eat? As they walked through the courtyard, the stench of their body odour hit my nose—*owack*!' Mrs Hem made a retching sound.

Observing her becoming increasingly agitated, Dr Hem cautioned his wife, 'Come on, lower your voice, the road's right in front. People going by will hear you.' Then, lowering his own voice, he said, 'Tell me, how was I to know? Did I know beforehand that this would happen? I had just said in the course of conversation that I'd treat him to payesh. That was long ago, when the cow was purchased. Who knew they would remember and demand it! Let it be, whatever had to happen has happened. Don't be agitated any more. I won't make such a mistake ever again.'

Could one be calmed just by someone's saying 'don't be agitated'? Mrs Hem had the dirt of the miyas washed by a Nama. But now she was angry, wondering who she would get the dirt of the Nama washed by! Those people were beef-eaters, while this one was a pig-eater. Winter was still in the air. Although one didn't shiver, nevertheless one felt a bit cold. Despite that, Mrs Hem vented some unknown anger on Jibon. 'Go, wash the dung-bucket and then immerse yourself in the pond. I'll wait until you're done!'

Jibon spent entire days with Hamid, Javed and Khaled. He never took a bath after that. He only bathed in the afternoon, just like everyone else. So why now, today, and at this time? Was that for purification or just to wash down the rage inside her? Jibon did not have the courage to ask Mrs Hem about that. He did not feel like provoking her either, by disobeying her. He was terribly hungry. This was not the time for doing anything rash. He walked towards the pond with the bucket and broom. He had to immerse himself once in the pond and then scrub himself with clay using a handful of straw. But just as he reached the bank and was about to enter the water, his feet were rooted to the ground. He saw that three people were standing on the path in front of the house. They seemed to have turned to stone. They were the same people, Rahmat Mollah, Nurul Huq and Amjad Sheikh. Nurul Huq had forgotten his radio on a shelf in a dark corner of the side verandah. If it had been on, they would have been aware. But it had been turned off, so that they could enter the house silently. So, no one remembered about it. Now, returning to get it back, they could not re-enter the house. Observing the whole rigmarole with the bucket, broom and dung-water, and hearing Mrs Hem's loud voice, they stood, frozen, near the entrance.

16

Anger and Animosity

Jibon had heard many accounts of riots from various people. He did not know what those who started riots looked like. He had seen butchers. But he did not know about the cruelty that lay beneath the calm demeanour of the butcher. The fire of humiliation, hatred and anger that shone in the expressionless eyes of the three men turned to stone, was full of the birth pangs of innumerable Noakhalis, all waiting to be perpetrated by many cruel butchers. For some reason, Jibon was sure another terrible riot was imminent. The bosoms of thousands of mothers would become bereft. Many pyres would blaze with flames. There would be lots of bloodshed, lots of destruction and a great flood of tears. This dark night, this worthless, injudicious night, had planted the seeds of riots in the secret recesses of men's minds. Such seeds were being planted in various places, in various people, in various ways. It would not end, and there was no safeguard against that, unless awakened collective conscience stood up and declared: Stop! Enough! No more! Put an end to it now! Or else we shall set upon you and stop you! We will counter the poison fruits of hate!

Darkness was a curse. The ignorance bred by absence of good education made the darkness inside the mind even denser and proximate. It created a solid wall that defied sound judgement. It hindered healthy and free thought. It didn't permit one to recognise or realise who was one's own and who wasn't, who was an enemy and who a friend, who should be strangled and who embraced. In the explosion that would follow after this dark night of unalloyed hatred, would Javed, Khaled or Hamid recognise his correct identity? Was that possible? Or would it be that after tonight's inhuman conclusion, his small role too would be evaluated with typical blind hatred? Which happened in every riot. Which was a riot's own religion!

Riots were imminent. Some would have weapons in their hands, while some would be unarmed. But no one would be impartial. That wasn't possible. Whether someone was nearby or faraway— everyone would become involved in the riot, either physically or mentally. Someone would set fire, someone would burn to death, someone's skin would be scorched, some would only feel mild heat—but no one would be spared. No one could be safe or impartial.

Impartiality was actually a role that aided the attackers. Would Jibon be able to continue playing that role without letup? He thought: when there were riots, a mountain of corpses would grow and a river of blood would flow, but which side would he be on? Whom would he kill? Whose houses would he burn down? Which bosoms would he lay bereft and whose mothers would he cause to grieve?

Jibon had been born in a Namasudra household. The Namasudras were earlier called Chandals. True, that name was no longer used in government documents now, but that did not mean that Hindu society had restored to them the social dignity they were entitled to. Even now, high-caste Hindus considered them to be untouchable and polluted. The doors of temples, monasteries and other religious sites were closed to them even today. And they were supposedly Hindu! The pillars of the Hindu religion were high-caste folk like Hem Chakraborty. In their eyes, there was no difference between Namas and Muslims. The Namas were like the fabled Ghatotkach, son of the ogress Hidimbi, who arrived at the battlefield of Kurukshetra to fight on the side of the Pandavs against the Kauravs. After he was killed by the divine weapon hurled by Karn, the Pandavs rejoiced because that fearsome weapon could no longer be used against their great archer Arjun. Bhim had planted his seed in Hidimbi's womb, but he had not been a father to Ghatotkach. In the same way, the Hindu religion had not been a father to the Namas. It would never be. So what would Jibon gain by supporting it? If the Hindu faith ever disappeared or was destroyed or wiped out, what would Jibon—the son of an untouchable—lose?

And what about Javed and Khaled, who were Muslim? On religious considerations, Jibon was, after all, of the same ilk as Dr Hem: a Hindu kaffir. Following the directives of the Holy Koran, a mountain of hatred for the alien race of kaffirs lay piled in the storehouse of the mullahs and maulvis. They would spread that hatred in the minds and hearts of their fellow-Muslims. Reflected in the mirror of religion, they would then identify the person named Jibon as an enemy. And if his identity was that of an enemy, he could not be forgiven.

Who would he consider his friend now, and which side would he stand on? Jibon was unable to figure that out. He did not know what would be correct. He did not want to be on the side of those who were attacked. He would definitely side with those who did the attacking. But who would he pounce upon, and who would be by his side? Whose blood would he bathe in? That was very complex arithmetic. He could not figure out the additions and subtractions, the multiplications and divisions of this arithmetic. A child's mind could be swayed by emotion, he could be moved to offer his own life. But emotion could not tell him how to accurately calculate gain or loss and set out on a particular path. Children did not have such shrewd minds. Because of that, they were prone to being used by shrewd people. They were directed from one wrongdoing to another.

Overcome with emotion, Jibon now thought: it would be fantastic if I and Mongla, Fatik, Maran, Javed, Khaled and Hamid, if all of us together could declare an all-out war against those who create discord among people, and pluck all of them out like lice or bugs and crush them. The world around us will then become beautiful, and fit for human habitation.

But all that was beautiful and fit would not come about so quickly. There was a need for more and more blows. Through the blows, the limits of what people could put up with would be breached. The harsh wall of cowardice going by the name of neutrality or impartiality would come crumbling down. Men would then stand up and declare war against hatred. The chapter of peace would follow the chapter of war. Peace: fulsome, undisturbed, infinite and eternal.

Finally, the inevitable happened. Without that, it would not have been possible for anything else to happen. The eternal beggar for food overcame his enchantment with hot rice and fish curry, and gave up his comfortable cowherd's job. Jibon had already been feeling broken inside, but finally a stout stick was broken on his back. It was inevitable. Nothing could be seen in isolation. An apparently trivial incident, outside the range of one's perception, can subsequently turn out to be the cause of a big incident. Who knows, perhaps this thrashing would change the course of an entire life, and determine a different path altogether. That story is hidden for now in the womb of the future.

Someone had said: there's no such thing as the present. The present was only a tiny bridge to go from the past to the future. The ugly and sinful misdeed committed that dark night in the past was eating Jibon up from within. He wasn't able to meet and mingle as easily and normally as before with the Muslim boys. When he looked Javed or Khaled or Zuleikha in the eye, he was struck by a strange sense of guilt. On the night of the payesh invitation, he had been made to bathe for purification of the pollution by Muslims. That bath had erected a mountain of weariness in his mind, which hindered embracing and advancing together, holding one another's hand. Something that wasn't required to be done if one touched dogs or cats had to be done when one touched certain men. And *I* was the one who did that. How despicable! Who knows more than I do how humiliating and agonising that is.

So Jibon gave up the company of Javed, and kept his inner anguish to himself. He had gone alone and far away with his herd of cows, where he would not have to be shamed by meeting them. He went all the way to the field of cane-grass, by the rail track. Leaving the cows to graze, he went and sat in the shade of a tree near the rail track.

Jibon loved watching trains. While living in the refugee camp, he would sometimes go to the rail track to see the passing trains. When a train sped by, emitting a *koo-jhik-jhik* sound and puffing out a cloud of smoke, it seemed as if a huge ship was racing crazily along the rail line, tearing and throwing away all bonds, all doubts and conflicts, having got intimation of some faraway land somewhere. What he liked most was gazing in the darkness of night at the illuminated engine as it shot ahead at great speed, pulling its train of carriages. The sheer speed of the massive mechanical contraption raised a mad storm inside Jibon's chest. Then, a child's eyes ran behind it, and rural Bengal's fields, riverbanks and villages, as well as towns, cities and ports were all left far behind and lost in the fabrication of the scenery of an unknown, unseen, new world of his imagination.

But creatures that could not speak were not in emotional turmoil like Jibon. Nature had assigned them merely three tasks: food, rest and reproduction. And it had given them a sense of fear, that whatever was unfamiliar and unknown was dangerous. As soon as you spot danger, you must flee and escape. And so, while Jibon was standing near the rail track watching, rapt, the train's massive engine advancing, the loud roar of the train terrified the cows grazing near the rail track. They began running helter-skelter to save themselves. Their tails flailing, they ran in whichever direction they could. One cow slipped and fell from the boundary ridge of the field into a compost pit. It lay prone there, with a broken leg.

What was Jibon to do! He ran and informed Dr Hem, who came and saw the cow's plight. He asked Jibon to explain why he had gone so far away with the cows. Not convinced by the explanation, he snatched the cowherd's staff from Jibon's hand and began venting his anger over the cow's injury by bringing it down wildly on Jibon's back. Drenched in sweat, he only stopped when the stick finally broke into two.

That day, Jibon hadn't been able to cry the least bit. Not once did he ask to be forgiven. One cruel blow after another had rained down on his back. There were bleeding welts on his skin, but the wound in his young mind also bled secretly. Sitting in the Shiromanipur camp and hearing the tale of the police's cruel oppression, he had developed a fierce hatred towards the word 'police' and the khaki uniform. Today, because of Hem Chakraborty's inhuman thrashing, the same feeling against him and his symbol, the Brahmin thread, were born in young Jibon's tender mind.

Dr Hem had beaten him and gone away, leaving him lying on the field. The thousand-rupee cow had broken its leg, he had to organise people to carry it back to his house. He was overwrought because of that. There was no scope for thinking about a boy then.

After Dr Hem left, Jibon got up and dusted himself. The sun was right above his head. He began walking. Ahead of him, snaking away into the distance, lay the railway track, one end of which reached the bank of the Matla river, while the other went to the heart of the metropolis, Calcutta. He walked slowly along the rail track.

Jibon's body was racked with waves of pain. He was covered in ugly welts. There were black and blue contusions in some parts. In some other parts there was swelling, like an angry boil, which was painful to touch. Jibon felt a bit feverish. Besides, he hadn't had anything to eat all day. Just a bit of dry muri in the morning. He had only had some water after that. Now he was in great pain. Man is actually a slave of habit. Earlier, the absence of food for a week or ten days did not torture him so much. After having eaten rice twice a day for almost two months at a stretch, the habit of going without food had been lost. His tongue had become greedy, as had the demands of his belly. Hunger assailed his body now, mocked it. He could not stand on his legs. His knees wobbled. His whole body throbbed with weakness. He became short of breath.

Jibon had heard the name 'Jadavpur' so many times from his father that it had been etched in his memory. He used to go there to work as a casual labourer. When Jibon had left home, he had hoped to go there. Jadavpur was also Calcutta. But it wasn't the real Calcutta, or else his father too would surely have got some of the money flying in the air there. Jibon did not know yet where the real Calcutta was. But he was certain he would find it. Jadavpur was where he would alight first in his quest to find the real Calcutta. He boarded the train at Ghutiari Sharif, and it was evening by the time he reached Jadavpur. A fire raged in his belly. It felt as if his intestines were writhing like a burning python in the fury of the fire. Hunger had its own law. When the day reached its peak at noon, so did hunger. Then it began to feed on itself. Like the goddess, Ma Chhinamasta, who sated her thirst by drinking her own blood. After sunset, the conflagration inside Jibon's belly abated. Evening had turned to night. Jibon was more feverish now. His head felt heavy. He couldn't figure out where he would go.

There was a small paan-shop on the platform at the Jadavpur railway station, and behind that was an iron railing. Jibon sat down beside the railing. After some time, he slumped and lay down right there, amidst the dirt, paan spittle, cigarette stubs and assorted bits of trash.

⁓

There was fierce enmity between hunger and slumber. When one arrived, the other just did not want to be there. But his feverish condition and the stinging welts on his body saved him from the agony of a sleepless and hungry night. He slept through the night. When Jibon woke up in the morning, he felt a bit better. His child's mind realised that as the day advanced, the void in his stomach would only grow. Just like the hands of the clock went from one to twelve and came back again to one, hunger too followed a similar clock. It went from one to nine or ten, and then came down to eight and seven. In Jibon's hunger clock, it was now seven or half past seven in the morning. It was the same in time's clock too. He had to find some decent work before noon, by any means. Something that wasn't as lowly as grazing cows and cleaning their dung and urine.

If one crossed the rail track at the Jadavpur station, took the road on the right side and walked a bit towards the east, one came to a triangular park. That was where Bade Lal had his tea-shop. Jibon walked until he reached the shop.

'*More kaje rakhben? Mui kamer talashe aichhi.* Will you give me a job? I've come in search of work.' Jibon had heard that small boys easily found work in the city, washing plates and glasses in roadside tea-shops and eateries. He got the job of cleaning cups. There was a lurking fear in his mind, regarding his caste identity. What if they came to know that he was a Nama and belonged to the community earlier known as Chandal? They wouldn't let him work there. So he took on a new name, which was the name of the tutor who came to teach Hem Chakraborty's daughter Gayatri. But Bade Lal Sahoo, who hailed from Benares, in Uttar Pradesh, wasn't interested in names. He needed someone to work. He himself gave Jibon a name: *naukarba,* 'servant-boy'.

Hardly any Bengali customers came to this tea-shop. Those who came were Bade Lal's brethren from U.P. and Bihar. Most of them worked as masons and construction workers. And there were some milkmen, coal-sellers, cart-pullers and so on. In the morning, the shop served tea, toast and eggs. At noon, there was ghugni and alur-dom. The shop did fairly brisk business. U.P. and Bihar were the states where the high-castes killed dalits on the most trivial grounds. One could never arrive at a correct estimate of the number of low-caste folk who had their skin ripped off their backs for the crime of drinking water and quenching their thirst from the wells of Brahmins and Rajputs. The customers of this shop had left home and come to West Bengal. But they had brought along with them their hatred for the low-castes. Their conservatism in matters relating to caste, and their clear expression of the same lacked the genteel cover of Calcutta's civilised caste overlords. Among the former, it was etched in black and white, absolutely barbaric. Within a month, Jibon thought he was done for. Suddenly one day, a group of men arrived and informed Bade Lal that they would never visit his shop again, because they were served food by a low-caste.

They had spoken with Bade Lal without raising their voices. Yet Jibon had heard them as he washed the cups. Although the boy hadn't yet fully learnt Hindi, nevertheless, with whatever could be picked up in a month, he surmised everything. At first he was extremely surprised. No one knew him in this city. Then how was his caste identity revealed? Was there some kind of smell or mark or sign on the bodies of low-caste folk by which other people came to know all about their identity? A tremendous fear took hold of him. He would lose this job, which paid a salary of ten rupees a month. Finally, there was relief—no, the declaration of war by them was not against him. That was against one of their own countryfolk, the boy who made tea in Bade Lal's shop, who was blind in one eye and whose elder brother sat and mended shoes in front of the police headquarters in Lalbazar—thus revealing his Chamar caste. The uproar was against him. Their verdict was unsparing: they could not consume water touched by a Chamar and thereby lose their caste.

Because he had left his home state long ago, Bade Lal himself was not so conservative in regard to matters of caste. But to a shopkeeper, the customer was king, or rather Ma Lakshmi. He could not run his shop if he did not heed their wishes. How would he survive then? And so the boy lost his job.

In common perception, losing a tea-maker's job wasn't such a big calamity in human life. But that didn't happen in the case of this boy called Kanai. After he lost his job, he did not take up any other work. Whatever he did finally made a jailbird of him. But that came some years later. It wasn't only Bade Lal—no one had any answer to the complex question pertaining to an ordinary shoe-mending boy.

Every morning, eight or ten people with buckets and brooms came to the shop to drink tea. Who knows why, but they never dared to leave their work implements outside and enter the shop, and go and sit on the benches or chairs in front of the tables, like all the other customers. Like poor beggars, they sat on their haunches outside the shop and drank tea from clay cups. They were sweepers. They cleaned the shit in people's houses. That was their crime. That's why they were dirty, low-caste. Jibon wondered why doctors and nurses—who also handled people's shit, piss, puss, blood, vomit and worms, who handled dead bodies—did not belong to low castes, and if they could enter the shop and drink tea with everyone else, then why was there an objection when it came to the sweepers?

☙

After Kanai left, the pressure of work on Jibon increased. The responsibility of making tea was added to that of washing cups. He had to wake up at dawn and begin his work, first lighting the oven. By the time he finished work, it was half past ten or eleven at night. As his hands and feet were wet all day, they became blotchy and blistered. Especially the soles of his feet. At night, the pain and itching on his feet was unbearable. After some days, his blisters began oozing blood. But who would understand his pain? After all, his employer was not a parent. The farmer doesn't think about the bullocks' suffering, he only looks at how much of the field has been ploughed. One heard that once upon a time, people were very compassionate, and sensitive to others' suffering. Who knows when, how many hundreds of thousands of years ago that was. Jibon did not know. This country was supposedly 'blessed with wealth and adorned with flowers' at one time and people lived in great comfort then. Perhaps that was long, long before Jibon, Garib Das and his father Har Kumar were born. According to the Hindu scriptures, it was now supposed to be the Age of Kali. Its duration was supposedly sixty thousand years. And before that had been the Dwapar Age. In that age too, other than a handful of the vast numbers of people outside the fold of Aryan society, everyone had great difficulty finding food. Enticing hungry folk like the Nishada brothers and their mother with food, the Pandavs had lured them to the forest of Varnavrat and then had them burnt alive in the house made of lacquer. After all, in order to befool Duryodhan, they badly needed the dead bodies.

Bade Lal Sahoo's tea-shop was right in the middle of where the Sukanta bridge in Jadavpur now stands. There was a mud-and-brick road in front of the shop. No vehicles other than rickshaws plied on this road. One day, Jibon saw groups of people hurrying along that road with bamboo poles and roof tiles loaded on handcarts. They were going eastwards, in the direction of what is now the Eastern Metropolitan Bypass. Jibon got to hear that a few thousand bighas of land there, belonging to zamindars, were being squatted upon by people who were setting up a new colony there. Many such colonies had already sprung up earlier in this vast region of south Calcutta. However, the background was somewhat different here. Which was why after a few days, the sky turned red one night with blazing tongues of fire. The distressed screams of stricken folk rent the night air. A new chapter of history was written, as the frenzy of destruction unleashed on the new colony by the police and hoodlum squad of the zamindars was engineered to resemble the re-enactment of a riot.

After night turned to day, handcarts and rickshaw-vans laden with broken people lying on bamboo litters returned along the same road on which they had walked, full of hope, a few days ago. Some were dead and some were about to die. Everyone was scorched, red, cut and broken, testimony to the heinous frenzy of destruction that the police and hoodlum squad had jointly enacted all night long. Jibon had seen a lot of deaths. His infant eyes had witnessed the death of Radhakanta's aged father in the moving truck, and after that it had been like a procession in front of his eyes. But, however grievous those deaths were, they were not as ugly and blood-curdling as this. Jibon was shaken seeing the bloodied bodies. At the time of the agitation in the Shiromanipur camp, the police had beaten up Jibon's father, hauled him into a van and left him in a desolate field. From that tender age he had harboured a suppressed rage and disregard towards the police. That grew fiercer now. It found another name—zamindar. Those who were zamindars, were oppressive and evil. After the inhuman treatment meted out in the doctor's house, his animosity against the high-castes was already sky-high. Jibon's life now coursed along the stream watered by the confluence of anger and hatred against police, Brahmins and zamindars.

17

A Black Night in Calcutta

While working in Bade Lal's tea-shop at the triangular park in Jadavpur, Jibon tried to find out the whereabouts of the Calcutta he sought. He gathered that the fabled city that he hoped to find—where money flew in the air—was not north or south but central Calcutta. Where night never descended, kept at bay by thousands of bright lights. It began from Sealdah station. Once he found out about that—then why delay! Why not set out to see that Calcutta! He needed lots of money now. Lots and lots of money. Durga Puja was approaching. He would buy new clothes for the occasion for his parents, brothers and sister—with his own money. A frock with red tinsels for his sister, and full-sleeved shirts and trousers for his brothers. Dhuti-panjabi for his Baba, and saris, blouses and petticoats for his Ma. His Ma would need two sets of those.

Quitting his job one day, Jibon set off on foot from Bade Lal's shop towards the unknown city. But where, how far away was it? He spent many days on the streets of Calcutta in search of that magical city. Jibon had worked for two months in Bade Lal's shop. The few rupees he had received after deductions—for breaking two glasses and spilling two litres of milk—were soon spent. After that, he wandered around aimlessly, roaming the streets, hauling his starving belly. The whole day was spent in this manner. When it was night, he just lay down wherever he happened to be, on the pavement, or a rail station, or under a tree. How could he return empty-handed to his parents after so long?

In these few months, Jibon had gone round and round the entire city. He had seen every part of the beautiful Calcutta, which was among the largest cities of the world and some two-hundred-and-fifty years old. Jibon thought it was its variety and contrasts, its vanity and wretchedness, its exaltedness and niggardliness that had given it its pre-eminence. He had already got a taste of some of its fare. On one side of the city were tall buildings that arrogantly touched the sky. Inside the buildings were all sorts of means to impart dull wantonness, comfort and luxury. Heartless, mechanical people lived there, who were bedecked from head to toe in expensive garb of exquisite colours. They laughed, walked and talked like machines—everything was measured. It was hard to find any shade or scent of human feeling in their love and lovelessness, virtuousness and immorality. Everything seemed to be governed by mechanical rules. Ordinary frailties like kindness, caring and affection did not trouble or influence them. All of earth's resources lay at the feet of these machine folk. They had erected between themselves and the lowest man a mountain of barriers, which hindered the development and expansion of society's tender nature. That was how their interests were fulfilled. The story of money flying—yes, that money did fly, but it entered their own vaults through the route created by them. Which no one else would ever go near or catch sight of.

Opposite their mansions were run-down, broken huts and shanties of impoverished folk. Starving, ill-fed, sick, defrauded and jobless people lived in those damp huts swarming with mosquitoes and flies. They too were inhabitants of Calcutta. In order to secure their daily existence, these people, perforce, provided services, deference and obedience to the inhabitants of the tall buildings. In return, they received stale bread and a few measly rupees.

There were big hospitals in the city. But they were not for everyone. Those who were excluded lay on the streets and died like cats and dogs for want of treatment. There were shops and markets and big hotels and eateries here. People went there, and some of them spent as much as a thousand or five thousand in a single instance! In the same city, one saw a few people, with battered bowls in their hand, crying, 'I haven't eaten for two days, babu, please give me one paisa.' There were big colleges and universities. But not everyone was able to enter the educational institutions. Whatever was precious and beautiful in this city was set in motion, controlled and protected by a group of mechanical men. For two-hundred-and-fifty years had this metropolis survived in this way.

The poor boy gazed wide-eyed at Calcutta, at the loathsome visage of the city. Truly, millions of rupees flew in the wind here. Those who were shrewd enough to catch the flying money could have sackfuls of it. The ones who did not know could not do the same. Toil, sweat and honesty had no value in the great city. There was cunning, fraud, artfulness and intrigue everywhere. The ones who were skilled in employing these won everything. And the ones who did not know were failures. Those who were born of the womb of poverty, who were simple and straight-forward, who were sons-of-labour, could not acquire the requisite skill and artfulness. So they lived in acute hardship and died on pavements, rail stations, beneath trees and in the slums or shanties alongside canals and rail tracks. All their desires, dreams, hopes and wishes died with them.

Who knows why, but seeing all this, without his being aware of it, a great cloud formed inside Jibon. But that did not pour down any rain. There were only bursts of thunder and lightning which left him feeling tattered. So many people had so much—why did he possess nothing? That unresolved question cast a shadow on the innermost recesses of his mind.

Someone or the other had once told Jibon that the wages for minor work were low. The more important the work, the higher the wage. Jibon could not figure out why the work of men who ploughed the land under sun and rain and provided the country food, of those who risked their lives during storms and cyclones and caught fish in rivers, of those who enabled the good health and the development of the faculties of the people of the country, of the workers in farms and factories who worked their hammers and tools and made the country wealthy, was considered small, and why were their wages so low? And how was it that the tonsured Brahmins muttering *om-bom* and ringing bells before stone images in temples, the babu sitting on a chair in his office and sipping tea, dozing and gossiping, and the loudmouth breathing fire before a mic were considered 'big'? So big that there was a mountain of money in their homes! Who made this classification of work? Who determined the remuneration whereby the coolie who carried a load of a quintal on his head would not earn enough to allow him to eat to his fill twice a day? Why was Garib Das compelled to sit all day without food at the railway station? Why did he have to suffer ailments stemming from not eating? Why could he not get a drop of medicine?

Jibon's young mind minutely sought the answers to these questions, but he could not find any. Hundreds of philosophers had pondered over such questions, over centuries. But they were at a loss, unable to agree on the correct answers. Marx, Gandhi, Ambedkar and Lohia had all been bewildered—so how could an illiterate boy find the answers?

⚶

One day, in the course of his aimless walking, Jibon reached Howrah Bridge. It must have been around noon. He stood there, leaning against a railing. He gazed at the Ganga flowing far below him. The riverbank was far away. Lots of people were bathing there. Bathing in the Ganga was supposed to wash away all sins. Jibon wondered how many times he would have to immerse himself in the Ganga so that the sin for which he was unable to get food was washed away.

Quite a few motor-launches and country boats plied on the river. Jibon had never been on such a vessel. Who knows what it was like on the boat when he came in his infancy in his mother's arms from the other Bengal. He observed a cargo-laden ship coming from far away. His eyes followed it for a long while. It finally passed by, and with the ship his mind too set off on an endless voyage without destination. Jibon had heard someone narrate the story of Chand Saudagar and his seven ships. Like the ship he had just observed, those too used to travel to many countries with goods to trade. If only Jibon could be on such a ship! He would go away to a country where hardship did not pursue him relentlessly. There was surely such a place, somewhere or the other, in the world. He believed that if he kept searching, he would definitely reach the place.

Jibon was unaware how long he stood there lost in his thoughts. Suddenly, he turned around to see the object of his infinite terror and hatred, a policeman, standing behind him. He had no clue when the armed policeman, who was part of a battalion force, put his hand on his shoulder. '*Ki re*, why are you leaning like that, do you want to die or what? Where do you live? Where are you going? What do you do?'

Jibon had heard that hoodlums caught the children who roamed the city streets, blinded them, broke their limbs and made them beg on the streets. If they were caught by hijras, they would take them away, cut their cocks, castrate them and induct them into their band. And if the police caught them, they were taken to jail and thrashed twice a day.

'Why are you crying?' asked the policeman. His voice and his eyes were not exactly like a policeman's, he seemed to be much gentler. So Jibon regained something of his confidence. He did not think it was necessary to tell any lies to such a soft-hearted policeman. He told him the truth.

'Babu, we live in Jadavpur. My Ma died. My Baba married again. My new Ma beats me up and doesn't give me any food. My Baba has a tea-shop at the triangular park there. I used to wash the cups there and got blisters on my hands and feet. My new Ma didn't give me any medicine either. That's why I left home. When I don't have anyone of my own in the world, what's the point of living? I'll drown myself in the Ganga.'

The soft heart hidden beneath the policeman's uniform was moved seeing the sad boy with blisters on his hands and feet, torn clothes, scrawny body and big eyes full of tears. He wanted to take Jibon along with him, but not to the police station or the juvenile detention centre. He would take him to his police mess, in the Shibpur Reserve Police Line, where a hundred-and-fifty Bengal policemen ate every day. 'Do you want to come with me? You can stay there, eat and work. You'll get a salary too. If you want to come, let's go. My duty gets over at two.' The policeman was part of the squad that had come from Rayna police station in Burdwan. He took Jibon to a police lorry parked nearby and sat him down there. 'Don't go anywhere, sit here. As soon as the relief squad arrives, our duty will be over and we'll leave.'

Shibpur was nearby. The lorry reached the place in twenty minutes. On the way, the policeman told Jibon, 'Stay there for some days, grow up a bit. After that, I'll put you in the police force.'

Jibon did not know how to read or write. Whether or not someone like him could join the police force—he wasn't bothered about such things right then. He was only thinking about today. He hadn't eaten for several days, so he thought—let's eat to one's fill today! When an opportunity had presented itself—why let it go!

The person who was the manager of the police mess also seemed to be a kind man. He gave Jibon an old shirt and a pair of shorts of his to wear. And he told him that there were only five days to go before the end of the month, so he would not pay him for the five days. But he would pay him twenty rupees the next month onwards.

There was a cook in the police mess, whose name was Amulya Thakur. He had been working there for almost ten years. His salary was sixty rupees a month. The members of the mess came and left; after all, the policemen's jobs involved regular transfers. But the cook's job was a stable one. The mess manager changed every month. But the cook was never transferred. His was the final word in the mess.

The very first day, he told Jibon, '*Ei chhokra*, you must do whatever I instruct you to do. If you do that, you'll keep your job. Or else you won't have it. After you wake up, go and break coal, light the oven and then bring water from the hand-pump at the far end of the police lines and fill all the drums. It's this water that's used for cooking, drinking, washing the utensils and for the members to wash their hands and mouths. After that, you have to cut the vegetables and wash the fish and meat. Once the cooking's done, you have to serve the food, and after the members have eaten, you have to clean the tables and then wash the utensils. After that, you have some time for rest in the afternoon. In the evening, it's the same work again, and in addition, you have to prepare the dough and make rotis.' But as far as Amulya Thakur was concerned, these did not comprise Jibon's real work. What the real work was—Jibon figured out a few days later.

It must have been about ten at night. All the members of the police mess had eaten dinner and gone back, some to their barracks and some to their duty. Jibon had finished his work, joined two benches and lain down to sleep. Suddenly he saw Amulya Thakur looming over him, standing against the light coming from the far end of the dining hall. He pulled up his dirty, oil-stained lungi and held out his hideous, black and long male organ whose foul smell made Jibon want to retch. This was the real work. Jibon had to pleasure him. The tumescent organ had to be made limp and normal. Without any restraint or consideration of modesty, Amulya promptly put it in the palm of Jibon's hand. 'Here, rub it!'

It seemed he had applied something like coconut oil on it. As soon as Jibon touched it, it was as if his whole being was filled with revulsion. The thick, black, smelly, hot organ was like a repulsive leech he had once seen clinging to a buffalo's rump. But what was Jibon to do then, he held his nose, turned his face away and continued to rub it. And he waited for Amulya Thakur to tell him when to stop, but Amulya Thakur was unwilling to let the hapless boy off so easily, with so little. It was Friday, the day on which the authorities in the police lines supplied an intoxicant called rum very cheap. After gulping two shots of the rum, Amulya Thakur did not care to distinguish between female and male. He said, 'Turn around!' So far, although intolerable, somehow Jibon had gritted his teeth and put up with it. But he couldn't take it anymore. He said a firm no. Who knows what he had in mind, but Amulya Thakur pulled out a red two-rupee note from somewhere, held it in front of Jibon and said, 'Go and see a cinema tomorrow. Don't say no, come now, take it.'

Jibon wasn't willing to debase himself like a dog for the red-coloured note. As if from the core of his being, he shouted, 'I've come here to work. Don't ask me to do that!'

Don't ask him? Amulya Thakur wanted to do something. And he had to do it now, and to hell with whatever happened thereafter! He held Jibon down and began to take his pants off. It was the manager's pair of shorts, which was tied to Jibon's waist with a string. Amulya Thakur began pulling at the string. Who knows where Jibon—emaciated from starvation—found the strength in his body. He pushed Amulya Thakur hard, throwing him on the floor, and ran into the kitchen. He grabbed the large cooking spud and held it over his head, like a spear, or like Shiva's trident, and said, 'If you come near me, I'll kill you! I'm warning you!'

After that, Amulya Thakur went nowhere near Jibon at night. But from the very next morning, he began finding fault with all his work. If he ground the spices, it wasn't fine enough, when he washed the vegetables, he found dirt on them. When he made rotis, he said they were burnt. When he argued with him, he slapped him too. Jibon realised that satisfying Amulya Thakur was beyond his capability. And it was difficult to work here if he was dissatisfied. So one afternoon, without telling anyone anything, he decided to quit and went away. Once again, he lost a secure shelter, regular food and the monthly salary of twenty rupees. He was unemployed and shelterless. Once again, Jibon spent the next few months on the streets. He roamed here and there all day, and when it was night, he slept in a park, or a rail station, or a vacant garage, or even on the pavement.

⚘

The long-awaited day finally arrived. The secret fear that had lodged deep in Jibon's heart when he stood at the bank of Hem Chakraborty's pond one night, now became a reality, baring terrifying fangs. Barely had the year 1964 begun, when fierce communal riots between Hindus and Muslims broke out. Something called Hazratbal had gone missing in some mosque in Kashmir. Muslims suspected Hindus to be behind the removal of the sacred relic. As a result, killings began all over the country. The atmosphere in the country was already like a simmering cauldron, full of hatred, mutual suspicion and animosity between the two communities. It only needed something to ignite it. As soon as that happened, they pounced upon one another like bloodthirsty dogs.

That a piece of hair of the Prophet had been stolen somewhere, from some mosque, was not significant. What was significant was the launching of a yagna of human sacrifice on that pretext. Like in other regions of the country, it took hold of Calcutta too, a city that was considered the centre of literature and culture. Where the first outbreak of riots occurred was no longer important, because now Rajabazar, Sealdah, Mominpur and Khidirpur were all engulfed in flames. No lane in any neighbourhood was safe any more. Assailants roamed the streets at night with daggers in their hands. Anyone could get killed now. Who was killing, why they were killing, who they were killing, who gained from that—all that was of no relevance to anyone on either side. The main point was, people would die. People murdered, and people died. Only numbers mattered. The numbers would determine which side had won and which one was roundly defeated. And so, just as people were dying, so was kindness, pity, love and affection, as well as conscience and sound judgement.

During this period of madness, Jibon found a new job in an eatery in Park Circus. He could not overcome the temptation of the salary of thirty rupees a month. Risk and danger did not matter to Jibon now. He just needed money, lots of money.

Park Circus was a predominantly Muslim locality, and until then there had been no riots there. But the situation was extremely tense, and it looked like something could happen at any moment. That was the possibility that seemed to be manifested on the streets. When evening descended at such a time, no loving father or caring mother would let their child out of their sight. They would not let them step out of the house. Jibon wasn't a child of anyone in this city, no one was supposed to be caring and compassionate towards him. For that matter, he was an unidentified boy, and if he went missing, no one would ever search for him. If he died, no one would mourn his death.

Every person has his own likes and fancies, which do not conform to any reason. And so Ram babu went all the way to Gobinda Pramanik's saloon, which was three miles away, for his haircut and shave. No other saloon satisfied him as much. Shyam babu only went to Robi Bagdi to buy fish, as if no other fish-seller could be trusted to provide him fresh fish of the correct weight and at a good price, as if they were all thieves and frauds. Similarly, when Jodu babu was ill, he only called Dr Abinash Pradhan. In Jodu babu's opinion, even Dr Bidhan Roy wasn't as fine a doctor as him. Madhu babu could never enjoy the curry made with banana flowers unless his cook Buro-ma had made it, and who else but Madhu babu knew what a fine cook old Buro-ma was!

The owner of the eatery where Jibon worked had a similar fancy regarding the beedis he smoked. It couldn't be just any other beedi, it had to be the one with the flat top and red string, made by the bearded man in the small shanty-like shop across the rail line. It was such a fine beedi that when one took a deep puff of it, one felt as if one's very soul was cooled. The eatery closed at ten o'clock every night. Before that, Jibon had to go and fetch a bundle of the special beedis. Like every day, tonight too, the owner of the eating joint instructed Jibon, 'Go and get the beedis!', at a time when butchers lay in wait in the darkness, with daggers drawn, to slit the throat of anyone who came near. If he had the slightest sympathy for the boy, he would not have sent him so late at night to that locality, given the frightening environment that prevailed then. But Jibon did not have the option to refuse. He could not say that he was afraid. That would have been grounds for him to lose his job. And so he began to walk—towards what would be a terrifying experience.

The Park Circus rail station hadn't yet come up. The place was covered with trees and bushes and somewhat resembled a jungle. And it was quite desolate too, as well as dark. But the only positive aspect was that so far there had been no killings in this area. People were still peaceful. That's why Jibon could still go there. Once news of the riots spread across the city, the streets turned desolate as soon as it became dark. Especially in the localities where both Hindu and Muslim communities resided, people did not have the courage to go out at night. They felt insecure. They trembled and choked in fear. But Jibon didn't feel so scared. Or else he wouldn't have been able to set out alone.

Actually, fear was the name of an experience, the sting of a memory. How would one who had never got scorched know the agony of that? He could cheerily walk towards the fire. It was ignorance that lay at the root of his courage. How could one who had never been underwater ever feel the indescribable agony of death by drowning?

Jibon hadn't yet witnessed riots. He had never confronted a killer's terrifying dagger. He had not seen thousands of bloodthirsty people, armed with choppers, spears and guns, baying for blood and pouncing upon another group of people with terrifying ferocity. Besides, a certain notion was still stuck in his head: why would those whom I have never harmed, never thought of harming, harm me? Especially such major harm as slitting my throat! So, compared to others, he was somewhat fearless.

That's why, like every day, he walked in the darkness, singing the song, '*Sundor zarina tomay ami korbo biya moner bashona*. Oh lovely Zarina, it's my heart's desire to wed you'. He made his way there all right, there was no problem. The problem arose when he was returning after buying the beedis. He found his way blocked. Breaking through the womb of pitch darkness in a lane, there emerged four children of the mother of darkness. They were all of about the same age as Jibon. However, there was no childlike playfulness in their voices. There was only the crookedness of adults, there was only the violence of a merciless butcher. 'Hey, which community do you belong to?'

The whole area lay in darkness. There was no light anywhere in sight. No people, no life. It was as if the stillness of some gigantic crematorium had enveloped the place. In that great darkness, the faces of the boys were not really visible. He guessed they were like Javed, Mamud, Fatik, Mongla and Maran. Only the few pairs of eyes were visible, which gleamed like sharp knives.

'Hey you fucking bastard, which community do you belong to?'

A most difficult question! Jibon realised they wanted to know whether he was Hindu or Muslim. When they received the answer, they would either abuse him or run their knives over his throat.

Once a pack of jackals had surrounded Jibon in a dark jungle of undergrowth in Kalikapur. Fire gleamed in the eyes of the bloodthirsty creatures. They were furious about humans trespassing into their kingdom. The city was slowly expanding and encroaching on their habitat. Their food was scarce. Enraged by all that, finding a human child all alone, they had attacked him. That day too, Jibon hadn't given in to fear. Or else he would surely have been eaten alive by the jackals. Like Abhimanyu trapped in the wheel formation, all alone and in grave danger, almost in the flash of an eye, Jibon had picked up half a brick lying on the ground and tied it to one end of the gamchha on his shoulder. Then holding the other end of the gamchha, he had swung the brick round and round. The pack of jackals had fled in panic.

Another time, where the Sukanta Setu in Jadavpur now stands, there used to be a very large drain carrying the city's sewage. To the left of the drain, there was a dirty pond and a dense jungle of wild grasses and shrubs. Across the jungle was the T.B. Hospital. One could walk from Raja Subodh Mullick Road to the Jadavpur rail station, going along the bank of this drain and then through the T.B. Hospital. Once Jibon was going somewhere along this route. However, he had gone prepared for potential danger because once it became dark, the path along the drain was infested with snakes. So before setting out, he took a thick iron rod with him.

Walking beside the drain that day, as soon as he was inside the T.B. Hospital precincts, out of the blue, a pack of dogs belonging to the sweepers began barking very loudly and attacked him. Perhaps they could not tolerate an unknown face. They were unwilling to heed the deadly weapon carried by the boy. But the dog that led the pack and sank its teeth into Jibon's leg could not escape. The heavy rod in the boy's hand came down with full force on its head. The dog yelped, fell and lay dead. That was the first time Jibon had killed any living creature.

Confronted by the hostile boys now, Jibon was full of regret. He was completely empty-handed. It was terribly wrong to have set out without adequate preparation.

'Why don't you speak? Come on, speak up! Tell me which community you belong to! Hurry up!'

What would Jibon say? Did he know which community he belonged to? If he was Hindu, then why did the Hindu Hem Chakraborty call him untouchable? If he was Muslim, why did the Muslims consider him to be a kaffir? Jibon knew that now there were only two communities of people in society, one of which was getting killed and the other was doing the killing. Which of these communities should he choose? Which community would he enlist in? He did not know which identity he ought to adopt.

But he did not think they would accord any value to or respect this sense of humanity in him. Their only question was whether he belonged to their community, and if he did not, then he definitely belonged to the enemy community. It was a very simple arithmetic, in which there was no scope for any addition or subtraction.

Jibon was in an acute dilemma. What should he say now? What would the correct answer be?

The one who was the biggest of the four advanced and halted before Jibon. Now Jibon saw that he had a knife in his right hand. It wasn't the kind of tiny knife Dhiren used to roam around with, back in the Shiromanipur camp, to frighten them. This was a spring-controlled knife with a brass handle, a full eighteen inches long. It was known as a 'rampuri'. Ratan Roy, the big hoodlum around the triangular park in Jadavpur, had a knife like this. It was with a knife like this that he had cut open a person's stomach a few days ago.

The boy with the knife asked again, in a menacing tone, 'I'm asking you for the last time, tell me which community you belong to! Are you Hindu?'

'No, I'm not Hindu.'

'Don't lie or I'll kill you! Tell me the truth!'

'I told you, didn't I, I'm not Hindu.'

'So you're Muslim? I'll take your pants off and look.'

'No, I'm not Muslim either.'

'Are you Christian then?'

'Not that either.'

'Then what are you?'

Looking at the boys, one could not guess which community they belonged to. There was no sign whatsoever on them of any community. If one removed the knife from the boy's hand and replaced it with a pen, he would look like a school student. Or if he had a cow-stick in his hand, a cowherd like Javed and Khaled. If he sat down and washed cups, then he would look like Jibon. That was the difficulty with this age—one couldn't make out anything. If he could have discerned anything, Jibon could have said that he was one of them and gone away. The boys did not have much time. They had to go elsewhere, prey on someone else. They harried him, 'Come on, hurry up!'

Jibon had to say something. He could not be on his way unless he spoke. He had made up his mind. It wasn't the time for an appeal, or a submission, or a request or solicitation. They would not heed any of that. He had to respond to them in the only language they knew. Not Hindi or Bengali or Arabic or Sanskrit, but the formidable language that everyone understood.

Jibon hadn't yet learnt to read the writing on the wall. But it hadn't yet begun to be written on the walls of Calcutta that 'offence is the best means of defense'. That lesson was learnt on this dark night. The unimaginable offspring of night. In a flash, Jibon picked up a brick lying on the ground next to his feet, which was known as a 'thanka' in the language of the street. There was no more time to think. Without so much as a blink, with unbelievable speed, he landed the brick with all his might right on the forehead of the boy with the knife. There was a sound like a coconut being broken. The knife slipped from the boy's hand. Blood gushed out from his head, covering his eyes and face. The boy let out a moan, slumped and fell on the dirt.

Jibon had been very ill when he was an infant. Thereafter, let alone nutritious food, he had never eaten to his fill all his life. So he was skinny and weak. Today, after the attack with the brick, all the skinniness and weakness was submerged beneath his self-confidence.

Picking up the knife from the ground, Jibon stood boldly and said, 'Come, who'll come now!' Just then, he remembered his rage at being called 'Chandal'. He screamed out, 'My name's Jibon, I'm a Chandal. What more do you want to know?' But none of them came forward. Abandoning their stricken companion, they fled into the black womb of darkness. As if the mother of darkness once again concealed her newly-born offspring in the pus, blood and faeces of her womb. Jibon complimented himself on his presence of mind and courage. He realised that life wasn't merely the name of a journey, an experience and an agony—it was also the name of a battle.

But he ought not to remain here any longer. Wasn't there a saying, that after eating one ought to go to sleep, and after thrashing one ought to escape! Leaving at the right time was absolutely vital in order to hold on to the victory. He walked ahead quickly. The hard courage endowed by the knife's brass handle was clenched in his hand, with which he could cut through any danger and make his way to safety. He wasn't afraid anymore. His heart did not thump. The fresh warm blood of his aggressor had washed away all fear today. Now Jibon was like a warrior. He walked ahead with the unfaltering and radiant stride of a warrior. But he did not return to the eatery. Jibon knew he was all alone. He had no one to help him, protect him or ally with him. He had nobody. Who knew whether the three boys who ran away knew where he lived? What would he do if hearing about the incident from them, the brother or uncle or father of the one who was lying on the road came looking for him? And so, he had to escape, far away from this place. That was what life demanded of Jibon now. Run, Jibon, run!

THE

SCHOOL

OF LIFE

18

Raja

Sealdah railway station. Perhaps the name was a reminder of the time when this was a marshland where jackals roamed. After walking long, a boy who had slipped and fallen into the pit of perilous time reached there. His name was Jibon. An unknown fear stalked him. It was as if a pack of bloodthirsty hyenas were chasing him. He feared that as soon as they got to him, they would tear him to shreds with their sharp teeth. After all, how old was Jibon now! Compared to this child's age, the firmament of unknown fear was vast. Which was why Jibon had come here to hide.

Like a couple of rabbit kittens might hide themselves in a forest, Jibon wanted to conceal himself among the crowd of thousands of unknown faces. He was now very scared of desolate places, and especially the desolation of black nights. Someone would surely be lying in wait in the womb of darkness, knife bared, who would suddenly pounce on him and run the knife over his throat. All the roads, lanes and neighbourhoods had been taken over by rioters, murderers and looters. The moment evening set in, flames erupted somewhere or the other. Country bombs exploded and people were murdered. Not a single person in the city was safe at this time.

Sealdah station—like every other station—also had a formless but sensorial soul. To see or understand that, one had to have a mind given to philosophical equanimity. At the aboriginal root of the secret, limpid, subterranean, stream of humanity was a profound bonding of the eternal human soul, transcending race and caste. There were thousands of people here, of various ages, wearing different kinds of clothes and speaking all sorts of languages. No one knew anyone. But it was as if an adept garland-maker had sewn together an invisible garland of all the flowers on a single string.

When the first train of the day arrived at the platform in the morning, it delivered swarms of people from its womb. After that, the procession advanced like a column, through the movement of each foot, all moving to the same metre, rhythm and sound. The life of labour blossomed in civic responsibility. But in the afternoon or in the evening or at night, the homeward-bound feet were tired and weary. People were eager to reach home, but also anxious. What if the train didn't come? What if the train didn't leave? What if it stopped midway? There were myriad dangers with trains nowadays. During the rainy season, the rail-tracks could get submerged. The overhead cables could snap. A thief could cut and steal the cables. There could be a power cut, or a sudden civic or political blockade or strike. Then the trains wouldn't run. If the train services were disrupted, the faces of all the passengers would be marked by the shadow of the same anxiety. The same kind of clouds would gather in their hearts, and sometimes there could be rain too. Everyone's folks at home would be waiting anxiously at the doorstep, with the same hope: may the person return home safely. No one looked at, spoke to, or knew or was familiar with anyone else, and yet everyone heaved the same deep sigh, with the same apprehension. Jibon was not a philosopher. He was too young to ponder over profound philosophical truths. Actually he was at the station in order to conceal his identity, a simple biological imperative. He did not want to die. At least, not at the hands of some insane murderer. And definitely not like a slaughtered goat.

For the last one month, Jibon's haunt was a spot behind a concrete bench on Platform No. 1 of the south section of the station. After roaming here and there all day, once it was night, making sure to avoid everyone's sight, he made his way to the spot. He was not alone at the station. Like him, many vagabonds, beggars, lunatics and homeless persons lived here. The addition of another new boy was not going to cause anyone any headache.

One afternoon, Jibon was walking around in the station. The station was not so crowded at this time. The red-shirted railway porters lay here and there on the platform on their spread-out gamchhas. Some were sitting and playing cards. Beyond the platform, a few women were cooking rice in soot-blackened pots on brick ovens lit with twigs and leaves. A few naked boys and girls hovered around them. Several mangy street dogs roamed around near the families and utensils. Just like the people of the time, they too were fighting and biting one another.

Tired after roaming around for a long time, Jibon drank some water at a tap and sat down on an empty bench. He had been at the station for a long time now, and he had no money with him. He ought to go somewhere now. But the whole city was in panic. All the streets would be empty once it was evening. There were hardly any customers in shops, markets and eateries. Who would give him work, shelter and food at such a time? That was what Jibon was thinking about as he sat on the bench. Just then, a boy who was two or three years older than him came and sat next to him. He was tall and dark-complexioned, with long, dishevelled hair. His eyes had a restless look, as if bearing the stamp of some deep agony. He was dressed in an ill-fitting pair of trousers and a sleeveless vest, and had a lighted beedi on his lips. The boy was a newcomer here. Jibon had never seen him before. Sitting beside Jibon, he asked, a tone of great familiarity, 'What's the point of sitting here? Come, let's go and sleep under the water-tank.' Jibon did not pay any heed to the unknown boy's conviviality. The fresh memory of a black night terrified him. Who knew whether he would take him to some desolate spot and ask him which community he belonged to? He said, 'I'm going to sit here.'

After a while, the boy spoke again, 'Hey, what's your name, boy?'

'Why do you want to know my name?'

'How will I call you unless I know your name?'

'Why would you need to call me?'

'Won't I have to call you if we are together in the same place? People need one another so much and so often. I think I'll spend a few days here! That's why I asked you your name. Or else why would I want to know your name?' There was a mix of simplicity and truth in the boy's tone.

Jibon said, 'My name is Jibon.'

Hearing the name, the boy raised his eyebrows. Jibon wasn't such a special name. But at least it was a name to carry on with, like Bhuto, Nede, Bente or Kelo—Fatty, Baldy, Shorty or Blacky. The boy said, 'Do you know what my name is? You'll be surprised when you hear it. Raja, my name is Raja. I must be four or five years older than you. But you don't have to call me "dada" or anything like that, you can call me by my name.'

Jibon did not object to calling someone who seemed to be worse off and more unfortunate than him, by the name Raja, meaning 'king'. If a butcher's name could be Dayamay, or 'kind', why couldn't a street urchin's name be Raja or Maharaja or Samrat!

By now Jibon had spent a long time in tea-shops, rail stations and pavements. He had heard people telling tales of how sometimes even kings lost their kingdoms and became beggars, like Harishchandra, or like Nawab Siraj-ud-Daulah. And sometimes kings themselves set out on journeys, disguised as beggars, fakirs or sanyasis. It wasn't clear yet why Raja had come here. After a hearty laugh, he explained, 'I'm going to Assam. You could say I'm in the business of travelling to Assam. I go there once a year. A friend of mine has said he'll go with me this time. He lives in Taldi. I have to wait for him here until he can run away from home. I'd have flown away long ago. But it's a long journey, you know. If someone's travelling with you, then you can while away the time talking. I don't like travelling alone.'

The name 'Assam' was not unknown to Jibon. A man used to come to the Jadavpur station to sell amulets. He also performed tricks, making a boy lie down on the ground and then raising him in the air by uttering a mantra. He could put a one-rupee note in the palm of his hand and make it into a ten-rupee note. Apparently, he had learnt these tricks in Assam. It was a remote place, full of mountains and forests. It was where the Kamakhya temple was located. It was said that no male could go there, or else the female sorcerers there would catch him and cast a spell on him, and transform him into a ram. And then he could never get back to his original state. The man who sold amulets and performed tricks had been able to return only because an old woman had helped him across the border of the city of magic. It was she who had taught him a few tricks.

But this boy named Raja had supposedly been to Assam several times. How was it that he had not turned into a ram, how had he been able to return? And he was going there again. Was he telling tall tales? With a mixture of both belief and disbelief, Jibon asked, 'Have you been to the Kamrup Kamakhya temple?'

'Many times.'

'Really?'

'Why should I lie to you?'

'But a man told me that no man can go there, and if he does, then the women there catch him and turn him into a ram.'

Raja said, 'He was lying. It's all lies. Here I am, sitting beside you. Do I look like a ram?'

'They mustn't have seen you then.'

'How come they could not see this big body of mine? Not only did I see lots of people, I also talked to so many people. I also held a person's hand.'

Raja seemed to be lost for a while in the remembrance of holding someone's hand, which had knocked at his memory's door. Then he said, 'Who knows what substance God made the women of that country with. They are like golden scimitars, simply sparkling! And if they touch you, your whole body turns numb. If you speak about magic—they have it, because if any Bengali is so fortunate as to find such a woman, then, why a ram, he'll gladly become even a shoe on her foot! Have you ever been to a cinema? Each and every one of the women in Assam is as beautiful as Vyjayanthimala or Mala Sinha. You can't take your eyes off them!'

The tale about women didn't go very far. How long could Raja alone speak? Jibon had not yet become an artist. He liked to look at women, but that was only from the corner of his eyes. If he ever looked directly at anyone, who knows why, he trembled from head to toe. Once, at the triangular park in Jadavpur, having observed the raunchy boys of the neighbourhood doing so, he too asked a girl walking on the road what the time was. But even before she could tell him the time, he ran away in fright, while behind him, the girl shouted, 'Cocky boy, playing the fool with girls ...!'

After a while, Raja asked Jibon, 'Would you like to smoke a beedi?'

'I don't smoke beedis,' replied Jibon.

Raja was surprised. All the boys of his age who lived in the station indulged in so many vices including drinking and smoking ganja, and this boy was averse to a harmless beedi! How was he faring in the station with his 'vegetarian' ways? 'Then what do you do? What habits do you have? What about gambling?'

'I eat rice. Since childhood, I've had just one obsession. And that's rice. I don't have any vices other than rice.'

Raja heaved a deep sigh and said, 'I too had that obsession earlier. I had to have a handful of rice at least once a day, even if it was rotten, burnt or stale. Now I'm not obsessed with it. If I get it, I eat it, and if I don't, I have no worries. What would I gain by worrying? It's not as if someone would come and put a plate of rice in front of me just because I haven't eaten.'

Below the platform, at some distance, in the shade of the tin-roofed godown, a beggar woman had sat down to eat with her children. What they were eating was not visible from so far. But it wasn't difficult to discern from the way they were eating that they were very hungry. They scooped out the food with a ladle from a black pot and put it on a battered aluminium plate, blew on it to cool it and quickly popped it into their mouths.

Glancing for a moment in that direction, Raja asked Jibon, 'Hey, tell me, how long can you go without eating anything?'

'I can't go even a day without food,' replied Jibon. 'If I don't eat, my hands and legs begin to tremble, my eyesight becomes hazy. Words buzz past my ears.'

Raja said, 'Going without food is no matter at all—once you learn how to do that. Actually, you can learn to do anything whatsoever.' Leaning back on the bench, crossing one leg over the other and sitting with a regal air, he said, 'Do you know how long a camel can stay without water? A month. Do you know how hot a desert is? Is it so simple to go without water for a month in the desert? Can anyone do that?'

Jibon nodded his head. 'They can't.'

'All right, tell me how long a snake can go without food?'

'I don't know.'

'Three whole months! Once it starts becoming cold, it eats one final time and then it gets into its hole and it doesn't emerge for the rest of the winter. It doesn't eat anything at all. So tell me, if they can do that, why can't men do the same?'

A train had arrived at the platform. The morning's pace was missing in the passengers' movements. They were very sluggish. As if the world outside the platform was not as familiar and dear to them as it had been earlier. An inauspicious gale was blowing over the city. Rajabazar was nearby, and just a stone's throw away behind the station was Park Circus. There were reports of fresh disturbances in both the places.

After the throng of passengers had moved away, Raja continued, 'I have an uncle. Not my own. I used to live somewhere, and so I called the man there Uncle. Everyone called him that. My Ma too called him Mad Uncle, "Pagla Mama". I've never seen him eating rice or bread. Every morning, he drank a mug of black tea with two biscuits, and the same in the evening. But if there was ever a wedding somewhere and food was left over, and Uncle was called there—then one got to see what eating really meant! He would polish off a bucket or a bucket and a half of mutton, fifty or sixty luchis, sixty or seventy rossogollas, two or two and a half kilos of curd, and then walk back home. Sometimes Uncle was invited to the babu neighbourhoods just so they could witness the spectacle of Uncle eating like that. But that was always the morning after whatever the occasion was. Not before that. I learnt the trick of staying without food from Uncle.'

'What's the trick?'

'Just don't think about hunger. Try it and see, you'll be able to do it too. All the time, think—"I just finished eating. My tummy's full." You'll see, you won't feel hungry at all.'

A man needed to be a sage to say profound things—that rule evidently did not always apply. Sometimes a foolish, ignorant, illiterate man may utter something that transcends the knowledge of the greatest of sages. Long ago, many thousands of years ago, man did not know whether the sun was bigger than earth or smaller, or whether the sun revolved around the earth or it was the earth that did that. He didn't know why an apple on a tree fell to the ground and why it did not float in the air instead. But he had pointed to the sky and said, 'That's where God lives!' For thousands of years, thousands of sages had been compelled to accept that without question.

The boy named Raja did not know that what he had said today was actually the final path of the Eight-Fold Path, and the ultimate teaching of *Porom Marg*, the Great Way. It had been given the name '*Nivritti Marg*', or the Path of Turning Back, by many sadhaks, munis and tapasvis. Travellers on this path were not attached to anything, whether wealth, pleasure, or indulgence. They had declared that attachment, that is to say, craving or desire, was the root cause of every kind of suffering. If attachment could be uprooted and the mind made inert, lifeless and unperturbed, that was moksha or the final liberation. Once moksha is attained, hunger, thirst, joy, sorrow, love, yearning—nothing at all remains. Everything comes to an end and the living being attains permanent liberation from the state of bondage. He then sees no difference between true and false, male and female, and between payesh and stale rice. The free soul, wearing a loincloth and with an empty stomach, can then lie beneath the shade of a tree and consider himself greater than any lord or master of a million rupees.

For millennia, thousands of great souls had been striving untiringly to take human society on the path towards such liberation. Thanks to the compassionate efforts of the Koran, the Puranas, the Vedas and the Bible, and monasteries, temples, mosques and churches, there had been partial success. Some people had seen the light. Once the rest of humanity could be made aware, the heavenly paradise would descend to the dust of earth. Becoming free of jealousy, malice, sin and violence, man would live in great bliss.

A man with a four-wheeled handcart came and stopped before them. There was a coal-fired oven on it, with round, puffy luchis being fried in a pan of hot oil. Golden luchis, and alur-dam prepared in a thick gravy. The price was four for a rupee. Its aroma filled the air. The aroma in the air had no price. Hungry Jibon inhaled and filled his lungs with as much of it as possible. A great lament arose in his mind. If only he had a rupee now. Observing his altered mood, Raja rebuked him, 'What are you looking at so greedily? Do you think you'll be able to eat it just by looking!'

Jibon replied shamefacedly, 'No, no, it's not for eating. I'm looking at the appearance of the luchis. Aren't they lovely to look at! And they smell terrific too!'

'That's rubbish!' Raja said scornfully. 'Are these luchis at all, when they're fried in Dalda! If you ever go to Assam, you'll see what real luchis are like. Fried in pure ghee, and this big.' He gestured with his hands. 'Do you know what it tastes like? Put it into your mouth and it simply dissolves! I'll be in Assam in a few days. As soon as I'm there, I'm going to gobble eight or ten of them.'

'What's the price of ten?'

'How much can it be, maybe ten rupees. Can't be more than that!'

'Ten rupees!' Ten rupees was ten days' wages for Jibon. Ten rupees was like having ten arms. He could buy a handloom sari for the amount. One could get two fine gamchhas for the price. Five kilos of good rice could also be bought for ten rupees.

Jibon asked, 'I suppose you have lots of money?'

'No, I don't.'

'Then how will you eat ten rupees worth of luchis?'

Shaking his head, Raja replied, 'Hey, am I going to Assam just to gallivant? I'm going to earn money. Assam is a money factory. Do you think it's a land of beggars like Calcutta? There are notes and coins lying on the streets there.'

'Notes and coins on the streets?'

'I told you, money on the streets. You've been sitting here all this while, but did you find a single paisa? Do you think you'd have to sit idle like this in Assam? No! People will come and call you to work and stuff money into your hands. Suppose you carry a small load from here and go and drop it into a rickshaw outside. How much will people pay for that here? Eight annas. But in Assam, they wouldn't pay less than two rupees. Money is like dirt in people's hands there.'

Jibon did not like the city of Calcutta any more. Every man here seemed to him to be a violent, cruel, lustful murderer. It was as if all the people here went around concealing their real appearance beneath decent clothes. It was better for him to stay as far away from them as possible. But where would he escape? In Khola-Doltala, where his parents lived, a greater enemy than any assailant was lying in wait, whose name was hunger. The agony of one's own hunger could nevertheless be borne silently, but what about his little brothers and sister, and his parents? How could he bear to see their agony? That's why Jibon hadn't returned home. He would die if he had to, but he could never return home empty-handed like this.

After a long pause, Jibon said, 'Will you take me with you to Assam?'

'You'll come with me?' Raja asked in astonishment.

'I will, if you take me along.'

'Where's the need for me to take you along? Are you a baby that I need to carry you in my arms? You'll go on your own two legs. But yes, come along. There's nothing to stop you from going there. It's not as if I've bought Assam for myself! Anyone who wishes can go there. If you come along, then I won't wait for that friend of mine. The bastard—can't say whether he'll come or not. How long does it take for someone to change his mind. So let's set off today! What do you say?'

'Today?'

'Why, is there a problem?'

Jibon replied, somewhat morosely, 'But I don't have even a rupee with me.'

As if he were truly a king, Raja said, 'I don't have it either!'

'That's why I say, let's wait for a few more days.'

'Will someone give you a bundle of money in the next few days? Have you bought a lottery ticket that you'll win a prize? What do you hope to achieve by waiting? After all, we'll go by the fucking train, without tickets. What do we need money for?'

'We may not need the fare, but what about food on the way?'

Raja became furious at the mention of food. 'That's what's wrong with you lot. That's why you'll never advance in life. You're surviving perfectly well here, aren't you? You go without food for several days, and just sit or lie somewhere. You don't talk about hunger then. But as soon as one talks about going somewhere, you bring up the question of eating. Anyway, I give you my word, I'll feed you hot rice once on the way, and after that I'll take you to Assam. You don't have any objections now, do you?'

'No, but I mean ...' Jibon said hesitatingly. 'You said you don't have any money, so how will you feed me? One needs money to eat rice ...'

'I don't need it.'

'How's that?'

'How! Oh you idiot, do you think we won't be caught even once by the ticket checkers? If they don't catch us, then we'll go ourselves and surrender to them. Once they send us to jail, where's the worry about food! We'll eat for ten days or so, get a bit strong and then set off once again!'

Jibon remembered his fear of the word 'jail'. Instead of being taken to jail, his father had been taken twenty or twenty-five miles away and dropped in the jungle. What if something of that sort happened with him too, and the ticket checker took them along for another twenty or twenty-five stations and then made them get off? What would Jibon do then, with this starving, weak body of his?

As if blowing away Jibon's apprehensions with a puff, Raja said, 'If they'll take us twenty-five stations ahead, let them. However far they may take us, after all they can't take us to Assam. There aren't even any rail lines there. Besides, once you cross the border and enter Assam, it's another country.'

No, there was no more doubt, hesitation or fear. Whatever had to happen would happen. Making up his mind, Jibon said, 'Let's go then!'

'I hope you won't start crying midway, saying "I'm missing my Ma, take me back!" If that happens, I'm warning you, I'll leave you behind and carry on. You can't then say that Raja is a scoundrel. Think about it. Do you really want to go?'

'I'll go.'

'Great, then let's go!'

The unbelievable journey of two crazies began. Perhaps it would make more sense to call it a conceit. Neither of them had a single paisa, yet they were setting off for Assam. They knew no one in that country, they had no clue about where they would stay or what dangers lay ahead. Yet, deceived by hope, the two boys set off on the journey to the enticing land.

The bridge at Farakka had not yet been built. Trains from Howrah station halted at Farakka, on the bank of the river Brahmaputra. After that, one had to take the ferry across to Khejuriya Ghat. Boarding a train from there, one reached New Jalpaiguri, from where one then took the Gauhati Mail. If there was no delay en route, it was a journey of about sixty hours. Which had to be completed without any expense! This was no less romantic, difficult or courageous than any tale of adventure. In fact, one could say it was even more so.

There was no ticket checker at the exit gate in Sealdah station. They went through the gate at ease, and once outside, began walking towards Howrah. In those days, the tram fare from Sealdah to Howrah was only eight paise. But they didn't have even that. They walked ahead slowly but resolutely, heading westwards, in the direction of where the sun set. The sun had already set by the time they reached Howrah station.

Raja knew which platform the train to Farakka departed from. It was also nearing the time for it to leave. But the problem was how they would enter the station without tickets! The gates here were not unmanned, as in Sealdah. There were two or three ticket checkers at every gate. Besides, there was something that rotated like a wheel which blocked entry, which every person entering had to push to get through, one at a time.

After walking up and down, looking around, Raja spotted a gate where there were no ticket checkers. The wheel-like impediment was locked. The checker must have done that and gone off somewhere. Raja immediately lay down on the ground there, and then in the manner of a soldier advancing on the battlefield, crawling on his chest, he went under the wheel and entered the station concourse. He called out to Jibon, 'Come along, hurry up!' Jibon entered the same way. And then they ran towards the train. The train guard was swinging the green lamp in his hand, signalling to the engine driver to depart. They ran and boarded one of the carriages of the train.

The carriage wasn't so crowded. The passengers were sitting quite comfortably. There were a few vacant seats, they could have sat there if they wanted. But they didn't do that. For one, they had no tickets, and on top of that, to occupy a seat—that would be a great offence in the eyes of both the ticket checker as well as other passengers. And so they went and sat down on the floor at the open door on the opposite side, one boy on each side of the door-frame, their legs resting on the steps below. The platform wasn't on that side. They could enjoy the breeze and look at the scenery outside. In very little time, leaving the brightly lit city behind, the train entered the womb of night's dense darkness. As the train advanced, the lights on the Howrah Bridge slowly receded into the distance.

Jibon had never ventured out from Calcutta on such a long journey before this. As the train moved ahead, as Calcutta was slowly left behind, he was filled with a kind of sadness. He had spent a long time on the streets of this city. All that he got was humiliation, injustice and oppression. The city had also denied him food for days on end. And yet, who knows why, he was sad to be leaving. His father, grown old ahead of his years, used to wait expectantly with a basket and spade in a corner of this city in the hope of finding work. His famished brothers and sister used to wait for their father to return home. His helpless Ma used to wipe her tears as she looked at his brothers' and sister's worn faces. This city hadn't bothered about their woes. That's why they had never been able to eat to their fill. They had never gotten any medicines when they were sick. When it rained, water seeped in through the tattered roof of the shanty and wet the emaciated bodies of the six unfortunate humans inside. When winter came, they shivered in the cold and wept. Jibon wasn't able to figure out whether he was sad for the helpless folk or for the hard-hearted city. But his eyes brimmed with tears. He thought to himself—Oh dear Ma, I am a worthless son. Forgive me. I could not fulfill any of my duties. That's why I'm leaving you behind and running away like a thief. I don't know where I am going. I don't even know what I shall get there, and yet I'm going. And even if no one knows or understands why I'm going, I know that you know and you understand. If I have done wrong, forgive me.

'Hey, are you crying?'

'No, I'm not.'

'Then why are there tears in your eyes?'

'Some insect or something got into my eye.'

'Where, let me see!'

Raja blew into Jibon's eyes. He put his arm around him and drew him close to him, and then said, 'Actually, I feel like crying. Who knows whether I'll be able to return. If I die or something, I won't be able to come back.'

There was a mesmerising quality in the sound of the moving train. When one listened attentively and for a long time to the sounds of the wheels of the speeding train thundering down the track, and to the chugging of the engine—altogether, the sweet music made one drowsy with intoxication. After that, after a long period of the same kind of instrumental music, when the train stopped at some station—the chorus of vendors' babble, and the shouts and busy running around of porters—all that was like a dead town suddenly bursting into exultation, festivity and joy at coming back to life, awakened by the touch of some magician's wand.

Jibon had now forgotten the melancholy of dusk, and he became immersed in the indescribable, intoxicating touch of the depths of night. The more the night advanced, the more his intoxication intensified. He found a poetic beauty in the hoarse-throated, double-syllabic cries of the tea-sellers, the nasal cries of the pakoda and sweetmeat sellers, and mixed with all of those, assorted, complex, incoherent waves of sounds, it seemed to him that the lingering trace of that orchestral music pervaded the slumbering night.

There had never been a night like this in the life of the boy named Jibon. It was a night that seemed to enrich life and usher in a new melody and beauty. And so, he was overcome by a wave of euphoria. The tiny boat of his life was rocked by countless waves of delicious elation.

After some time, Jibon found Raja resting against the door and singing, '*Amader jatra holo shuru ogo kornodhar tomake kori nomoshkar. Ekhon bancha mora tomar haate phirbo naki aar ...* Greetings, O Lord, our journey's begun! Life and death are in your hands now, I know not whether I shall return ...' Raja had a melodious singing voice. The tune was captivating. He had not learnt it from any maestro, after painstaking effort. He had just picked it up effortlessly. It was as if a sorrowful Baul had poured his life's essence into the tune and was now giving voice to the song of his lonely life. It wasn't a song, it was like an upsurge of a helpless man's distress, a surrendering to the god of life. Jibon didn't know who had composed the song, but whoever may have written or composed it, it seemed to have been done specifically for a vagabond youth, who had set out on an uncertain journey on a dark night and sat down on the dirt at the door of a moving train, to sing and derive inspiration from. As if he was the rightful heir to this song. The song was no longer simply a song for him, it was as if it had become his life-prop, which one could clutch firmly and, notwithstanding one's hungry stomach, race ahead towards an unknown destination.

Raja sang one song after another. They went past one station after another. The night advanced. As Jibon sat listening to the songs in the blowing wind, he turned drowsy. After a while, he lay down in front of the door, in the dust and dirt, on shreds of paper and butts of beedis and cigarettes, with his hand resting on Raja's lap. He fell fast asleep.

$$19$$

'Live Up to Your Name!'

When Jibon woke up, the eastern sky was alight. Gradually, beyond rural Bengal's vast green paddy fields, thickets of bamboo and groves of mango, jamun, coconut and palm, the large golden face of the sun became visible, like a red dot of vermillion on the forehead of a shy bride. Little by little, it began to rise higher in the sky. Its first light spread over all the fields, trees and plants, marshlands, houses and people. There was life in this light. Nature, that seemed to be almost dead in the night, now began to smile on receiving the light and warmth. A flock of white storks were flying on their journey across the sky. Forming a large 'V', the storks made their way in the northeasterly direction.

After he awoke and sat up, Jibon saw Raja holding the door handle with his left hand, resting his head against the door and gazing fixedly at the storks in flight. Jibon asked him, 'Didn't you sleep?'

'I didn't feel like sleeping. I was missing my Ma a lot. It's been such a long time since I saw her.'

'Didn't you go to see your Ma before leaving?'

'How could I visit her?' Raja heaved a deep sigh and then said, 'I don't know where she lives now.' Wiping the tears that had begun to form in the corner of his eyes on his arm, Raja slowly said, 'How old was I then, must have been three or four years old—Ma dropped me at the Sealdah station, left me there and said, "Sit here, I'll go and get some food for you". That was the last I saw of her.'

'Don't you have a father?'

'I don't know whether I have a father or not. Ma knew about that. She never told me anything about my father.'

Jibon thought for a while and then said, 'Before that, I mean before your Ma left you at the station and went away, where did you live? Don't you remember that? You could go and search there.'

Raja replied, 'I can't remember where I lived earlier. I vaguely remember we lived in a shanty beside the railway line. There was a large saw-mill nearby. They used to cut wood there with large saws. There was also a big lake nearby, where we used to bathe. I don't remember anything else.'

Raja did not have anything more to say. Jibon did not have any more questions either. It was as if all the questions and answers were lost in a blind alley. All of Raja's past had been wiped out, it had disappeared. He had no other identity, he too was just another of the countless failed, defeated, unnoticed, unnecessary people, who were all merely the discarded garbage of the world in the eyes of civilised folk, towards whom no one felt any empathy or compassion. This boy—born of a father who gave birth to him and then vanished and a mother who then cast him away and freed herself from all responsibility—now tramped the streets of the world and was growing up like a wild weed. Like a weed, he would give birth to a few more weeds and one day die like a weed. And yet, in him too lay the raw material with which men became great and famous. But that was withering for want of a little bit of attention.

Jibon asked Raja, 'Raja, you sing so beautifully! Who did you learn that song from?'

'Whatever I learnt was by hearing my Ma sing. I was very small, but I still remember the tunes I heard then. I sing whenever I feel sad, and it makes me feel better.' Raja sat silently for a while, and then he said, 'I thought so many times that I won't return to Calcutta, that I'll remain in Assam—after all, who do I have in Calcutta? Who will I return to? But I'm unable to do that. After six months or a year, my heart begins to cry for Calcutta. I then come running back like a lunatic. I search the Sealdah station frantically. Perhaps I'll see my Ma sitting in some corner. After all, she doesn't know where I live now ... If she comes to look for me someday, where would she go? I once saw in a cinema that a boy was separated from his mother at the Kumbh Mela. His mother turned insane with sorrow. Twelve years later, when she had recovered from insanity, she returned to the mela and found her son. Who knows, maybe my Ma really went to get food and was knocked down by a car or something, and lost her memory. Maybe she'll get back her memory one day. And then she'll return to the bench in front of which she left me. That's why I go there and search for her. What else can I do, tell me?'

Oh you fool! The ways of life are nothing like the cinema screen. Here, the scene and dialogue cannot be changed at will. Hoping for any repetition is futile. On this road, once anyone was lost, they remained lost. The ways of the world were very difficult, harsh and winding. While it may be easy to set out, it wasn't at all easy to remember the way back and return as the same person to the old address.

Jibon said, 'After all, you have an umbilical connection with Calcutta. But why did you go away to faraway Assam? Did someone take you there, or did you go all by yourself?'

Raja laughed a bit now. He said, 'Like you, I too used to believe that one could learn magic if one went to Kamrup-Kamakhya. After a sadhu told me how to get there, I set off all by myself one day. I've been going back and forth ever since.'

At about eight in the morning, the train reached Farakka station. Unlike in Sealdah or Howrah, there was no railing, gate, shed and so on in the station. There weren't so many streets or any procession of cars and vehicles, big and small. There were no tall buildings or bustling crowds of people. The ferry station was about a mile and a half away. All the passengers who got off the train were walking in that direction. Raja and Jibon followed them.

Arriving at the ferry station, they saw two or three steamers anchored at the riverbank, perhaps waiting for passengers. There were also quite a few large cargo boats there, which were being loaded with goods. There were some small fishing boats too. Some bare-bodied, dark-skinned fishermen in loincloths were unloading basketfuls of various kinds of river fish. There were lots of hotels and eateries fringing the ferry station. All of them had bamboo-mat walls and tin roofs. They were all crowded with people now.

Passengers were boarding the steamer that was going to depart first. People were slowly climbing the gangway with their luggage. At the end of the gangway, in front of the entry door of the vessel, two or three skinny, lungi-clad men were checking the passengers' tickets before allowing them to board the steamer. Raja and Jibon did not have tickets. Jibon looked inquiringly at Raja. Raja did not pay any heed to Jibon's unease. He said, 'Just be patient, wait and see.'

'But the steamer's about to leave!'

'Let it leave. There will be so many more after this, there's one every half hour. We'll get our chance in one or the other.'

The hooter of the steamer blared once again. It was the last hoot. It had already been sounded twice before. All the passengers had boarded. The lungi-clad ticket checkers flicked the beedis from their lips into the water and prepared to remove the gangway. Just then, a woman with a large bundle in her hand and a brood of kids came running towards the steamer. Probably most of the shopkeepers here were employees of the ferry service, and all of them seemed to know the woman well. Because as soon as they saw her, laughter and various kinds of remarks sprang out from several shops. Roundly cursing their filthy language as she climbed the gangway, the heavily-laden woman was about to board the vessel with the kids, when—perhaps after the new employee asked to see her ticket—she added in a tone that was a scream, wail and abuse all at once: 'Ticket! Why, don't you have a mother or a sister at home!

Why don't you go and check their tickets? If you want to see my ticket, come with me, I'll show you the ticket!' Flabbergasted by the woman's crude language and bizarre gestures, the poor ticket checkers moved aside in fright and the woman boarded the vessel together with her brood. Almost as soon as the woman climbed the gangway, Raja ran, following her and folding his hands in a plea before the stupid beedi-puffing checkers, and said, 'Babu, don't be angry, babu, after all my Ma's a bit cracked.' He had addressed them as 'babu', and on top of that the apology with folded hands. The ticket checkers were felled by the two-pronged assault. Before they could recover their senses, pulling Jibon along by the hand, Raja disappeared into the bustling crowd inside the steamer.

'Phew! We're in, let's see what happens now!'

Jibon wasn't assured by Raja's relief. 'What if someone catches us now?'

'If they catch us, they catch us! What can they do if they catch us? They have to drop us off at either of the two sides. They can't push us off the steamer, throw us into the water, can they?'

The vessel had departed almost as soon as they boarded. The water was muddy and red. There were small waves rippling on the surface. After the steamer had been moving for a while, visible on the right side, far away, was the greenery of the mango, jamun, coconut and areca-nut trees of a village. Just in front of that, fishermen on boats were casting their nets in the waters of the Brahmaputra.

Raja said, 'That's East Pakistan.'

'Our country! We used to live there earlier.'

'I know you're from East Bengal, that's why I showed it to you.'

'And you?'

'Mohun Bagan!'

After half an hour, the vessel reached Khejuriya Ghat on the other shore. There were no ticket checkers at the gate on this side. The two of them got off with ease. The railway station here had been built very close to the river, by laying tracks on the sandy soil. Seeing the station, anyone would figure out at once that it was not a permanent affair. Once the Brahmaputra rose, it would be dismantled and moved back. The same with the shops. Everything was temporary. Tea-shops and eateries had sprung up on the sand of the riverbank, one separated from the other by reed or bamboo matting. There was a train waiting at the station. It was as if the engine that would haul the carriages was asleep. There was no sound of the rapid puffs, accompanied by the hot exhalation of steam. The engine now was just like a bullock that rested in the shade of a tree, chewed cud and let out an enormous amount of piss.

Raja said, 'I think it will be quite a while before the train leaves. Come, let's find something to eat.'

A bazaar had come up parallel to the rail track. Farmers from the nearby village had come there to sell various kinds of crops and fruits, especially ripe mangoes. The mangoes, four or five of which would comprise a kilo, was selling for an anna each. If one bought a rupee's worth, one could get eighteen, and some sellers were offering even twenty for a rupee. Raja went up to the basket of an old farmer and asked, 'Are the mangoes sweet? Or are they sour?' The old man responded with his hands—he held out a slice of a cut mango. Raja took a bite and gave the rest to Jibon. 'Try it.'

In this way, going from one vendor to the other, the two of them tasted slices of mangoes from all the baskets in the market. This was a lot like sucking the nectar of those yellow flowers from the camp, or like breaking the tender stalks from the paddy field and pressing them between the teeth to drain the milky juice inside. It did not wipe out one's hunger, but it did offer some consolation.

Raja said, 'I don't think the mango harvest this time has been so good, or else there would have been many more people here, selling mangoes. We could have eaten to our fill. But at least we got something, and that's better than nothing! Even if we don't get anything else all day, we can carry on, isn't it?'

The train departed for New Jalpaiguri at about ten in the morning. All the carriages were quite vacant. With only five or ten passengers in each carriage, the train slowly advanced along the tracks laid on the sand. Raja and Jibon occupied their favourite spot, sitting on the two sides of a door. They gazed at the sun, the smoke from the engine, the paddy fields, the marshlands, orchards and cows grazing in fields, the villages speeding away in the distance, and the village folk.

Was all this new? Had Jibon not seen it before? Of course, he had seen it all. But he had never seen this scenery with the kind of mind-frame he was in now.

As the train left behind one station after another, gradually the number of passengers increased. But throughout the day, the train was never really crowded. After running continuously the whole day, and without any hold-ups on the way, the train reached New Jalpaiguri in the evening. There were no more trains going to Assam tonight. They would only be available the next morning.

Jibon was going crazy with hunger now. His limbs were trembling. When he tried to speak, it was as if the words exited through his ears. He felt as if someone was trying to tear out his intestines. As if the bird of life raised in the cage of his ribs did not want to remain bound inside any longer. As if it would leave the cage behind and fly away somewhere right now.

Raja was hungry too, but unlike Jibon, his hunger did not turn into agony but anger. He said very angrily, 'Did you see the scandalous state of the bastards, Jibon? Is it possible? We've travelled a thousand miles, all the way from Calcutta, but did you spot even a single ticket checker? Two people merrily travelling without tickets, as if it's their dad's train! And no one to catch them! All the *banchods* are useless! The bastards collect their salaries and go home and sleep! Tell me, what can we do now!'

Jibon couldn't really understand the rage of his ticketless-travel companion against ticket checkers. His brain had probably stopped functioning under hunger's duress. Raja explained the matter to him. 'If there had been ticket checkers and if they had caught and thrown us in jail, we could have eaten comfortably for a few days. I'm not saying this for myself, I can go on for a couple of days without even water. It's because of you. Looking at your face I know you're in agony. Aren't you hungry?'

'What? What did you say?'

'I know you're hungry. Your head and ears are surely ringing, that's why you can't hear what I said. Come, let me see whether I can arrange for some food for you from somewhere.'

It had turned dark by then. Although the electric lamps on the lamp-posts had begun to come on all around, the light was not so bright as to wipe out the blood-curdling darkness. The hill-station town of Darjeeling, situated on the crest of a faraway mountain, was visible from here. The lights of the local streets, houses, shops and markets that had just come on looked like a host of stars that had fallen from the sky and spread out in all directions. It was as if the stars had fallen on the branches of trees in a dense green forest and were twinkling in unison.

Emerging from the rail station, they walked in the direction of the distant lights. It was a bit cold here at this time. There was nobody on the road. It was completely desolate. Only a few people had arrived by the train, twenty or twenty-five people at most, and they had all left for their destinations by now. To the eyes of one used to the lights, people, cars and carriages of Calcutta, the desolation, the mountains and forests and the whole environment here was frightening. Jibon held Raja's right hand firmly in his left hand. He understood how safe the touch of the hand of someone who had become a friend only twenty-four hours ago could make him feel.

After walking for about fifteen or twenty minutes, they reached a crossroads. There was a banyan tree there. The base of the tree was ringed with stones to form a seating platform. There was a row of shops on the road on the right. The first one was a sweet shop, the one after that was an eatery. The owner of the first one was Bengali, and that of the next one, Nepali.

Raja said, 'Come, let's go near the shop.'

'We've got no money, what will we do in the shop?'

Raja's eyes scanned the place, and then he said, 'There are two options. The first one: we can eat as much as we want and run. Can you do that?'

'If they catch us, they'll thrash us badly.'

'They won't thrash us badly, they'll only slap and punch us a few times.'

'I can't take any beating, it hurts too much.'

'Then there's the second option: we'll go and say we want to work. If they give us work, they'll give us food too. Will you work? We can work here for a few days, eat properly, get refreshed, and then set out for Assam.'

'That's what we should do.'

Raja went to the sweet shop and, in a simple, intelligent tone, said to the shop owner, 'Excuse me, the two of us live in Calcutta. We have come to see this place of yours. We want to stay here for a few days. Can we get any work in your shop? I have the bad habit of smoking beedis, if you can give me a few that would be nice, but it doesn't matter if you can't.' The Bengali shop owner called the Nepali owner from the shop beside him. The two of them laughed heartily for a while, and said enthusiastically, 'You'll definitely get work. We've been looking for workers. There's such a lot of work piled up for lack of workers! Come, come boys. Stay as long as you like, eat, enjoy yourselves, see the place!'

Raja and Jibon were immediately recruited at the Nepali's eatery and the Bengali's sweet shop respectively. From the godowns at the rear of the two shops there emerged huge pots and pans, basins, ladles, spuds and so much more! Pointing to the small mound of utensils, they said, 'We aren't giving any more than this seeing that you're tired today after a long journey. Wash and clean these thoroughly, and let's see you make them shine.'

There was a bamboo fence between the two shops. Both Jibon and Raja sat at the taps on either side. There was a mountain of utensils in front of each one, which looked like they hadn't been washed for many years. They had been given ash and soda and told, 'As soon as you've finished the work, you'll get hot rice.' The temptation of food made the two boys begin their gruelling, two-to-three-hour-long wrestling match against the utensils. Finally, after he had finished, before he went inside with a large basin, Raja said to Jibon, 'We'll get out in the morning. The train to Assam leaves at seven. Don't forget that! If we don't leave, the bastards will make us work till we die!'

Deeds followed words. In the morning, Raja set off in the direction of his destination. Jibon knew he would go there, just as he too was supposed to. But is everything accomplished in a timely manner just because it is supposed to be? After he had eaten, Raja had been asked to sleep outside, on the verandah of the eatery, from where it was easy to slip away, while Jibon was inside a locked wooden room on the upper floor. He could not come out unless the door was unlocked from outside. Besides, tired after a twenty-four-hour-long journey, he hadn't been able to wake up on time. When he did wake up, he heard shouting and a volley of abuse in Nepali outside: 'The fucking thief, he's slipped away!'

There was a huge difference between 'slipped away' and 'stole and ran away'. But that difference was judged according to place, time and person. When was a weak, poor child from a faraway land ever favoured with such precise specification! Someone caught Jibon by his hair and dragged him outside the shop. He slapped him hard on his cheeks. 'Get out, you fucking thief! Run!'

Where would the friendless Jibon go in this foreign land? He began crying, not because of the stinging slaps but thinking about his helpless plight. He felt as if he had fallen into a well with his hands and legs bound. He was helpless now, as if certain death were staring him in the face. Any second it would swoop down like an eagle and grasp him in its sharp talons.

Walking away from the shop, Jibon came to the crossroads and sat down under the banyan tree. His eyes frantically searched in all directions. He could not spot anyone before whom he could supplicate, 'I am in great danger. Please save me.'

Jibon wasn't aware of how long he sat alone in the friendless seat under the tree. Nor did he know when the tears in his eyes dried up. The face of Maran, the boy who roamed the cremation ground, whom he had last seen years ago, floated into the pupils of his dry eyes now. Maran, the one who never accepted defeat under any circumstance. Who, despite being alive, had died, so that he could defeat death. Who had said one day—'Your name is Jibon. Live up to your name, don't piss and shit and die out of fear of death!'

Jibon steeled himself now and stood up. He began to walk ahead slowly. After walking a few steps, he thought, yes, I can. He would be able to walk alone, even without anyone's help. The road wasn't a winding one. In fact, it was as straight as a bowstring. Walking along the straight road, Jibon reached the railway station, from where he had walked yesterday, holding Raja's hand. The station wasn't as vacant now as it had been yesterday evening. Feeling somewhat assured at the presence of people, Jibon went and sat down by himself on a bench.

He began to long for the crazy Baul named Raja. It was as if he had disappeared like a gentle breeze. Like a river that had run dry and vanished, not a trace remained anywhere. And when he departed, he had taken away with him everything that he had brought along.

Yet, it seemed he hadn't been able to take away everything. A disorganised person had inattentively left something behind, whose name was memory, which remained in some secret chamber in the recesses of the mind of the boy named Jibon. This memory would stay with him all his life like a shining star. It would never turn grey, dull, or colourless.

20

Spring Thunder and Swindle
in Siliguri

Raja wasn't at the New Jalpaiguri station. Nor was he supposed to be there. The train that was meant to depart at seven in the morning had done so on time. Raja had left on that train. The next train to Assam was at twelve o'clock, and there was another one at four in the afternoon. It was only about ten o'clock now. How would Jibon while away the two hours? After dawdling awhile, he got up to look around the station. Once he was done scanning Platform No. 1, he climbed the over-bridge to Platform No. 2. But his eyes could not spot the familiar signs of a railway platform. There was no clay oven here, surrounded by the emaciated children of a beggar mother. There was no torn, dirty kantha spread out on the railing to dry. There were no drunks expostulating. No groups of railway porters playing cards. No one was quarrelling or fighting. The atmosphere here was utterly peaceful and without any kind of disturbance. Roaming along seeing all this—or not seeing anything—Jibon whiled away the time. When the clock showed twelve o'clock, a train arrived at the platform from the car-shed. All those who had to travel slowly boarded the carriages. Jibon too had to get on. There was no reason why he should keep sitting. He got into a carriage and sat down beside the door as of old, with his legs dangling.

The train departed from New Jalpaiguri and arrived at Siliguri shortly after. Thousands of passengers stood waiting there with their large bed-rolls, trunks and suitcases to board the train. The moment the train came to a halt, they rushed to get into the carriages. With all the screaming, shouting and commotion, it was as if the station had suddenly been transformed into a battleground. People stepped on each other's toes, elbowed and pushed one another to get ahead in the competition to occupy a seat of their choice. When all that ceased, the one who could not be glimpsed even after the past few days' tapasya, that unexpected figure, suddenly appeared and stood in front of Jibon—a giant of a ticket checker, in his black coat. 'Ticket!' Shaking both his head and hands simultaneously, Jibon responded, 'I don't have one.' The ticket checker did not need to hear anything more. In exactly the way an eagle swoops down and takes away a baby mouse, he grabbed Jibon with his huge paw. After that, in the way a prisoner of war is tied to a horse and taken away, he dragged him from the train to the station's exit gate. Finally, a hefty push: 'Go!'

Observing Jibon's clothes—a pair of shorts, a sleeveless vest, a gamchha around his neck—and bare feet, the ticket checker had realised that someone like that did not possess the resources or capability to pay either the fine or a bribe. Getting into a train without a ticket was not such a heinous act. What was heinous was not having the means for either, the fine or a bribe. Such people deserved to be ejected. In every sphere of their life, at every step, they were constantly pushed out. And that's what the ticket checker too had done.

Beyond the exit gate was the ticket counter. Beside that was a vacant wooden bench. Sitting on that, Jibon cast his eyes once again at the station and the Assam-bound train. Black-coated ticket checkers and khaki-uniformed railway police seemed to be everywhere, around the train and all over the station. Jibon had never seen so many policemen and ticket checkers even at Howrah and Sealdah. He did not know how he would board the train, evading so many pairs of eyes. Raja, the one who would know, was no longer there.

What would Jibon do now? He could not get into the train, and so would he now have to be alone in this foreign land, and die of fear, anxiety, hunger and thirst? If he had to die, then why had he come to this faraway place? Was death at all scarce in Calcutta? He had come so he could survive. He still wanted to survive. He needed to survive in order to save everyone else. If he had to save everyone, then going to Assam was necessary too. That was where money lay on the streets, money with which the means for survival could be purchased.

Sitting on the bench pondering over such things, Jibon became drowsy. A face floated into his dream. Jibon couldn't exactly figure out whether the face belonged to Fatik or Maran or Raja. It said, 'If you really want to go to Assam, then if you can't travel without a ticket, just buy a ticket and go! That should be simple!'

Jibon brushed off his drowsiness and stood up. There was a large stall in front of the ticket counter. Various kinds of edible items were arranged in its showcase. Kachoris, singharas and so much more were being fried on a stove. Tea was being prepared, thick with milk. Jibon went up to the shop and, adopting a tone like Raja, said, 'Do you need someone to work in your shop? I've come from Calcutta in search of work.'

The owner of the shop, long-haired and clean-shaven, had an effeminate look. With the sweet intonation of a Vaishnav devotional song in his voice, he replied, 'Where was your homeland?'

'It was in Barisal district, in East Pakistan, sir.'

'We are from Dacca district. Don't they say, learning, brains and money are all in Dacca! What's your name?'

'Jibon. I'm Jibon Krishna Dutta, sir.'

'Such a nice name, a Kayastha. Yes, I do need someone.'

'How much will you pay me?'

'Pay you!' He laughed and said, ' Learn the work first. Without seeing how you work, how can I tell you about salary? You're from my country, we belong to the same caste—we are Saha. Why would I cheat you!'

'No, but please say something. I badly need money. I can wash cups and make tea.'

'All right! Since you're insisting, after the first month, take forty rupees a month.'

Jibon would get forty rupees after merely sixty days. Only sixty days and then he would have the train fare. After those few days— Jibon would have the entry-pass to the magical city! Once he reached there, the happiness he yearned for would be within hand's reach!

❧

Jibon had been running hither and thither like a chased dog. But at the same time, unknown to him, the tide had turned in the political history of West Bengal. The political party that had been firmly ensconced in power ever since India's independence—the Congress—had been rocked. Because of the somersault by Ajoy Mukherjee, an influential leader of their party, together with his friends and associates, the party was no longer in power.

A United Front, comprising fourteen parties, came into office. Ajoy Mukherjee became the chief minister of the new government and Jyoti Basu, the leader of the Communist Party of India (Marxist), or CPI(M), became deputy chief minister. The police department was under Basu. As a result, there was a revival of hope among the workers, peasants and labouring folk of rural Bengal. Workers thought that when the police department was in the hands of a leader of the party of the working class, the industrialists would no longer be able to stifle—with the help of the police— the workers' movements to demand their legitimate rights. The peasants too, who had been hearing all along that the natural owner of the land was the one who ploughed the land, were galvanised with hope. 'Those whose feet never touched the soil were the ones who owned the land'—that old, unjust credo would finally be changed now.

That was in the beginning of 1967. Autumn had turned to winter, and an extreme one at that. While people who lacked clothes trembled, the green stalks on the paddy fields turned golden. In time, that too passed. Came spring. Spring is called the season of love. But this time, for the region of north Bengal, it was a rebellious spring that arrived, with a resounding clap of thunder.

Jibon was at the station tea-shop in Siliguri at the time. People from various places used to visit the shop. From hearing scraps of their conversation, he too had gathered that the spring hadn't brought any good news for the happy and peace-loving folk of Siliguri. The town was abuzz. As if everyone was trembling in a fever of fear. After a few days, Jibon saw that the whole of Siliguri, including the station and markets, was awash in the colour of khaki. The district police headquarters was in Siliguri. It seemed like a whole army of policemen had arrived in trucks, vans and jeeps, carrying rifles, Sten guns, and SLRs. They were all from the Central Reserve Police. And then the convoy left in the same vehicles. With their arrival and departure, a battle-like atmosphere set in, seeing which, one might have thought that they were now going to avenge their humiliating defeat at the hands of China in 1962.

Not far from the station, in a red-coloured, two-storey house, lived a lawyer. Every morning, after a half-hour walk, he came and sat on a wooden bench in front of the ticket counter. A vendor there sold newspapers. The lawyer sat and went through the pages of all the papers, one by one. In the course of doing that, he had two cups of tea. He paid for one cup. The second cup was courtesy of the tea-shop owner. After that, the two of them discussed the various problems afflicting the world. At around eight o'clock, the lawyer would leave.

One day, he said, 'Saha babu, have you heard the news?' The tea-shop owner, Binod Saha, shook his head. 'No. What's the news?' There were so many newspapers right next to him, so many policemen had arrived and departed in front of his very eyes, and yet Binod Saha did not keep himself apprised of anything. But the lawyer wasn't surprised. There were some people like that—in all countries, at all times—who had no time or taste for anything other than thinking about, smelling and counting money. But Binod Saha wasn't entirely like that. And so the lawyer said, 'Police stations are on fire in Naxalbari, Kharibari and Phansidewa.' All three places were near Siliguri. Binod Saha had never been to any of these places, but he had heard their names. He said, 'If they are on fire, why are policemen going there? How will the police deal with the fire? Fire-engines should have gone instead!'

'*Arey moshai*, it's not that kind of fire. Ten people, including seven women and two children, were killed in police firing. Apparently some landlords and policemen too died. Thousands of Santhal peasants and workers, armed with bows and arrows have gathered there to wage war. A complete state of anarchy! The law and order situation is dire. It's like what happened at the time of the Tebhaga movement ...'

Saha babu did not have the time to read newspapers. He didn't really need to either. He got all the important news from other people. That's how he knew about the Tebhaga movement. Those were terrible times indeed. Hearing that such times had now returned, he said, 'So that's why there are so many policemen coming and going.'

The lawyer said, 'Thirty battalions have arrived. More will come if required.' Finishing the second cup of tea, he said, 'But this time, it's not going to be so easy. The peasants are not so scared of the police this time. They are confronting the police head-on. With choppers, *bontis*, spades, axes, bows and arrows. Can you imagine, are these any weapons at all when compared to rifles?'

'I've heard that the Santhals are very peaceful and good-natured, that they don't unnecessarily engage in fights. What's the reason for them suddenly getting so enraged?'

'It's not their fault. It's the fault of those who are now sitting in government. It's they who had once filled their heads with the idea that land belonged to the tiller. So now the Santhals are saying, the landlords are nothing, simply parasites, and the true owner of land is the one who harvests grain with the sweat of his brow. Can you imagine! In that case, the bullock who pulls the plough should also be the owner! Does it become the owner? Or does it get a handful of paddy? The party leaders did not think then that all that they said in order to come into power would come back like a bamboo up their backside. And so whatever had to happen is happening now. The peasant bumpkins think that they now have a parallel government of the poor and are dancing with joy. They are cutting the paddy on thousands of bighas of land, looting the granaries of landlords, and carrying away the grain to their own granaries. Of course, at the final moment, Jyoti babu's good sense finally dawned. He realised what ought to be done at this time. He asked the central government to dispatch the C.R.P. forces. But the C.R.P. too are facing arrows when they try to supress the peasants. The situation is extremely volatile.'

Binod Saha smiled and said, 'Then it's a great time for you! The more killings, riots, anarchy and settling of scores there are, the more lawyers and court clerks will benefit. They can get their hands on some money. If there's peace in the country and if everyone becomes a good boy, what's there to gain then! Are you getting cases?'

'*Na moshai*,' said the lawyer, sorrowfully. 'Go to the court some day and see for yourself. Every day the police are bringing in twenty or twenty-five people. You should see their plight. Not one of them has the means to buy a shirt to cover his body. All are naked. How will they fight cases and pay the lawyer's and clerks' fees? One needs the strength of money to fight cases in court. None of them has that. All of them are being sent to prison. All of them will rot and die in jail. I heard that there's no more space in the sub-jail. Five or seven thousand people have been crammed there when there's space only for fifteen hundred.'

After this, it became like a ritual for the lawyer to say something or the other about the peasant movement in the areas under the Naxalbari, Kharibari and Phansidewa police stations. One day, he had just finished his tea, put down the cup and turned the page of a newspaper, when a school teacher he knew appeared there. In those days, members of the teaching community did not have huge salaries and shining visages like they have today. Dressed in a panjabi which had been darned, rubber slippers on his feet, his face unshaven and his hair looking like a crow in a storm—that was their typical appearance. Seeing a school teacher like that, the lawyer laughed out aloud, 'What's happening, sir? What's all this your people have started?'

'What have they started?'

'This business of slitting the throats of landlords and looting grain. Do you think all this is right?'

Probably the teacher wasn't in a good mood then. Responding to the lawyer's provocation with fire in his voice, he asked him in turn, 'In your opinion, what would have been right, then? That those who do back-breaking labour in sun and rain and grow paddy should deliver the harvest to the granaries of those who don't let the hot sun touch them, or a drop of rain wet them, or let their feet touch the soil, and then simply tie a gamchha around their bellies and lie down? The eternal law, the way things had always happened—it would have been good if that's what prevailed, isn't it?'

'No ... not that ...' stuttered the lawyer. 'There are laws, there is a judicial system in the country. Besides, there's a government in office that came to power with the votes of poor folk. Wouldn't it have been good if everything was done peacefully and resolved constructively through discussions? But instead of doing that ...'

'Do you think it's possible to convince a tiger, through discussion, that instead of eating meat, eating tender blades of grass would be much better for its health?'

'Are tigers and men the same?'

'Each one of those landlords is more terrifying than any tiger. A tiger doesn't hunt unless it's hungry. But these people—they kill for no reason! Their greed knows no limits. Unless they are wiped out, labouring folk won't be able to survive. That's the lesson of history.'

After a pause, the lawyer said, 'So you want to say that government, law, the judicial system, all these amount to nothing? That people need not rely on these? That one can do whatever one thinks is right?'

'I'm not saying that. Who am I to say anything? From their own experience, people are realising that they can cast their vote, but there's no certainty that the government will be theirs. Everyone can see what the role of those who are now in power was before they came into office, and what it is now. Their hands don't tremble before firing at women and children. It's clear whose interests they are serving. So what will people do? Those in whom they had vested their hopes for so long are betraying them. And so, people are standing up on their own feet and fighting for their rights, their own way.'

'But I think this path is a wrong one. By fighting like this, they won't achieve anything other than death.'

'What's the point of you and me, two urban babus, discussing whether it's right or wrong while we sip tea, far away from the battlefield! If it's wrong, those who are fighting will correct themselves. If it's right, they'll be successful. When we are not beside them or behind them through their joys and sorrows, what do they care about our opinions?'

⚛

Jibon wanted to visit Naxalbari and Kharibari. He had been to Mongla's hamlet, back in Shiromanipur. He had seen with his own eyes how difficult Santhal life was. Now the poor Santhal peasants and farm-labourers were fighting a brave battle. Their leader's name was Jangal Santhal. Under his leadership, the peasant masses had declared rebellion against exploitation, deprivation and oppression.

Jibon felt this was also his battle. He had witnessed communal riots between Hindus and Muslims. A few drops of blood from those riots had stained his hands too, whose stench perturbed him till this day. He had never thought that those battles were right, or that they were his own battles. But now he thought that the current battle was like his own.

Although Jibon wanted to go to those places, he was unable to. He remained at the tea-shop, beside the pile of soiled plates, glasses and cups. Eight or ten months had passed by in this way. Saha babu had said that he would pay him from the second month onwards. As soon as that month was over, Jibon stood with outstretched hands before the tea-shop owner. 'Babu, give me my salary.'

Saha babu, with his shining, well-oiled hair and seemingly calf-like innocence and effeminate looks, heard Jibon and smiled meekly. 'Salary? Why won't I pay it! Of course, I'll pay it! I'll certainly pay you, but I don't have it now. Take it at the end of next month.'

Jibon was dejected at not receiving his salary, but he got over that. Two months had gone by already, he could wait another month. In fact, that would only be better for him. He would have some more money in his hands. He could go to Assam, eat well and roam around for a few days and then look for a nice job. But, oh you unfortunate! The next month, as soon as he asked for his salary, Binod Saha replied humbly, 'I don't have it, dear boy. Take it next month.' In this way, six or seven months passed by, with Saha constantly deferring the payment of Jibon's salary.

One day, affecting an aggrieved and angry tone, Jibon said to him, 'Every time you say you'll pay me the following month. It's been six or seven months, but you haven't paid me a paisa yet. Give me my salary now! Just see, my gamchha and vest are all torn. I need to buy new ones.'

'What do you say! Has it been six months? Are you sure you counted correctly?'

'Why don't you count and see? I joined work in the month of Kartik, it's Boishakh now.'

'Oh my, you're a calendar! All right, but it has only been six months and not six years! Forty into six is two hundred and forty. That's what I owe you. Why don't you stay another six months, I'll pay all your dues then. It'll be useful for you too if you get all the money at once.'

Jibon became very distressed now. He was about to burst into tears. He said, 'Babu, we are very poor. I have small brothers and a sister at home. They don't have any food. My father has a stomach ailment, he can't buy medicines. That's why I came to work. Give me my money, babu. I'll send it home.'

Saha babu was extremely annoyed. 'I see you're a little moneylender's father! I told you I don't have it and yet you go on nagging me. If I knew you'd behave like this, I would never have employed you. I took you on because I took pity on you. Don't they say, tigers eat do-gooders. That's my plight. I made a big mistake. I'm telling you, I'll pay you next month. God has given me a lot, and will continue to do so. Why would I steal a few rupees of yours?'

Jibon said, 'Babu, I've been away from home for a long time. I'm missing my Ma terribly—who knows whether they are alive or whether they are all dead. Settle my dues next month. I want to go home.'

Saha babu replied in a magnanimous tone, 'I'll surely pay you. In fact, I'll pay you a little more. Go and work dutifully now.'

The next month, it was the same story. 'I don't have it, dear. I have no money at all in hand. I had kept money aside to pay you, but, you know, I had to suddenly buy a fridge for the shop. All the money was spent on that. But it's all right. When it's been so long, no harm in waiting another month. I'll definitely pay you next month. I give you my word.' The next month, too, Binod Saha did not pay Jibon, but gave his word: 'I'll pay you for sure next month.'

A boy from Bihar used to work as a servant in a house near the triangular park in Jadavpur in Calcutta. One night, he had slit his employer's throat and run away with all the jewellery and money in the house. A desire like that now played on Jibon's mind. But he could not do anything other than shed tears in secret. Those tears did not move even a leaf on any tree. Who was it that had once said—it's a sin to lose faith in mankind! He had trusted Saha for almost ten months now. Finally, he lost all trust in people. Jibon was now angry with himself, the country, the society and people at large. One day he told Binod Saha, 'You aren't going to pay me my money. I've figured you out. I'm not going to work anymore.'

With a sweet smile, without the slightest bit of anger, Binod Saha said, 'Whether you work or don't work is entirely your wish. In a free country, a free citizen cannot be forced to do anything. If I want I can hold you back until I find someone else. But I won't do that. But, about your money, I say the same thing—next month.'

'How will I come all the way from Calcutta to collect the money next month?'

'You don't have to come. Leave your address with me, I'll send it by postal money order. I've never cheated anyone in my life, I won't cheat you either.'

Jibon could not say anything more. Who knows why, tears streamed down his eyes. Tears, the cheapest and most useless thing in these times. He walked away silently, his eyes blurred with tears. Friendless, the destitute boy spent a few days and nights roaming, on bare feet, the streets of the small town of Siliguri, and sleeping on an empty stomach. At first he thought he would return to Calcutta. If he could not board a train from Siliguri, then he could walk along the rail track until the next station. And then his eyes fell on his own two poor hands. Because of endless washing of cups and plates and the perpetual wetness of his hands, the blotchy hands had nothing in them to carry back for his parents and siblings. There was only the endless ridicule of nothingness. It was as if the hands were mocking him: you are a failure, you are a useless failure. You can't go and face your parents empty-handed.

21

Father by Life

One day Jibon remembered Assam again. He remembered Raja, who had spoken a lot about Assam. Raja had never spoken ill of Assam, everything he said had only been in praise of the place. So that proved Assam was different from all other places. The people there were surely not as devoid of pity and kindness.

And then it occurred to Jibon that if he could walk from Siliguri to the next station to catch the train bound for Calcutta, then it should not be difficult to walk ahead to the next station to catch the train to Assam. He was annoyed with himself for not thinking of this simple means in the past so many days, while he had been tramping the streets of Siliguri. He had almost walked himself to death. If he had followed the rail track instead, he would perhaps have reached Assam by now. He didn't want to waste any more time. He began walking towards the railway track.

It was about seven in the morning. However far it might be, he would surely be able to reach the next station by twelve. He knew the usual distance between one station and another. So where was the need for any further thought! After he left the town, he came upon a well. Some women were filling pots and pails there. He asked one of them for water and drank some, cupping his palms together. Who knows whether he would find water on the way. Having drunk water on an empty stomach, he felt full. The water seemed to be bouncing around inside his stomach as he walked. But Jibon did not want to waste any time thinking about such a trivial matter. He kept walking.

After walking two or three kilometres, he saw the railway line splitting and going in two different directions, one to the left and the other to the right. The track on the left side was narrow. The train that ran on this line was just a bit larger than a tram. It was called narrow gauge. That train went to Darjeeling. Jibon took the broad track on the right side. That was the way to Assam.

After walking for some more time, Jibon saw no trace of any house, settlement, vehicle or people. Dense forest emerged now. Just beside the rail track were chest-high, wild bushes, and behind them were tall trees that seemed to touch the sky. Bands of monkeys swung from the branches of the trees. He could also see lots of birds of various hues. The air was full of their chatter and songs. The monkeys swinging from trees looked with astonishment at Jibon and emitted strange noises from their mouths.

Jibon had seen forests in Bankura, when he was at the Shiromanipur camp. He had roamed a lot in those forests, all by himself. But the forest here was completely different. And so he felt a bit scared. Every forest had its own distinctive fragrance. The nature of a forest lay hidden in its fragrance. Those who were experienced in such matters knew this. Jibon did not know anything about these forests. That's why he could walk alone here. If he knew, he would never have done so. There were tigers here, as well as leopards, which were deadlier. They were smaller, but terribly fierce. A few days ago, a leopard had killed a cow there.

After walking for over two hours, Jibon reached the desired station. But what was this? There was no one at all at the station, which lay in the middle of this dense forest. There was no sign of the station-master—without whom trains could not run—or the signal man or any porters. Seeing the station, it seemed like it had been closed down and left to the forest. It must have been lying abandoned ever since. No trains with their chugging and metallic sounds went by here. No passengers boarded or alighted amidst commotion and hustle and bustle. That's why the station remained in slumber and never returned to life. Beyond the forest area that had been cleared for the station, there was no sign of any village or town or human habitation amid the bushes and trees. But at least as far as Jibon could see, there were no creatures hiding in that frontier, under the hot summer sun that was beating down now.

Jibon realised that even if some trains did stop at this station, the mail train would never do so. This station was too small for a mail train to stop there. The Gauhati Mail would leave Siliguri at twelve. He still had three hours in hand. He could reach the next station within that time without much difficulty. And that is what he must do if he really wanted to go to Assam. So he began walking ahead once again. Now the forest was more dense and deep. More terrifying. He felt a bit tired, for he hadn't eaten for the past few days and had been walking continuously for a few hours. But he willed himself on. A long time ago, someone who had sat in a mountain cave and meditated deeply had made the wise exhortation—'*Charaibeti, charaibeti, charaibeti!*' Keep moving. Keep moving on. This message was resonating everywhere in the world, on water, on land and in space: move, move on. Life was about moving on. Only the one who was moving was alive. The one who stopped moving died. Jibon now invoked this great wisdom within his inner being. If he stopped and sat down in this forest, even the few days he could have survived would be denied him. As soon as night fell, some wild animal would devour his spent body.

Who knows whether it was because Jibon was walking slower than before, or whether the next station was far away, or whether it was because the hands on the clock were speeding—but the sun was directly over his head now, beating down on the rail track that ran through the forest like a parting on a head of hair. Jibon felt he was burning. The soles of his feet were getting scorched. He was also feeling very thirsty.

He was yet to reach the station. Just then, the Gauhati Mail that left Siliguri at 12 o'clock came speeding down the track. Hearing the sound, he turned around and saw the train approaching. He got off the track and stood in the clump of chest-high grass beside it. The train raced ahead towards Assam, making the earth and forest tremble, leaving dry leaves billowing in the air and frightening the birds of the forest. As Jibon stood on the side, he felt as though the train was running over his very chest. What was he to do now? He went back to the rail track and stood there despondently for a while. But how long could he remain standing there? He realised nothing would be achieved by waiting there. He had to reach the next station. There was no other option.

He began walking again. Hauling his spent body and the useless, senseless, now throbbing head on his weak legs, he moved ahead. After walking another couple of hours, he spotted another station. Jibon was astonished when he reached there. Had he walked in the wrong direction after getting off the track when the train approached? Or else why was this station desolate too, resembling some city of the dead? The station was blazing under the hot sun, but let alone people, there wasn't even a crow or dog to be seen there.

What was Jibon to do now? There was nothing to be done but to keep walking. By any means, he had to reach a station where there were people, where mail trains stopped to drop and pick up passengers. It was foolish to wait where there were no houses, shops or people, nothing at all. And so he plodded on, through the forest along the rail track. His knees were aching, his throat was choking with thirst, there was a fire raging in his belly, his whole body was burning under the sun's fury. Disregarding all that, he walked on like a lunatic. The monkeys of the forest were surprised to see him and seemed to be chattering among themselves about something. If their talk could have been translated, perhaps Jibon would have died of mortification hearing their opinion of people!

Be that as it may, Jibon was completely exhausted now. His body seemed a burden to him. Hauling the burden, just as he reached the next station, the Assam Mail of 4 p.m. shot past him like an arrow. This station too was not good enough for the train to halt even for a minute.

After the train went by, Jibon spotted a man, the first person he had come across since morning. He came walking down the platform, holding a flag in each hand, one red and the other green, and stopped in front of Jibon. The railway office was on the right, he was about to go back there. He would signal for a train to pass on the other side of the platform. Waving the flag and signalling the engine driver to pass by—that was his job.

Seeing Jibon, he looked at him incredulously. Who was this who had emerged from the dense forest!

He said, '*Ae bachcha, kahaan jayega?* Where do you want to go?'

Jibon answered plainly, '*Hum Assam jayega.* To Assam.'

'*Toh paidal kyun?* Why on foot then?'

Jibon replied, 'I don't have any money for train fares. That's why—Assam.'

The man with flags could no longer control his astonishment.

He said, 'There's a train going to Siliguri now. Sit on that and go back. Do you want to die? Assam is very far away, you can't walk all the way.' Without speaking further, he entered his room.

No, Jibon could not walk anymore. And there were no more trains to Assam leaving today. The station looked eerie even now, and Jibon was terrified imagining what it would be like once night fell. There was no other option but to go back now. If he went back to Siliguri, he might get caught once again by a ticket checker. He would push him around and slap or hit him. He could take him to jail too. Let it happen! Thinking along these lines, he went and sat down in front of the station's ticket counter. He saw two more people there: one was the station-master, while the other was a fisherman. He had come with some fish in a wicker-basket, hoping to sell it here. The station-master was his customer.

The signal-man had said, 'The train is about to come now.' But it was evening by the time it finally arrived. Jibon promptly boarded the train. Halting at every station on the way, the train finally reached Siliguri. Getting off, Jibon walked past what seemed to be countless ticket checkers and policemen and climbed up the steps of the over-bridge. Now no one looked askance at him. As he climbed the steps, he felt dizzy. He sat down on the bridge. After that, he spread out his gamchha and lay down flat on his back. He fell asleep. No one bothered him. The night passed without any disturbance. When Jibon woke up and rubbed his eyes, the first thing he saw was the sky. It was still dark, clouds were floating by. Who knew where they were going, where, impelled by the pull of soil, they would unleash their load on the earth, dry and parched under the sun's fierce heat. The rains had not yet arrived this year. But they would. The clouds and thunder signalled that. Once the earth received water, crops would bloom, awakening people's hopes and desires with the promise of survival. If man survived, then so would human society and civilisation, and all of man's construction, art and creation.

But now everything seemed to be moving in the reverse direction. Man had altered the laws of nature. With his adroitness, he could create drought, flood, epidemic and famine. He could render people destitute and make their lives akin to an agonising death.

Jibon turned on his side and saw the owner of the sweet shop in the station carrying a basket on his shoulder, of yesterday's unsold singharas, nimkis and kachoris. He walked to the edge of the platform and began throwing them one by one as he called out to the crows, *'Aay, aay ...'*. Seeing that, Jibon's stomach rumbled in hunger. It was painful, he felt like crying. He knew that even if people starved to death, no one would give them leftover food. They would rather feed it to crows and dogs, precisely because they were not human. The schoolteacher at the Siliguri station had said that this was apparently the nature of the capitalist system. In this system, there was no place for emotions between humans such as pity, compassion, affection and love. The only relationship possible was commercial, of buying and selling. Before anything was given, calculations were made, about whether what was given would come back by way of profit.

Because of such arithmetic, Jibon was now a worthless person. And so Jibon and thousands of people like him had to go without food. That was astonishing. In this country, the son of a Baniya used to go on a fast from time to time, for two or ten days every month or two. He had become a leader by doing that. Later, he became the father of the nation. But the names of Jibon and many more like him—who began fasting from the time they were in their mothers' wombs and ended it only when they finally died—found no place in history. No one spoke about them. No one wanted to hear about them. Could there be anything more incredible than that!

Jibon sat up. A passenger hurrying to the train that had just halted had stepped on his hand. He looked up and saw that the sun had risen eight or ten feet above the horizon now. It had been concealed by the canopy of a large tree and so its rays had not been cast on the bridge-top. Jibon asked someone, 'Which train is that?' As the man hurried by, he said, 'It's the Gauhati Mail!'

The Gauhati Mail! Jibon cautiously descended the steps and looked around. Yes, there was a chance. When the train began moving, it would not be difficult for him to run and get into the empty carriage he had spotted. The ticket checkers and policemen were all on the platform. What could they do once he got into the moving train. He did just that shortly after. The guard waved the green flag in his hand and blew on the whistle in his mouth, instructing the engine driver to depart. The driver blew the whistle of the engine and prepared to start. The train began moving. Jibon ran and entered a carriage. He went to his own spot, at the door on the opposite side, and sat down there. This was a proud train, it did not stop at minor stations. The station it halted at after about half an hour was an impressive one. It was called a 'junction'.

After two or three hours, it reached another junction. Perhaps water was being loaded in the engine or maybe the engine was being changed, for the train's departure was delayed. It was about ten in the morning now, the time passengers ate their tiffin. Jibon was sitting at the door away from the platform, dangling his legs on the steps. Suddenly his eyes fell on the window of the train on the other side. A fair-skinned, hirsute arm emerged from the window. There was a sal-leaf packet in the hand. With great disdain, the packet was thrown on the rail track below. As it fell to the ground from that height, it burst open. Jibon saw that it contained a thick, reddish-brown roti made of wheat and some cooked vegetables.

As soon as he saw the roti, Jibon remembered that he hadn't eaten for several days. And what had been discarded disdainfully was something to eat. In that moment, he strangled and killed his very soul. And he did what he had never done before, what he had never thought he would ever have to do. In a flash, he jumped down to the track. He ran and picked up the leaf-packet as if it was something precious. Seeing the food, a few mangy dogs too had come running to claim it. They lived in the station and so they knew that there were still lots of people in the world who had plenty of food to throw away. That's why they walked along the tracks once a train halted. They looked up at the doors and windows and whined. So far, they knew that whatever else people did, they would never become like dogs. But now they saw that one like them was hiding in human society, in human disguise, and he was snatching away their food! A man-turned-dog was depriving the dogs of their dog-rights!

They began howling in protest, all at once, against the inhuman and unfair behaviour on the part of Jibon. They ran to snatch away the leaf-packet of food. Jibon was alone, while they were many. Jibon was harmless, unarmed and hungry, while their vicious fangs were sharp. Jibon turned and ran. After running a safe distance, he hopped into another carriage. He sat down again at the door, with his legs dangling. After that, he took out the thick roti made of fine wheat and turned it round and round and gazed at it for a long while. He brought it to his nose and smelt it. It seemed to have been fried in ghee. But it had not been made today, it must be from yesterday or the day before. The vegetables too were as stale. The stiff and hard roti and stale vegetable curry gave off a strange smell. The smell could evidently tempt man to descend to the level of a dog and free himself of agony for at least a day. Jibon surrendered to the temptation.

After eating the roti and feeling somewhat full, Jibon drank some water. But now he was overcome with self-reproach. It was as if someone wept inside him and was reviling him. You finally sank so low! Snatched food away from the jaws of dogs! How much lower will you stoop, Jibon! But how could the helpless Jibon respond now? What did he have left in him that he could offer in response? He had no answer. Perhaps thousands and thousands of people in this country did not have any answer. The fierce agony of the belly did not know any answers. That's why, driven by that agony, people rummaged for scraps of food in garbage bins. A mother sold the child born of her womb and bought rice with the money. A father made his daughter stand, with make-up on, at the kerb of the alley in the red light district.

The carriage Jibon had boarded was quite vacant. He sat resting against the door—like someone who had no possessions to lose, no hopes or prospects of getting anything; for whom all seeking and getting in life was over, who was now indifferent to any kind of suffering; who had surrendered himself at the feet of God and to the hands of the future, resigned to whatever might happen; like a sadhak or tapasvi, or a despondent person devoid of hope. Once the train started, the pleasant breeze bearing the fragrance of the soil, fields and forests of north Bengal blew over him. It seemed that it wasn't a breeze but the soft, gentle hand of a mother stroking the body of her beloved child, at the touch of which he fell asleep.

Jibon had spread out his gamchha in front of the door and lay flat on his back. With his eyes shut, he could not see the unspoilt beauty of nature on the way. Beyond the thin cover of trees and plants rose the mountains that had been in slumber for ages, from whose bald summits the sunlight was reflected, as if from a mirror. It was as if someone had placed the mountain on some unseen river, which was carrying it towards the estuary like a sailboat. The more the train moved ahead, the more the mountain retreated in the opposite direction.

After a while, a more dense and deep forest appeared. A primeval, all-encompassing, sylvan darkness seemed to shroud the immense length of the train. It wasn't just the forest, there were also small hills in some places. The hillsides had been cleared to lay the iron train tracks. The Gauhati Mail sped ahead along the tracks with a resounding roar. And Jibon, plagued by inner anxieties, lay sprawled beside the door, as if surrendered to an irreversible trance. He wasn't sleeping but only dozing, as if he was waiting with his eyes shut for some outcome.

When his drowsiness passed, it was past noon. The measly roti that had dropped into the sea of hunger in his belly a little while back had evaporated. The rumbling in his stomach had commenced once again. His eyes seemed to turn blank, and his head and ears were ringing. Man is a slave of habit. His mouth had turned greedy. He could no longer control himself.

Suddenly, as if he had fathomed Jibon's distress, a man came and stood in front of him, like some great soul inspired by God. The man was middle-aged, with a bit of grey in his hair. There was a kindly smile on his lips. His eyes seemed to be overflowing with divine tenderness, something rare in human society today. There was deep love, affection and caring in his voice. 'Where are you going, my dear?'

The man looked like he might have been a village schoolteacher. He looked up at him. Almost in a whisper, like a gasping invalid, Jibon replied, 'I'm going where the train is headed.'

'Do you know where it's headed?'

Jibon nodded his head to convey he knew. After that he said, 'I've set out in search of work. I'm going to Assam.'

'Where is your home?'

'We have no home. My parents live in a refugee camp.'

The kind man befriended Jibon and found out everything about him. He spent his own money and bought a cup of tea and a loaf of bread for him, and then began talking about himself. He said, 'I too was like you when I was a child. I wasn't afraid of anything. I too ran away from home once. You wouldn't believe it if I told you how much I roamed around, and all the places I went to. Mountains, deserts, oceans—I saw so much!'

Jibon had encountered many people in his brief life. But he had never experienced such humane behaviour before. No one had ever spoken to him so caringly and with such intimacy. His dirty clothes, unfamiliar and unattractive appearance, and his pathetic plight always aroused revulsion in people, or sometimes they affected sympathy. But this man who looked like a rural schoolmaster seemed to be of a different kind. It was as if he had understood Jibon's unbearable plight and was fulfilling the duty that, naturally, only a kind-hearted person could. And so Jibon felt gratified.

The man said, 'Once I was travelling by train. It was nighttime. It was on that train, in exactly the way I met you, that I met my father. You're wondering how that could be, isn't it? No, it wasn't my own father, but my *dhorom-baap*, father-by-life. Do you know, a father-by-life is far greater than one's own father? How can I tell you how much that father loved me as soon as he set eyes on me! You should know it happens, such things happen—when one suddenly meets someone—like how I met you and loved you as if you were my son! That is an amazing ploy of God, there's no way of knowing who one encounters and likes, who one cares for. After that, the man whom I called my father-by-life got off the train and took me along to his house. He gave me so many things to eat. You see, he didn't have any children of his own. Through me, his wish for a child was fulfilled.

I stayed for almost ten days in his house. After that, he bought me new clothes and shoes, and gave me five hundred rupees. Can you imagine what five hundred rupees from back then would be worth today? He gave me all that and sent me home. Yes, such people do exist. Not everyone in the world is like that Binod Saha of yours. How could he cheat a small boy like that!'

The man was then quiet for a while, as if wrestling with some inner anguish. Finally he said, 'You haven't eaten anything since yesterday, you poor boy. I'm getting off at the next station, come with me to my house. I can't ... I can't sit still when I see people suffering ... I too had received someone's kindness. I always remember that. And so, I try to ease people's suffering as much as I can. Come with me, stay for a few days in my house, eat well, and after that, if you want to go to Assam, do that. If you want, you can take some money from me for your travel expense. That's what my father had done for me.' What the man said was full of empathy, it was tempting, nay, infatuating. Jibon could not disregard it. When the train stopped at the next station, he followed the man. And so Jibon walked towards another experience. After all, life was just another name for learning about the world every day through a new journey. Of stumbling, bumping, getting injured and wounded and dripping blood on the streets.

The station was not a large one, but it wasn't so small either. Stepping off the platform, there was a brick-lined road going southwards. Trees fringed the road, their canopies creating a pleasant shady environment. The evening market on the roadside had commenced. The local farmers had come to sell various kinds of produce from their fields. Farther down the road, there were some shops selling garments, saris and petticoats. These were all shops for humble folk, in a poor region. The shopkeepers were not of the class of shrewd businessmen either.

The man entered a shop and said to the shopkeeper, 'Please show me some good saris. And a pair of shorts and a shirt for my son here.' Jibon had never known fine clothes. Seeing the colours of the clothes and hearing the price, he was filled with joy. But before he could hold the clothes in his hands, the man told him, 'Do something, son, go and have a haircut first. Meanwhile, I'll select a sari for your Ma.'

The saloon was across the street. The man took Jibon there and sat him down on a chair. Then he returned to the sari shop and began selecting the ones he would buy. He was not concerned about the price. After all, something good would command a good price. His only concern was whether his wife would like his choice. He looked at many saris, and after much thinking, he finally said, 'Do something, bhai, if it's not inconvenient, give me four or five saris. I live close by, only five minutes away. I'll buy two or three that my wife likes. When my son has had his haircut, ask him to come and sit here.'

The shopkeeper was a simple fellow. He was thrilled at the prospect of a good sale. Besides, how could one not trust someone who was leaving his son there? He let the man go with the saris.

Jibon wasn't aware of the proceedings because he was sitting in the saloon. After all, it wasn't intended for his ears. And even if he had heard the man, what sense would he have made of the sentences; they would have only been words. After all, had he attained, at his age, the capability to ascertain the hitherto undiscovered secret of human character? There was still some time left for him to learn that. After Jibon emerged from the saloon, the shopkeeper called out to him, 'Hey boy, come and sit here. Your father will be back in a few.' He told the saloon owner as well, 'His father will be back, he'll pay you.'

What else could Jibon do but wait. He waited eagerly for his father-by-life. An hour and then two passed. Evening turned to night, but the man did not return. Since he hadn't returned, the shopkeeper did not allow Jibon to leave the shop. He said, 'I won't let you go until your father returns. Where's your house, how far away is it?' Word spread around the market. A lot of people arrived there and surrounded Jibon. They began questioning him. They slapped him, which was the punishment for thieves and cheats. After one round of ordinary beating, Jibon was taken to the office of the market committee. An inquisition began. For all his protestations that he did not know the man and that he had only met him on the train, no one believed him. And disbelieving him, the committee members became ever more aggressive in their bid to unearth the truth. Someone landed a mighty punch on his chest: 'Tell us where your gang-leader has gone.' Jibon's frail body, weak and tired from hunger, could not take the force of the powerful punch. He fell to the floor and fainted. One advantage of fainting was that one did not feel the pain of any further thrashing.

22

The City of No Magic

When Jibon came to his head and face were wet. That was a result of the usual efforts of ordinary people to bring someone back to their senses. After he fainted, and did not respond even after a couple more blows—'the bastard's pretending'—they had splashed water on his face and eyes. Realising that there would be a serious problem if he died, the shopkeeper brought him a glass of hot milk after he came to his senses. He cursed his own stupidity, accepted the loss incurred, and in order to avoid any further damage, he accompanied Jibon to the station. The train going to Gauhati that left New Jalpaiguri at 4 p.m. reached this station at 10 p.m. Jibon boarded the train. By that time, the pain from the thrashing had subsided. Jibon considered himself extremely fortunate to have got away. Those people had talked about sending him to jail. And what if they had killed him instead under cover of darkness! They had threatened to do exactly that. 'Tell us where your gang-leader lives. Or else we'll kill you and throw your body on the rail track!'

With a host of apprehensions in his head, and racked with physical pain, he now lay down in the passage adjoining the bathroom, right on top of all the spittle, beedi and cigarette butts, peanut shells, squeezed lemons, discarded sal-leaf packets, shreds of paper and other such garbage. He could not think of anything beyond rest. In fact, he did not want to think about that either.

The train roared ahead through the night. The commotion that one usually heard during the day was absent. After running for half an hour or an hour, the train would halt at some station. A group of passengers would get down and another group would board the train and occupy the seats that had been vacated. Jibon did not pay any attention to all that. He just lay there, like a patient afflicted with an incurable disease, to whom the doctor had said there was no hope. 'Pray to God, only he can do something now. Everything is in his hands.'

Jibon had been diligent about doing everything that he should have done for himself. There was no fooling or cheating about that. There was nothing more that he could do. Whatever had to happen could happen now. There was no longer any fear, worry, restlessness or excitement in him. He lay there, like a dog curled up to die. People crossed over him to enter and exit the bathroom. The night advanced.

'Ticket!'

Jibon rubbed his eyes and gazed in the direction of the voice. Standing silhouetted against the light was a hefty, moustached ticket checker, wearing a black coat. Without rising, Jibon waved his hand, 'No ticket.'

'*Utar jaa!* Get off!' the ticket checker said.

The train had stopped somewhere, in some station that lay in darkness. Like an obedient boy, Jibon got off. After going past a few carriages, he got into another carriage and once again lay down in the same way, in the same place. Just as the train began moving, another ticket checker made him get off. Unfazed, Jibon got into yet another carriage. And so did morning arrive.

At about ten or eleven in the morning, the train arrived at the yearned-for destination: Gauhati. The platform was quite empty at this time of the day. A few people were moving around here and there, some were huddled in groups. There weren't any crowds of customers at the stalls in the station. There seemed to be a lazy air hanging over the station, like the way a cow chewed cud. The only exception was an old sweeper, wearing a blue shirt and shorts, who was cleaning the platform with a long-handled broom. The station appeared to be quite clean. There were no lunatics, drunkards, gamblers or beggars to be seen. Jibon sluggishly exited the platform and went and stood under the open sky. The sun was quite hot now. Far away, over the horizon, were rows of small and larger hills, covered with green scrub and trees. But this was not the time for gazing raptly at scenic beauty. Just as the sun blazed overhead now, the fire of hunger raged in his stomach. But no one would give him food just like that. Raja had said, 'It's as if money lies on the streets there.' But seeing the world outside the railway station, Jibon began to doubt his words now. He began to have misgivings about the place. It was no different from Calcutta or Siliguri. The streets, houses and buildings, shops, marketplaces and people, all seemed just the same as elsewhere. Jibon realised that all the hopes he had arrived here with, after going through so much hardship, would remain unfulfilled.

But for now, Jibon needed something to eat. Everything else could come later. What would be the easiest way? There was only one way: taking up what he knew, washing cups and plates in some tea-shop or eatery. He needed a job now. And so, he began to walk along the main road.

'Do you need someone to work?'

There was a large shop run by a Sikh man on the left side of the road. He sold tea, sweets and savouries. Various kinds of items were displayed in his shop's glass-cabinet. The shop was bursting with customers. Five or six employees were running around busily. As soon as he stood before the shop, the shop owner drove him away, as he might shoo away a dog, assuming he was a beggar. *Jah! Bhaag! Nahi to badan pe garam pani daal dega!* Go away! Or else I'll throw hot water on you!' Jibon then explained, 'I'm not a beggar, I'm looking for work. I've worked in a sweet shop before. I know all the work.'

The shopkeeper was a middle-aged man. He had a turban on his head, and he was bearded and wore a thick steel bangle on his wrist. He asked Jibon, 'Where did you work earlier?'

'In Siliguri.'

'From Siliguri directly to Assam!' The shopkeeper was surprised that someone had journeyed by train all the way here to work in a sweet shop.

'Weren't there any more shops in Siliguri?'

'I don't have time to waste in useless talk. Tell me if you'll give me work. I don't need a salary, only food. Or else I'll go.'

'Who knows you here?'

'How would anyone know me, I've just arrived today.'

'Then there's no work for you here. What will I do if you steal something and run away? Go away, move on.'

It was the time when a mass of dark clouds hung over the fortunes of Assam. Which would soon turn into a super-cyclone called 'Bongal Khedao' (Drive out Bengalis) and ravage all of Assam. A destructive frenzy would be unleashed—spreading across Digboi, Dibrugarh, Tinsukia, Jorhat and Gauhati—that would continue for almost a decade. Houses would be burnt down, shops would be looted and people would die. Some signs of that had already begun to be felt. A few days ago, there had been a fierce clash between Assamese and Bengalis. Broken bricks and soda bottles still littered the streets. But unaware of all that, driven by a primordial impulse to survive, the starving boy walked along those streets.

Now that he had reached Assam, Jibon had to find a way of staying there for some days. After that, he had to find the Kamrup-Kamakhya temple. Jibon had heard that it was surrounded by an impenetrable jungle of prickly cacti, which was extremely difficult to go through. The temple was supposedly guarded by a squad of beautiful, splendidly-attired women, who knew magic spells. Apparently, as soon as they spotted any male, they cast a spell on him and turned him into a ram. If any brave man overcame all these obstacles and dangers and reached there, and somehow managed to learn a few spells, he would have the whole world in the palm of his hand. Jibon had heard such tales many times over since his childhood. Apparently, it was only after going to Kamrup-Kamakhya and getting the blessings of the Goddess that P.C. Sorcar had become such a big magician. Whatever might be the dangers, Jibon would definitely go there once. Raja had said, 'All those are simply lies!' Jibon would see for himself whether it was true or false. What more was there to this life? Having snatched and eaten food from a dog's jaws, he had already descended to the level of dogs. If someone now turned him into a ram—let them! What was so bad about a ram's life? Whatever else they did, at least they did not starve!

Jibon ruminated along such lines as he walked ahead on the street, and whenever he spotted any tea-shop, or eatery or sweet shop, he stopped there and enquired, 'Do you need someone to work in your shop? I am in great difficulty, babu. I'm very poor. No one is giving me a job. My father could lift a sack of paddy to his head all by himself and carry it for two miles. I'm the son of a father like that. I can work very hard. People were very happy with me where I worked earlier. Will you keep me?'

Who would keep him? Why would they do that? It was a time when people were full of suspicions, and suspicion was contagious. No one trusted anyone. Who knows if he wouldn't take everything and decamp? The honest folk also tended to be wary of unknown persons. 'Who knows you?' That's what they all wanted to know. 'Who will guarantee your honesty?'

No one, there was no one like that anywhere in Assam, or for that matter, anywhere in India or anywhere in the world. No one who would say, 'I know him very well—not only do I know him, I can also vouch for his honesty.'

And so it was unlikely that anyone would employ an unknown person like him. But Jibon did not give up trying. He realised that nothing would be achieved by sitting on the street in this foreign land, throwing up his hands. He walked ahead.

The sun was directly over Jibon's head now. He felt as if he was melting in the heat, and as if his intestines were twisting and turning like a burning python. His legs could no longer support him, he felt like a tree hacked at the base, as though he would collapse at any moment. But, like a snail carrying its shell, Jibon dragged along his weak body and stopped in front of a ramshackle shop. This was a Bihari man's tea-shop.

Although the shop sold tea, its main business was milk. The owner was a Yadav. The milk left over was made into curds. With which lassi was prepared. Jibon found work in the shop as soon as he enquired. '*Haan haan, kaam ke liye to aadmi chahiye!* Yes, of course, I need someone to work!'

Sensing the man's eagerness to employ him, Jibon asked him, 'Will you pay me a salary?'

'*Zaroor, zaroor, kyun nahi dega!* Of course!'

'How much will you pay me?'

'How much do you want?'

'No, you tell me how much you'll pay.'

'Food twice a day, and twenty rupees a month. Will that do?'

It wouldn't just do—it was fabulous! Jibon thought over the matter. Whatever the work may entail and however it may be, if he could get the salary every month, then there was nothing like that. If someone wanted to cheat him, they wouldn't be able to cheat him out of more than a month's salary. He did not want to trust anybody anymore. It was as if all his trust had died, rotted and become useless. His life, reduced to that of a dog, had taught him that there was no empathy or sympathy left in human society. As far as society was concerned, he was an unwanted creature. People would go on cheating him as much as they could if they got the opportunity. And so, this time, with some forethought, he concealed his vulnerability and laid down a condition. 'I must be paid my salary every month.' The Bihari owner, who looked like someone playing the role of Shakuni in a poor man's jatra troupe in the countryside—skinny, with a thick, salt-and-pepper moustache, and clad in a fatua and lungi—said loudly, 'You'll get your salary every month. That's better for me. It won't become too much of a burden.'

⁂

Jibon began working for the Bihari milk-seller. Work meant carrying a drum of milk on his head and walking behind the man. The son of the father who could lift a two-and-a-half maund sack of paddy did not succumb carrying a weight of twenty kilos. But he did feel overcome when he sat down to eat in the afternoon and at night. The milkman had a wife and daughter back in the village and lived here with his two sons. The two sons were not only experts in grazing and milking buffaloes, but also equally adept in wielding lathis and wrestling. There wasn't another pehelwan to match them in the whole Barak valley region. Every morning, they religiously performed their exercises. And in the evening, they went to the wrestling akhara. When they returned home to eat after all the pummeling given and received, most days they forgot that there was one more person who had to eat, for whom something had to be left. Unlike Bengalis, Biharis were not so fond of rice, and sattu and roti were their staple food. But Jibon hungered for rice. Even if he somehow bore that inconvenience, how could he go without food? Especially when in return for being fed twice a day, he was made to carry a load all over the city. Another reason why he was very perturbed was because of what pilgrims returning from the temple of Kamakhya Devi had to say. There were no magic spells or suchlike there! Perhaps that had existed long ago, but there was nothing like that now. And there were various kinds of explanations about why it wasn't there any longer. One devotee said that apparently all that had been destroyed by man's greed and sinfulness. The Mother Goddess's gift had to be preserved carefully. It could only be used for the good of the world. But people did not do that. How would the Mother tolerate it if the mantric powers attained from Kamakhya were used to harm people? All the tantriks, shamans and healers only misused their mantric powers. They used spells to harm people, they caused still-births and helped scoundrels win court cases. And so, as a result of such malpractices, there were no more mantric powers to be had.

Little by little, Jibon's naive consciousness descended from fanciful flights to the hard ground of reality. He observed the world around him. The stretch between the rail station and the crossroads leading to the Barak valley, for instance. All around him were hungry, destitute, stooped folk. Who, despite living in this magical land, had not yet found the magic wand that would have made their lives beautiful. Their bellies were sunken. Their ribs like teeth bared mockingly. And eyes that, faced with the dance of the black shadow of an uncertain future, had forgotten to dream. Where were the streets laden with the pieces of copper that people called money with which food to fill the belly and clothes to cover one's body could be bought? No, there was none of that here. So what was the use of staying on in Assam?

Jibon was like a bullock that carried the burden of sacks of sugar all its life, without ever tasting even a single grain of it. He carried a large drum of milk on his head all day, but he never got to taste even a drop of the milk. The owner himself, who dealt with large quantities of milk, did not so much as touch a drop, and Jibon was only a common servant! Why would a profit-minded owner waste any of his milk when it could be sold for a price.

There is a strange custom in human society. The sweet-maker who makes huge quantities of sweetmeats never eats sweets. He just cannot. He desires only hot and spicy food. The vendor who fries fritters in oil loves to eat things like peanut candy and cottage cheese and never touches a fritter. Even if he did, he would not really enjoy it. Who knows whether it was because of this custom or otherwise—but this milkman never drank milk. After sundown, he scooted to the country liquor shop. And after drinking, when he was a bit intoxicated, he would begin to remember how, when he had gone and lived for some time in Calcutta—who knows how many years ago that was—Bengalis had misbehaved with him. Then, for no reason, he would rain foul abuses on Jibon, simply for the crime of being Bengali. Before this, Jibon did not know how flawed this race called Bengalis was. There was no such thing as chastity among the women of this race. Apparently, as soon as they saw a robust man, they went and lay down in front of him. They had no taste in regard to food and ate just about everything. They ate fish even if it had been rotting for a few months. They were physically weak, but if there was ever any quarrel or fight anywhere, they forgot about everything else and jumped into the fray. And they only lied and never spoke the truth. They scorned even those who were kind to them. To the extent that they even cheated him of the price of his milk. Jibon's ears were sore listening to this cursing of Bengalis almost every day.

If it had been anyone else, perhaps he would have left long ago. But Jibon had stayed five months despite wanting to leave. There was only one reason for that. On the tenth or twelfth of every month, the milkman paid Jibon his salary for the previous month. Like a miser guarding his wealth, Jibon hid his hard-earned money inside his pillow-case. He did not know then about sending money to his parents via the post office. He was worried the money would never reach the address; it would be pilfered on the way. And so, he planned to work and accumulate a small amount that he could then go and give to his Ma.

But that was not to be. However carefully and secretly he hid the money, it wasn't actually a secret. The people around him knew about it. Jibon had spent a bit of money buying this and that, eating this and that. But he had kept a single blue-coloured, hundred-rupee note. One morning, when he returned to the shop after delivering milk, he saw it had disappeared from the pillow-case. The younger son of the shop owner was in the shop then. Jibon lost his senses. He directly pointed his finger at the younger son: 'It can't be anyone but you! Before I left for work I saw it was there, and there was no one else in the room after that. Give me my money back.'

Stealing was not as shameful as an accusation of theft. The younger pehelwan, a doyen of the wrestling arena, was furious. '*Saale, hamara khata hai, hamara peeta hai, aur humhiko chor bolta hai!* You bastard, we feed you and then you accuse us of being thieves!' He picked Jibon up and threw him out on the street. '*Ja saala kutta, bhag, nahi toh maar ke tabiyat bigaad dega!* Scoot, you fucking dog, run, or else I'll break your bones!' Jibon had thought the people present there, and especially the few Bengalis among them, would come to his defence. Someone who would at least say that this was wrong, give the poor fellow his money back. But that did not happen. Many standing afar actually seemed to derive pleasure from seeing Jibon weep. Perhaps some felt bad about it, but they did not come forward to protest. So once again, after five or six months of fruitless toil, Jibon was back on the streets in a penniless state.

⚬

It was about three in the afternoon. The street was completely deserted. In any case, these parts were not so congested, especially to eyes that had seen the crowds of Calcutta. Heartbroken, reduced to emptiness, Jibon walked slowly and reached the railway station. He did not know where he would go or what he would do. He could not find a single person before whom he could break into tears. To whom he could narrate his tale of woe. From whom Jibon could hope to get some succor, so that this rudderless boat of his destiny, with tattered sails, could touch shore and find land. So that a small plant could spread roots and survive there.

Jibon had no more expectations or demands from the world—all he wanted was two handfuls of rice, twice a day, a piece of coarse cloth, and a shelter above his head. But even that was too much for this miserly world. It was simply unwilling to open its arms to him. His father used to say, 'The one who makes you hungry will provide you food. There are borers that live inside wood, but the Lord makes sure that they too don't go hungry.' That's what his father had told him. By what conviction, Garib Das—who was flailing in the ocean of hardship and writhing like a slaughtered goat in the throes of the agony of his untreated stomach-ache— told his son all this, like a parrot's recitation, as he sat weeping in front of the dead body of his infant daughter who had died of starvation, bemoaning his incapability to obtain a piece of cloth to protect the modesty of his unclad wife—was indeed an amazing puzzle. Jibon had still not been able to figure out the meaning of that sentence. He could not see any trace of the munificence of the so-called munificent one. He would never be able to tell anyone that God did everything for good.

After spending some time sitting at the Gauhati station, Jibon finally got into a train that was departing. Why he boarded the train, where he was going—he did not have any answers to that.

The train was impossibly crowded. The carriage was spilling over with passengers. No ticket checkers ever got into such crowded trains. How much jostling could they endure! After all, it wasn't just for a day or two, this was their daily job. Jibon could not find any place to sit. He stood in the crowd of people in front of the door. Observing the clothes and appearance of those who were standing there, one knew they were labouring folk. They were going somewhere in search of work. From Assam, they were going to a place called Alipurduar in neighbouring West Bengal.

After some time, Jibon was able to squat down on his haunches in the same spot. The crowd thinned after two or three hours, and so he found enough space to lie down there. Gradually he fell asleep. At four, just as dawn was breaking, the train halted at Siliguri. Who knows why, but Jibon got off there. All that Siliguri had given him was betrayal. A murder of trust. Yet he got off there.

It would be daylight soon. Every night had an end. That was nature's own law. The only night of darkness that did not end was the one created and nurtured by man for his own purposes. People nurtured every kind of darkness in their own hearts. Living in the darkness he had created and nourished, man too turned into a black, ugly, ghoul-like creature, devoid of form and devoid of ideals, who worshipped only darkness, darkness, darkness. From the womb of that darkness was born ever more darkness, which was eternal, infinite ...

Nature's darkness now lay like a thin sheet over the sky. Then, as if peeling off the cover, a faint streak of purple emerged in the east. A multitude of birds in their nests of twigs and straw, made on the branches of trees of various kinds, awakened from slumber. Their chirps and tweets were audible. How happy they were! They had two small wings. But with those small yet free wings, they occupied the vast sky. As long as greedy men did not cast their dark shadows on the lives of animals and birds, they lived in joy.

Jibon walked absent-mindedly along the rail track. He did not know where his restless feet were taking him. The vast space outside the illuminated precincts of the station still had a sleepy look about it. As the darkness paled, a slight thin, smoke-like mist became visible, which clung to the trees, verdure and mountains in the distance. Jibon stood awhile in the middle of the desolate field, pondering over something. He now felt like the fabled shepherd boy who got lost in the forest, before whom there was no trace of any path. Or like the fawn that had stepped on quicksand, sinking little by little. It knew what was to come, but had no recourse whatsoever.

The sun had emerged over the horizon. Shedding the golden hue of dawn, the sun was now like a bloodshot eye whose arrow-like rays shot past mountains, hills, rocks, foliage, greenery and fields and pierced the environs around Jibon. Just then, Jibon saw a strange-looking vehicle with three or four carriages arrive and halt on the rail track in front of him. It was smaller than a train, but larger than a tram. The engine too was as small. After a while, Jibon saw a group of well-dressed, beautiful people boarding the vehicle. So this was the narrow-gauge train. From the people's conversations, he gathered that the train was going to Darjeeling.

Visible in the crisp sunlight of morning were the matchbox-like houses of the town atop the mountain that seemed to be touching the very sky. They looked like tiny, colourful toy boats strewn on a still, green sea. The boats were gleaming in the rays of the sun.

There was an old saying that one could say, by looking at the morning, how the day would go. Jibon too knew that. That the day would not bring any glad tidings for him had already been intimated. It would be the same tale of tramping the streets with his heart full of distress and stomach full of hunger. When there was no other option, what was the harm in going to Darjeeling? Someone had called Darjeeling 'Alakapuri'. That was the name of the abode of Kuber, the god of wealth. Even the lorries carrying ash, sand and rice that plied on the road going there dropped a little bit on the way. Jibon was a small boy, and his desires too were small. Surely he would be able to scrape something from Kuber's town, which could satisfy his small desires. The only way to ascertain that was to go to that abode.

Jibon would go. When there was no hope of anything good happening, and the worst that could happen was known, why not try out Darjeeling instead of rotting in Siliguri! Even if he died there—at least, before he died, he would have the consolation that he had tried out a few fruits in life, despite knowing they were sour.

The engine was at the front. After that were the luggage van, the first-class carriage, the second-class carriage, the general compartment and finally the guard van. It was a small train and the crowd of passengers was also a thin one. Most of the people who travelled to Darjeeling from Siliguri preferred going by jeep rather than by train, and especially sitting on the front seat of the jeep. The fare for that was also a bit more than for a seat at the rear. The jeep took less time than the train and also offered the thrill of driving along the mountain edge. But one could not travel on a jeep without paying the fare. That was possible on the train. Jibon only had to avoid the three or four ticket checkers who stood around the train, and get into a carriage.

Jibon moved to a position slightly ahead of the engine and waited for the train to depart. This train moved rather slowly. It would not be difficult for him to hop onto the train while it was moving. He would do that once it moved ahead a bit and left the ticket checkers behind.

There was no platform as such where the train was standing, it was in the middle of an open field, under the vast blue sky. A flock of migrant birds were flying in the sky. They had come from some faraway land, flying, crossing the mountains of the Himalayas. They would spend three or four months here and then, around February, return to the place they had come from. It was October now. After a few days, according to the Hindu shastras, Ma Durga would descend from the Himalayas to the plains with her children to be worshipped. There was already a slight chill in the air. The scent of the approaching Durga Puja also seemed to be in the air. Of course, that was not something that concerned Jibon. All he was aware of was the fire raging in his belly. All festivals had been burnt to ashes in the flames of that fire, and what remained was something quite ugly.

The engine had been languid so long, like a pregnant maiden, a torpid wisp of smoke rising from its chimney. Now the lazy spell was over. With coal being shovelled into the boiler, clouds of white smoke rose and seemed to fill the sky. The whistle sounded twice— *koo-koo!* The train was ready for its run.

Jibon was ready too. The engine started. After some huffing and puffing, mechanical force was suddenly exerted on the lever controlling the rotation of the wheels, and it began to move ahead. One, two, three, four. After the wheels had turned four times, the four black-coated ticket checkers turned back to return to the station cabin. There was no need to wait any longer. Jibon ran behind the moving train. The train had gathered speed by then. In comparison, Jibon's body was somewhat out-of-control, his legs wobbly and arms devoid of strength. But somehow he managed to grasp the handle of the door of the carriage. Seeing him trying to board the moving train, some passengers inside became terrified. They shut their eyes apprehending a calamity. He's going, going, gone—but Jibon did not go. He did not lose his life or limbs. He managed to get into the general compartment and stood in front of the door. A couple of passengers, who had been worried that the train would halt if an accident occurred—thus delaying the journey—showered a volley of abuse on him and then turned to gaze at the scenery outside.

The first station at which the train halted after leaving Siliguri was Sukna. The train began moving uphill after that. The mountainside was covered in thick forest composed of many kinds of trees. Jibon began to feel a bit cold now. He saw the passengers had shawls, sweaters and coats on. Jibon had only his sleeveless vest and gamchha. He wrapped the gamchha tightly around himself.

23

Alakapuri Unvisited

As the journey progressed, it became colder. But that did not trouble Jibon as yet. Rather, he gazed in awe at nature's incomparable creation, the small, middling and large hills and mountains and their peaks. It was as if a huge green carpet of waves had swathed the whole terrain, which was embroidered with a multitude of flowers. A flock of sheep grazed far away, adding their own charm to the beauty of the scenery.

Owing to the mountainous terrain, the train track could not run straight, it had to follow the curve of the mountainside and wind itself over the slope. Jibon was amazed imagining the hard labour that must have gone into constructing the railway. All accomplished by the sons of Vishwakarma. What couldn't man achieve if he tried! But who remembered the men who created such a flawless work of art by blasting the mountain, using chisels and hammers and dripping their sweat on the earth? Who knew whether or not they too had attained the plight of Garib Das, who could once carry a big sack of paddy on his head!

There was a deep abyss on one side of the mountain along which the train snaked, like a gigantic centipede, hissing *tikis-tikis*. If the train toppled over, who knows where it would tumble and fall. And on the other side stood the mountain itself, almost touching the train. Myriad wild flowers, multi-hued, red-white-yellow-blue, bloomed on the mountainside. One imagined that someone had artfully planted them there. Five or six Nepali boys of about Jibon's age got into the train at some station or the other. They too were crowded around near the door. The boys, bursting with restless energy, stretched out their hands and plucked the flowers. After that, whenever they spotted a girl walking on the road, they threw them at her. Those to whom the flowers were flung also waved and smiled and flung back their loving response. Those who were a bit braver threw back a flying kiss.

Beside the track along which the train moved, accompanying it, and sometimes winding round and round like a snake, was a tarred road. There were many jeeps on the road, taking and bringing back tourists. The travellers on those jeeps were bursting with joy and exuberance. Because of the time and place, no one felt inhibited. Almost all the passengers on the train were laughing in glee. Perhaps in the whole world it was only the language of laughter and tears that everyone could understand without translation. Laughter, joy, delight and bliss—the intoxication spurred by the mountain breeze—were infectious and transmitted from one person to the other. The only one who was an image of joylessness amidst all the cheer was a person named Jibon—neither child nor adult, neither alive nor dead. With his small gamchha wrapped tightly around him, he sat huddled away on one side, braving the cold air, observing the happy folk and heaving deep sighs.

The journey seemed unending. Sometimes the engine pulled the train from the front, and sometimes it pushed the train from behind as it ascended the gradient. Sometimes the rail track was visible above one's head and sometimes directly below one's feet. This winding route was called a loop. There were supposedly eighteen loops between Sukna and Darjeeling. The restless, spirited Nepali children knew all the curves and loops of this route like the back of their hands. At each of the loops, they jumped off the train and onto the road along which the jeeps moved, and after answering the call of nature or drinking water or tea, and plucking a bunch of flowers, they climbed the mountain-slope on foot and then waited at the next loop, which the train sometimes reached only as much as twenty minutes later. They resumed their boisterousness once they got into the train. This was the natural exuberance of youth. After doing all this for a few hours, they got off at some station. Someone said the station was called Ghoom. The up- and down-trains crossed each other here. All the boys got into the train going from Darjeeling to Siliguri. Now they would descend the mountain with all their boisterousness.

It was about one o'clock in the afternoon. Water was loaded into the engine. The passengers were given the opportunity to have lunch. After the train departed sluggishly once again, it grew much colder. Jibon's vest and small gamchha could do little to push the cold back. There was no other passenger like him on the train. Everyone was in trousers, jackets, caps and scarves. One could see there were some passengers who were poor, because their trousers and jackets were dirty and torn. But whatever condition they were in, at least they kept them warm. Jibon did not have even that.

The train continued on its journey for several hours, leaving many stations behind, till it reached Kurseong. It must have been about five in the evening then. The departing sun shone like a powerful searchlight on the crest of a high mountain. In another fifteen or twenty minutes, it would disappear behind the mountain. The day ended much earlier here than in the plains.

Most of the passengers got off at Kurseong. There were only seven or eight people left in the carriage. The train set off once again. Jibon found a vacant seat and sat hunched, making himself small with his knees drawn and arms wrapped around them. It was less windy here and so less cold. After a while, he could see the lights had come on—looking like a garland—on the crests of the mountains, high and low, wherever there were habitations. The train shooting forward through the stillness of the mountains seemed to be like a celestial vehicle advancing through the kingdom of stars. Jibon was sitting on the right side of the train. On his right was a huge descent, covered with pine and devtaru forest, and beyond, set against the sky, were slumbering hills, mountains and peaks.

Jibon did not have the time now to be captivated by such scenery. He was wondering how much longer it would be before the train reached Darjeeling. After that—what would happen there? What astonishments, dangers, events and accidents were awaiting him there? He was already assailed by the biting cold. It would get even colder as the night grew. What would he do if he did not find some warm place to shelter himself? It was raining from time to time now. It wasn't the torrential rain of the plains. These were wandering clouds, which floated along until they stopped somewhere and shed rain for a while. And so sun and rain alternated. This game of hide-and-seek went on continuously in the mountains. But when the rain struck him, it felt like needles penetrating the skin and making their way all the way to the bone. Perhaps it was the frozen ice on the mountain peaks that had turned to water and was raining down.

At about half past eight in the evening, as icy rain drizzled, the train reached Darjeeling station. It was completely desolate. It was as if winter had suddenly pounced down here, extinguishing all heat and turning the very breath of life cold. An eerie darkness that made one shudder, shrouded the whole place. Porters picked up the luggage of the few passengers who had alighted here. The porters here did not carry the luggage in their hands, but on their backs in rope slings. They carried the luggage through the rain as the passengers headed to their respective destinations. Jibon got off the train and looked around. He felt very dejected. A tremor of fear arose inside him. He realised he had made a big mistake in his calculations.

While living in the refugee camp in Shiromanipur, Jibon had once walked, alone, all the way to Bishnupur. There were two large lakes there, called Lalbandh and Ranibandh. The Mallah kings had had these lakes dug to alleviate the water scarcity faced by their subjects. Owing to lack of maintenance, the water was no longer potable. Reaching the bank of Lalbandh, Jibon had seen a clump of lilies that had bloomed in the middle of the lake. Water-lily was a plant that could be boiled and eaten. In the hot afternoon, driven by hunger, without so much as a second thought, Jibon had taken off his shorts at the lakeside and entered the water. Although he had learnt to swim with Mongla in a pond when he visited his hamlet, that pond could in no way be compared to Lalbandh. Who knows with what conviction or courage Jibon had entered the deserted Lalbandh all alone. He had even swum and reached the middle. He had gathered a bunch of lilies too. But when he was swimming back with his haul, he realised he shouldn't have done that all by himself. He had managed to return to the shore, but while swimming back, he had encountered the obstruction of a host of vines and leaves spread out by the water-lily clump, which had got entangled in his legs while swimming. The lake was not very deep, but it wasn't so shallow that it could not drown a child. And it wasn't as if that hadn't happened a couple of times either. Just the previous year, a shepherd boy had drowned when he entered the water to pluck a lotus, and his body was found floating on the surface. He had turned blue, because of which some people suspected snakebite. Yes, there were snakes too in Lalbandh, which some people had seen lying coiled up on the lotus leaves.

When Jibon's arms and legs had tired as he swam, when the sheer terror of death by drowning seized his heart—just then, he had heard someone's voice, the voice he had heard again and again during times of danger: 'Don't lose courage, Jibon! Don't give in to the fear of dying. There's no one nearby, don't hope for anyone's help. No one is going to come all the way here to save you. If you have to survive you have to do that yourself. Make the effort!' It's said that a drowning man firmly grasps any stray branches he comes across. But there were no branches near Jibon. There were only a bunch of lilies in his clutch, for which his life was now in danger. Jibon held on to the lilies and kept himself afloat, resting awhile to catch his breath. Then he swam a bit more and rested again. In this way, he crossed the wild jungle of vines in the lake and reached the shore. Jibon had vowed that day never to make such a mistake again.

But now it seemed, he had done the same thing yet again. He had fallen into the dark, icy, unfathomable waters of some shoreless sea. Here too there was no friend or kin to save him.

There was a man sitting in the station with a black blanket wrapped around him, warming himself over a coal-oven. Jibon went up to him and asked, 'Can you tell me where I can stay the night here?'

The man appeared to be an employee in a food shop at the station. He looked at Jibon without interest. He was annoyed and unwilling to engage in futile conversation.

The man said, '*Koi hotal mein chala jao.* Go to some hotel.'

'But I don't have any money. Can't I stay here in the station?' Jibon asked.

The man seemed even more annoyed now. '*Yahaan to teshan mein pulis machchar tak rehne nahi dete to kaise rahoge!* The police don't allow even a mosquito into the station, so how can you stay here!'

As Jibon stood, he warmed his hands at the oven. The man asked him, 'Where do you live?'

Surmising that it would not be correct to say he was from too far away, Jibon said the name of a place that was nearby. 'Siliguri. Our house is on Burdwan Road in Siliguri.'

'So why have you come here?'

'I've come in search of work.'

'Work!' The man stuck out his lower lip in scorn. 'There's no work here. The people here go to the plains in search of work. And you've come here from the plains!'

The man's words broke into pieces and ground into dust the imagined golden edifice of Kuber's palace. The people in the mountains were dying of hunger and poverty. The mountains looked very beautiful from afar, but once one came near, one saw how many abysses and sheer drops there were.

Jibon asked in dismay, 'So what will I do now?'

'What will you do! Die! After all, you've come here to die!' The conversation was over. The man got up, picked up the clay oven and went into the shop, shutting the door behind him.

Suddenly the shrill screech of the train whistle made the very air of the drizzling night tremble. The train seemed to be moving backwards slowly. Although no one said so, Jibon figured out that the train was returning now. He got into the train, he would go back. Yes, he would return now, what else could he do but return? Alakapuri had not been waiting with glad tidings for him.

The empty train reached Kurseong after about an hour and a half. The onward journey had taken twice the time. That had been an ascent, while this was a descent. This was the rule in every aspect of life. It took a lot of time, effort and determination to climb up, but when one descended, it seemed effortless.

It was about ten at night. After the train halted at the mountain station of Kurseong, it did not move again. The engine driver and guard seemed to have disappeared, leaving the train carriages behind at the platform. Their duty for the day was over. They would only return tomorrow. In the morning, Kurseong had seemed to be even colder than Darjeeling. And wetter. For Jibon, this was like being thrown from the frying pan into the fire. What would he do? He got down from the train, stood on the platform and looked all around, terrified. There was only darkness everywhere. This wasn't a power cut. There were electric lamps burning, but they were too dim to illuminate the environs.

The platform was completely empty. This was the off-season, the tourists preferred not to come here at this time of the year. Besides, it had been rainy today. And so, people who were usually out on the streets had all returned home and shut their doors much earlier than usual, in fact almost at sunset. Walking slowly, Jibon went ahead to the jeep-stand outside the station. There were a few vehicles parked there, standing under the drizzling rain. But there were no people there. Perhaps the jeep drivers were sitting or lying inside the vehicles.

As he turned around to look at the train from there, Jibon shuddered. A railway employee had come out of the railway cabin and was locking all the carriages of the train. The keys would be with him. He would return with them tomorrow morning and unlock the doors so that passengers could board the train. But what would Jibon do now? Where would he sit and see through the terrifying, icy night? If he found shelter inside the train carriage, it would have been different.

Jibon had heard a story from someone about a land like this. Where it was apparently very cold. Cotton-like snow fell from the sky all day and all night. Apparently the water in the river there also froze. As soon as it was sunset there, people would shut the doors and windows of their houses. And they never opened them, come what may, before the sun rose again. For if they did that, the cold that blew in would freeze them. One day, a guest had come to some house. For some reason, he had been delayed and arrived late. By then, the door of the house had been shut. The guest could hardly speak because of the cold, his limbs were near frozen. With his stiff hands and faint voice, he tried to knock and call out to the people inside to open the door. But the house had been built in such a way that they did not hear anything. When they opened the door the next morning, they saw lying in front of the house the dead body of the man, covered in snow.

Jibon pricked his ears. As if floating from across the sea of darkness, from some cave in a mountain that rose to the very sky, or from some unknown planet across the cloud-covered firmament, came the great death-defying mantra: '*Charaibeti, charaibeti!* Move ahead, Jibon, move ahead! Don't succumb to the fear of death.

Don't give up before drowning.' The voice was extremely familiar, it was a beloved voice. Jibon knew it very well. It was the voice of the boy in the crematorium, Maran. The one who did not know the meaning of defeat!

Jibon went back into the station, and stepping down from the platform, he walked to the other side of the train and looked around. His eyes were like that of a creature of prey that hunted at night. No, no one was watching him. He could do whatever he wanted at this time. He went up to a carriage and pushed the door. Just as he had anticipated, the door opened. The railway employees could not deviate from the conduct of all government employees. They had locked the carriage doors on the platform side of the train, but left the doors on the other side unlocked, thereby saving themselves half the labour.

Jibon got into the carriage through the open door, and lay down on a berth, curling up his knees to his chest and shrivelling himself into a ball. Naturally, it wasn't as cold here as it was outside. Jibon thought it would be hard, but he could get through the night like this. At least he could cheat death.

❧

Who knows what time of night it was. It seemed an illusory slumber had descended upon the mountains at the wave of some imaginary magician's wand. The mountains, the trees, the houses, the streets and the vehicles all seemed to be immersed in the bottomless pit of sleep. There was no sign of life anywhere, only the howl of the wind and the soft pitter-patter of rain. The lamps on the light-posts and those hanging from the platform-shed shone dimly like the thousand eyes of some tired demon. Some light trickled in through the shuttered windows of the rail carriage and fell around Jibon. But that did not remove the darkness inside the carriage, it only became somewhat thinner. Jibon had dozed off. Suddenly there was a loud noise inside the carriage. He woke up at once. He became aware of the foul stench of *cholai* liquor that pervaded the whole carriage. Jibon could discern a drunken man standing in the shadowy darkness. His head and face were covered and he was wearing a knee-length coat. His legs were tottering and his voice had the tone of a cat about to catch a fresh mouse.

Who knows how he figured out that in this inclement night, there was an unprotected guardian-less, destitute, feeble boy in the carriage. He advanced, tottering, towards Jibon. He moved aside the gamchha to look at his face. He was already drunk, and so in the darkness of the carriage, he imagined Jibon's hairless, young face to be that of a woman. He moved closer on his wobbling feet and pulled at the button of Jibon's shorts. He was impatient, as if he would tear off the pair of shorts if unbuttoning proved too slow.

Jibon wasn't prepared for such a sudden attack. He was petrified. In a bid to protect himself, his right leg shot out in hatred and rage. It struck, unfortunately, exactly where the man's testicles were. This was the most vulnerable spot in the male body, where, let alone a kick, even the slightest knock could fell a hefty wrestler. The man dropped to the floor. The sound that he emitted from his throat then could be compared to a moan, a groan or a whine. Hearing either that or Jibon's terrified cries, two men from the jeep-stand near the platform came running. They promptly entered the carriage. The drunken man was probably known to them. Probably the acquaintance wasn't made under pleasant circumstances. One man shouted, 'Who's that ... bastard! At it again ...?' As soon as he heard that, the drunken man ran away, hauling his wounded body.

These people were the drivers of the jeeps outside. The one who had run away, as well as the two men standing inside the carriage, were Hindi speakers. They did not look like Nepalis. They looked at Jibon and asked him brusquely, '*Kaun hai re tu?* Who are you?'

In a terrified voice, Jibon summarily explained why he was there. The man who was the taller of the two, who looked to be about thirty or thirty-two years old, asked Jibon to come with them.

'Where to?'

'With me.'

'Why?'

'Or else you'll die in the cold.'

The jeep driver took Jibon along and made him lie down on the rear seat of his vehicle. He gave him a torn coat to cover himself with, and said, 'Go back as soon as it's morning. You won't find anything here. It's completely futile to come here!' After that, he went and lay down on the front seat. These were people who lived in this mountainous region. The winter had just begun now. For one who was used to the bitter cold of winter, the cold at this time of the year was nothing. In a little while, he began snoring loudly. But Jibon could not sleep. The uncertain situation, an unknown place, the hunger raging in his belly, and add to that the shock to his fragile mind from the sudden assault, did not allow him to sleep. He spent the night tossing and turning this way and that.

⁂

The sun rose atop the high mountain. The early morning sunlight seemed to smile like a young woman as it fell on the leaves of the devtaru, pine and teak trees towering over the green, rain-washed tea gardens. A few people were already on the streets now. The shops and markets had opened. The day had begun in the small mountain town of Kurseong. The jeep driver woke up and took Jibon to a shop. He bought him a cup of tea for fifteen paise and two slices of bread for ten paise. 'Have it. The train leaves later in the day. Get on it. Don't ever come back here.'

Jibon was overwhelmed with gratitude at the jeep driver's generosity. Never before had anyone spent even a penny on him without expecting something in return. He said, 'I'll do exactly what you said. I'll go back.' At about two in the afternoon, the return train arrived at the station. A defeated Jibon was compelled to return on that train. He returned to Siliguri. From the mountains to the plains, from the dizzying heights of the city of gold created in his imagination to the harsh ground of reality. Back to familiar skies, earth and people. It wasn't yet unbearably cold here. The biting cold, like piercing needles, was absent. The nights too were less dark, less scary. And so it was not at all difficult for Jibon to spend another ten or twelve hours here. Even if he examined the nooks and crannies of his mind, he would never be able to arrive at an explanation of why he halted there. Perhaps the only reason was that he was unable to decide what to do next. The easiest thing for him to do would be to go to some shop and ask for work. But when he thought about that, a fear pricked his mind like a sharp thorn. What if he was again made to slog like a donkey but not paid. Unable to come to any decision, Jibon roamed around near the station and whiled away the whole day and most of the night.

When it was approaching dawn, the Lucknow Mail arrived at Siliguri station. It had come from Gauhati, in Assam, the magical city that Jibon had left behind. Jibon thought to himself—Lucknow was in Uttar Pradesh, which was near Delhi, the capital city of India, where all the leaders of the country lived. There was no harm in going and taking a look there. After all, what did he have to lose. For one who seemed to be engulfed in misfortune, there was nothing to fear about a new misfortune. But perhaps something different might happen, the tiniest bit of something favourable might transpire. Perhaps there would be some change in his life that had been unfailingly cruel and hellish so far. At least, there was nothing wrong in playing one hand in such a hope.

While living in Khola-Doltala, Jibon had found a spoke of a broken umbrella. He had sharpened it by rubbing it against a stone and tied it to the top of a bamboo stick to make a fishing rod. He had never made a fishing rod before that, nor had he done any fishing. Actually he had no experience at all in that regard. He had only seen, on a couple of occasions, how a fishing rod was made and used. That was a lot like learning to cycle by standing afar and watching someone cycling, or learning to swim by standing at the bank of the pond. So naturally, even after going around the whole day with his fishing rod, and trying his hand at the canal and the paddy fields, Jibon met with no success. He could not catch a single fish. Returning home crestfallen, he thought the fishing rod was useless and flung it away towards the paddy field. But just then, something astonishing happened. The pointed spoke of the fishing rod pierced the eye of a baby eel. The eel was only about five days old, it was an inch-and-a-half long. Perhaps the Almighty had assigned exactly this liberation to its destiny, and so it died in that way.

One shoots an arrow skywards and it pierces the prey. One throws a stone into darkness and it hits the target. Does that ever happen? It does, when one is lucky. Not everyone but some people had definitely been so fortunate. Thinking deeply about all this and coming to a realisation—or perhaps without thinking about or realising anything—Jibon got into a terribly crowded third-class carriage of the Lucknow Mail.

24

The Havildar

Thus did Jibon begin a long, two-day train journey. People got on and got off at stations. The train would empty out a little during the day and become more and more crowded as the night progressed. At some station, Jibon got down to drink water at the platform, but was unable to re-enter his carriage because it was so crammed. It wasn't just him, many others too couldn't find a place even to park a foot. Risking their lives, they went and sat on the metal connector joining two carriages. Flaming flecks of coal emitted with the puffs of smoke from the coal-fired steam engine flew into Jibon's face, eyes and hair. The grit stuck to his dusty, matted hair. The flames scorched his exposed skin. There was no way of escaping the scorching. If he tried to brush away the flecks of flame with his hand, there was the danger of falling off the connector on to the rail track below. Jibon was no circus trapeze artist.

Jibon encountered a ticket checker on the long journey. It was about ten in the morning. He was a bearded, elderly man, who had boarded the carriage at some station. He began checking the passengers' tickets from one end of the carriage and finally reached Jibon. He stretched out his hand—'Ticket?' Jibon knew only one answer to this question: 'Don't have one.' The ticket checker then asked him softly, '*Kahaan jayega?* Where do you want to go?'

Jibon knew the name of the place he had decided to go to when he had boarded the train. But he didn't say that now, he only said, '*Jayega bahut dur.* I'm going very far.' The elderly checker was a bit hard of hearing. Given the sound of the moving train, and Jibon's feeble, famished voice, he heard something else. 'What did you say? Gorakhpur? Gorakhpur is far away!'

The checker appeared to Jibon to be of a somewhat kindly nature. He could tell him his tale of woe and beg for some assistance. He hadn't eaten anything for several days. He was on the verge of collapse. If Jibon requested him, the kind checker would definitely send him to jail for a few days. Raja had told him that food was provided in jail. If he was to eat something, it was essential that he be sent to jail. Who knew how far away Lucknow was. And it wasn't as if someone would hand him a trayful of food once he reached there. If only some arrangement for food could be made right here. There was no harm in resting for a few days and then resuming the journey. He followed the advancing ticket checker and stopped behind him. 'I don't have a ticket. Meaning, I'm ticketless.'

Turning his head around to look at Jibon, the ticket checker said, 'You've told me that already! So what do you want now?'

'I'm saying, can you take me away?'

'Why?'

'Because I don't have a ticket.'

The kindly disposition of the elderly ticket checker suddenly turned to rage. His eyes turned bloodshot. He retorted, 'Go! Stand quietly in that corner. Can I take you away? Fucker, the people who can afford to buy tickets travel without them and I'm unable to haul them away! What can I do alone? They should assign a force to accompany me. But they won't do that. Should I die in the course of duty? You're just a poor fellow. Looking at you, one can see you're starving. What's the point of catching you? I won't do that. Go and sit on that side.'

Jibon's humble plea had angered the man, but it wasn't the kind of anger that could benefit Jibon. Before he got off from the carriage at the next station, the ticket checker assured Jibon, 'My duty is until Gorakhpur. Go, my son, no checker will come after that.'

Jibon did not encounter any ticket checkers or police personnel for the rest of that day and the whole night. The long journey, without a ticket, from Bengal, through Bihar, to Uttar Pradesh, finally concluded without any mishap. The train arrived at the Charbagh station in Lucknow. It was seven in the morning. There was a nip in the air. Jibon got off the train and joined the procession of hundreds of passengers walking towards the exit gate. If only he could cross the gate, he would be free, with nothing to fear. On the other side of the gate was the soil of Lucknow, the capital city of Uttar Pradesh, with its streets and people. Lucknow was the famed city of nawabs and badshahs of yore, the city of ghazal, thumri, courtesans and dancers, palaces and monuments. Jibon wasn't at all in a sound condition. He would not be able to carry himself very far unless he ate something. So he had to stay here for a few days. He had to find some food. He would resume his journey after that.

Two black-coated ticket checkers stood on either side of the gate. They examined the ticket of each passenger before letting them pass. Jibon wasn't worried about that. After all, what could the checker do? What power did he have? They would either catch him or not do that. If they hauled him up, then he would either be taken to jail or be released. Either way, he would gain. He walked ahead confidently.

But Jibon could not reach the gate. When he was about twenty or twenty-five feet away, a loud, grave voice made him halt—*'Aiy, ruk!'* It wasn't a ticket checker but a havildar of the Railway Police who stopped him. He was middle-aged, fat, bespectacled, with a bushy moustache. He was dressed in his uniform of a white shirt and khaki shorts, with boots on his feet and a cane in his hand. In Jibon's eyes, he resembled a wild boar. He blocked Jibon's way and grunted, 'Where are you going?'

Because Jibon had worked for quite some time in Bade Lal's shop in Calcutta, he had no difficulty in understanding Hindi. The difficulty was in speaking it. He replied to the havildar in his poor Hindi, with his East Bengali accent, 'I'm going there. Outside the gate.'

'*Kahaan se aaya?* Where did you come from?'

Calcutta—but would it be appropriate for him to say that? If he admitted to travelling so far without a ticket, then the jail term and quantum of punishment too would be commensurate with that. So he should mention some place that was not so far. Then he would be in jail only for about a week. Jibon replied, '*Gorakhpur thika aaya.* I'm coming from Gorakhpur.'

Gorakhpur meant a journey of about ten hours from Lucknow. The havildar was surprised to hear that. 'Do you know where you've arrived?'

'Yes, I do. This is Lucknow.'

'Why have you come here?'

The havildar wanted to find out whether he had committed some crime and run away from Gorakhpur. But what was Jibon to say now? What could he say so that the policeman would believe he was telling the truth? 'Always tell the truth'. 'Satyameva Jayate'. However sweet-sounding such pious talk was, actually it wasn't at all sweet. The real truth was that the truth did not work at all times, and sometimes the truth became a blatant lie. Despite his meagre years, Jibon carried that learning in his very bones. If he hadn't told Binod Saha that he was from Calcutta, and had instead mentioned New Jalpaiguri or the name of some other nearby place, would Binod Saha have had the courage to cheat Jibon out of his money so flagrantly?

Be that as it may, at this crucial moment, Jibon could not tell the havildar, 'I'm very poor, that's why I left Calcutta ...' Calcutta was one of the biggest cities in the world! Whoever else that may sound credible to, it would not sound true to a policeman, someone who apprehended thieves and rascals day and night. So Jibon was compelled to fabricate a story. Like everything else, truth too could be constructed, embellished and given life to. Like a rubber band it could be stretched long. That's why a great sage had said, 'Greater than the birthplace of Ram in Ayodhya is the soil of the poet's imagination.' Whether it was a poet or a storyteller, how he presented it was the main thing. Through his compositional skill, untruth became truth, and the truth became a great truth.

Bringing tears to his eyes, Jibon said, 'We are refugees. When riots broke out in East Pakistan, we left behind our homes, our land, a granary full of grain and a pond full of fish. We left everything behind and crossed the border risking our lives. The government allowed us to live in a camp. They took us from there by train to Dandakaranya. I was travelling with my parents, brother and sister. When the train stopped at a station on the way, my Ma asked me to fetch some water to drink. I went to get the water, but the train left before I could return. I could not get on the train. I lost my parents and brother and sister.'

Wiping his eyes with the back of his hand, Jibon continued, 'I don't know where Dandakaranya is. Someone told me it is near Lucknow. When I heard that, I came here in search of my parents. Can you tell me where Dandakaranya is?'

The havildar shook his head. He did not know. Jibon's tearful face darkened in dismay. He said, 'You don't know ... no one knows ... how will I find them? What will I do now in this foreign land? What will I eat? How will I survive? You look like a good man. Can you help me? Can you find me a place to work? I can work very hard.'

'Do you know how to cook?'

'I do,' Jibon said. 'I can cook everything.' Jibon knew how to cook. He had done a lot of that in Gauhati.

'Come with me.'

The one who has cancer does not need to be afflicted with any other disease. Similarly, when a policeman had already apprehended Jibon, what more could a ticket checker do! The two checkers moved aside from the exit gate. Holding Jibon's arm firmly, the havildar led him to the rickshaw-stand and made him get into one. The twenty-minute ride, for which the fare was fifty paise, took them to one end of the city. Beyond that lay open fields and the railway track. The rickshaw came to a halt in front of the railway quarters there. The havildar got off the rickshaw, took out a key from his pocket and unlocked the door. There was no sign of anyone else in his quarters. There was no furniture as such in the two rooms except for a string-cot in each of them. Hanging on a wire strung across a room was a gamchha, a lungi and a couple of police uniforms. On the floor was some wheat flour in a tin container, a few potatoes and onions, a bottle with mustard oil, and another with some masala, a few plates and two buckets. In the verandah outside was a clay-oven with some pieces of coal and chopped wood. In front of that was a large drum.

The havildar asked Jibon, 'Do you know how to light an oven?'

'I do.'

'Then light the oven and prepare the dough for rotis.'

The havildar removed his uniform and sat down in his undergarments on a string-cot. His arms, legs and chest were all covered in hair and he had a Hanuman tattoo on one side of his chest. A dirty thread ran across his chest. He was sweating, letting off a pungent odour. The kind of odour there was on an old goat.

The havildar had measured out the flour and dal for Jibon to use. Jibon prepared the dough and made rotis. He prepared a potato curry and arhar dal, garnished with garlic. After Jibon had finished cooking, the havildar told him, 'Bring some oil in a bowl.' He then lay down, sprawling on one side of the verandah. When Jibon came with the oil, he said, 'Come, massage me now.'

What with a sea of hunger in his belly, the murderous aroma of dal and garlic assailed his nose. It was like a cyclone raging in his belly. This was a very vulnerable time. He could not afford to lose control now. Jibon began to massage the man. At first his arms, and then the legs, back, head and whatever else there was. Forsaking all modesty, the havildar had all his parts massaged by the soft hands of the boy. Oh what comfort, what bliss! His body seemed to tremble at the touch of Jibon's fingers. After having his whole body massaged, using almost fifty grams of mustard oil, he felt utterly refreshed. Now he would bathe. So he instructed Jibon about his next task.

'Go to the road outside, turn left and go straight, you'll find a well there. Bring water from there.' Jibon drew water from the well, filled the buckets and returned to fill the empty drum. He made three trips to fetch six buckets of water before the drum was full. After that, the man bathed for a long time and then dressed, combed his hair and sat down to eat. His duty began at 8 a.m. The havildar had measured out the flour for Jibon, he knew that six rotis had been prepared. After eating four, he left two for Jibon, washed his hands and mouth, sat down on a cot and began kneading tobacco with lime. Stuffing the prepared tobacco into his mouth, chewing it, and spitting out a stream of spittle, he said to Jibon, 'Go, have a bath and eat. Hurry up!'

There was some water left in the drum. Jibon bathed quickly, ate the rotis, dal and potato curry left for him, washed all the utensils and put them back in the room. The havildar put on his boots, locked the door with two large brass locks and left for his duty. Before he left, he said, 'Stay in the verandah. I will return by eight.'

Jibon had not bathed, eaten or slept for several days. After having a bath today and eating something at least, he felt somewhat revived. He swept the verandah clean with a broom, lay down there and fell asleep. He was fast asleep and had no idea that the whole day went by. He woke up in the evening to the chortling of children. The place belonged to the railways. They had constructed fifty or sixty quarters for the employees to live in. The quarters were built around a small field. There was a six- or seven-foot-high wall encircling it, with an iron gate. The doors of all the quarters were open now and children had come to the field to play. Waking up, Jibon sat in front of the havildar's door and watched the children playing. Their laughter, games and commotion filled Jibon with delight. And tears of anguish filled his eyes. He too had had a childhood once, he too was supposed to laugh and play like this. But he hadn't been able to do that. It was as if someone had conspired to rob him of laughter, play and joy. All these children had either a father or brother or someone who was a government employee. The government had assumed the responsibility for their food, clothing, comfort and every convenience. That's why their children were growing up amidst laughter, play, food and comfort. A government employee was like a pet son of the government. He would get his salary as well as bribes, and he did not have to work if he did not want to. It was a very comfortable job, providing a very comfortable life. Their children too were growing up in comfort on the earnings from the comfortable job. Who else but them could laugh in this way!

The children's playtime was over. From a mic far away, the melodious call of the azaan came wafting. And close on the heels of that sacred twilight came the terrifying, midnight-loving, necrophagous ghoul of the new-moon night, black as tar.

The havildar returned home at eight in the evening. Seeing Jibon, a smile appeared on his face. He unlocked the door and brought out the wheat flour, dal and potatoes. 'Make the food,' he said. Like in the morning, Jibon once again prepared rotis, dal and potato curry. The havildar served himself the food and ate, and after that Jibon ate whatever remained. It was about ten by then. Spreading a sheet provided by the havildar on the floor, Jibon lay down in the verandah. The havildar lay down inside the room, but he could not sleep. A fresh, fifteen or sixteen year old *londa* was nearby, in his own quarters—in his custody—in darkness. How then could he sleep! After tossing and turning for quite a long time, he opened the door and entered the verandah. A bird of prey that hunted at night swooped down on a chick sleeping in a nest on the branch of some tree. The chick's mother flapped its wings in terror and grief and cried out plaintively. Its loud screeches pierced the silence of the night and filled the air.

This night was a disgustingly black and ugly one. It was as if the earth had altered the speed at which it rotated and the path along which it revolved. It had started rotating in the opposite direction. All the laws and rules of nature, human civilisation, cultivation and culture, which had been built with great difficulty over thousands of years, were ruptured. A creature who took pride in having risen to manhood descended to a role which would make even animals shudder with revulsion.

The havildar saw Jibon. He was shrouded in darkness. It was the darkness that resided at the other pole of light. Light meant radiance, lustre, sight. Light meant the sun, it signified truth. But darkness meant only darkness. Dense, black, seamless. The darkness in whose womb dwelt sin, injustice, cruelty and oppression. That could conceal the true form of Satan's offspring. It was a golden opportunity. Like a hungry hyena, the havildar pounced upon Jibon, as if he was a juicy fawn. Jibon could not resist, he did not have the strength to do that. He could not shout because there was a strong hand on his throat, together with the threat, 'Don't shout, or else I'll strangle you'. Jibon lay on the ground, compelled, gritting his teeth, biting his own hand. The havildar ejaculated his sticky perversion, humiliation and oppression into Jibon. He had been able to protect himself in the Shibpur police mess and on the train in Kurseong. But now he was unable to protect himself from the clutches of someone who was responsible for protecting law and order and the security of the citizens of the country. A pitiless creature, estranged from human and police codes, had raped him—raped his soul, his dignity and his very being.

The thrusting of the policeman's rubbery piston into his anus had continued for a while. Jibon had been in great pain. A few drops of blood had dripped from his body.

He had had to endure grave humiliation. But nothing so terrible as today's incident, such filthy indignity, had happened before.

And it would never happen again. As long as he lived, the incident would cloud his mind. It would teach him to view men and their mentality differently.

Rape is such a brutal act that those who suffer it lose all their self-respect and dignity in the eyes of society—as well as in their own eyes. Life then becomes heavier and more painful than death. In current thinking, rape is seen as always being perpetuated by a lustful man upon a weak, unprotected woman. But in common perception, rape of a man by a woman, or of a woman by another woman, or of a man by another man, is not seen as something worrisome. People find it difficult to believe that such things happen. But the truth is that such perverted crimes happen all the time in society. Let alone another man, some men do not even spare dogs and cows.

Jibon remembered an incident that took place in the Shibpur police camp. At about nine in the night, a man had spotted a young bitch on the open ground on which football was played and parades took place. He had become aroused and fucked it. But the matter did not remain secret. Some people saw it happening and spread the word. It was a subject of conversation for a long time. But no more than that.

⚘

It was morning. The havildar's quarters faced west. So it was only later in the morning that sunlight entered his premises. Jibon had fallen asleep around dawn. When he woke up, he saw the havildar had left. He had gone for his morning walk.

Jibon was filled with self-hate. He wanted to cry. He felt like a dirty drain in which people pissed. He felt as if a maggot was running all over his body and eating him alive, the way they ate up unclaimed bodies in a morgue. He thought that all the people on the other side of the wall must know what had happened to him. As soon as he opened the gate and stepped outside, they would raise their eyebrows, smirk and break out in laughter as they ridiculed him, 'Look, there he goes, the bastard who got his arse fucked!'

Jibon felt his body scorching in shame. In his inner being, an untamable wild buffalo shook its head in rage. It wanted to pierce the bastard havildar with its sharp horns. His blood boiled, as on the stormy night in Park Circus. His hands itched. He could still smell blood on his hands, the smell of human blood.

Rage made people blind. But Jibon had not become so blind that he forgot about his present situation, or forgot about the consequences. Here was a government employee, weighing eighty-five kilos, and over six feet tall, who had learned combat and practised physical culture. And shielding him like a mountain was the all-powerful Indian state's judicial system, which would protect him with all its might. Pitted against that was a helpless teenager who, by virtue of his very birth, was a wrong-doer, poor and weak. What power did Jibon possess, to penetrate the armour of state and social protection and reach the offender, and ensure that he was punished in a manner befitting his crime?

There is a law book called the Indian Penal Code, according to which, if a man rapes a woman and the rape is proved in a court of law, the rapist can be imprisoned for a maximum of seven years. And if a man rapes a boy or a youth, then the punishment is imprisonment for life. In this country, one woman is raped every fifty-four minutes. Even if it wasn't as much, the number of rapes of boys was not so insignificant either. Although one heard about a few cases of punishment in regard to those who raped women, when it came to rape of boys, and for that matter, animals too, there was not a single instance of punishment.

So, however much Jibon scratched his head, he could not see how he would get justice. Who would bring the man to justice? As the saying went, how could the owner of the paddy field get justice from the one whose cow had consumed the crop? Had anyone ever got it?

But there was one thing Jibon could do. He himself could judge and punish the one who had committed the outrage against him. He could lock the door from outside when the havildar was asleep in his room at night, set fire to the room and escape in the darkness. Perhaps even a needle could be found in a haystack, but in this vast country of millions, it would be impossible to find a boy who lacked a name or identity. Given the inferno raging inside Jibon, it would be an easy matter to burn the havildar in the same fire. But where would he get the ten or twenty litres of petrol or kerosene to do that? After all, it wasn't a thatched hut that could be set aflame with a single matchstick.

So what could Jibon do? Would the scoundrel be spared? Would he go scot-free? As he pondered over the matter, Jibon thought up a way which would be cheap, reliable and fatal. There was a shelf on one side of the verandah. There was a small mirror on that, as well as a razor beside it, together with a few new blades. A very ordinary thing. The havildar combed his hair there after he took a bath. A sharp blade could be of use to Jibon—a slash at the base of the male organ was all that was needed, just a single slash.

Jibon shook himself awake and rose up. He got over the incident of last night that had weighed down on him like an immovable stone. Nothing had happened. Whatever had happened was not so terrible. It was merely a misunderstanding, arising out of a lack of prior preparedness. The havildar returned after a while from his morning walk. Jibon easily completed all the tasks that he had done yesterday. He lit the oven, prepared the wheat-flour dough, made rotis, fetched water for bathing, and massaged the havildar's whole body with oil. Jibon's oil-smeared hands effortlessly reached the parts where they had hesitated to go yesterday. The havildar was satisfied. The *londa* had fallen in line. *Londa* was a very commonly used word in Hindi, whose meaning was 'fucked-arse'. The *londa's* business was to get his arse fucked. In a cheerful state of mind, the havildar ate and left for work. And Jibon sat waiting with a blade for the night.

But the havildar was fortunate. He must have left home at an auspicious moment that day. A message reached the Railway Police office in the railway station: 'Come home at once, son'. The havildar did not have the power to disregard that summon. His younger brother had beaten his father and left him with a gash on his head. Being a policeman, he did not get too perturbed about fights, murders or riots. However, since this was a family matter, it was a bit worrisome. He set off at once for his village home. But before leaving, he got Jibon a job in the railway engine repair workshop.

The loco workshop lay on the right side of the road going from the havildar's quarters to the station. Jibon's work involved collecting ash from the rail track and carrying it to the dump. He worked together with twenty or twenty-five more men, under a contractor. His salary was fifty rupees a month. On the days he did not work, there was no pay. Fifty rupees a month, which meant about a rupee and ten annas a day. It wasn't normally possible to get people to work for such a meagre salary. But they were able to find willing workers because at the end of the day, each worker was allowed to take back a basket of coal foraged from the rail tracks, which fetched a rupee or a rupee and a half when sold outside. Jibon too would get the coal. With the money he got from selling the coal, he bought flour and dal. The havildar took pity on Jibon and left the oven, frying pan and griddle in the verandah, so that he could cook his food. He had told the contractor to give him a rupee or two if he asked for money.

Jibon worked from eight in the morning until six in the evening. One person shovelled ash into a basket and lifted it to Jibon's head. He then walked a long distance and dumped it on the heap. In the evening, he carried the basket of coal to a neighbourhood nearby. There were plenty of buyers for the coal. After selling the coal, he went to the market and made his purchases. He cooked his food and ate, all alone. Jibon had seldom had the opportunity to eat well and stay comfortably somewhere. Who knew what lay in store for him in the future. He had got seven days. He ought to enjoy it.

The havildar returned not after seven but ten days. But he was not alone. His wife and daughter had accompanied him. They would stay here henceforth.

⁓

Someone had observed that life was a drama and that the world was a stage. The havildar now concealed his animal instincts like an innocent and began playing the role of a most devoted husband. But there was no change in Jibon's fortunes. He continued to buy food, cook and eat by himself. When the havildar's family retired for the night, Jibon would light the oven with his coal and cook two meals. And for the rest of the night, he would lie in one corner of the verandah.

It was a small verandah, open on one side. Because Uttar Pradesh was close to the Himalayas, winter arrived here earlier than in Bengal. It had begun to get cold. Jibon would turn stiff by dawn. But at least he had some sort of a shelter. By rule, it definitely commanded a rent. Jibon could not afford to pay rent. So, without any compunction, the havildar's calculating wife exacted the rent by making Jibon wash utensils and clothes, fetch water for cooking and bathing and so on.

A month passed by in this way. Came the day for receiving wages, and all the workers were in high spirits. Jibon too floated in a tide of joy. In a little while, he would have fifty rupees in his hands. He, or for that matter, even his father, Garib Das, had never seen or actually held so much money all at once. His gamchha was torn and tattered. He would get a new gamchha. He hadn't eaten rice for a long time. He did not even possess a pot to cook rice in. He would go to an eatery and eat rice today. Thinking about the Bengali eatery near the Charbagh station, Jibon waited, with fond hopes in his heart.

At exactly 4 p.m., the payment of salaries commenced. Everyone's name was called out, one by one. They all got their salary. Only Jibon's name was not called. Dismayed, Jibon went up to the contractor. 'Where's my salary, sir? You haven't paid me.'

The contractor was a fair-complexioned, round-faced Muslim. The blood of nawabs and badshahs could have been flowing in his veins. He lived in a huge mansion in the middle of the city. He had two or three wives. His youngest wife was supposedly only twenty-two. He had married her about a year ago.

He said, 'I can't give you your salary. The havildar has forbidden me to do so. I believe you stay and eat in his house. I don't know anything about the arrangement and terms you have with him. He was the one who put you on the job. Actually, it's like he is the one you are working for. Tell him whatever you have to say.'

Jibon said, 'I buy the food that I eat at his house. I stay there, but for that they make me do all the housework. Sometimes I also give them a basket or two of the coal that you provide.'

'I don't know anything about that. It's between you and the havildar.'

Jibon had been caught in a rat-trap. He was just not able to get out of the trap, or out of the invisible spider's web that had been laid—worldwide—to destroy him. No one would incarnate as an avatar to come to relieve him. What would he do now?

He realised that if he had to work here, he had no option but to stay in the havildar's quarters. But once there, he would be burdened with all the housework, just like in the story about the load on Sindbad's back. Massaging him, fetching water, washing utensils and so on. And after all that, at the end of the month, he wouldn't even get the wages for his labour! To expect any kindness or mercy from a wretch like the havildar was to live in a fool's paradise.

The contractor said, 'It's not as if I don't understand your plight. You belong to a poor family. You've come to work in order to earn some money. But there's nothing I can do. My hands are tied. When I dwell in water, can I afford to offend the crocodile? You know that workers take some coal, as part of their wages. To tell the truth, that is against the law. The law is that even the dust of the workshop is not to go out. If I don't abide by the havildar's instruction, he'll get angry. And then he won't allow the coal to be taken. He'll confiscate everything. It's happened a few times earlier. The workers will starve to death if that happens. If the work stops— tell me, how will I survive.'

Lucknow was the famed city of the erstwhile nawabs, badshahs, courtesans and dancers. The city of the poets Ameer and Umrao, the city of ghazal and thumri. So much of history and so many tales and legends lay in the very dust of its streets. But a cheated youth heard none of that. Saw none of that. He had to go away from there now.

Sensing that Jibon was thinking about leaving Lucknow, the contractor helped him to move forward with his resolve. 'I know your situation. I think it's best for you to go away from here. But yes, if you go to Kanpur, I also have a contract there. I can give you work there. Then the havildar won't be able to take your money. Do you want to go there?'

Jibon spent the night in a room on the ground floor of the contractor's house, and before sunrise the next morning, he set off for Kanpur. A manager who looked after the contractor's work in Kanpur had come to Lucknow to collect payments. He had to be in Kanpur before eight in the morning to supervise the workers. Jibon left with him.

Kanpur was not so far away from Lucknow. Jibon reached the loco shed there in an hour and a half. It was a very small workshop. The volume of work was much less than in Lucknow, there were fewer workers too. But could Jibon remain there? Especially when the earth beneath his feet was slippery? He had kept slipping and sliding all the time, so would he be able to stand firm in this land?

There was no facility for cooking one's food in Kanpur. Jibon had to eat in eateries. If someone with a salary of fifty rupees a month ate in eateries throughout the month, how would he save anything of his earnings? Twice a day, only twice a day, could he eat his fill—and even then he would be left with nothing. Four rotis, the price of which was eight annas, together with a dal, which was for two annas. That was the meal he ate at night. But in the afternoon, he could not manage to eat lunch for under a rupee. He needed at least eight rotis, as well as a plate of vegetables, which cost four annas.

The ash that was thrown out of the engine also contained burning embers. So water was poured on the ash to put out the embers. The weight of a basketful of wet ash wasn't less than fifty kilos. As Jibon carried the heavy basket on his head all day long, the fire of hunger raged in his belly. How long did it take for eight or ten thin rotis to be consumed in that fire. The additional income from coal that was available in Lucknow wasn't available here. The family members of the workers foraged that before Jibon finished his day's work. There was nothing left for him.

While in Lucknow, Jibon's fellow-workers used to help him out a bit because he was the youngest of them. But his colleagues in Kanpur were not like that. When he stood before them, for the basket of ash to be loaded on his head—they saw him as the contractor's man. They hastily loaded as much ash as they could in the basket. The ash shovelled from the track and loaded into the basket was wet. The water would drip on his head and all over his body. He would get drenched.

Jibon endured it for a month. But it wasn't just the behaviour of his fellow-workers that made him quit. The cold weather was also significantly responsible. Winter made people in Uttar Pradesh shiver and claimed a few lives every year, before moving to Bengal. Jibon had a place to stay in Lucknow, but that was not the case in Kanpur. Amidst all his various preoccupations, the contractor did not think about this matter at all. Big people thought about big things and such a trivial matter could not find a place in their thinking. For the first few days, it wasn't very difficult for him to spend the night at a mezzanine in the workshop. But it became increasingly frightful as the winter set in. The open space was no longer suitable for sleeping in.

So Jibon quit his job and began walking again. But this time he did not suffer any further financial loss. He had received his wages in full. And all of it had been spent too.

25

A Place to Live

Garib Das had become accustomed to suppressing the pain in his stomach with the help of baking soda. Another man suffering from the same ailment had told him about this great medicine. As soon as a stomach-ache began, Garib Das would stuff a handful of soda into his mouth and drink some water. It provided immediate relief. That cost him an anna each day, but he felt fit enough to go to Jadavpur again to work as a labourer. And he was able to work too, unless the job was very strenuous. The wages here were quite good, he was paid three and a half rupees a day. Sometimes a tiffin of stale rotis was also provided by some of the households he worked for.

In this part of Jadavpur, all the people of means who had arrived from East Pakistan had chosen not to go to the government's refugee camp or rely on the government's assistance or kindness. Instead, through their own efforts—some said, using the local idiom, with the strength of four bamboo posts and one staff—they had established a few colonies. These were *jabar dakhal* colonies, set up on land that was forcibly occupied. Construction, reconstruction and repairs went on continuously in their houses.

These people had all been reasonably well-to-do in East Bengal. So they had never learnt to undertake any kind of physical labour. They only performed intellectual labour and viewed physical labour as something demeaning. So even after coming to West Bengal, they were unable to do that, although the situation demanded it. They had to rely on the eternal means. They had to take the assistance of those who had eternally served and assisted others—the Muslim masons of this country, most of whom lived in Murshidabad district, and poor folk from south Bengal belonging to the Kaora, Bagdi and Pode communities. And there were starving Namasudra, Podes and Jaliya folk from the refugee camps where the dole had been discontinued. All of them arrived at Jadavpur station in the morning with their work-baskets and spades, travelling without a ticket on the suburban train. They waited at the roadside kerb to be called to work. Those who needed workers took them away. At the end of the day, they collected their wages and returned home by the evening train.

They did not have to pay the railways anything for their outward and return journeys. Without going into the question of whether or not they would have been able to survive on such low wages if they had to pay for the travel, one could say that, as a result, the womenfolk of all these low caste communities were able to work in middle-class houses, washing clothes and utensils, sweeping and mopping the floor, and thus earn ten or twelve rupees a month.

Hemanta Dasgupta of the Ramakrishnapur colony was quite a well-to-do person. He had a goldsmith's shop. At one time, he used to be in politics. He had also been jailed once for participating in a satyagraha, so he knew some people at higher levels. Everyone in the neighbourhood regarded him with respect. In a way, he could also be called the founder of this colony. Garib Das worked for two or three months at a stretch in his house. He was first a mason's assistant and had been involved right from laying the foundation to erecting the roof slab. But there were many aspects to the project of constructing a house, and so a lot of work needed to be done even after the mason's work was over. Garib Das found a long period of employment under Hemanta babu to do all that work. Hemanta babu was also very pleased with Garib Das's conduct. Unlike other workers, he didn't sit idly, smoking beedis. He worked like a donkey for eight or nine hours at a stretch. If he was given two rotis, he melted in gratitude. It was difficult to get such a man nowadays. Hemanta babu had said, 'The house construction is over, but don't stop coming because of that. Come here from time to time and find out if there's something to be done.'

For that reason, and because he could keep his basket and spade in a corner by the wall, under a guava tree inside the compound of the house, Garib went there every day. On some days, he also got a cup of tea and a couple of rotis. It wasn't as if they were dry, stiff, burnt or stale on all days, they were also fresh and hot sometimes. Just day before yesterday, they had also given him some potato curry with the rotis. Hemanta babu's wife too was a nice person. After he had eaten the rotis, she had said in a very kindly tone, 'Garib, the drain is completely blocked, the water is not going through. Will you please run a spade through it?'

Garib Das hadn't been able to work today. The train had halted at Champahati station for all of two hours. It just did not move any further. Apparently an overhead cable somewhere had snapped. By the time it was repaired and the train departed, it was already nine o'clock. All the masons began working at eight o'clock. They worked until five. Who would call Garib to work if he reached after nine? So Garib went without work sometimes on account of such delays. The old coal-fired engine was more reliable. At least it wasn't unpredictably left stranded like the electric trains.

When Garib Das called on Hemanta babu's house, he saw that preparations for a big feast were underway. The house was full of guests. Garib Das had never seen them before. Hemanta babu's brother-in-law and his wife, together with their two children, had come to spend the day in the newly constructed house. They hadn't been able to attend the grihapravesh ceremony, and so they had come today. But there was a problem, something terrible had cropped up. Hemanta babu's wife was elated to see Garib Das just then. She said to her husband, 'Garib's here! Why don't you tell him? He'll be able to do it. They are used to doing all that.'

Jibon had been acquainted with one Hemanta babu, the doctor, and now his dad was acquainted with another Hemanta babu. Both of them were very soft-spoken. This Hemanta babu called out to Garib Das in his usual courteous tone, 'Come, come Garib. You've come at just the right time. There was a big problem, my dear. God's sent you here now! Just see, I had purchased a goose. Now tell me, who'll cut it? Do we know how to do all that! Please cut it before you go.' Garib Das sat under the guava tree with the goose and a big knife. It was shady there. Even if it was cold at night these days, it was quite warm at noon. Nearby, under the shade of another tree, Hemanta babu and his brother-in-law, Sanjoy Sen, sat down on two chairs next to each other. The two brothers-in-law were always engaged in friendly banter, teasing, taunting, one-upmanship and putting the other down. Today was no exception. The game of words commenced. Hemanta babu smiled, looked at Sanjoy Sen and said in a theatrical tone, 'So tell me, oh respected mister secretary of the famed Bijoygarh, the very first *jabar dakhal* or forcibly-occupied refugee colony in West Bengal, what's happening in your locality? How's everything going?'

Hemanta babu was one of the founding members of Ramakrishnapur colony. He was averse to according Bijoygarh the status it flaunted. And so he always spoke tauntingly and provocatively about Bijoygarh. The residents of Bijoygarh were very proud of their locality. Forty colonies had sprung up in the city of Calcutta by now, adopting means that the denizens of Bijoygarh claimed they were the first to devise in West Bengal. One could say they were the pioneers. That was the reason for Hemanta babu's anguish.

Sanjoy Sen too was proud of Bijoygarh. And he was a temperamental man. From time to time, for no apparent reason, he fell into a bad mood. For instance, when he got into a rickshaw and it wasn't going as fast as he thought it should, he got into a bad mood, and an altercation resulted while paying the fare. Or when he went to the market and the price of fish was too high. The same outcome. Presently, he was annoyed that the tea was slow in coming, and now this verbal attack. The provocation rankled. He retorted agitatedly, 'Do you have any doubts about that?'

'About what?'

'That Bijoygarh is the first forcibly-occupied refugee colony in West Bengal. Which inspired all the other colonies to come up in the same way—and I have no hesitation in saying that your Ramakrishnapur also came up in the same way.'

'I'm unable to concur.'

'Why's that?'

'Because it's not correct.'

'Why isn't it correct?'

The tea arrived. Hemanta babu was about to sip his tea. Instead of doing that, he put down the cup and said in a soft but pained tone, 'It's said that whoever drinks from the Chambal river becomes a dacoit. I think the water and air of Bijoygarh is also the basis of a special quality like that. Whoever drinks the water of the place becomes a hot-headed, quarrelsome ruffian. If you are not like that, if you can be level-headed and patiently make the effort to sit still, then I'll tell you something. You'll then realise how wrong you are.'

Sanjoy Sen said brusquely, 'Tell me.'

'You won't lose your temper, will you?'

'No.'

'You won't interrupt me before I finish what I have to say?'

'I told you, I won't.'

'You won't feel anguished?'

'No, no. Tell me.'

Hemanta babu sipped the tea now. He took two quick sips and then put down the cup, lit a No. 10 cigarette, blew out a mouthful of smoke and looked at his brother-in-law with squinted eyes. He was quite agitated. Let's provoke him some more! Nothing yielded as much fun as provoking people!

He said, 'Yes, what was I saying? The first forcibly-occupied colony. I have no objection to accepting the word "first". The objection is to the term "forcibly- occupied". After all, there's a kind of heroic quality to saying "forcibly-occupied". But Bijoygarh is not a forcibly-occupied colony at all.'

'Then what is it?'

'Don't go back on your word.'

'I'm not doing that. You tell me then what Bijoygarh is.'

'It's a government colony, established by people affiliated to the government, with the help of the government.'

'You can't just make such an allegation! Give me proof.'

Garib Das had slaughtered the goose and was skinning it, but his ears were pricked up for the babus' conversation. That was a lifelong habit of his. He loved to hear discussions, explanations, speeches and conversations. So much could be learnt and understood thereby!

'Listen to me patiently, and your misconception will be cleared.' Taking another puff of his cigarette, Hemanta babu began speaking. 'In order to house the American army during the Second World War, the British government acquired a few thousand bighas of land in this country, I mean from the zamindars of this region. You surely know that there's a law whereby the state can take over any land for public use by issuing an order. That law first came into effect in 1894. It was used to take over many people's land and property in the past, and the same will happen in the future too.'

'Skip the theoretical talk, and tell me what you have to say in brief.'

'That's what I'm doing. After the government acquires the land, legally speaking, the land no longer belongs to the zamindar. The government becomes the owner of the land. The war ended, the American soldiers went back to their country. The zamindars had hoped that once the war was over, they would get back their land, but that did not happen. It remained in the government's custody. After that came the transfer of power. The British left and the Congress government came into power. In between, there was the partition. A flood of people gave up their country.'

'I know all that.'

'So you should also try to know about what you don't know, which lies at the heart of whatever you know!'

'Tell me.'

'The chief minister of West Bengal at the time was Bidhan Chandra Roy. A close associate of Bidhan Roy was one Santosh Dutta. Now this Santosh Dutta was in the Congress Party. He had also gone to jail once for a few months. When he came away from his homeland in East Bengal, he went and met Bidhan Roy. Whether you people agree or not, I know for a fact that it was only after Bidhan Roy's secretary advised Santosh Dutta that he began preparations to set up a colony, by occupying the land. Santosh babu found an associate in another person like him, who everyone knows by the name of Kala Bhai. Under the leadership of these two people, about twenty thousand people speedily erected their shelters on this tract of vacant government land. Am I correct? The zamindars did not have any legal right to hinder that. Only the government could have prevented it. After all, they were the owners of the land. But because of the proximity between the chief minister of West Bengal, Bidhan Roy, and Santosh babu, and also because of practical considerations, Bidhan babu did not obstruct them. He must have thought—if a part of the refugee problem is solved this way, so be it.'

'Taking the last sip from his cup of tea and a last puff of the cigarette, Hemanta babu continued, 'Whether you people agree or not, the truth is that without the tacit consent of the administration, it wouldn't have been possible to occupy thousands of acres of land without any hindrance. It was only after getting Bidhan Roy's consent that Santosh babu was emboldened to move ahead. I believe it's said that Bijoygarh is Asia's largest forcibly-occupied colony, which came up without any kind of assistance from the government. The residents of Bijoygarh are very proud and arrogant about this. But if you take away the term "forcibly-occupied" from forcibly-occupied colony, then only "colony" remains—and the real honour goes to Israel! That's why those who are of a somewhat dim-witted but belligerent nature firmly hold on to the term "forcibly-occupied". I say that it was not forcibly-occupied at all! All the big leaders and ministers would never have come to Bijoygarh to encourage the occupiers unless there was support from the government. They would have let loose the police instead. Do you want to hear the names of those who came? Chief Minister Bidhan Roy was there of course, as well as Pandit Jawaharlal Nehru. And from West Bengal there were Prafulla Ghosh, Triguna Sen, Samar Guha, Sarojini Naidu, General Satyabrata Sinha and many more. I can't remember everyone's name now. Which bastard would have the guts to evict them when such stalwarts stood beside and behind them, with their hands raised in support!'

Hemanta babu smiled a bit, savouring the delight of seeing the embarrassed look on his brother-in-law's face, and then resumed his narrative. 'And so, Bijoygarh can in no way say with pride that "we built a colony by forcibly occupying the land". Rather, one could say the opposite, that it is a colony established on government land, by people affiliated to the government and with the assistance of the government.'

The soil under the guava tree was wet with the blood of the slaughtered goose. Having skinned it, Garib Das was now cutting the meat into small pieces. Hemanta babu had eaten goose flesh many times when he lived in East Bengal. But this would be the first time since his arrival in India. Actually, the meat wasn't so tasty. It was a bit dry and stringy. But because referring to goose flesh had a kind of aura, one felt somewhat regal while eating it. That was satisfying and joyful.

Sanjoy Sen's face was flushed. Hemanta babu paused to relish that and then said, 'Forcibly-occupied—if you accept that "forcibly-occupied" means occupying land by relying on one's own power, without depending on anyone and without hoping for anyone's help or assistance, then it is we in Ramakrishnapur who have done that. We can rightfully be proud about that. There was no assistance of any kind from the government. We occupied the land and built our houses, and we relied entirely on our own strength. All the land in this colony belonged to a Muslim owner, I forget his name. We occupied one hundred and fifty-two bighas of his land one night. Five-kattha plots were marked out and allotted to all the households. We had to deal with the police, courts and cases, you know.'

'Court cases!' Sanjoy Sen was now angry with his brother-in-law. His anger was evident in his voice as he retorted, 'Court cases against whom, my dear brother-in-law? All these stories have been fabricated by a handful of your people. People were not so aware then, and so everyone used to believe what some of you, who were the leaders, told them. You lot floated the story about court cases. You collected a hefty amount every month on that pretext, by way of contributions from the people. No one ever saw the accounts of that. I know the person who owned this land. His house is on Prince Anwar Shah Road. He's a fine person. He had nothing to do with courts and cases. Actually, one day he told me, "Allah has given me plenty. This life will soon be gone. Why should I take back that little bit of land. The people are in a bad way, let them stay there". You people are unnecessarily denigrating a good man like him.'

'A good man indeed!' Hemanta babu now began to get agitated. What was the bastard saying? How could a Muslim ever be good? He replied, 'Good and bad depend on a person's mentality. What's good to you may not be good to me. But there's one point on which we need to agree. You ought to thank us, because you had to flee your country on account of Muslims. We had to abandon our homeland because of them. But we could at least exact a little bit of revenge on one of them for the loss of our homes, land and property.'

'I can't understand your logic. You could not say or do anything against those who were responsible. Instead you denigrate the one who deserves to be praised and thanked. It won't be correct to talk only about yourself. This tendency to pin the blame on someone else is also common among some people on the other side. It's not that all Hindus hate and decry all Muslims, but the whole community has to bear the consequence of that fault.'

Their loud arguments and counter-arguments filled the air. People outside would have thought they were quarrelling, but those at home knew that this was routine. It would subside on its own as soon as the food was ready. After cutting the goose flesh, Garib Das washed his hands at the tap. He then came up to Hemanta babu and said, 'The goose is done, what should I do now?'

There was a break in the conversation. Hemanta babu turned towards Garib Das: 'There's no other work. You can leave now. Come tomorrow, let's see if there's something to be done ...' As he spoke, he put his hand into the side-pocket of his panjabi. An eight-anna coin came into his hand. He held that out to Garib Das and said, 'Have some tea.' Hemanta babu's wife was sitting by the tap, washing the meat. Seeing her there, Garib said to her in a most humble tone, 'You had told me that you would give me some old clothes. I'll be most grateful if you could give it.' As she washed the meat, she said, 'You can see how busy I am today. Remind me tomorrow or the day after tomorrow.'

The Jadavpur rail station was about a mile away from Hemanta babu's residence in Ramakrishnapur. Garib Das walked to the station. Tiny shanties had come up along both sides of the rail track. They were made of gunny, hogla grass matting, wood and suchlike. Those who came to live here weren't just people from the Sundarbans, who had lost their homes for a variety of reasons. The people who had arrived from East Pakistan and not found a place in any refugee camp, had also started living there now. They had not been able to establish any 'forcibly-occupied' colonies. One such person was Rakhal Das. He had been a schoolmaster earlier, in some school in

East Pakistan. Now he spent his time teaching the children in the shanty settlement. One of his sons was killed when he was run over by a train. Another son was a fish-seller in Sandhyabazaar. He had two daughters. The elder daughter was twenty years old. She was of a marriageable age. Rakhal Das was always worried about not being able to get her married. What would happen if she became a bad girl like Shefali, Kanak, Kali and Kajal, her neighbours in the slum?

Garib Das would go and sit with Rakhal Das sometimes. He had found out the whereabouts of this distant relative of his after much difficulty, and established a fraternal relationship with him. He looked upon him as an elder brother. Rakhal Das was a literate man. He kept himself informed about national and international affairs. Garib Das used to visit him so he could ask him what the future held for them. Was there any sign of a ray of light anywhere? Were the rulers of the country at all concerned about them? And so he had come today, but not just to hear Rakhal Das. He also had something to say. Whatever he had heard in Hemanta babu's house was buzzing inside his head. After a while, he said, 'Master dada, I have seen hundreds of people in Jadavpur setting up so many forcibly-occupied colonies and living there. They are doing very well. So why are you languishing here beside the rail track? And why am I languishing in Khola-Doltala? Come, let all of us find a good place and occupy it. One can't be certain about being able to live beside the rail line forever, they can evict you at any time.'

Rakhal Das was in a somewhat troubled frame of mind then. A child in the morning batch had just not been able to recite the seven times table. Even after breaking two sturdy twigs on the child's back, the schoolmaster was unsatisfied. Garib Das's idiotic talk, when he was smarting from that frustration, was like rubbing salt on his wounds. He flared up: 'What's your caste? It won't do if you're a Nama, Pode, Kaibarta or Jaliya. Once they find out about you, they'll kick you on your arse and evict you. Only the high-caste can carry out forcible occupation. Go and see the colonies and find out for yourself. All of them are Brahmin, Kayastha and

Baidya. Show me a colony where there's a single low-caste family. You won't find any. Do you think I didn't try? I tried very hard to find a colony where I could get a tiny bit of space to park my two feet. Do you want to know the secret of how all these colonies were born?'

'Tell me. I've come only to hear you. My train back is only in the evening. There'll be ticket checkers before that.'

'Have you eaten anything? If you haven't then there's some chira inside, let me soak it in water for you.'

'Don't trouble yourself, dada. I had some tea and bread. Please tell me.'

Rakhal Das's shanty was about ten feet in length and about six feet wide. One almost had to crawl to get inside the shanty, and once inside, one had to stoop down. There was no one else in his house now. Everyone had gone out to work, they would only return in the evening. Food was cooked once a day, which they ate over two meals.

Sitting in the room, Rakhal Das began speaking as if he was teaching his students. 'It's not as if I can set up a colony merely by deciding to do that. There are several stages involved in this. First, eight or ten people of the elderly variety come together, and then they form a committee. The committee goes around searching for a suitable place, they find out what the history of the land is, who the owner is and so on. Once they've done that, the elders contact some leader or minister. There's sure to be a cousin or an uncle of some committee member among the leaders and ministers. Do you have any cousins or uncles among them? No! Why not? Because all the leaders and ministers are high-caste people, they are Brahmin or Kayastha or Baidya. The elders on the committee are the same. The hearts of the high-caste go out to high-caste refugees. The leaders consider all the aspects and give their opinion. But first there's a secret understanding between them—that no poor, illiterate, low-caste folk will enter the colony. All those who get plots must be educated *bhadralok*. People of means. The committee has to be paid fifty rupees at first, and then ten rupees every month. How will you pay if you don't have money? Some of this money goes into the pockets of the leaders and elders, and some of it is spent on laying roads and installing water-taps.'

Rakhal Das began coughing. He expectorated and spat out a thick glob of yellow phlegm. Then he continued: 'Next comes the building of the colony. If you don't believe me, go and find out for yourself. So many colonies have sprung up in and around Calcutta. See if you can find even one where there's a family with the title Ghorami or Biswas or Das or Mondal. You won't. All are high-caste. And affluent. One or two families of our folk may be found in each colony, who have concealed their name and caste. They have joined the babu group and become like them. But anyone who revealed his name and caste origin was driven away.'

Rakhal Das paused for a while and smiled. That was by way of scoffing at the thought. 'There was one such bastard in our own village. He posed as a Brahmin by wearing a thread on his chest and found a place in Azad Nagar colony. I ran into him one day and recognised him at once. He recognised me too, and then he almost touched my feet in panic, asking me not to tell anyone. He said he had found shelter after much difficulty. If I opened my mouth, he would be in trouble. What else could I do, I kept quiet ...'

When Rakhal Das stopped speaking, there was a deafening silence in the shanty. After a while, Garib Das said, 'Master dada, I don't know how to read or write like you. How would I know about these secrets? I go to places like Bijoygarh, Swadhin Nagar, Azad Nagar and so on, and I am amazed. They are all so well laid-out, with fine roads. There are lights on the road at night. It's as bright as daylight. There's running water in the taps. A kattha of land in such places is apparently worth as much as five or ten bighas of land in a village. How is it that people got such land just like that?'

Rakhal Das replied impatiently, 'I told you what the secret was. All those roads and so on in Bijoygarh were built by the government. There used to be a military camp there earlier. But if they didn't provide all the comforts and facilities, there would have been a mutiny. That's why they made roads and arranged for water, electricity and so on. Those who were fortunate enough to get a place there are enjoying themselves now.'

'I had heard that the refugee camp where we lived earlier also used to be a military camp. But the facilities there were not so good.'

'You mean Shiromanipur, isn't it? Who knows how long ago that was! The military camp in Bijoygarh existed until two or three years before the country became independent. People occupied it before anything fell into ruin.'

Rakhal Das was silent for a long time. Then he spoke again: 'The land there is as valuable as gold. They gave it away for free to fellowmen from their own caste. And because we are low-caste in their eyes, they don't want to give us even a place to die in West Bengal. They want to drive out people like us from Bengal with their truncheons and bullets. What justice! It's like a stepmother's behaviour, feeding her own child on her lap while driving away the stepchild.'

Garib Das added, 'Milk and curds for one, and parched rice for the other.'

'Even parched rice is not allotted to us, only ashes.'

'Will it always be like that?'

'If not—then who'll change that? It can change if our people get educated, if they also become clever and cunning and get into politics. Who else but our own people can understand our pain? This government does not belong to us. It does not matter to them whether we live or die. We need our own people in the government. But before that, we need to get an education.'

Garib said, 'I know that if one doesn't know to read or write, it's like being blind although you have eyes. That's why I tried to send my son to school, but then …'

Interrupting Garib Das, Rakhal Das said, 'That's good. But what news of your elder son? Did you find out anything about him?'

'No, there's no news. Who knows whether he's dead or alive.'

'No, don't say that. As a father, you shouldn't think ill about him. He's certainly alive and well. How long has it been since he left home?'

'It must be four years, I think.'

'Just you see, he'll come back with a lot of money. Once he returns, all your troubles will vanish.'

When would that day arrive? An outpouring of sorrow and pain rose to Garib Das's throat, choking his voice. 'I can't take it anymore, Master dada. There's nothing left of me after the illness. I push myself to go to Jadavpur, or else everyone at home will starve to death.'

Rakhal Das thought for a while and then said, 'You don't have anything in Khola-Doltala. You only go there for the night. I tell you, bring your family to Jadavpur. Build a shanty beside the rail line. Then your wife can also earn a few rupees. Your sons and daughter too.'

'It's not a bad idea. But let me go back home and think about it.'

'Do that quickly. There's still some vacant space here. If you delay, you won't get anything.'

Finally, Garib Das decided that he would wind up his affairs in Khola-Doltala and move to Jadavpur. After all, he had no roots in the soil there, only a wobbly shanty beside the canal. He wouldn't be able to survive if he developed any attachment to the place.

⚮

Every night, Garib Das had to wake up as soon as the morning star appeared in the sky. Stuffing the tin of baking soda into his bundle, he would set off to walk towards the rail station. It would probably be three at night then. He had to walk all the way to the Ghutiari Sharif station. That was about seven or eight miles away from Khola-Doltala.

Garib Das had turned old before his age. So he could not walk very fast. It would be daylight by the time he would reach the station. The early morning train would arrive at the station at six o'clock.

He took the train and got down at Jadavpur. That took an hour. After that, he walked another two miles and reached the Baghajatin crossing. He sat on his haunches there, like a beggar at a pilgrim site, hoping that someone would call him for work. Jobs were few in the factories and farms in the country, compared to those seeking work. That was why the number of people unemployed was much greater than those employed. Those who were daily labourers were also subject to the same rule. Consequently, there was no certainty that everyone would find work on all days.

On the days that Garib Das found work, he could take an advance of eight annas from his employer, which took care of his afternoon tiffin. For eight annas, he could get one roti and a plate of alur-dam, and also have four paise left over for beedis. On the days he didn't find work, he went without food in the afternoon. There would be no food at night either, after returning home. On those days, he had to lie on an empty stomach in the station all day long. The ticket checkers started getting into the trains from nine or ten in the morning. They stalked every carriage like bloodthirsty hyenas. Apparently each checker had a quota. In order to fulfill that, the frantic checkers pounced on ticketless travellers as soon as they spotted them. 'Pay a fine or go to jail.' Garib Das could not afford to buy a ticket. No daily labourer could afford that. They sat waiting for the 'office time' to be over. The checkers would then finish their duty and leave. But by then, the day was over. Night would have fallen by that time; it would be dark all around.

If Garib Das found work and got a wage, he went directly to Sandhyabazaar near Jadavpur station. By the time he reached home, it would be very late. All the shops and markets in Khola-Doltala would be closed. He bought broken corn, milo flour or rice fragments from Sandhyabazaar. Of course, there was a lot of dust, dirt and grit in the rice particles. It was a bother to dust and remove all that so late at night. Yet, from time to time, it was rice particles that Garib Das bought. It was like getting a taste of milk from its foam. For a rice-eating Bengali from rural Bengal, lack of rice made the heart distraught. Garib Das placated his heart with the rice particles.

Whenever a thin gruel was made with the rice particles, if Garib Das could afford it, he also put some potatoes into it to boil. He added a bit of salt and chillies. Oh, it was as if life itself leapt up to embrace that! Whatever be its form, it was after all Ma Lakshmi's grain. Rice meant life, rice meant a full life, rice was a delight to the heart and soul. On those days, he would wake up his sleeping children and ladle out the steaming gruel either on a banana leaf or the battered and patched-up plates. The children scorched their tongues as they slurped and ate it with glee. On the days Garib Das didn't find work, he did not have to wake them up.

Those were days of dire difficulty. The nights were terribly long, as if in a state of suspension. After a day of wasted effort, when he reached home very late, dragging along his tired and famished body and trudging the long distance, he spent the whole night gazing at the sky, awaiting the morning star, the Dhruva tara. Once it was sighted, he dragged along his weary body once again, and reached Jadavpur the same way.

On such mornings, there was less of a chance of finding work. Because anyone with experienced eyes could see that his belly was shrunken and so his body must be weak. Some even expressed their doubt: 'The old fogey can't even talk, he's gasping. How will he work? By the time he lifts up a sack of cement, he'll soil his clothes!'

The additional toll of going and coming back was even more arduous than eight hours of work. His body was simply unable to bear it any longer. The easiest way of getting out of this was to move with his family to Jadavpur.

And so one day, Garib Das packed his meagre belongings into bundles and arrived at Jadavpur. The shanties of bereft people that had sprung up along the rail track grew in numbers like a procession, coming to an end at the edge of a large storm-water drain. The drain passed beneath the railway line and flowed towards the Chowbhaga canal in the eastern fringe of Calcutta. All the sewage of the city flowed along this drain. A row of makeshift toilets had been built over the drainage channel by the shanty-dwellers. As a result, the whole place gave off a terrible stench. It bred mosquitoes and flies. And when it rained, the water level in the drain rose. It was in such a place that Garib Das built his shanty. No better place was vacant.

After coming to Jadavpur, Garib Das's wife, Bimala, found work as a part-time maidservant in two homes. She was paid a monthly salary of ten rupees in one house and eight rupees in the other. But they gave her two rotis and a cup of tea in the morning. Garib's second son, Jatan, started working in a tea-shop. He got food twice a day and a salary of ten rupees a month. The next two children were still very small. But they too had devised a few ways to help the family. They went with a cloth bag to Sandhyabazaar every evening. They foraged and brought home the dried up or rotten or worm-eaten vegetables thrown away by the vegetable-sellers. They were able to pick out something edible from that.

Like before, Garib Das went and sat at the Baghajatin crossing for work. Nowadays the crowd of workers at the kerb was much more than before. Because of the crowd, the shopkeepers at the crossing became terribly annoyed. There was a large sweetmeat shop there, and if anyone went and stood in front of that, the shopkeeper flung water on them. He hurled abuses at them. He was angry because they made it inconvenient for his customers to enter or exit the shop.

This was a terribly unbearable and frustrating time. It was like Yama was mercilessly raining deathly blows. Yet time kept passing. Man had been called the offspring of the divine elixir because he did not die. He survived even after coming so close to death. That was the only reason why Garib Das's entire family survived. Otherwise there was no logical reason for them to survive.

26

Coming Home

Getting away from the ash-heap in Kanpur, Jibon once again began a journey without direction or pause, in search of a soil of human warmth. He traversed thousands of miles on his small feet—Delhi, Agra, Allahabad, Mathura, Kashi, Vrindavan, Haridwar and many more small and large towns. A day or merely an hour somewhere, or a week somewhere else. In this way, he spent many days on the move. But he was never able to find a prop that would help him survive, which he could grasp firmly. Young Jibon's little cup remained empty. No, not entirely empty, for he had accumulated some tales of shame, humiliation and oppression, which pained him greatly. They only revealed how fallen and wretched he was.

The earth was round. So if one set out on a journey and kept going, eventually the journey would end at the place where it began. Who knows whether or not it was because of this truth, but one day the sound of the wind blowing against his ears sounded familiar. This was Bengal's soil, the air was Bengal's, the language was Bengali. And so at about eight one morning, Jibon emerged from a train that had run all night and arrived at Howrah station. His feet were dirty and chapped from walking through many towns of India. Many other people had got down from the train, someone or the other was standing at the platform or gate to receive them. But there was no one for Jibon. On the day he had left for Assam, Raja was with him, but today he was alone. On that day, the light of hope shone in his heart, but today there was only the darkness of despair. Jibon walked slowly, moved past the ticket checker at the gate and exited the station. No one seemed to notice him.

Jibon had spent days on end in railway carriages. His body still seemed to be rocking to the movement of the train. The mechanical clatter rang in his head. But now it seemed as if the whole city was speeding along with the same clatter. It shot forward like an arrow from left to right and from east to west. Jibon felt as if he had been stationary, as if he had not moved an inch all these days. All the running around had been in vain. Walking along slowly and avoiding the hurrying people, vehicles and horse-drawn carriages, Jibon reached Howrah Bridge and halted. A doleful sky above his head, and beneath his feet flowed the river Ganga, mother incarnate. How much water must have flowed along the Ganga in all these months and years! But there wasn't the slightest trace of that. It was exactly like Jibon's life. How many winters, summers and monsoons, how many storms and gales, how much of effort and trying—but even after all that, there hadn't been the slightest change in his fortunes; his life remained as worthless as it had been before

Jibon walked from Howrah to Sealdah. That was where he happened to meet Nirananda Haldar from Khola-Doltala. He was going to Thakurnagar, to his daughter-in-law's house. He did not see Jibon. But Jibon spotted him and went and stood in front of him. 'How are you, kaka? Where are you going?'

'Isn't it Jibon?' Nirananda Haldar stared at Jibon with wide eyes. 'It's been such a long time since I saw you. How are all of you?'

'Who do you mean?'

'Are your Baba, Ma, brothers and sister well?'

'You would be able to tell me about that. I don't know anything about them. You see, I wasn't here for a long time. How are they?'

'Who?'

'My Baba, Ma, brothers and sister!'

'How can I tell you that?'

'Don't you see them?'

'How would I see them? Do they live where I do?'

'Don't you live in Khola?'

'Where else would I live but in Khola! Is there any other place for us to live?'

'Your house is near theirs, so how can it be that you haven't seen my father? Tell me the truth, how are they? Are they all dead?'

'What's all this you're saying? Had they borrowed money from others to feed themselves that they'll die! Don't you know that they all left for Jadavpur? What kind of son are you who doesn't know the whereabouts of his parents!'

'Didn't I tell you, I wasn't here, I only returned today.'

'Where were you all these days?'

'Under trees, on pavements, in stations and in rail carriages.'

'Didn't you do any work? What did you eat?'

'Water and air, and the kicks and curses of people.'

'Do you think you can spend your life fooling around like that?'

'I've not yet been able to find out how to fool around and go through life. Actually I've spent my life trying to find that.'

Nirananda Haldar did not say more, he began walking ahead. Garib's son had come to the city and become a ruffian. He was playing the fool with elders.

Jibon took a train from Sealdah and got down at Jadavpur. Where would he search for his parents in this forest of people? How would he find them? Who knew their address? Then it occurred to Jibon that he ought to go to the Baghajatin crossing to find out. Garib Das used to go there earlier in search of work. For all he knew, if he went there he may well find out something. That was the only possible lead he had.

Lost in his thoughts, as he pondered about this, Jibon walked from one end of the station to the other a few times. The station was packed with people now. Those who came from the village to the city to sell fish and vegetables were returning home after the morning market ended. Thanks to them, the station was bustling with life. Cheap tiffin, consisting of muri and alur-dam, was selling like anything. Suddenly, Jibon's eyes spotted a familiar face in the crowd. It was Dhonai Sardar, from Ramdhari Bridge. He too used to go to the Baghajatin crossing to find work. In fact, it was Dhonai who had told Garib Das about finding work there. Seeing him, Jibon's heart leapt with hope. He walked quickly towards him. '*Aeyi*, Dhonai kaka, do you recognise me? I am Jibon, son of Garib Das. The one you took for work from Khola.'

Dhonai Sardar was a hot-tempered man. He never minced his words. He said whatever came to his mind. He saw Jibon, but he pretended as if he hadn't, and continued to eat his muri and alur-dam. He had not got work today. He would eat the muri and then spread out his gamchha and lie down on the station platform.

'O Dhonai kaka, don't you recognise me?'

Hearing Jibon's voice, Dhonai Sardar looked at him again. There was no civility in his response. He snapped, 'Why should I recognise you? Shall I dance? Garib Das's son! What son? The son who does not bother about his parents! You're grown up now, and the father who gave birth to you is dying of sickness, but you don't care to even look him up. What kind of son is that? I say that the son who does not look after his parents is as useless as piss!'

Jibon kept his head down and heard all the abuse. He knew that if there was anyone who knew about his father, it was Dhonai Sardar. He was sure they met and talked even now. That was why he was angry with Jibon. Even before he could ask him anything, Dhonai Sardar spoke: 'You've roamed around all by yourself, you've tasted everything that's good and bad. Think a bit about your parents here. You don't even know where they live. They're right here, in Jadavpur. Walk along the rail track. Go towards the shanties on this side of the canal. Go and see the terrible state they are in.'

With a heart full of shame, Jibon walked along the railway line and reached Garib Das's shanty. Standing in front of the door, he began weeping and called out, 'Ma, I'm back.'

⁂

Jibon had returned. Garib Das's son was back after such a long time. He had surely brought home a lot of money. Now they could at least eat to their fill for some days. Now they could eat rice, with a bit of fish curry. Garib Das could visit a doctor for his stomach ailment. Garib Das had been lying down. He sat up. He had not found work today. He wasn't feeling well either.

Seeing Jibon, his chest heaved and his voice choked. 'Where were you all these days? We were dying of anxiety, your Ma wept all the time, saying, "My son is no longer alive". Why don't you say anything? Where were you all these years?'

Jibon's youngest brother Jugal went and hugged him. 'Dada, what have you brought for me?'

Jibon was overcome with emotion. His eyes welled with tears. Holding out the palms of his incapable hands, he said, 'I couldn't bring anything.'

'You've come without anything! Nothing at all!' Little Jugal was filled with dismay and disbelief. How could this be! How could Jibon have changed so much!

'Didn't you do any work? Jatan earns ten rupees a month. Didn't you earn anything?'

'I worked.'

'Then where's the money?'

'I have nothing.'

'You spent it all on yourself?' Garib Das lost his patience now. A torrent of grievances shot out of his throat. 'Spend it! What's it to you, you've grown up now, you've grown wings. You roam around here and there, you eat whatever you like. What's it to you whether your parents and siblings are dead or alive? When a son grows up, the father feels assured. Because he thinks, I have a new pair of arms. I've worked like a donkey all my life, now I can get some relief. What a fate!' Garib Das was almost gasping now in agitation. After taking a few breaths, he continued: 'When a son doesn't understand his parents' suffering, it's as good as not having a son. When there's no son, one can't hand over the burden of responsibility. There's nothing I can do about that. No one is more accursed than the one who doesn't really have a son despite giving birth to one.'

Bimala had been silent all the while. She only gazed at her son with sorrowful eyes. Tears streamed down her face. As if the long frozen ice of agony within her had melted into a river of tears. Each wave of the river seemed to be like a bullet shot out of a gun, which pierced Jibon's heart. Every teardrop seemed to explode in condemnation. Fie, fie on you and your manhood a hundred times! The son who does not repay the debt of his mother's womb, the son who fails to pay the price of his mother's milk—curse him! Curse the very existence of the son who forgets his mother's unstinting love!

Jibon was standing on the rail track. The door of the shanty was only five feet away, but it seemed to him that it had gone five million miles away from him, a distance he could never traverse, to stand before his Ma. But arrows faster than the speed of sound were shooting out from the door. 'Did you come to find out if we are dead or alive? We are here, we are alive. The one who has nobody has God. You don't have to look after us. Go, eat to your fill, enjoy yourself and be happy. Be well. As long as you are happy, we are happy. You don't have to worry about whether we are dead or alive. Be well and be happy.'

Jibon's brother Jugal began weeping loudly with a great sense of hurt. 'I don't have a single shirt, I don't have a kite or a spinning-top. On the day you left, you said you'd buy me a new shirt, you said you'd buy me a kite and a spinning-top. Why didn't you bring it?'

Jibon's sister did not cry. She did not go near him, nor did she demand anything. She stood afar and looked at her unknown brother. An unknown brother who was like an ogre of selfishness, who didn't take her in his arms, didn't cuddle her or give her sweets. What kind of brother was he!

Jibon stood on the rail track like a tree scorched by lightning. His chest heaved, he felt devastated. Seeing the tears of crushed hopes streaming down his Ma's eyes, blood rushed to his broken heart. Ma, oh Ma, I'm really an accursed son of yours. I was cursed the very moment I was born. There's no pity or care or empathy left for me in this world, Ma. There's not a grain left in the pot for me in this cruel world. All that was divided up among others long before we were born. Those who got it are not willing to give us even a grain. How many days, months and years, how many thousand miles I've walked through the streets of this world. I met so many people and saw so many towns, cities and ports, but nowhere was there anything for us. Everywhere, our lives are unwanted, redundant and a burden on humanity. That's why no one paid me, Ma. These hands are still extremely tiny. What could I do, Ma, I could not snatch away my rightful dues. That's why my hands are empty.

Jibon felt terribly helpless standing before his family, whose hopes he had crushed, whom he had now rendered hopeless. Jibon's travel tales were of no use to them given the circumstances they were in. They too knew all those tales about how heartless and cruel the people of this world were, how as soon as they spotted someone weak and helpless, they squeezed him dry, like wringing a stalk of sugarcane. Such tales would not alleviate their suffering.

And so, in the same way as Jibon had returned—a failure, with the scent of his travels all over his body, mind and soul, his feet covered in dust—his chapped, cracked, dirty feet sped off once again in search of some means. He was unable to bear the gaze of his own folk. He had let them down. His mother was boiling wheat-flour dissolved in water over a fire of leaves and twigs. Everyone sipped it like gruel. Although he saw food before him, he could not say, 'Ma, I haven't eaten for many, many days. Please give me something to eat.'

The revolutionary poet Sukanta had written, 'In the kingdom of hunger, the world is prosaic.' A man walked along an old thoroughfare of the prosaic world, floundering in the ocean of an unfathomable quandary. His life was like a leaking dinghy, whose mast was broken and sails torn. Lacking the direction of any helmsman, it was adrift in deep, shoreless waters. Who knows when it would sink? As far as one could see, there was no one who could help him now. The eternal moral claim of one human over another had been overturned. In other words, he had been told— this country and this time considers you to be dead, you have been declared non-existent. You have been thrown away like bad, rejected garbage. Go, go away now! Go to your destiny!

27

The Dream

There was a park in front. Next to the park were rows of houses of happy, affluent folk. The doll-like infants from those houses were playing in the park. Their mothers or their families' maidservants were watching over them. Seeing the children laughing, playing and running around, the youth thought—so play, fairy tales and naughtiness had not yet been lost from the lives of all children; there were still some people who ran behind their children with a bowl of milk, cajoling them, 'Come here, my darling boy, drink the milk'.

The innocent children did not know how many mothers there were, who, when their children pleaded for food, secretly thumped them—'How much do you want to eat, you devil! Shall I give you everything? As if there isn't anyone else who has to eat!' The children who refused to drink milk did not know that there were hundreds of thousands of children like them who, let alone milk which was just a dream, could not get even a taste of rice-foam.

The youth had walked a long way and arrived here. He was extremely tired. His sleepy eyes were falling shut. Seeing an empty bench on one side of the park, he went and sat down there. There was a pleasant breeze. He dozed off. Death-like sleep wrapped him up entirely. Suddenly his eyes fell upon a long, wide road. A boy like him was walking along the road. He had a big sack slung on his shoulder. He foraged and picked up torn bits of paper, pieces of plastic and cardboard, torn flip-flops and so on from the trash lying on the road and stuffed it into the sack. How old was he? Jibon had run away from home at the same age and come to this city. He had found shelter in the city's railway stations, on pavements and under trees.

With keen eyes, the youth, whose name was Jibon, observed the rag-picker. He looked very familiar, as if Jibon had seen him many times. He had surely spoken to him, walked together with him and had lain with him, holding him tight, in some station or on some pavement. His eyes, face, nose and eyebrows, the way he walked, for that matter, even the scar on his forehead—all seemed extremely familiar. As the boy walked along, he suddenly halted with a start beside the milk depot. There was a filthy garbage bin there, surrounded by buzzing flies. 'An endeavour by the Calcutta Corporation towards safeguarding the health of citizens.' The boy climbed into the garbage bin. Looking at the change in the expression on his face, it seemed like he hoped to find something or the other that was valuable there.

Everyone in this locality had big jobs. Thanks to big government or private sector jobs, they were all well-to-do. Everyone had cars, dogs and watchmen at their doors. A glittering wedding reception had taken place in a house here yesterday. There had been a lot of eating and drinking, which had gone on until midnight. All the used banana-leaves, clay glasses and food waste from the function had been thrown into the garbage bin. The boy was sorting through all the leaves and waste, searching for something.

After a while, Jibon saw the rag-picker boy laying down a plate and putting into it bits of leftover food from last night's reception, which he had picked out from the garbage. He had a sharp rod in his left hand with which he moved aside one used leaf after another, and as soon as he spotted something, he picked it up with his right hand and laid it on the plate. Pieces of luchi, half-eaten sweetmeats, a few pieces of fish and meat, vegetable chops—taken together, he had collected quite a lot by now.

The boy was engrossed in going through the soiled leaves lying in the dustbin. He seemed to be in a world of his own. It was as if he was consumed by some primordial obsession, which made him lose all sense of his surroundings. As if something astonishing was emerging from the soiled plates. As if the closed doors of destiny had suddenly opened wide today. The metal rod in his hand seemed to be like some magician's wand. At the touch of which, all kinds of foods emerged beneath the discarded banana-leaves. Oh wow, a whole fish-fry—completely unbroken, no one had taken even a single bite! And this, what's this? Must be something wonderful—I want more, even more. He kept rifling through the soiled leaves like one possessed.

Suddenly, Jibon spotted a dog. It had no hair on its body, and there was a festering sore near its ear. Maggots, fluid, blood and pus oozed from the wound. The dog stealthily advanced towards the food heaped on the plate. It had a birthright to this food. It began wolfing it down. After ferreting around for quite a long while, when the boy turned around to put down the foraged food from his right hand, he saw all his labours being turned to naught. All the precious treasure that he had mined was being looted. He stood up. An all-destroying fire blazed in his eyes. He transferred the sharp rod from his left hand to his right hand. He took two steps forward with the intention to slaughter. He looked fixedly at the dog. It had its head down and was busy eating. The boy looked in all directions, he ran his eyes over the houses, the people, the road and the cars and vehicles, and then he rushed forward and plunged the sharp rod into the dog's belly. Blood gushed out. With the rod embedded in its belly, the dog howled loudly, ran ahead and fell on its face. It moaned a few times, its legs trembled, and then it became still. The soil under its body became wet with blood.

The boy walked ahead and pulled out the rod from the dog's belly. He wiped off the blood on the rod with a piece of wastepaper. He then folded up the plate with the remaining food, put it into his sack, lifted it onto his shoulder and prepared to move ahead. But he could not advance even a single step. He saw another boy like him blocking his way. 'Wait, don't go!'

This boy too looked very familiar to Jibon. But although he sifted hard through his memory, he just could not remember where he had seen him. His voice too was very familiar. The ghostly boy Maran had this kind of brave voice, the voice that Jibon heard from time to time even now. But Jibon could not figure out why he was standing like a wall in front of the rag-picker boy now. It seemed as if someone had pushed him from behind and made him stand there. It could also be that someone had pulled him along from the front. If the one who pushed him was his past, then the one who pulled him was certainly his future.

The rag-picker boy said combatively, 'Tell me what you have to say.'

The boy with the grave voice ordered him, 'Throw away all the stuff which you put into the sack.'

'Why should I throw it away? I took pains to collect it.'

'There's the dog's saliva, drool, pus and blood on that. Don't eat any of that and don't give it to anyone else either.'

'How will I survive if I don't eat it? My parents and little brothers and sisters at home are dying of hunger. What will they eat?'

'They can't eat that.'

'Will any of us survive if we don't eat? Are you calling the luchis and sweets shit?' the rag-picker boy flared up in anger.

'Tantriks of the Aghora sect consume their own shit and piss. This is even worse than that—dog's pus and blood. Throw it away, throw everything away!'

'No, I won't throw it away.'

'I won't let you go unless you throw it away.'

As soon as the boy with the grave voice began moving towards the rag-picker, he raised the rod and growled. 'Don't you dare come near me. Let me go. The folks at home are waiting for me, they haven't eaten anything for several days. If you block my way, I'll stab you in the belly. Move aside!'

The boy who had blocked the way was angry. 'Are you trying to frighten me? Fear itself is afraid of me, and you're trying to frighten me! My dear, I've killed people, you know.' He puffed up his chest and advanced towards the rod pointed at him. 'Let's see how you hit me. Hit me or else throw away the stuff inside the sack!'

The rag-picker boy said, 'Don't move any more, I'm warning you ...' As he spoke, he moved back, one step at a time, until his back was against the wall of the garbage bin. He had no more place to move. The boy with the grave voice suddenly grabbed and twisted the rag-picker boy's arm and snatched away the rod. He snatched the sack with his other hand and emptied it on the ground. All the fondly gathered food lay on the dust of the street. Seeing that, the rag-picker boy was overcome with rage, and he screamed out, 'You shouldn't have done that. You'll pay for this one day! I won't spare you! If I do, then you can raise a dog named after me!'

'What's your name?' the boy with the grave voice asked jeeringly. 'What shall I name the dog?'

'My name is Jibon Chandal.'

'What? What's your name?'

'Jibon. Jibon Chandal. I'm from Barisal district.'

'But that's *my* name. Where did you get my name from?'

'That's *my* name. My parents gave me that name.'

Now the whole being of the boy with the grave voice blazed in anger. 'What's the son of a bitch who licks dogs' spittle saying? He says his name is Jibon Chandal! Chandal is another name for anger. How can someone whose name is Jibon Chandal put shit into his mouth thinking it's delicious food? Can he ever do that? Doesn't his soul cry out? No, whatever may be his name, he can never be worthy of the name Jibon Chandal. The one who has such a despicable life does not have any right to be alive. If he lives, the name Jibon Chandal would lose all its dignity and worth.'

He suddenly thrust the rod forward forcefully. The rag-picker boy began writhing, this way and that. All the astonishment of the universe shone in his eyes. He wailed, 'Why did you strike me? I didn't harm you in any way ...'

'You did,' said the boy with the grave voice. 'You disgraced my name. If you stay alive, you'll do that even more. That's why there's no need for you to live any more. What will you do alive? It's better that you die.' The boy with the grave voice moved aside the garbage in the bin and buried the rag-picker boy under it. After that, just as he turned around and was about to go away, Jibon recognised him. It was Maran! Dear Maran, here I am, come! But the boy didn't stop. He went away.

⸎

'Hey, who are you? Get up, get up now. Is this a place for you people to sleep?' Jibon opened his eyes and saw that it was evening. There were dark clouds in the sky.

A pack of mangy dogs surrounding the garbage bin in front were fighting among themselves and biting one another. The horrible dream had left him feeling heavy-hearted. He slowly walked out of the park. A rainstorm was likely to come down soon. He ought to find a shelter somewhere. But before that, he had to eat for the night. Nights on a hungry stomach were infinitely long.

So what would Jibon eat today? Rice or rotis, vegetables or meat? Thinking that he would decide once he reached the eatery, he began walking in that direction. It was far away. It wouldn't be bad if he went by bus. But he did not have the bus fare. Nowadays, Jibon ate at eateries. He could eat very cheap. But he had to eat in a different eatery each day. Something new every day. He liked the look of the restaurant he had seen in Garia yesterday. That's where he was going to eat now.

Boudi's eatery was at the foot of the farther end of the Garia Bridge, on the right-hand side. By the time Jibon reached, the eatery was busy. Customers came, ate and left. There was a drum of water placed in front of the eatery. That was where people washed their hands and mouth before and after eating, it was where used utensils were washed. Jibon took some water in a mug from the drum, washed his face and hands, and went and sat down on a bench in a corner. 'What's there to eat?'

Boudi was quite young, but her husband was old. She cooked and so on, while he looked after the cash. Their son and two daughters served the food. Boudi's younger daughter now came to take the order and said, 'There's egg curry, potato and soya-bean curry and fish curry.'

'Isn't there any meat today?'

'No, only fish.'

'What kind of fish?'

'Small whole carp, pieces of carp and tilapia.'

'Give me a piece of carp and rice. And half a plate of vegetables. Bring some lemon, onions and green chillies too.'

There wasn't much of a crowd in the shop at this time. A man had sat down to eat in front of Jibon. Observing him, one could tell that he was very hungry. Possibly a *khalasi* from some truck—there was grease and dust all over him. He was eating the small carp curry. As he ate, Jibon asked the man, 'How's the fish?'

'It's fresh,' replied Boudi's elder daughter. 'If it's not nice, you don't have to pay.'

Jibon asked, 'Is there any fried fish? If there's any, give me a crisply fried one.'

Once he finished eating, Jibon went to wash his hands and mouth. It had begun to drizzle. Looking at the black clouds in the sky, it seemed it would rain heavily in an hour or two. There were lights on the lamp-posts along the road, but that did little to remove the darkness. Jibon washed his mouth and placed the mug atop the drum. He took a deep breath—and then shot away like an arrow and plunged into the darkness. He thought someone was chasing him, shouting, 'Thief, thief, catch him!' And so he did not stop running. Taking the hospital lane and going behind the police station, he kept running in the direction of the crematorium.

He ran from light towards darkness, from death to life, a solitary journey. He did not know what the final outcome of the journey would be. He only knew that he had to run now. As long as he could run, he would survive.